T0290449

OCCAM'S RAZOR

T.R. RYDEN

BEAUFORT BOOKS

For inquiries about volume orders, please contact:
Beaufort Books
27 West 20th Street, Suite 1102
New York, NY 10011
sales@beaufortbooks.com

Published in the United States by Beaufort Books www.beaufortbooks.com
Distributed by Midpoint Trade Books, a division of Independent Book Publishers
www.midpointtrade.com
www.ipgbook.com

Cover Design by Dan Yeager
Interior design by Mark Karis
Charts and Illustrations by Sasan Kayyod www.sasankayyod.com

All Biblical quotes are from the King James Bible:
The Holy Bible, King James Version. Cambridge Edition: 1769; King James Bible Online, 2019.
www.kingjamesbibleonline.org

Printed in the United States of America

For my wife who was my high school sweetheart,
I love you as much today as I did that first day I saw you.

To my three boys, I love you more than you know.
Always be honest, true, and humble,
and you will never want for anything.

OCCAM'S RAZOR
DEFINITION

THE SIMPLEST EXPLANATION IS USUALLY THE CORRECT ONE. When competing hypotheses are equal in all other respects, this principle recommends selecting the hypothesis that introduces the fewest assumptions, postulates, and entities while still sufficiently answering the question. The principle, used as a rule throughout the sciences as a guide in developing theoretical models, was an important rule in the formation of special relativity by Albert Einstein, and has been used in the development of quantum mechanics by Ludwig Boltzmann, Max Planck, Werner Heisenberg, Louis de Broglie, and others.

The bottom line: the simplest answer is usually the correct one.

Sometimes fact is more terrifying than fiction.

The historical and scientific aspects of this book are based in fact. If you think the information is too fantastic to believe, I challenge you to research it yourself. However, be careful; the rabbit hole goes deep. What happens when all the whistleblowers are dead, and no one can hear the warning?

"In a time of deceit, telling the truth is a revolutionary act." But beware, because *"in an empire of lies, truth is treason."*

—QUOTATIONS ATTRIBUTED TO GEORGE ORWELL

NOTE TO READERS

THIS STORY TAKES PLACE IN 2015; HOWEVER THERE are instances where a character remembers previous events that are out of chronological order, which are identified in the section heading.

PROLOGUE

WADIA STOOD BEFORE THE GAPING MOUTH OF THE VAULT, the lights behind him barely penetrating its darkness. He knew the gods had chosen him for this. His willing sacrifice would bring honor to his children and his descendants. Throughout the ages, his deeds would be told in stories and sung of in songs.

Trembling with fear and excitement, he pulled himself from his reverie. He took a lamp from one of his escorts and slid it through the small opening ahead. Then he pushed through the carefully wrapped books of gold before crawling into the chamber himself. Standing in the small room, he ran his hands across the large, smooth, granite-block walls as shadows flickered across them. Wadia was a scribe. His family had always been scribes from the time of his great-grandfather's grandfather, and so would be his son and grandson, young Taluk.

How many times had he been here before? This time he would not be leaving. Those few slaves standing outside the chamber were the only ones aside from the gods who knew of this room's existence, and with that knowledge their fate was also sealed. The thought made him feel as if the weight of the whole imposing structure was bearing down on him, shortening his breath. Before he could change his mind, he walked to the small wooden lever near the stone door and pulled it, as he had been instructed. Once the stone-block door slid into place, those outside sealed the chamber with wax, ensuring that the chamber was airtight.

Doing his best to control his growing sense of panic, he picked up the first of the three golden books and carefully unwrapped it from the cloth in which it was wrapped. After setting it on the stone table in the center of the room, he looked at it intently, then did the same with the other two books. Then he sat down on the floor behind the table with nothing left to do but wait. Time passed slowly.

The flame began to flicker, and Wadia struggled to find air. By the time the flame on the small oil lamp went out completely, he had already passed into total darkness . . .

1

KHALID AL HASSAN
MYKONOS, GREECE, JULY 2015

Therefore I will shake the heavens, and the earth shall remove out of her place, in the wrath of the Lord of hosts, and in the day of his fierce anger.
—ISAIAH 13:13

KHALID AL HASSAN LOOKED DOWN AT HIS WATCH. This would be a quick trip. It was late afternoon as he sat at a small café table a few buildings over from a scooter rental, and a warm breeze blew off the Mediterranean. He wondered if he had missed his mark. He looked around the square in frustration. Looking down at the prepaid phone he had been given, Khalid checked the address. This was the right place. *Maybe there has been a change of plans*, he thought. He took one more look at the photograph in his pocket. He then tore it up, burned the small pieces in the ash tray on the table, and lit a Cuban cigar. The sun was hot and reflected off the white painted buildings and the water. Several boats were tied up at the Old Port of Mykonos City, swaying gently in the waves—but the beauty of the location was lost on Khalid. He had a job to do.

Khalid Al Hassan had honed his skills in the Palestinian Authority's National Guard (PNA) under Arafat. He had trained soldiers in munitions, explosives, and IEDs. His entire life had been about jihad as a young man, and he had been groomed and molded into an elite killer. After Arafat's death in 2004, and an internal power struggle at the PNA, Khalid fled Palestine and applied his proficiencies in a much more lucrative manner as part of an ancient Islamic sect, the Hashashin. It was a strange twist of fate when he considered who he was now working for.

Khalid was growing impatient. He knew his employer did not accept failure. He was just about to break protocol and make a telephone call when a small taxi pulled up to the scooter rental. Three older men exited in shorts and sandals, smiling and talking loudly as they entered the rental office. Khalid smirked. One of them was his mark: Professor William Steiger of the University of Edinburgh, the current head of the Institute for Astronomy.

Khalid had been informed by his employer that Professor Steiger had a reservation for a scooter rental today to tour the Greek island, but nothing was said of there being a party of three. This could complicate matters. Khalid remained seated at the café table. He pretended to be texting as he watched the door of the office intently over top of his phone. When the waiter approached, Khalid waved him off. He needed to remain focused. His mind raced.

The three men walked out of the scooter rental office's front door and stood talking for several minutes. Soon someone emerged from the office and motioned the professor over to a scooter. It seemed as if the man was giving the tourists instructions. Professor Steiger sat on one of the scooters and started the engine. The other two men seemed to be leaving; they waved to the professor and began walking toward the pier. *Perfect* thought Khalid.

He left a few Euros on the table and walked across the square to the small delivery truck he had stolen just hours before. He started the truck and backed out of the parking spot, straining his neck to follow the professor's direction of travel. This had to be perfect, and it has to look like an accident—like the others.

"Another astronomer," Khalid muttered. He was curious of course as to the motive of those he served, but he dared not ask questions. Questions in this business could get you killed.

The narrow streets of Mykonos wound through the hillside. The streets were treacherous on a normal day, bordered on both sides by small, jagged-rock retaining walls that usually had large drop-offs on the downhill side. There was just enough room for two cars to pass each other going opposite directions. Khalid followed the scooter for several minutes, lagging behind so he would not draw any attention to himself. The professor seemed to be taking in the sights. He was constantly looking around but seemed oblivious to the fact that he was being followed. The small red scooter wobbled as the professor attempted to become proficient at navigating the meandering roads on the small Vespa. He looked ridiculous, unable to control the scooter with much skill, and he had no helmet—his hair was blowing wildly. *What a fool*, Khalid thought, *in his shirt, shorts, sandals—not the right outfit for a treacherous drive.*

After a few miles the professor's scooter slowed down. So did Khalid. The professor stopped to park his scooter and began to take pictures from the edge of the road. *Shit*, Khalid thought. He continued driving past the scooter; he did not want to raise any suspicion by coming to a stop and waiting. He drove down the road about a mile and turned into a gravel lot where a house was being constructed. This was good cover. He parked by several construction vehicles and waited, looking in the rearview mirror for the scooter.

The hot sun was turning the cab of the small truck into an oven.

Heat radiated from the black dashboard that was cracked and caked in dust. He fumbled with the fan controls on the dash, to no avail. Nothing seemed to work in this forsaken vehicle. Sweat ran down his back. Khalid slammed his hand on the steering wheel in frustration, and spittle flew from his lips as he cursed.

After a few minutes Khalid saw the professor approach slowly. He tossed his cigar out onto the gravel and spit. Khalid was patient, letting the scooter continue down the road a bit, and then slowly he pulled back out on the narrow street and resumed his position far behind the professor.

Khalid looked in his rearview mirror to ensure there were no cars around. There was nothing. The road ahead was clear as well. There were no houses nearby. He knew it was now or never. Without a pause he gripped the steering wheel and slammed down on the accelerator. The engine whined as the truck lurched forward. He quickly closed the distance to the small, red Vespa. The van's engine screamed loudly, and the exhaust belted out a cloud of black smoke from the poorly serviced old truck. The engine stuttered. A brief moment of worry flashed through Khalid's mind—*was this beat-up pile of crap going to break down?*

Cleary hearing the sound, the professor attempted to look over his shoulder, likely in near panic. As he did, the back wheel of the small scooter shifted on some gravel and the professor nearly lost control, but recovered. The truck ran down the center of the road and took up most of the two lanes. The professor wobbled again as the bumper of the truck quickly approached the rear of the Vespa. The professor gunned the engine of the scooter, and gravel flew out from the rear wheel as he looked wildly from side to side, trying to find an avenue of escape. There was nothing.

The professor throttled the Vespa as fast as it would go. He drove dangerously close to the edge of the narrow wall, beyond which was a precipitous drop down a jagged rocky embankment. The truck sputtered again, and Khalid felt the engine about to stall. Fearing he was flooding it, he backed off the accelerator just a bit. This gave the professor just enough time to pull ahead as they approached another sharp curve in the road. The Vespa flew around the turn. Khalid had to slow down considerably to make the turn. The rear wheels of the truck slid through the turn, casting gravel and dust into the air. *Shit*, Khalid thought. *He's getting away.*

Khalid gunned the engine again. He shifted gears, the engine screamed, and the truck shook as he pressed the pedal to the floor. He had only one chance to catch the Vespa before they neared homes and perhaps other vehicles. The engine held up. Belching black exhaust, the truck accelerated quickly to 60 kilometers an hour. The Vespa was just a few yards away. Just as the professor looked over his shoulder, Khalid's truck slammed into the Vespa with a deafening crunch. The scooter and the astronomer were smashed against the cab of the truck. The professor's face bounced off the windshield, breaking the glass on the passenger side, smearing it in blood. The Vespa careened into a small retaining wall. The professor was thrown from the front of the truck into the wall, his head bent back at an impossible angle. The scooter and the professor then flew over the wall, and the professor's lifeless body bounced to the bottom of the steep hill of rock.

JAMES ANDERSON
PARIS, FRANCE, SEPTEMBER 2015

[S]hut up the words, and seal the book, even to the time of the end: many shall run to and fro, and knowledge shall be increased.

—DANIEL 12:4

He found himself in Paris, again. It seemed he was always in Paris. Sitting at the old zinc bar, watching the local drunks argue with each other while he drank alone, added to his depressed mood.

For James, this trip had been very different from the many others which he usually enjoyed reminiscing over. James had been in the city for a week, alone. He had never come to Paris alone; in fact, this was the first time he had no family with him and no friends visiting. It was supposed to be a celebratory trip, a gift to himself for closing on the sale of one of his portfolio companies to Roche Diagnostics. It had been a big deal, over $125 million, and involved a tremendous distribution to himself personally.

The transaction experience always began with the same sense of exhilaration. It started in the pit of his stomach and enveloped his senses. *Adrenaline. Focus. Total control. Power.* It was hard to recreate the feeling in any other environment. Even sex didn't measure up. It was spontaneous and only occurred in the heat of battle—when he was negotiating a deal.

Business transactions, mergers, and acquisitions, were not bound by ethical rules. They were pure one-on-one contests, true negotiations. You could hide the ball when deal-making. But having come through this one successfully, he found he did not feel like celebrating. He'd lost the exhilaration of the deal in a myriad of other emotions he was now experiencing for the first time.

James Anderson ran a large private equity firm, Diamond Capital. He leveraged his background and cut-throat instincts to invest the firm's capital in up-and-coming or disorganized enterprises, which he then grew and sold to strategic buyers. Having graduated Magna Cum Laude from Stanford with a degree in Chemical Engineering before receiving his MBA from Wharton, he applied his ChemE background when possible and understood scientific complexities many other investors did not.

At forty-three, James had been uncommonly successful. Though, it had never really been about the money, the money was certainly nice. But the constant travel, meetings, missed dinners, and generally being an absentee father and husband left some holes in his life. Now he was in Paris, trying to repair the biggest hole yet. His divorce from his wife of seventeen years, Kerri, was official this month. And it killed him. He had come to Paris to try to deal with being single, and to try to figure out who he was: a strange concept for a forty-three-year-old man.

He ran his fingers through his black hair and took a drink of his beer. Nothing he'd learned over his years of success in business had prepared him in any way for this personal failure. In fact, he never even knew he was failing. He just did what he did. Now, looking back, everything was much clearer. Revisionist perspectives always were. It should have been apparent to him that his relationship was suffering. He just had not been paying attention. He had taken his marriage for granted. *What the fuck happened?* he thought, taking a drag of his cigarette.

James got up from the café and crossed the busy Boulevard St. Germain. He needed a change of atmosphere.

His love of Paris stemmed from the times he'd spent here as the student of a prestigious boarding school. James and his American classmates had felt it was their charge to personally liberate Paris for the third time. More specifically, their aim had been to liberate Paris of its cigarettes, its beer, and, most importantly, its women. During the year he'd spent in Paris as a student, James had become proficient at navigating the meandering neighborhoods and streets, mostly out of necessity. It had become his and his friends' cultural standard to try to visit at least one attraction in Paris upon waking up, usually between two and three o'clock in the afternoon on weekends after a night of bar-hopping. This had required discipline, as most attractions closed around 4:00 p.m. Once they'd visited the cultural imperative of the day, they retreated to the cold, dark corners of the bars near Rue Mouffetard, St. Germain, St. Michel, and occasionally Chatelet Les Halles.

Those raucous evenings had turned into months, and instilled in James a deep love of French culture, people, and nightlife, as well as of the smells and sounds of the city. Friendships from that time still held true. Every time he returned, James enjoyed grabbing a drink with Killian, Gary, and Sean, whom he had met nearly twenty-five years earlier. The three bartending, fight-loving, binge-drinking Irish expatriates had changed a lot over the years. They loved to talk and laugh about the old times, but now they too were responsible, respectable fathers and husbands. Times changed, even in Paris—although Paris itself stayed the same.

James was not a loner, and he could never understand those people who liked to travel alone. *What the hell good is having interesting experiences if you have no one to share them with?* he thought—and now was no exception. He hated being alone. He needed to be with someone for comfort, support, and—yes—probably validation. Finding himself alone at this stage in his life was unsettling and depressing. What good was all this success when you were alone?

One of his older divorced friends had once said, "You know, James, you work your entire life to buy time to spend with the ones you love. But by the time you've earned enough, there is no one left to spend it with." As he thought about it, James felt he was now a glaring example of that tragic, barroom truism.

AGENT DEVON STINSON
FLASHBACK: THE WHITE HOUSE, DECEMBER 16, 2009

And the stars of Heaven fell to earth as a fig tree drops its late figs when shaken by a mighty wind.

—REVELATION 6:13

Agent Devon Stinson rubbed his temples. His journey at NSA had been dramatic. No one would believe it, even if they were presented the facts. How had he ended up here? Would his grandmother believe what he had been through—what he now knew? Probably not. It would probably scare her to death. He smiled as he thought about his sweet grandmother, who had dragged him into that Southern Baptist church at least three days a week.

Devon Stinson was from a small Mississippi town. He'd never known his father; his mother struggled with addiction and was in and out of either jail or rehab for most of his childhood. He almost wondered himself how, as a poor black boy living in a three-room shack, he'd ultimately made it to the pinnacle of the intelligence world. But he knew how: it was because of his grandmother. She had forced him to focus on his schoolwork, even when Devon really only cared about sports. Thank God he'd excelled at both. The only student from his school ever to be accepted to the Naval Academy in Annapolis, he'd both played football there and was honored at graduation as a Cadet of Distinction. Soon after he'd gone to work for the CIA as an analyst and was later recruited by one of his college mentors to the National Security Agency.

He sat at his desk and reflected on the shock that had come with this position deep inside the NSA. No one would believe the information he held so close—even President Brooks had been in disbelief when Stinson had begun briefing him as the new Commander-in-Chief.

Agent Stinson thought back to that day. When President Brooks had walked into the conference room, where NASA Administrator Charlie Hastings, Deputy Administrator Suzanne Leonard-Rich, NASA Associate Administrator for Public Affairs Mitchell Goodell, OSTP Head James Holester, and NASA Chief Engineer Thomas Kramer were assembled, Stinson was sitting in the back of the room in a chair along the wall, lacking the pedigree to sit at the "big" table. Brooks had stepped to the head of the table and quickly surveyed the room while everyone stood patiently beside their chairs. Many were eager for their first meeting with the new president. Stinson himself had looked forward to this meeting for several weeks. It wasn't often he was in the presence of the president, and he felt a deep sense of pride to serve under the first black Commander-in-Chief. William Brooks was a tall and handsome man, with a strong jawline and piercing eyes; just a hint of gray had begun to accent the sides of his tightly trimmed hair. The president himself had called the meeting to gain a deeper perspective on NASA's projects, including the current status of the crew exploration vehicle program, the replacement for shuttles.

"Good afternoon," President Brooks had said, taking a seat and opening the folder set before him. Those present returned the greeting. Stinson could tell the president was in awe of NASA's capabilities, its achievements; his sincere interest was palpable and focused. But the president had hidden his hand—no one in the room that day had known anything about the stunning announcement he would make at the end of the meeting.

Over the first hour, Charlie Hastings had discussed the Augustine Commission, the Constellation Program, and other important issues. The director updated the president on the latest operations of the Mars rover and the geological, topographical, and atmospheric information harvested from it. It was clear that the NASA personnel believed this information paved the way for a future Mars mission.

"I am sure we have all reviewed the advice of the Augustine Commission," the president finally interrupted. "Contrary to the priorities of my predecessor, this administration plans to broadcast its intent to put human space flight first. I will need your support to do so. However, I know I don't need to remind you of the current economic disruption under which this country suffers. We are in the midst of a breakdown of the financial system, of a magnitude not witnessed since the Great Depression. This financial contagion has rocked Wall Street and the global financial community, and it will continue to impact the folks at home.

"As you know, more and more people are losing their homes, unemployment continues to rise, and many have lost large portions of their retirement nest eggs. My financial advisors will tell you that we are likely to suffer for quite some time, maybe even years, until things begin to improve. It is my intention, as part of my economic stimulus plan, to fund many new programs at NASA."

Stinson joined the others in exchanging excited looks around the room.

"Now, my team believes that NASA stands to play a unique role in our economic recovery." President Brooks continued "One, its programs will create jobs within the organization, with a multitude of suppliers, contractors, and partners. Two, these programs will help America compete, and remain the envy of the world in technological advancement. And three, NASA programs, unlike any other governmental programs, have the ability to inspire national interest, pride, and excitement while generating new, cutting-edge technologies that can spur growth in the private markets."

"Mr. President, I know you are aware that the shuttle program is way past its life expectancy," interrupted Hastings. "When our shuttles were built, we felt we would use them maybe ten years at the most. Unfortunately, with one economic downturn after another, most presidents have seen fit to continue the program on a minimal budget, which has led to highly public accidents."

"Mr. Hastings, rest assured, I am not under the belief that we should attempt to continue the shuttle program," Brooks replied. "Frankly, based on what I hear from you and others at NASA, it's time to send our shuttles to the museums. We are not going to risk the lives of the brave young men and women who are willing to serve in our space program, using antiquated technology. It is my understanding that you have been working on a new multipurpose crew vehicle with an Ares rocket?"

A few of the men shifted uncomfortably in their seats.

"We have," Thomas Kramer responded, looking at the unopened folder before him. "We think this vehicle would be a suitable replacement for the shuttle, and would fulfill the primary missions of delivering satellites into orbit, transporting astronauts to the space station, and performing scientific and maintenance missions."

"Gentlemen" the president said, pausing significantly, "we are not going to limit our aspirations to delivering satellites into orbit or astronauts to the space station. I believe it is time for a greater challenge. I believe it's time for America to return to the moon. My economic team came up with the idea," he concluded, smiling, "and it met with no small amount of support from myself."

The room went silent. Several of the men seated tried to conceal smiles. The president knew no one had been briefed on this plan; he and his cabinet had conceived it without consulting any of the intelligence agencies. All those at the table were blindsided, and all were very excited—all but a few.

"Sir, with all due respect," Mitchell Goodell finally said, "the funding necessary for such an endeavor would require tremendous public support."

"Actually, we are going to ask Congress to increase NASA's budget to $20 billion, and we will seek to fund certain components of the mission through a hybrid of public and private funds," the president stated matter-of-factly. "My team is already at work on that."

"But in the middle of this economic downturn, with all the other agencies seeing budget cuts, how are we going to gather public support?" Goodell asked.

"Well, first I am going to suggest we privatize portions of the space program," Brooks replied. "I am confident someone in Congress will step forward to fight against that, of course. But we are going to bring in private money by incentivizing companies with the intellectual property that results from the effort."

Stinson gave NASA Chief Engineer Thomas Kramer a knowing look. He knew this was dangerous territory, and they needed to get a handle on it immediately. Kramer nodded at Stinson subtly before interjecting himself into the conversation.

"Will potential patent rights be enough to encourage private companies?" he asked.

The president frowned. "Mr. Kramer, it has come to my understanding that NASA has developed more than six thousand patentable materials, and most of those patents eventually went to private companies," he said "The space program has led to advances in all fields. We need to rejuvenate our economy and invest in long-term growth. A new moon initiative is just what we need. I have explained my stance on achieving sustainability for the manned space program, although we will keep the idea of a new moon mission private for now." President Brooks looked pointedly at Goodell. "We will allow most of the other information out about what NASA is doing, to go public."

Mitchell Goodell leaned forward on the table, frowning to himself. "Mr. President, I think that it is a good idea to release as much information as possible, but don't you think that if you take a public stance to support NASA in these harsh economic times, it will result in some backlash?"

"Mr. Goodell, like any good PR man, you worry too much," the president said. "I'm not worried about my image, because I'm doing this for the economy. Increasing funding to NASA will not only create more jobs within the organization itself; it will also encourage private companies to invest in the new technologies. They will then hire people to deliver those technologies, and Americans will see a return on their investment." He stood and smiled charmingly. "If there are no further questions, we will adjourn."

As everyone filed out of the room, Stinson and Kramer, lingered.

"Sir, if you have just a moment?" Kramer asked.

The president raised an eyebrow. "Yes?"

Mr. Kramer looked around uncomfortably and turned slightly toward the wall to shield the conversation. "We can get the Ares V to the moon for certain, sir," he said. "But—we can't send an astronaut there."

The president looked in Kramer's eyes, gauging his intense expression. "Perhaps your reluctance is the very reason we should go," he said steadily.

Kramer took a deep breath, put his hands in his pockets, and continued in a hushed tone. "Mr. President, we need to schedule a classified meeting on this topic—right now. NSA Chief Perkings will explain more and brief you on Project Aquarius. However, I'm afraid we cannot go to the moon."

JAMES ANDERSON
PARIS, FRANCE

James sat at a street-side table at the Bonaparte, a chic café on Place Saint-Germain-des-Prés. It was here that he always felt most at ease.

"*S'il vous plait, avez-vous le Seize Soixante Quatre?*" he asked, knowing they carried his favorite French beer before hearing the response. He had ordered it here a thousand times. He just liked trying to communicate in a foreign language, even being as limited as he was with French.

The waiter, a rude Asian man in his sixties who must have worked at the café for a decade, delivered the beer without a word and stuffed the bill under the ashtray. James took a sip, lit a cigarette, and took a long drag, watching the embers burn and the resulting small line of smoke emanating from its tip. As the ash grew long, he carefully tapped the cigarette on the edge of the small green plastic Carlsberg ashtray.

He never smoked elsewhere—only here. It seemed that he could not fully enjoy Paris without a cigarette. When he first came, everyone smoked; many still did, although not as they once had. He was shocked when the French passed a smoking ban before most major U.S. cities. It was incomprehensible to him how something like that could possibly have passed. No one smoking in Paris bars anymore? *Crazy.* He sifted through random memories and tried to steady the small café table that sat on uneven paving stones.

He saw a couple holding hands, walking across the street as they laughed at some private joke. Now that he thought about it, it seemed he had very few memories of his life before his marriage to Kerri. And certainly, all the ones that mattered included her. Most important were those involving their four kids: Allen, 16; John, 14; Daniel, 11; and little Amy, 6. Together they had all experienced the rollercoaster ride of his entrepreneurial life and its resulting successes and failures—but none more so than Kerri.

Over the years, they'd begun to spend less time together as James ran from deal to deal and Kerri ran from soccer games to dance recitals. When they'd first had kids, they were adamant about keeping date-night once a week, but soon that slipped away. Their relationship soon revolved almost entirely around their kids: the soccer and softball games, school-work, music lessons, parties, after-school clubs. They seemed to forget about making time for themselves. Things just got in the way. It was no one's fault; there had been no terrible fights.

"Nah," he muttered, taking another drag. As he thought about it, both of them were to blame. He had withdrawn from his involvement with her, but she had done things that he'd never believed her capable of doing. He looked down at the ashtray, his sense of the loss of his love burning in his chest. He had never experienced the gravity of such pain. He felt as if his body had tripled in mass, and any moment the chair would crush under its weight. How could these feelings manifest themselves so physically? His chest felt compressed, a suffocating sensation. He lit another cigarette. The smoke wafted into his eyes, making it more difficult to hold back the tears that threatened to escape.

Kerri had been screwing the tennis coach. It was such a cliché that it was almost funny. Ironically, they had often laughed together about which of their neighbors was fucking the tennis coach. James always found it strange that once you had money in his social circle, all the wives played tennis. *Maybe,* he thought, *they were all fucking their tennis coaches.*

James was a proud man and finding out had not only caused him great pain, it had humiliated him. The affair was widely known about, of course. When talking to mutual friends, he found it nearly impossible to look them in the eye. He knew what they were thinking. It was the proverbial elephant in the room. And it killed him. He couldn't stand the hushed comments, people quickly turning their heads, or the social climbers at the country club obviously discussing his problems.

It's always the catty, fat women with money. Don't they have anything else to fucking do than revel in others' misery and gossip constantly? he thought to himself. That kind of cattiness pissed him off. To avoid it, he got out of town—thus Paris, alone.

James had always been clever in his business dealings, outmaneuvering his competition: getting the better end of the deal. Ironically, the same cleverness was how he'd discovered Kerri's infidelity.

One Friday evening, Kerri had gone out with some girlfriends, while James stayed home, working on a Letter of Intent for the acquisition of a software company.

As the night progressed, the Chicago weather turned nasty. It was

January, and snowing hard. James got nervous and called Kerri's phone. She didn't answer until his tenth call or so, at which point it was after two in the morning. She told him that when she'd dropped off Stacy, her tennis friend, she'd decided to go inside for a glass of wine.

"One glass turned into a bottle, because Stacy is upset with her boss. I need to be here for her," she'd explained.

But something wasn't right: it was too quiet on the other end of the phone. Kerri's tone was hurried and nervous, too, and James had heard the soft clanging of two beer bottles as they were lifted from a table. Having drunk more than his fair share of beer, he knew it wasn't the sound of wine glasses, and neither Kerri nor Stacy drank beer.

He'd had a sinking feeling in the pit of his stomach as he hung up the phone. For several minutes he'd considered what he should do as he stared at the keypad, trying to convince himself he was over-thinking this.

Finally, he'd picked up the phone and called OnStar. He'd told the operator that his 15-year-old son had taken the car, and he needed to know where it was immediately. The weather validated his excuse, and after a few minutes of sweet-talking the operator out of her suggestion to call the police, she provided him with the exact location of the car.

It was not Stacy's address. Kerri's car was parked in the driveway of a small subdivision home, and when James had knocked, it was the tennis coach who answered.

James was normally a volatile man, and reflecting on that night, he often wondered why he hadn't gone crazy and beaten the shit out of the guy. But he hadn't. Through the door opening, he had seen his wife in the living room; their eyes had met for a moment before he'd calmly turned around and left.

His life had changed the night he found out. He was forced to deal with feelings he never believed he would experience, the kind of problems he thought only happened to other people. Kerri had partied hard the entire spring and summer after they separated; it was as if she were back in college again. She was always out with the tennis coach—always drinking too much. James was amazed at her blindness to the fact that the guy just wanted her lifestyle: the cars, the huge house, the pool, and the boats. He wasn't screwing her; he was screwing James's wallet. The tennis coach was probably in his mid-twenties, and Kerri was forty-two. James knew it was not going to last, and for a while, all he wanted was for her to realize it and come back to him.

Instead, she tried to act like she knew exactly what she was doing. In fact, she threw it in his face, punishing him with her self-righteous air. Deep down it seemed to him as though she knew she'd made an incredible mistake, and just couldn't bring herself to admit it. But the thought brought him little comfort. Had he really deserved all of that?

James took another drink of his beer, and then he flipped his hand around to look at the burning ash. He wished he were drunk enough to stop feeling the pain.

"Une autre, s'il vous plaît," he said, attracting the waiter's attention as he finished the pint.

While he waited for his next round, James adjusted the small round table so that it would face the square and crossed his legs, hoping the view would distract him until the alcohol stifled the hurt. He gazed out at St. Germain-des-Prés, the oldest church in Paris. Dusk cast a dark, pinkish hue across the rough limestone surface of the steeple, which still bore the scars of World War II. Although this church lacked the grandeur of the more famous churches in Paris, it was his favorite. It had endured because of what it represented, not because of its rich sculptures or artwork. It was just an old church. Ivy hung from its southern wall, accentuating its age. It almost looked as if nature were trying to reclaim the stones from which it was built.

James lit another Camel, consciously acknowledging that it was his fourth cigarette in rapid succession since sitting down. After he finished the Kronenbourg 1664, he slid some Euros under the ashtray.

He slowly walked over to the church; the cool evening air blew down the street as he crossed it. As with most churches in Paris, the doors were open. He paused before entering.

People were scattered throughout: tourists photographing the artwork and windows, a few people sitting in the chairs facing the altar, some servant of the church—perhaps a young priest—ducking into a side alcove between the tall green columns.

James chose to sit alone in a chair near the back. He stared at the church's well-lit altar and glanced at the blue ceiling painted in stars. *What have I done?* He pulled a small, folded sheet of parchment paper from his pocket and looked down at the few handwritten lines upon it.

He had planned to give it to Kerri on their anniversary, knowing things were bad. Opening it, he reread what he had written:

Happy anniversary, my love. I know we haven't seen much of each other lately—it's awful how life gets in the way. It keeps pushing us forward. I never know where I am going anymore, and time only seems to drive me further from you. I'm sorry.

When I take time to pause and realize that the important things are right before my eyes, my path clears before me. I realize that all that matters is to be with you ... always.

You are all that matters to me. I am void without you. I'm sorry for not showing you the love you that you always deserve. I promise, that will change.

He'd learned of the affair two days before their anniversary. After his discovery, anger had prevented him from giving her the note.

He needed to calm himself. He stood up and took a long look at the small cross above the altar and the stained-glass windows just barely glowing from the evening light of the city. Then he walked out of the church without looking back at the note he'd left on the chair. It was time to close that chapter in his life.

2

FATHER MATEO PEREZ
CASTEL GANDOLFO, ITALY

"From my perspective, the Big Bang remains the best explanation of the universe's origin that we have from a scientific standpoint."
—FR . JOSÉ GABRIEL FUNES, FORMER DIRECTOR OF THE VATICAN OBSERVATORY

FATHER MATEO PEREZ WAS BUSY WORKING on the observatory dome door. *What was I thinking? I shouldn't be out here messing with this*, he thought, overly aware of his short, rotund body where it stood on the small circular walkway that wrapped around the metal telescope housing. Once again he rummaged through a bag of less-than-adequate tools and cursed under his breath, looking around to ensure no one had heard. The slight wind from the south carried the smells of the early fall countryside gently toward him, but the beauty of the day was wasted on him and did little to lift his sour mood.

He was so lost in his thoughts, he scraped his hand attempting to use the wrench. After swearing to himself, he threw it back into the tool bag, simultaneously wiping grease from his hand and sucking the blood off his index finger. He shouldn't be doing this without assistance. He should stick to what he was good at—he was a respected astronomer, well known for his publications, mostly around properties of galaxies, and for his radical comments about extraterrestrial life.

Cardinal Russo emerged onto the observatory walkway, inadvertently slamming the door open. Father Perez jolted upright and nearly fell over the edge. Had there not been a railing, he surely would have toppled from the suspended walkway. No one ever journeyed up to the observatory, let alone someone with the stature of Cardinal Russo. Father Perez knew the cardinal liked to think of himself as merely the political arm of the Vatican, but to many he was the most powerful official in the Roman Curia: the Secretary of State and Camerlengo of the Holy Roman Church.

Cardinal Giovanni Russo was an old man. His face was creased by time, but his piercing brown eyes were bright and very alert. His close-cut white hair was thinning and mostly obscured by his zucchetto.

"Are you quite all right?" Cardinal Russo asked.

"Oh, excuse me, Your Eminence! Y—you startled me," Father Perez stammered. He glanced self-consciously down at his grease-covered clothing. This was not the way he imagined meeting such a high-ranking official from the Vatican.

"Not at all, not at all, my son," the Cardinal chuckled, slowly working his way along the narrow walkway toward Father Perez. Russo was considerably older than Mateo but enjoyed good health. His clear eyes revealed his depth of wisdom, owing perhaps to having more secular knowledge than most who were dedicated to the clergy. "You look very busy."

"Yes, the door has been giving us problems for several days, Your

Eminence. Sadly, I am too impatient to wait for a repairman." Father Perez shifted his weight nervously. He began to mentally review all the work he had recently completed, trying to remember what might had offended those above him.

"So, what have you observed that is new and interesting lately?" the Cardinal asked.

"Actually, there is a solar storm that we are tracking in an effort to calculate its potential impact on Earth . . ." Father Perez began. After a brief pause, the Cardinal Secretary responded with a very stern glare.

"You know, in the 1600s we had Giordano Bruno tortured and burned alive for suggesting the earth was not the center of the universe," he said.

Father Perez felt his heart fill with terror.

Father Russo laughed aloud. At first, Father Perez did not know what to make of this, but after seeing the warmth in Father Russo's eyes, he smiled back.

"Here we are four hundred years later, and we know we were wrong. I suppose it's too late to apologize to him!" Cardinal Russo said, still chuckling. "Ah—well—what are we going to learn tomorrow? Come with me. I have something to share with you." Without waiting for a reply, Father Russo turned and began his slow descent.

"I'm sorry, your Eminence, I'm in the middle of this . . ."

Cardinal Russo continued down into the observatory. "Yes, yes, I am sure it will wait. Come with me," he said over his shoulder.

Father Perez stood gaping at him for a few seconds before closing his mouth and carefully ambling after the old man. Despite the slow pace of the Cardinal, they were soon in the courtyard, where Father Perez felt he was close enough to speak. "Excuse me, Your Eminence, I do not exactly understand. Where are we going?"

The Cardinal Secretary did not turn around this time, but held up his index finger. "All in good time, my son," he said. "All in good time."

DR . SOFIA PETRESCU
GENEVA, SWITZERLAND

Prove all things; hold fast that which is good.

—1 THESSALONIANS 5:21

It was unusually cold and gray for mid-September in Geneva. Dr. Sofia Petrescu sat at a small table in the cafeteria at the United Nations building, eating her lunch. She tried to act like she didn't notice Professor De Vos sitting nearby and hid her face behind her thick blonde hair, realizing as she did how fruitless the attempt would prove. It was rare that she escaped male attention anyway, given her looks and slim, athletic figure. Those were not the ostracized professor's interests, but she knew very well he had others.

Her position and background made it almost inevitable. She served as a consultant to the United Nations Office for Outer Space Affairs in Vienna, primarily on subjects dealing with technology use in outer space. UNOOSA focused on maximizing the peaceful use of space by member countries; its director, it was rumored, had officially been designated by the U.N. to be the first contact for any extraterrestrial communication. That thought always made Sofia laugh—like the U.N. would have control over the situation.

Sofia had grown up in Romania, raised by a harsh, bitter grandmother, bitter over the obligations thrust on her to raise a child on her own after both of Sofia's parents had been killed in an automobile accident. She barely remembered them now. She had very few fond memories of her childhood, and she'd lost contact with her grandmother after she'd left home.

Her grandmother had sided with the Nazis during the Second World War, just as Romania had, and she had a militant, abusive way about her. After the war and the Yalta Conference, Romania was subjected to a forced armistice that gave the Soviet Union unlimited control and military presence in Romania. Sofia had been educated in Soviet-run schools and had never understood her grandmother's hatred for the USSR.

Not that she cared what her grandmother thought. Her grandmother had treated Sofia like more of a house servant and a nuisance than a family member. Sofia had retreated into her books and schoolwork, and looked forward every day to the long walk to school and the reprieve it granted her from the pain that surrounded her home. That house held so many bad memories. Even at an early age, Sofia knew that her only way out was through education. In Romania there was little opportunity for women, and she knew for certain that her grandmother could not afford any secondary education. Nor would she approve. Sofia excelled in school and obtained a scholarship to the University of Bucharest.

Professor De Vos was making a beeline over to her.

Dr. Jonas De Vos was a member of the United Nations Intergovernmental Panel on Climate Change and a chemistry professor at the Université Catholique de Louvain in Belgium. Sofia had known him from her brief time as a post-graduate astrophysics researcher at UCL, where Professor De Vos was one of her doctoral advisors. At that time his reputation had been pristine. But no longer. Although he was still recognized as an accomplished researcher, Sofia knew things hadn't been going well for him lately: he had lost his research grants, and his papers had been rebuked and criticized among his peers. She barely knew him otherwise—or cared to, anymore.

"Sofia, please—I need your help here," the professor said as he abruptly sat down at her table, scattering his files on the table inadvertently. "You have not responded to my emails."

"Professor De Vos, I'm sorry, but I have no environmental science background—you know that," said Sofia, sighing. "I don't think I can be of any help." She had hoped to avoid this conversation in person.

"You are precisely the person who can help. Sofia, you know what they have done to me here," he added motioning around the room. "I'm fearful I'm going to lose my position at the University. My removal from the IPCC Working Group, and the recent, very public criticism from my colleagues at the U.N. does not bode well for me." He looked down at the floor self-consciously. "My research will prove my postulate correct," he said quietly, motioning to his files. "I just need your help in verifying some data."

Sofia stifled a cringe. She knew that Professor De Vos's recent publications had challenged the notion of human causal impact on global warming and climate change, a central theme to the U.N.'s IPCC plan and a foundational battle cry for its controversial Agenda 21.

"Professor, with all due respect, I don't want to get mixed up in your climate-change argument. It's really not my place . . ."

"Sofia, please listen," he pleaded. "You must understand, as a scientist." He broke off, collected himself, and started again.

"CO_2 is not a pollutant; it is a nutrient, and there has never been any direct evidence of human activities causing temperature change. Yes, that is a hypothesis, and a reasonable one—one which I've studied to see if there was a causal connection. But it has now become a religion, a sacred cow you dare not speak against. This is not science. If you vary from the U.N.'s party line one iota, you will be ostracized. The IPCC is made up of alarmists. The mentality around the U.N.'s climate change forum is cult-like. This is not what I signed on for. The IPCC was set up by the World Meteorological Organization and the United Nations Environment Programme to assess the scientific basis for climate change. However, they have made their decision already: the party line is that global warming is caused by man-made carbon dioxide—end of story. The goal of the program, when I joined it, was to provide a rigorous and balanced scientific study of the issue. That is not happening. I have been urged by several of my counterparts on the committee to reconsider and revaluate my findings—can you believe that?"

"Even more of a reason for me to steer clear of the debate," Sofia said.

"Please, Sofia, you above all people will be interested in what my research is showing," the professor pleaded as he fumbled through his files. "Please bear with me for just a minute."

Sofia sighed and did her best to simulate a polite smile.

"All throughout human history we have many periods of time, and I mean centuries, that were much warmer periods than the present—the

Medieval Warm Period, for example," he went on. "The theory that global warming is man-made is an abject hypothetical with little evidence, and frankly, I'm beginning to believe it is more about global governance controls and taxation. That is all Agenda 21 is. Too much is at stake now. The U.N. could never admit they were wrong, especially now that they have architected a global control and taxation system around CO_2 being a pollutant and the cause of global warming. Any pure scientist wants to test the hypothesis from a neutral perspective, free of bias. But any research that contradicts the U.N. and the IPCC is scuttled. That's where you come in." Professor De Vos scooted his chair closer to hers and leaned in. "I do believe in global climate change," he said. "Yes, it is happening. But a real scientist should seek the real causal factors. And I think I have identified the real primary cause." He let the statement hang.

"And?" Sofia demanded.

"The periodicity of sun spots is the culprit," Professor De Vos said in a whisper. "As you must know, the periods of solar minimums, the periods of least activity in the eleven-year solar cycle of the sun, occur contemporaneously with decreases in global temperature. The sun has the volume of 1.3 million Earths. How could something so massive and so close *not* have an impact on temperatures? It's 99.8 percent of the mass of the entire solar system, for God's sake." His voice was rising as he became more agitated. "How could it not be rational to question whether global warming is causally related to the sun, that massive thermonuclear furnace next door to our planet?"

"Okay, Professor. I've heard that argument, and it's reasonable enough, I suppose but how do I fit in?" Sofia asked.

"There are specific periods of sunspot activity. This has been documented diligently since William Herschel noticed the correlation in the late 1700s. We have a documented *Little Ice Age,* as it was called in the 18th century. What was unique about that timeframe? There were virtually no sun spots during this period. And we're heading into another such period now." Professor De Vos pulled out a paper from the folder and handed it to Sofia.

"This is a report by Knud Lassen from 1860, showing solar variations and how they impacted global surface temperatures. This scientific precedent and others are being ignored and persecuted, purposefully. My own research demonstrates that clouds form with increased magnetic fields—I call it ion-induced nucleation of the troposphere."

Sensing that Sofia wasn't following, he went on. "Here is the bottom line," he said. "When there are fewer sun spots, as is the case during a solar minimum when there is less solar activity, more solar radiation reaches the earth. The radiation proximately causes cloud cover which leads to a cooling effect. Believe it or not, we are not in a warming phase now. My data suggests we are headed into a long cooling period. Likewise the inverse is true: the earth will heat as solar activity increases, and we have less of a global cloud cover."

Sofia considered this for a moment. It made sense; in fact it was a rather simple postulate. Was this sort of hypothesis really what had aroused such a violent protest against the professor's research? She decided to find out. "Professor, I'll take a quick look," She relented. "Please understand, though: I'm not putting my name on anything."

Professor De Vos was elated. "Thank you, Sofia. Thank you," he said, pushing the files toward her eagerly. "Here are some additional findings that correlate. I think you will find them interesting. And troubling," he added nervously, as he got up to go.

JAMES ANDERSON
PARIS, FRANCE

"The most likely [scenario]: We find an intelligent civilization and there's no way in creation we can communicate with them because they're so alien to us."
—GUY CONSOLMAGNO, DIRECTOR OF THE VATICAN OBSERVATORY

The ringtone James Anderson had assigned to his friend Robert was playing from his pocket as the phone vibrated. Before he'd even said anything, Robert's voice came through.

"Hey, James."

James rolled his eyes and wondered why he had answered the phone. "Hey, Robert—uh, look, I'm kind of busy right now. I am at the Polidor in Paris, eating a fabulous *confit de canard*, or *duck* to you non-Francophiles," he said, chortling at his own joke.

"Sorry, but you need to hear what I found," Robert blurted. "It's something very strange, maybe an anomaly. I do think, however, that we need to take a deeper look at it."

James sometimes found it hard to talk to Robert after his decades in academia. Those locked in the world of *University* who dedicated their entire existence to researching a single protein string, and limited their interactions to those measured by a micropipette titration set, tended to develop their own language, syntax, and cadence of speech. It was a little unsettling for some, James included.

"Look, I really don't like it when you start sounding like a mad scientist," James said. "If you found some special biological pathway, can you at least wait until I am back at the apartment actually *trying* to fall asleep?"

"That's funny, James. I'll call you tomorrow."

"Hang on. If this is about more funding, the answer is *no*."

"No, it's not. I'll talk to you soon, okay?"

James hung up the phone. *Shit. Why didn't I turn that off?* James thought to himself. *Probably just needs more money. I'm sure of it.* He had just enough alcohol in him to feel especially in tune to the injustices of his life without having a completely foggy brain.

He reflected on his friendship with Robert. Dr. Robert Matson had been a lifelong friend, and was now a business partner; he was the one friend James had maintained from childhood. James had grown up rich, really rich—and as a kid, he knew it. From grade school through high school, he had defined himself by what he and his family had: the biggest houses, the nicest cars, the best clothing. James had gathered friends who glommed onto him, wanting to be part of that lifestyle. And even at a young age, Robert was the only one who challenged James about how he treated others. He used to say, "James, everyone knows you're rich; why do you throw it in other people's faces? You constantly talk about money and belittle others who don't have what you have. Stop being such an asshole."

James had met Robert in middle school, and they'd both attended St. Paul High School in upstate New York, a private boarding school catering to the elite. James's father paid his way in. Robert had been accepted based on his intellect, and awarded a scholarship available to families with bright children who couldn't afford the tuition—helped along by a nice recommendation from James's father, which James use to hold over Robert's head. Nevertheless, James, who had always been athletic, was willing to stand up for the slighter, nerdier Robert, and the two had become fast friends.

As a senior, James went to Paris to study for the year through a joint program with The British School of Paris, where he partied and ran hard with the rich kids for the entire school year. Then in his second semester, he and his father had a very sobering conversation. His father had lost nearly everything they had when the Nikkei Stock Index in 1992. James only knew that his father worked in international finance, and they now had nothing. The tuition and school fees were already paid for James through the end of the year, but after that, he would come home to a new reality.

This forced a fierce introspection upon James. All that he had defined himself by was gone. He returned to a small two-bedroom ranch home with a single-car garage, fronting a four-lane highway. All his "friends" had vanished along with the money. This was a pride-crushing experience that laid him bare. He could tell some relished seeing that James had been thrust into a new reality. The only friend who still hung around was Robert. He had always been there.

For over a year, James struggled to find himself. He reflected often on how he had treated others, and made it a point to apologize to those he had mistreated, especially Robert. At the end of that time, James emerged a new person, much more sensitive and concerned with others' feelings and situations. He also realized he hated being poor, and decided to do all that it took to be successful in life and to give back and lift up those around him. He still felt like he had to look out for Robert, but he also knew he valued Robert's advice and judgment above all others.

James decided it was time for a walk along the Seine. He walked over the Pont des Arts, which was filled with pedestrians. A fantastically beautiful woman approached from the opposite direction, her long, black hair seeming to flow into her scandalously short, black dress. Her legs were tan and perfect. He held her gaze. *Wow,* James thought. She batted her eyes at him and smiled.

James continued walking, a little more confidently. *Maybe I still have it,* he thought. He stopped at a small shop and pretended to be looking in the window as he surveyed his reflection. Some slightly graying, black hair, maybe a few creases by his eyes. His jaw was still quite square—no double chin yet. He sucked his gut in a bit. *Not bad,* he thought. *Still got a bit of an athletic build, maybe with a little wear on it.* After a minute, he released his breath. *Crap, I need to lose at least fifteen pounds,* he lamented.

Later that evening, he found himself back at the Bonaparte. This time he sat outside, but under the awning since it had begun to rain. He sat at a small table nursing a beer and watching couples running here and there in an attempt to dodge the raindrops on their way to the small theater next door.

The phone rang. "Robert, again?" he said aloud. He picked up. "Bonjour, Monsieur Robert," he said in a Monty-Pythonish French accent.

"James, where are you?" Robert replied.

"Well," James retorted, "where in the hell do you think I am? I just talked to you a couple of hours ago." *This guy is a PhD, for God's sake,* he thought.

"I am fully aware of the country you are in, and I also am aware of the state I would probably find you in should I be in that country with you," Robert said. "However, when I asked you where you were, I was speaking metaphorically and wondered in fact if you were available to talk." His tone was hurried and exasperated, which immediately worried James. Robert was never emotional about anything.

"Yeah, go ahead," James sighed, extinguishing the last of his cigarette brutally in the ashtray and taking another sip of his beer. "All I'm doing right now is drinking a lonely beer at the Café Bonaparte, watching all the saps spending $16 on a beer across the street at Les Deux Magots."

"No, that's not good," Robert said hurriedly. "You can't talk there. You need to go back to your flat immediately and call me. And make sure you call from a landline—" There was a pause and a rustling noise on Robert's end of the phone. James looked at the half-empty pint glass he held between three fingers and frowned.

"On second thought," Robert's voice resumed so abruptly that James almost dropped his beer, "I'll email you a dial-in number. I'm a bit freaked out right now. There is a DNA anomaly here that is causing me some serious goose bumps."

"Robert, you aren't making that much sense right now, and I really haven't had enough beers to help that. What's this about?"

"There is something very—well, unexpected—here, to say the least. Oh, and James?"

"Yeah?"

"Hurry the hell up."

"Okay. Give me twenty minutes," James said, disconnecting. "Shit," he muttered to himself as he stood, fishing several Euros from his pocket. "I should have trusted my gut and stayed the hell away from investing in biotech companies."

AGENT DEVON STINSON
FLASHBACK: JOHN F. KENNEDY SPACE CENTER, APRIL 15, 2010

And a great war broke out in Heaven: Michael and his angels fought with the dragon; and the dragon and his angels fought, but they did not prevail . . .
—REVELATION 12:7 - 8A

"Mr. President, you will need to cancel any plans of a return mission to the moon," said Mitchell Perkings quietly.

Sitting in a small conference room at the Kennedy Space Center, the president was preparing to give a speech. He frowned and glanced at his watch, then looked around the small room. The table was occupied by Director of National Security Perkings, NASA Administrator, Charlie Hastings, and NASA Chief Engineer Thomas Kramer, as well as a young man unknown to him.

"Mr. Perkings, Mr. Kramer was quite insistent that we meet before this speech," he said. "Now I'd like to understand what is so important."

Agent Stinson had a sick feeling in the pit of his stomach. The president had yet to be briefed on Project Aquarius, and Stinson knew he was not going to like what he was about to find out.

"I'm very sorry, Mr. President. I know your agenda has been very full, but this is an extraordinarily important matter," Kramer said.

"From what I understand, you are planning to announce a return to the moon very soon," Perkings said.

The president glanced over the men in the room. "That is the plan at this point," he agreed sternly, "and I see no reason not to go forward with it."

"Mr. President, I'm not sure we have time to fully brief you as we anticipated before your speech," Perkings went on, unfazed, "but I think after we have some time to talk, you will reconsider this plan. You'll need to cancel or change your speech today."

"I don't like making changes without knowing what is behind them," President Brooks said. "If you want me to push this aside, you need to give me the full details, and now. What is this all about, gentlemen?"

The men around the table shifted uncomfortably, feeling the weight of the information that they needed to share with the president. For a moment they sat in silence, their faces stern in serious consideration.

"Mr. President, this is Agent Devon Stinson of the NSA," said Perkings finally, motioning toward the young agent. "He is our team lead on Project Aquarius."

"Nice to meet you, Agent Stinson," the president said politely.

Agent Stinson nodded. "Thank you, sir." He got up and closed the door to the small conference room "Mr. President, Project Aquarius is an above-top-secret, multinational program managed within the U.N. Security Council. It is the repository of all collective information we have on UFOs and any information we have on extraterrestrial biology. What I'm about to tell you may be a bit—well, unsettling."

FATHER MATEO PEREZ
THE VATICAN

"We are not split into a world of Spocks and Kirks."
—GUY CONSOLMAGNO, DIRECTOR OF THE VATICAN OBSERVATORY

Father Perez followed the cardinal through Castel Gandolfo. They continued to a silver Mercedes waiting on the street. The chauffer opened the back door and motioned for Father Perez to enter. He slid across, allowing the cardinal to join him. Once the door shut, the cardinal turned and smiled at him.

"Your work has attracted quite some attention, Father Perez," he said. "You are good at what you do. So good, in fact, that His Holiness would like to meet with you."

It took a second before Father Perez could respond. "Thank you, Your Eminence. My only wish is to please." Although this was not exactly true, he felt it was better than saying his only wish was not to bite the hand that fed him.

"I am counting on that fact." The cardinal turned away from him and looked out the window, abruptly ending the discussion.

Father Perez began to sweat. Now he was truly terrified. Going to the Vatican to meet the pope could not be a good thing, at least not for someone in his position. He was aware that some of his colleagues occasionally called him "the agnostic priest" behind his back, but he had never felt his position more precarious than at this moment. He had known that he would never obtain rank above a priest, and he had accepted that; he'd never been much interested in the religious side of the church anyway. But why he was being singled out now was beyond him. Although he had made a poorly received statement on extraterrestrials years ago, he could see nothing of controversy in the current area of his research—solar flares and their impact on the magnetosphere—that would put him at any risk.

Was he going to lose his job? He loved being an astronomer—it was the only thing that meant anything to him. And though he had always known he could be laicized, he had never known anyone subjected to this. As a priest, his earthly goods were all linked with the Church; what would he do if he were stripped of his title? He supposed he might find a teaching job somewhere, but would the church give him the time to find it before taking back the possessions they had bestowed upon him? The thought of applying to an upper-level university wearing the lay clothing he'd worn when he entered the seminary brought a snort that he suppressed in a fit of coughing. His head was spinning.

What could the pope want with him? He had met Saverio Ferretti before he became Pope Paul VII; as the cardinal from Venice, Pope Paul had served as one of his examiners when he'd joined the Jesuit Order. Perez knew that Pope Paul was also a scientist at heart and had been known to make statements against some traditionally held beliefs. Could that have something to do with it?

Near the end of their drive the cardinal's cell phone rang, and the cardinal listened carefully to the person on the other line. The few times he spoke, he did so in a hushed, cryptic tone, doing his best to keep his part of the conversation unheard. Father Perez felt almost as if he were intruding and shifted uncomfortably, trying not to overhear what was being said.

Whatever was going on, Father Perez felt very much in over his head. He'd never been the adventurous or aggressive sort. As a kid in the ghettos of Buenos Aires, he was never much of an athlete; instead, he had fallen in love with the stars. He began reading at an early age, and could always be found gazing at the sky or buried in a magazine reading about the latest supernova. He'd attributed his curiosity about outer space to his mother's intense Catholicism and faith in God and heaven, but he inherently knew—at least from the moment he could think for himself—that heaven was not really a place. He was painfully aware that it was not "up there beyond the stars" as his mother would say. However, there was *something* up there. Of this, he was convinced.

To make his mother happy, he'd done his catechism, made his confirmation, and accompanied her to mass every day. But he'd never allowed himself to believe that the whole practice was anything more than a cultural routine. Faith in an afterlife made his mother happy, and he believed it gave her peace of mind. At least, it answered those questions for which she wanted answers. He, however, had questions that went beyond the catechism.

A motorcycle screamed past the car, interrupting his thoughts.

He smiled to himself at the irony of his entrance into the seminary, glancing briefly at the cardinal. He'd told himself he did it for his mother. She rarely ever spoke of her own family; when she did, she limited her recollection to an older brother who had been a priest. But despite these associations, and although he'd never said it aloud to anyone, he knew his choice had really been made to distance him from the social concerns that served to motivate young men his age but seemed alien to him. The practical side had been real, too: although his mother made sure their stomachs were never grumbling, funds for continuing his education had not been available. Not only had the Church assumed the cost for his seminary, it had also paid for any continued education he desired.

His was not the typical path of a parish priest, and surprisingly, that had never been an obstacle. In fact, the Church had seemed to encourage his academic appetites, insisting there were many roles to fill that required scholarly work beyond theology. Ultimately, he'd moved on from the seminary, and with the blessing of the church, began to pursue a master's degree in physics, concentrating on astronomy.

After that, he dared apply to the University of Padua, where he'd received his doctorate in astronomy. Then, as a nod to the Vatican for paying his way, he earned a degree from the Pontificate Gregorian University in theology.

Once his education was complete, Rome had sent him to Mount Graham, Arizona, to begin his research. He had first been worried that the Vatican would return him to Italy to teach at one of the seminaries, but apparently they'd had other plans for his life. When the call to return home finally came, it was with an appointment at the observatory in Castel Gandolfo to continue his work. That kept him busy, and gave him a sense of self-worth and accomplishment without demanding that he pretend to believe in something he didn't.

The day's frustration with the observatory cemented his preference for the much more advanced Mount Graham facilities. His staff at the Vatican observatory was very small, much like the town itself.

Soon they arrived. Upon entering the Vatican through a guarded gate, the cardinal hung up the phone and exited the car without comment. Father Perez followed the cardinal as he walked under the entry arch to the papal apartments. Perez was awed; he had never had a reason to venture inside the business area of the papal apartments. Although Pope Paul chose to live modestly in a flat nearby at the Vatican guesthouse, he still conducted business in the top-floor apartment of the Apostolic Palace.

The journey to the meeting room was slow as they proceeded through the Clementine Hall and past the colorful Swiss Guard, down the Seconda Loggia, and through more corridors guarded by even more Swiss Guard, until they finally arrived at the desk of the Prefecture of the Papal House.

"Father Perez," Cardinal Russo stated to the man behind the desk, whose sole response was a nod.

The cardinal then led him through several more passages before finally opening a door to a large room. After a pause, Father Perez followed him into the room through the camel-colored curtains framing the door. A table with one large white chair at the head and several smaller wooden ones sat in the center of the expansive room. All the walls were painted with intricate details. The floors bore a beautiful pattern of inlaid marble. The furniture looked to be from the 16th century. The room was furnished with only a few elegant pieces, perhaps to give the impression of modesty, while the exquisitely painted walls, marble inlay, arched ceilings, and elaborate chandeliers hanging over the table betrayed another intention. Cardinal Russo walked behind the table and took a seat next to the white chair. He motioned for Father Perez to sit across from him. As Father Perez seated himself carefully, Cardinal Russo smiled, leaned back in his chair, and began humming.

Father Perez had never been in this meeting room before, but knew it to be the Stanza di Eliodoro immediately upon his entrance. This was the smallest of the Vatican's Raphael Rooms, adorned with paintings by the famous artist on all the walls and ceiling.

The *Expulsion of Heliodorus from the Temple* dominated the room. It depicted the expulsion of Heliodorus from the Temple of Jerusalem after his attempt to take its treasures. *The Meeting of Leo the Great and Attila* depicted Saint Peter and Saint Paul floating through the air, wielding their swords in anticipation of battle. It amazed Father Perez that these works were completed in the early 1500s, and yet with careful preservation, had remained in prime condition. It was almost tragic that they were rarely seen by the public. Father Perez wondered if this room had been chosen today for a specific reason.

Father Perez shifted his eyes to a large, darkly stained cupboard on the opposite wall. As he had done since childhood in every mass he had ever sat through, he began blocking out the world around him and focusing in on the detail of the cupboard. It was a technique he'd learned in the Latin high masses he had suffered through with his mother before he could understand them. After his first fidgety experience when he had dared to complain, his mother had snapped at him, telling him that he should be looking at the stained glass to entertain himself. He had taken it to heart and used the method for every situation he found boring or uncomfortable thereafter.

The doors opened abruptly, jerking both Father Perez and Cardinal

Russo to attention. Cardinal Russo slowly rose from his chair and bowed as the pope stepped into the room, several guards in tow.

Father Perez remained frozen in awe. Until this moment, he had not believed he had truly been summoned to appear before His Holiness in person. The cardinal politely cleared his throat to gain Father Perez's attention, prompting Father Perez to his feet to execute a low bow. When he rose, his face was drained of all color, and his eyes were wide. The pope smiled with a twinkle in his eye and took a seat, his stark white hair adding an air of wisdom to his commanding presence. The smile betrayed the serious aura around the man. He tossed a stern look at the Swiss Guards, who glanced hesitantly at Father Perez before stepping outside the room.

The pope looked to make sure the doors were completely closed, then inched forward on his chair. "Well, it is all arranged then?" he asked.

Cardinal Russo nodded. "Yes, Your Holiness, we can begin immediately," he said.

The pope folded his hands on the table and held the gaze of the priest before him. "Thank you for coming today, Father," he said. "You continue to do great work for the Church." He took a deep breath, then said, "Father Perez, today we have a new task for you, a task for the Jesuit Order. One that may—shall we say—test your faith."

3

DR . SATI AM UNNEFER
GIZA PLATEAU, EGYPT

"You know, I do [think there's life out there], but that's just a hunch."
—GUY CONSOLMAGNO, DIRECTOR OF THE VATICAN OBSERVATORY

DR. SATI AM UNNEFER STOOD QUIETLY IN THE DARKNESS, his assistant not far from where he stood. The mortuary temple north of the Great Pyramid cast its shadow over him and hid him from the moonlight. Although most educated Egyptians had abandoned their traditional jalabiya and kaftan, which were associated with fundamental Islam or the lower social classes, he'd chosen to retain his. His colleagues wrote it off as an idiosyncrasy.

He came here alone often. His credentials afforded him access to these ancient structures at any time. Whenever he felt he needed a break from the politically charged world around him, this is where he came to get it; the one place where he could attempt to reconcile existence, religion, and purpose.

He breathed in the night air deeply as he stared across the plain. It was not uncommon for excavation work to take place at night, in an effort to avoid the day's sweltering desert heat. But on this night there were no sodium lights illuminating a dig; there were no workers, and the valley stood still. Sati leaned against a small ancient stone wall, resting his arm and the left side of his body against its radiant warmth. It was well past twilight, and the afternoon heat was giving way to cooler breezes blowing east off the Giza desert plateau.

Sati spoke softly to his assistant, Henku, who sat on the desert sand quietly beside his boss. "It's hard to believe that it finally happened this week, Henku," he said. "After years of releasing and retaking the reins as Egypt's Antiquities Minister, Dr. Mohamed Zaher has finally resigned." Henku looked up at Sati dubiously; Sati laughed "Yes—I, like you, doubt that his absence from the department will be permanent, as always. But maybe this time it is different."

Sati had reason to believe it would be. For years he had served under Zaher, sticking out the abuse when others quit. His sole goal was to become the Zaher-recommended replacement. Over the years, especially when Dr. Zaher was relieved from his position during Egypt's revolution, Sati had often wondered if it was worth it. He had not even been considered an option to fill the dictator's shoes. But he should not have doubted Dr. Zaher's power. When the man returned, Sati was also brought back under his wing. As of late it had been tedious work, since the senior archaeologist had grown crankier with age and refused to lesson his grip. Nevertheless, Sati felt confident that he was finally stepping down: Dr. Zaher had handed over all his files and given him his blessing.

"What will you do now, Dr. Unnefer?" Henku asked.

"We will reignite our dedication to true archaeology," he said.

Although it seemed to take a long time to reach this point in his career, Sati was a very young man to reach it. He had been hardened by the constant demands of perfection Zaher made, and his abusive demeanor. Few could work for Zaher—let alone dedicate their entire career to his tutelage. However, Sati was a quiet man, only speaking after much consideration. He never gave Dr. Zaher any reason to fly off the handle, because when Sati spoke, his comments were well thought out, deliberate, and usually correct. It also helped that even Zaher respected his intellect.

Everyone knew that Zaher enjoyed the power that he wielded. In fact, he often allowed excavation and research only with the understanding that he would be the one to release the findings, thus taking credit for the discoveries. Zaher did not make friends; he made work. He enjoyed catching people off guard, shocking them, and keeping them off balance. This was frequently his form of control, and Sati assumed that was why Dr. Zaher had told no one, including Sati, of his decision to resign until he had already done it.

"Henku—we finally have the power to truly crack open the answers to questions that have plagued me and others for a lifetime." Sati stared at the pyramid before him and allowed his eyes to trace its jagged outline in the moonlight. The night air in the desert had a distinctly ancient, earthy smell. There was almost a sweetness to it. Perhaps it was because tonight he was no longer the apprentice. Having chosen academia over a traditional married life, Sati had long buried himself in studying, writing, and searching for answers. He had no family; he had only his career. It had finally culminated in this moment—a moment he knew he would not be able to enjoy for long. He had no doubt that Zaher would remain hovering in the background; the retired minister had held the reins too tightly and too long to just let go. Although he would have preferred the old man to have passed on quietly in the night, or perhaps fallen to some tragic accident during the revolution, Sati took comfort in the fact that he would be signing the orders now—Zaher would no longer have the power to veto or ignore Sati. He would have preferred an unencumbered quest, but he could handle the complicated scenario he was given. Sati felt a sense of empowerment.

It would be interesting to see Zaher's reaction when he discovered that the man who had once been so deferential and respectful to his mentor's beliefs and decision, was suddenly allowing his own deeply divisive thoughts on research and on department positions to surface.

Sati wondered if he would be able to contain the resentfulness that had overshadowed their relationship the next time they met.

"There are so many questions," Sati said to his assistant, "questions that Zaher refused to discuss or research. For example, the ancient Egyptian calendar found in these ruins, dating from 4,000 years ago, is more precise than the one used today. Where did this knowledge come from?"

Henku just stared out into the desert.

"And the Great Pyramid there," Sati continued, pointing, "was constructed of 2,600,000 limestone blocks weighing two tons each. Still, they were cut with a precision that would be hard to replicate with present day technology. How did they create and move these stones?"

In a quiet tone, Henku replied, "Zaher taught me that they rolled them on trees."

Sati's new assistant had grown up in a very poor family and had almost no formal education. But he was self-educated and a hard-working, affable young man. During the violent riots against Mubarak in Cairo, he had lost most of his family, and Sati felt good about giving him a chance to improve his life. Although Henku had more fundamentalist beliefs than he did, they got along well enough.

"There were no trees, Henku," Sati retorted. "It was desert, then as it is now. These ancients pieced together the internal blocks of the pyramid so precisely, a razor blade could not be inserted between the stones. I've had archaeologists estimate their tolerance to be within one-hundredth of an inch, and modern architects have confirmed that they could not build on this scale with this level of accuracy today. How?"

Henku just looked down at the sand without answering.

Sati gazed past the Great Pyramid, allowing it to blur in his vision. The stars were bright around the large canvas of sky blocked by the megalithic structure before him. It seemed to create a sizeable void in the fabric of space, a huge hole in the otherwise star-filled sky. His insignificance always felt pronounced here. The magnitude of the galaxy before him and the scale of the pyramid both stood in stark contrast to his small self, staring into the night. Although he had come here countless times, it was always awe-inspiring, and deep emotions welled within him.

He rubbed his sandal into the ground, and the warm sand covered his foot. He took a deep breath and regarded his thin shadow cast across the waves of sand. His boyish face and bright eyes betrayed the intellect behind them and the analytical frustration that drove him.

Sati had so many fantastic questions that had never been addressed, let alone answered, in all the years he served under Zaher. When he'd brought them up as possible future investigation, Zaher had promptly refused to investigate. And Sati never asked a second time; he simply filed each question away. But he knew Zaher had blocked excavations and archaeological work. His intuition told him that Zaher knew something—he knew more about these structures than he had let on. Something that he never shared with anyone, and something that scared him.

JAMES ANDERSON
PARIS, FRANCE

". . . Pope Benedict supported the Vatican Observatory and its scientific work."

—GUY CONSOLMAGNO, DIRECTOR OF THE VATICAN OBSERVATORY

James walked rapidly down Rue Bonaparte to his flat, hoping that the frantic call from Robert had not been because of some major bad news. Since making the investment with Robert in XNA Pharma, James had had constant acid reflux. All the risk, the damn regulations, and the scientific complexities drove him crazy.

The new company had developed a synthetic RNA gene therapy to target specific diseases. They were on the cutting edge of a new science: designer DNA-based treatment. It seemed that Robert had been right about the uniqueness of this approach, and James had to admit that its potential for making money was enormous.

He knew big pharmaceutical companies had been on a buying binge to snap up these small biotech startups; Merck, for instance, had recently purchased the unknown Sirna Therapeutics for $1.1 billion. Anomalies in DNA sequences were linked to so many incurable diseases: cancer, Alzheimer's, multiple sclerosis. It made sense that the latest Holy Grail in the pharmaceutical world was finding a way to deliver medication or therapy directly to the specific section of DNA or gene that was causing an ailment, and thereby repair it.

But interestingly, no RNA-based therapy had gained much market share yet. Most either caused a toxic response in patients or they could only be poorly delivered to the cell because of their particle size. XNA Pharma was different. The synthesized RNA they used was a quarter of the size of other gene therapies and offered a unique, patented delivery method. In addition, if the research done thus far was correct, XNA's technology produced no toxic response in the body. In James's eyes, XNA was a standout from its competitors.

But though James was a chemical engineer, he had no direct biotech or pharmaceutical background. He understood the scientific aspects of the research better than most, given his background—as long as the procedure was thoroughly explained by the experts. But normally when approached with this sort of venture, he would have steered clear of the investment opportunity. Even with all the advantages XNA exhibited, there were huge business risks associated with the years of research and development it still required, not to mention the bureaucratic backflips the company would need to do to gain FDA approval, or the time and advertising required to make the treatment palatable to the average American citizen.

Dr. Robert Matson, on the other hand, was one of the foremost experts in the world on synthetic RNA. He consulted with many companies and lectured all over the world on this particular topic. Granted, there were only a handful of people on Earth that could understand what in the hell he was talking about—but among those few, Robert was a rock star. James's otherwise perhaps hasty decision to invest in XNA made perfect sense, given Robert's expertise and their friendship. And although he hated to admit it, James loved that he had the opportunity to give Robert a piece of the action as the company's new Chief Scientific Officer—while of course, potentially flipping XNA to a big pharma company for a pretty penny.

They were cut from the same cloth. Both had a panache for mischief, exhibited, for instance, during their junior year of high school when they'd spontaneously snuck up to the auditorium catwalk and stole all the theater's track, stage, and spot lighting. They'd placed them in the band director's unlocked car just hours before the Christmas play. Obviously, that was not quite enough, so they then put the car in neutral and pushed it out into the middle of the muddy baseball field. The shit had truly hit the fan that night. They were never caught and had been best friends ever since.

James crossed the busy Boulevard St. Germain, which was crowded with people enjoying the cool evening. But he slowed down as he approached Saint-Sulpice. Inhaling deeply, he paused to look around. He especially loved the fountain in the middle of the square and the newly restored church.

When he'd first arrived in Paris decades ago, nearly all the Paris lime-stone buildings were covered with the pollution of a century of diesel fuel use. Then the French government had spent billions of Euros and many years systematically sandblasting the buildings; slowly, the elegant, white Lutetian limestone began to emerge, and the city was transformed. Every year the City of Light became brighter as the cleaning campaign reclaimed the beauty of its architecture and building materials. Paris was a renewed, vibrant Paris to him now. It was hard to even find a building with heavy soot on it these days. Place Saint-Sulpice, however, had been one of the last places to get a facelift. The fountain, long defaced with graffiti and now sparkling clean, and the strange, two-toned church with its mismatched towers, stood as a testament to its interesting architectural history.

Luckily, James had purchased his three-bedroom flat on Rue Palatine before Saint-Sulpice had been restored to its former glory. Although it was originally bought as a gift for himself and his family following the sale of one of his companies, James appreciated that it had also been a good investment. The small square had emerged as one of the most coveted real-estate areas of Paris after the restoration and as Paris real estate rebounded.

At his building James typed in his digicode, walked across the centuries-old black-and-white tiled floor, and climbed the stairs to the third-floor apartment. As he took off his coat, he removed his iPhone from one of the pockets and saw that Robert had left two emails since they'd talked. He hung his coat over a chair, walked across the herring-bone parquet floor, opened the floor-to-ceiling windows, and leaned heavily on the small black railing as he looked out at the fountain.

Shaking his head he returned inside, grabbed a cold beer from the refrigerator, lit another Camel, and dialed the number Robert had provided on the landline that was generally more of a decoration than a telephone.

"What took you so long?" Robert asked when he picked up, clearly a bit agitated.

"Jesus, I came straight away," James replied.

"Okay, okay, okay. Well, here's what we have," Robert went on. "I've been working on isolating a protein sequence. Not to rehash too much, but we needed a small string of non-coding DNA that was conserved across all human beings, so we could test the delivery methodology."

"Wait," said James. "Please remember that I'm not a biochemist. All those years in college when you thought I wanted to be a chemist have long left the memory banks, or were buried in Scotch. You're going just a little fast for me here."

"Look," Robert sighed, "you know this. Most human DNA is

identical from person to person. In its simplest form, we need to have a common protein string across all test subjects. Then we can test the efficacy of RNA therapeutic delivery to a specified protein. Basically, in this case we wanted a section of DNA that was identical in all patients so we could attempt to modify it with our RNA therapy. The protein string would need to be non-expressive: that is, if we cut out a functioning gene, it would be bad for the patient if and when we ever got to human trials." Robert paused.

"All right. Keep going," James prompted, taking another drag on his cigarette.

"Well, we identified a rather large inactive string of nucleotides for testing," Robert stated. "It looked good."

"By inactive, you mean *junk DNA?*" James interjected. The concept of inessential genetic matter had never made much sense to him, as astonishing as it was. Roughly 97 percent of the four billion nucleotides in the human genome, Robert had explained to him, were considered noncoding or "junk" DNA; only the remaining three percent were required to build a unique human being. Robert's best explanation for this—which even then had seemed like a bit of a cop-out—had been that those sequences had been "forgotten" during the process of evolution. But where else was nature so inefficient?

"Good. Yes, junk DNA—essentially all noncoding DNA. In this case, it's a specific type of junk DNA, probably an endogenous retrovirus that attached and was suppressed from coding or a LINE retrotransposon-related sequence." Robert sounded a bit frustrated. "I'm sure I've explained this to you before . . . "

"Yeah, I got it. Press on, my good man. What's the problem, and why are you calling me?"

"I identified and isolated a noncoding DNA sequence for testing our RNAi therapy," Robert said. "I was analyzing the protein sequence prior to the testing to ensure that there was no breakdown or change in the sequence across samples. When I finished mapping out the exact sequence of proteins in the selected segment, I just happened to notice a very strange anomaly in this particular isolated sequence." He hesitated.

"And?" James pressed.

"Well, this sequence with the anomaly was separated from the rest of the genome by an Alu sequence family. This is not too unusual, since Alu sequence families make up about five percent of the genome. Basically, these are commas in a sentence. DNA sequence patterns for a particular expression are almost always preceded and followed by an Alu sequence."

"What the hell are you trying to say?" James asked, beginning to wish he'd stayed at the bar. "One minute you're telling me you're looking for a bit of gibberish in DNA, and the next you're saying DNA has commas in it?"

"Well . . . yes," replied Robert. "Each sequence or group of sequences manifests as specific traits, like computer code." James rolled his eyes as Robert continued, inhaling and then blowing the smoke of his cigarette out through his nose. "In all this, I found a very abnormal sequence. The thing was offset in the beginning and the end by *two* Alu sequences that were identical. That, in and of itself, is beyond highly unusual. But then, between these breaks was a very long, very abnormal sequence that repeated itself five times. In all my years, I have never witnessed any sequence separated by two identical Alu sequence families, and I have never seen a section of DNA that had a repeating nucleotide sequence. This one repeated five times *across twenty-eight different test subjects.*" Robert's tone raised to a crescendo. "Can you imagine a 50,000-word sentence enclosed in double quotation marks, repeated five times exactly the same way, having been written independently by twenty-eight different people who had no idea the others had written it?"

James was beginning to wonder if perhaps Robert needed a vacation. But before he could say so, Robert continued.

"This is beyond peculiar!" he said breathlessly. "Obviously, I needed to confirm the results. So I reran the sequencing of each of the subjects separately, and the results were identical—"

"What?" James choked on a mouthful of beer, convinced his friend had been spending a little too much time in the lab. "You ran a $5,000 test on twenty-eight different samples to determine if this sequence was an error in the testing procedure or a naturally occurring anomaly?" James pounded on the window railing, his voice reaching to almost a shout. "Why would you do that when we're trying to conserve cash, Robert? I thought that 'unique but conserved sequences' were the point here, so we can deliver the medicine?"

James had learned the hard way—DNA sequencers were very expensive and not readily available. XNA was using the sequencer from the Lawrence Livermore National Laboratory's Human Genome Project. Sequencing involved determining the exact order of the four individual chemical building blocks, or nucleotides that formed DNA (Thymine, Cytosine, Adenine, and Guanine, or T, C, A, G).

"Shut up and listen to me," Robert interjected. "All humans have identical protein sequences of varying lengths, but not like this. This is an incredibly strange pattern."

"So what?" James pressed. "Keep in mind that the whole purpose of this project is to make money. How does this help us make money?"

"James, this isn't about money. This is about life itself. This looks like something that has been graphed into the DNA structure." Robert's voice had lowered nearly to a whisper, but he was clearly exasperated. "The odds of an anomaly like this occurring by chance—it would be like someone winning the lottery one million times in a row. There is something very big here. Like—like—I mean creation big."

"Robert—you're an atheist. Where are you going here?"

"I'm no cryptology expert, James, but it looks very much like a code."

"I thought DNA was all code."

"No—I mean a mathematical-type code, like a code that was placed there for a purpose and set apart and highlighted to make it obvious—so it would be easy to find," said Robert. "Look, you need to calm down and stop thinking about money. I need to develop a better way of explaining what I found to you. Let me put this on paper, and I'll call you back later."

"Robert," James said, his voice cracking in frustration. "Don't spend any more XNA money on this unless it is absolutely critical to our product-development path. Okay? Cash is a scarcer resource than you think."

Robert sighed. "I'll call you later," he said again, and hung up.

James closed his eyes and pinched the bridge of his nose. Snuffing out his cigarette, he reached for another, only to discover he had run through the entire pack.

"Shit!" he swore aloud, realizing again how alone he was; there was no one to hear him. He debated going to the *tabac* to buy another pack, then he realized he had already smoked an entire pack today. He settled on getting another beer from the refrigerator, then sat to calm himself down.

He glared once at his laptop and then changed his mind and leaned on the window railing to watch the night settle over the square. He needed to calm down before sitting in front of a computer.

After a minute or two, he began to wonder about what Robert had said. Was there some potential in this that he hadn't seen? If Robert continued on his mad-scientist rampage, XNA would need more capital, and soon. But James knew that primary funding and research in biotech could sometimes lead to very unexpected benefits. What if Robert's discovery could lead to a greater understanding of human DNA, with far broader implications than a cure for one disease? If it was a new find and exciting to Robert, the expert in this field, it was likely something no one else knew about.

"I guess you've got to be in the game to win the game," James said under his breath, watching as motley flock of pigeons winged their way around the fountain.

FATHER MATEO PEREZ
THE VATICAN

Canst thou bind the sweet influences of Pleiades, or loose the bands of Orion?
—JOB 38:31

Father Perez had again begun to feel like an outsider as the pope and cardinal discussed Vatican business. The things they said remained cryptic to him, and even after several minutes he could not fathom why the two most powerful men of the Vatican had summoned him. Just as he glanced at the door, wishing momentarily that he could leave, Archbishop Antonio Reggio entered the room and closed the doors behind him.

Now Father Perez was certain that this was either a dream or a nightmare. Archbishop Reggio was the Vatican's representative ambassador to the U.N.—his official title was Permanent Observer of the Holy See to the United Nations.

"Father Perez, we are on the edge of remarkable times," Cardinal Russo said abruptly, "and times of significant challenges, especially for the Church. You are a man of God, but you are also a man of science. We have a situation in which we need your . . . particular skill set and assistance."

"A—anything, of course, Your Eminence," Father Perez stammered.

"We have a special task for you, Father," interjected the pope. "One that will require your brilliance as an astrophysicist, your confidence, and most importantly your dedication as a Jesuit." The pope held his gaze for a moment, his brown eyes piercing. "This is a difficult project, Father, and it is one that we assign you with some degree of trepidation. We know you have been a little open about your feelings to the press. We are hoping that will help you transition more easily. But the position in which we place you may also be fundamentally challenging to you." Father Perez's heart began to pound in his chest. There had been rumors of murders and clandestine tasks that had been accomplished under papal directive, but he was sure that those were hundreds of years ago. He'd heard of very recent rumors surrounding the scandal-ridden Vatican Bank, and the heavy-handed tactics by some at the recent conclave that had bordered on blackmail. He wondered if he were about to be forced into some compromising position. He clasped his sweating hands in his lap in an effort to keep them from shaking.

"Father Perez, you know that the Vatican is a member of the United Nations," Archbishop Reggio stated bluntly. "But few outside of this room are aware that I work as a special liaison to the U.N. Security Council." He paused, waiting for Father Perez to grasp the importance of his statement, then continued "We, as a Church—as a people—are confronted with a threat. For several years, I have been the eyes and ears of the Church on worldwide security issues. I sit in on the council meetings, though I am not a voting member. Generally, they overlook my presence. However, I was recently asked to join a special working group, a task force begun by the United States and formally taken over by the U.N., known as Project Aquarius." There was a long pause in which the archbishop seemed to silently question the pope for approval to continue. After what seemed an eternity, the pope gave a slow, bleak nod.

"After the Second World War the major world powers—the United Kingdom, Russia, France, China, and the United States—began to collaborate and share certain security information," the archbishop went on. "This data has recently begun to suggest that we might not—*might not*—be alone in the universe."

A long silence filled the air.

"To be clear, Father," the pope broke in with a grim smile, "Project Aquarius, which is responsible for all its member states' sensitive information and decision-making, is focused on the possibilities of astrobiology or, as the lay people refer to it, extraterrestrial life."

Father Perez's head spun. Adrenaline coursed through him. He could not believe the pope was addressing the possibility of life outside Earth. He wondered if perhaps he'd heard wrong, and considered asking the pope to repeat himself.

"You see," the archbishop continued, "each country started its own investigative group regarding the possibility of extraterrestrial life. The genesis of Project Aquarius occurred in the United States, and the program has now been formally taken over by the U.N.

"I ask you, Father, what would happen if some form of intelligent, nonhuman life were discovered?" Archbishop Reggio's expression was severe. "How can the Church continue to claim that we were created in the image of God, if other and different intelligent beings are identified? I maintain that we cannot—but to be prudent, we must prepare for such a possibility. Science has come a long way, while unfortunately the doctrinal teachings of the Church have remained static. We have a lot of work to do."

"This is where you come in, Father Perez," the pope stated. "You will be our representative for Project Aquarius. You will help us craft our new message. From your observations, you will help prepare the Vatican's new position on intelligent life beyond Earth for the church. You see, our theological research needs to shift to support the new proposition that our *souls* are created in God's image, and that the universe shares the same God."

"You will need to view the Vatican archives," Cardinal Russo interjected. "Not the public archives, but the secret archives."

Father Perez always thought it interesting that the Vatican did not hide the fact they kept secret archives.

"There you will find some information that will be helpful to your task. I've identified that information in these reference materials." He slid a small brown envelope over to Father Perez.

"For hundreds of years, we have been collecting and protecting evidence on otherworldly phenomena. The Church has writings, specific philosophies, and scripture interpretations that will be helpful. Your task, like that of Project Aquarius, will remain secret." He smiled impishly. "It is one thing for the Vatican to have its own astrobiological research committee; it is quite another for us to admit that one exists!"

Father Perez felt his heart pounding, no longer out of fear but out of exhilaration.

The pope leaned toward him and almost whispered, "As of late, the archbishop has been hearing unsettling things in the Security Council."

"Yes," the archbishop agreed.

"So you believe that there really are intelligent beings in the stars?" Father Perez asked the group, no longer able to contain his excitement.

Cardinal Russo shot him a frown. "Those records will show you what we believe," he said, gesturing at the file. "From the dawn of pre-history it has been apparent that this was a possibility."

"But why has this information been kept secret so long?" Father Perez insisted. "Why didn't the Church just incorporate it into our initial doctrine?"

The pope raised a finger. "Once you arrive at Mount Graham, you will learn more." he said. "But know this: there is an occurrence, a culmination of events, coming. We have ancient records, religious prophecies, and biblical prophecies which speak to this precise time in our history. That is why we must act now, and why the Jesuit Order demands your diligent service. Preparing for this time is at the foundations of our work as an order. Extraordinary things are about to manifest, and our time is short."

Father Perez opened his mouth and then clamped it shut again, bowing his head in submission.

"Your job will be to begin a modern revival in the church," the cardinal smiled. "You will help us integrate new beliefs with the old. If asked, you will say that you were summoned here only to receive your new assignment. It would be best to tell the curious that you had been expecting a transfer. We do not wish to draw attention to your mission in the media before you have helped us prepare our new position. You will have some time to review the physical archives, but most of the data you need has been digitized. You will be able to access it from Mount Graham. Now we have other pressing business, and must leave you. Addio."

The archbishop and cardinal rose and left the room through a door hidden behind one of the curtains. The pope also stood and walked back to the door through which he'd entered, joining the Swiss Guard who awaited him on its other side.

Wide-eyed, Father Perez slowly stood from his seat, trying to digest what had just happened. His mind whirled, contemplating the theological challenges that extraterrestrial life presented. Would such beings be of God? If they looked different from human beings, were they still created in God's image? Had Jesus's death been for their sake too, and were they too Heaven-bound? Absurdly, he looked around the room, wondering which door he should leave through.

After several minutes, a young aide appeared.

"If you will follow me, Father, I will take you to your car," the man said.

*   *   *

That night Father Perez sat alone at a small table in his apartment, mesmerized. He was primarily an astrophysicist but had also been a student of world religion, and he had become very aware of the dilemma that Christianity and other religions of the world faced in light of a possible announcement of intelligent life beyond the earth.

The implications of this notion for the Church were unspeakable; other religions could potentially reconcile themselves to the existence of extraterrestrial life, but Christianity was defined by the incarnation of God in the Messiah, and His appearance in human flesh. That appearance had been for the salvation of the children of Adam, not for that of extraterrestrials.

The Church taught that man was created in the image of God. He wondered what the Vatican would do if faced with an intelligent alien existence, especially if it turned out to be intellectually superior to humans or more evolved in other ways. And would these beings be sinless? The fall of Adam in the garden was uniquely human. He did not know how the Church could justify its doctrine in the face of such findings.

In any case, he knew it was beyond his ability to resolve. The pope was worried about something urgent, that was certain. But Father Perez was far from convinced that he was up to the assignment.

4

DR . SOFIA PETRESCU
GENEVA, SWITZERLAND

The heavens declare the glory of God; the skies proclaim the work of his hand.
—PSALMS 19:1

DR. SOFIA PETRESCU RUBBED HER TEMPLES, removed the folder from her briefcase, and opened it with a sigh. She was only to be in Geneva at the United Nations Headquarters, Palais des Nations, for a week, and she had plenty of work to do for her role with UNOOSA. But, she had made her commitment to Professor De Vos to review his work, so she begrudgingly reopened his file.

Spreading the materials out again over the small conference-room table she'd reserved, she fumbled once more through the densely packed reports, graphs, and studies.

Looking over Professor De Vos's report in detail, she'd been surprised to find that it was well researched and clearly presented. The data seemed to support his conclusion that reductions in solar activity resulted in increased cloud cover and thus increased cooling; according to his premise, the earth was ending a period of global warming and just beginning to move into another protracted cooling period—potentially a mini Ice Age. Professor De Vos would be arriving any minute. She reviewed a few more aspects of the report and jotted down some notes.

The sensibility of the report made her even more anxious. Sofia had grave misgivings about helping Professor De Vos; she had struggled so long and hard to get to where she was in her career, digging herself out from under the barriers that life had erected before her, that she could not justify risking her career by participating in the professor's less-than-popular research. Was she going to bite the hand that fed her by openly challenging the U.N.? She couldn't. It would be academic suicide. She sighed heavily to herself. She had been singularly focused on her career, and on escaping the past. She was just getting to a point in her life that she felt like she had a future and maybe even time for a relationship.

There was a knock at the door. "Sofia?" the professor's voice called.

She sighed. "Yes, Professor, please come in," she said.

"Thank you." Professor De Vos entered, an anxious look on his face. "Well?" he asked.

"I've read through the report and your data," Sofia said. "It seems very compelling to me. But honestly, I'm still unclear as to where I can help you," she added, hoping to limit her involvement.

"Ah, yes," the professor said, his face sinking a little. "Well, first, of course, you could help me review these previous studies of solar sunspot activity and ensure you agree with their findings, as I'm basing my research on the terrestrial effects on cloud cover and temperature on their veracity."

"That I can do."

"But there are a few additional reports that are a bit concerning, and I'd like your thoughts," the professor pressed. He handed her a paper. "Here is a chart of CO_2 emissions and other greenhouse gases over the last two thousand years. You will note the very recent and marked rise in greenhouse gases. This is from an Assessment Report in 2007 issued by Intergovernmental Panel of Climate Change."

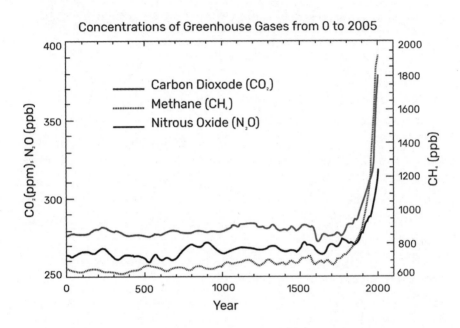

"Now, please take a look at these." He handed her another file labeled "Sofia," and she flipped through to a report with a Post-It note on it reading *Correlated Data*. The first was a United States Geological Survey Agency graph of worldwide destructive earthquakes of magnitude 6 and above, recorded over the last hundred years. Sofia looked at the graph and shot the professor a strange look.

"What's this all about?" she asked.

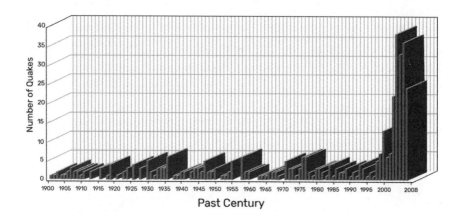

Past Century

"Please, just look at the graph," the professor insisted. "Does it look similar to the CO_2 escalation?"

"Well…it does," she agreed. "This graph clearly evidences a very recent and rapid rise in the number of earthquakes on Earth. Clearly, since 2000, there has been a marked increase. Very strange, but I'm not sure it's a correlation."

"True. But I have found no geologists who have been able to explain this."

"But couldn't it be from fracking, or better measurement equipment, or something like that?" she asked.

"Maybe," he said, "but there's more." He passed along another paper. "This is a graph of the massive increase in volcanism over the same period. Again, there are no other existing scientific explanations for this—or none that I can find."

Sofia frowned. "That…is striking," she admitted. "But maybe the CO_2 increase is a causal effect of the increased volcanism? We know that volcanoes produce vast quantities of CO_2."

"It's possible. But man is not creating this. Here is a graph of CO_2 levels as measured in Antarctic ice-core samples. Going back eight hundred thousand years, we have had many periods of increased CO_2 levels."

"So you think this is cyclical?"

"Yes. Why are we seeing, in all this data, all of these sudden spikes and anomalies at the same time—now? Explain to me this next graph," he added, sliding another page across the table toward her. "This is from the NOAA National Geographical Data Center, which maintains a data set of annual magnetic North Pole coordinates that go back to the year 1590. It shows over 420 years of movement of the magnetic poles on Earth."

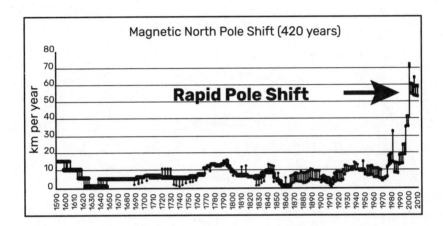

"I—hmm," Sofia said, rubbing her forehead. What this graph showed was clearly more concerning. Sofia knew that the earth, like all planets, underwent regular changes in the location of its magnetic poles; these movements varied from year to year, generally constituting just a few miles of movement each time. But what Professor De Vos's graph showed was much more grave. "This is an incredible increase in the movement of the poles," Sofia said, "and yes, I see the correlation with the other graphs. I'm not sure it's statistically significant, but—" She faltered at the words, forcing herself to remain calm. "I admit, there is something interesting here."

The professor nodded excitedly. "The poles are no longer moving a few miles a year; they are moving fifty to one hundred miles a year," he said. "The pole migration has exploded. I stumbled across this research when studying the effects of magnetism on temperature at the poles. The magnetic poles are now racing across the earth. The magnetic North Pole is moving across the Arctic toward Siberia. Look here," he said, handing her an image from the World Data Center for Geomagnetism at Kyoto University. We know that the magnetic poles flip from north to south with a periodicity of around 650,000 years," he said mimicking the motion with his hands "We understand that the fields weaken and then flip. But—"

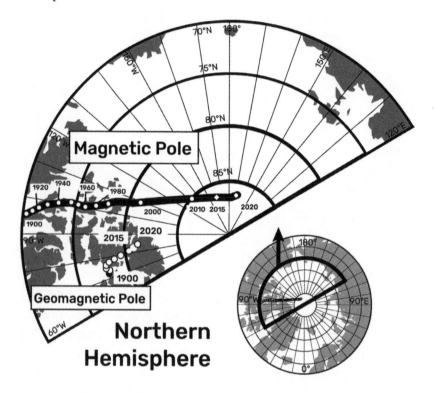

"This is different," Sofia finished for him.

"Yes," he said. "It appears that something, most likely the sun, is electromagnetically interacting with the earth—and is causing the movement of the magnetic pole across the earth. This, I hypothesize, is what's causing the recent climate-change phenomena, as well as the increased earthquakes and volcanism."

Sofia considered the implications for a minute. "Professor, I need to do a bit of research," she said carefully. "If these facts are causally related, and this pole-migration data is accurate, there are some who theorize that the rapid movement of the location of the magnetic poles could cause a geographic shift in the axis and rapid crustal displacement. And that could be cataclysmic in and of itself," she concluded.

"Wait a minute; what do you mean?" interrupted the professor. "Why is that cataclysmic?"

"It means," Sofia said, "that we could be heading for a change in the location of the geographical north and south poles, as well as the location of the equator. What we consider to be the top of the earth and bottom of the earth would change physically—not just magnetically. The U.S. might move directly onto the equator, and say, China might become the new Arctic north."

"Is that possible?" the professor challenged.

"Professor, I need to take a deeper look into this," she said finally. "But—well, imagine the earth spinning like a top in space. Its magnetic poles are like a bar magnet straight through the center, on which the top rotates. At the equator, the earth must spin faster to keep up with the poles. Centripetal acceleration causes the diameter of the earth to be forty miles wider around the equator than from pole to pole. If the locations of those magnetic poles changed, the axis of spin of the earth could change too—when it moves, so does the equatorial bulge. Lands would rise and fall immediately, based upon the new equator's location."

"Unbelievable," the professor urged, clearly excited that she was finally following him. "And that would mean…"

"That would mean massive tidal waves, floods, and earthquakes. Fifty percent of the world's population lives on the coasts. It would be—"

"Armageddon?" the professor asked.

"Armageddon," Sofia agreed.

AGENT DEVON STINSON
FLASHBACK: JOHN F. KENNEDY SPACE CENTER, APRIL 15, 2010

Stinson was preparing a report for the president on Project Aquarius. The long hours were getting to him. His stomach was in a tight knot with all the stress. He again reflected on the past, attempting to recall all the details of his early meetings with the president.

It had taken some pressing, but the president had agreed to change his speech, and he was not happy about it. Stinson watched him walk toward the podium at the John F. Kennedy Space Center on Merritt Island. With NASA Administrator Hastings and former astronaut Buzz Aldrin beside him, he placed his hands on either side of the lectern, thanked the many in attendance, and began.

"Citizens, I am here today to inform you that NASA and the dreams it represents will not be allowed to die simply because I have some opponents trying to make unnecessary cuts to our budget during times of great economic distress," he said. "I am not only dedicated to the continued exploration and the progression of technological innovation that has historically burgeoned out of the program, but I am one hundred percent committed to the mission of NASA and its future."

The president paused to allow the audience to applaud his statement.

NSA Chief Perkings stood tensely on the side of the stage.

"It is according to a uniquely American characteristic that our society has always demanded we push forward, explore the unknown, and challenge human intellect, resolve and resilience. We have always striven to satisfy that innate American desire to explore, and to reach new horizons. Now, once more, history is calling upon us to inspire a younger generation, provide a spark to technological innovation and creativity. In this moment, if we fail to press forward and search out the unknown, we are betraying what it means to be an American.

"In keeping with that vital trait, it is my plan to increase funding to our program by six billion dollars. Although this is a small percentage of the amount we truly need to fund the various projects we wish to pursue, it will allow us to move forward with robotic exploration of the solar system, including a probe of the sun's corona. It will allow us to begin new scouting missions to Mars, Saturn, near-Earth objects, and other destinations within our solar system. And it will allow us to create a new and even more advanced telescope than the Hubble, with which we have already accomplished so much.

"It is time for us to hold up a magnifying glass to the worlds beyond us, and peer deeper into the universe than ever before. Now, I understand that some believe that we should attempt a return to the surface of the moon. That is a laudable goal, and someday we will pursue it with the dedication it deserves. But we have been there before." He nodded respectfully to the aged astronaut beside him. "Buzz has been there. There's a lot more of space to explore, and a lot more to learn from it. That's why, right now, I believe it's more important to ramp up our capabilities to reach for increasingly demanding targets while advancing our technological capabilities with each step forward. It is time for America to take space travel to the next level. We need new innovation, and that requires us to address new challenges and unprecedented goals. That is how we will ensure that our leadership in space is even stronger in this new century than it was in the last."

Stinson saw the president glance over at Thomas Kramer, who nodded in approval.

When the speech concluded, there was great applause. But it was only afterward that things truly became interesting.

"Mr. President, please follow me," Thomas Kramer said.

Stinson, Perkings, and Kramer walked the president across the hall to a small conference room, where another man already stood waiting at the large central table. He was dressed in a gray suit with a burgundy-checked bow tie. His wire-rimmed glasses offset a thin face and hawkish nose, over which presided a dark, bushy pair of eyebrows and short graying hair. His entire demeanor was one of intense seriousness. Stinson nodded to him as he moved around the table, distributing a briefing document in front of each chair.

"Mr. President," Stinson said, "I'd like to introduce you to Nicholas

Innsbruck, with the British Ministry of Defense."

The president cocked his head, puzzled. "Wait. I'm at NASA talking with the NSA about what I thought was an American problem, and the British Ministry of Defense is going to speak?" he said, his eyes narrowing.

"We have been working hand in hand with the British on Project Aquarius, Mr. President," Stinson said. "Mr. Innsbruck has expertise in the topics we wish to address today. He flew in yesterday in anticipation of this meeting."

"Good morning, Mr. President," said Innsbruck as he took a seat. His voice was thickly accented. "At this point, it may make sense to give you a bit of history about Project Aquarius." He glanced at an open notebook in front of him. "In essence, Project Aquarius is the latest incarnation of a research program that has had many names over the course of several decades, it originated in 1946 through the British-U.S. Communications Intelligence Agreement, known to the public as BRUSA. Its publicly expressed intention was to channel secret communication intercepts between Britain's Government Communications Headquarters and the National Security Agency for better uniformity of intelligence gathering between the Allies, but like all public governmental agreements, it also had another purpose. In this case, the hidden purpose was its primary one: to compile any and all information associated with unidentified flying objects."

Stinson glanced at the president to gauge his reaction. It was clear he didn't know how to react to this. His relaxed demeanor visibly began to evaporate.

"The effort gained more steam in 1952 from an executive order signed by President Truman, following seven days of unidentified-flying-object activity that occurred directly over the White House and Washington, DC," Innsbruck continued, unfazed. "These objects were tracked on radar and followed by military aircraft. Similar but less publicized events occurred in London." He looked down at his notebook and folder introspectively. "We find it rather amusing that the U.S. public has all but forgotten this event. The federal government was never able to explain the events adequately but the people were calmed by several press releases stating there was nothing to worry about—that it was merely a temperature inversion that had caused a mirage," Innsbruck said grimly.

Stinson nodded his head, then added to the history. "Although we had been around for several years before this under a different name, the NSA officially came into existence on November 4, 1952," he said. "We were always charged to interpret and decode signals, from not only foreign countries, but, if the opportunity presented itself, from extraterrestrial sources. The events of July 1952 were the proverbial straw that broke the camel's back. The NSA directive became a top priority—after all, we couldn't have alien craft hovering over the capital of the most powerful nation in the world.

"John Stamford was promoted to Director of the NSA in 1956 by President Eisenhower. Since that time, the Director of the NSA has been briefed on all the activities involving the special projects dedicated to alien contact. It is also the Director of the NSA who generally has the responsibility to drop this bombshell on each new incoming president," Stinson concluded with a smile, looking over at Director Perkings.

Innsbruck chimed in again. "Due to changes in the administration over the following years and the necessity of maintaining the secrecy of the program, and in an effort to maintain plausible deniability, there have been many iterations of Project Aquarius—most notably under the names Project Blue Book and Majic-12. These programs, and those of our partners in other countries, have focused primarily upon compilation and analysis of UFO-based sightings. As of this moment, Aquarius is comprised of a small working group that reports directly to the security administrations of each member government and the United Nations Security Council."

"You should have seen the look on G.W. Bush's face when he was briefed on the program and given our recommendation to formalize the project under the NSA and the U.N.," Stinson interjected.

"The weight of this information is tremendous," Innsbruck went on, "and far more so than this damn financial crisis everyone's focused on right now. With viable businesses, appropriate taxes, and intelligent investment bankers, we can work out solutions to such financial problems. The particular quandary facing Project Aquarius has no known solution." He paused a moment before continuing. "Our member governments have agreed that a formal collaboration was necessary at this time for many reasons. Primarily, we need to collaborate and look in our shared data for consistencies, similarities, or the lack thereof, and for any identifiable patterns of behavior associated with the latest sightings. Secondarily, all member nations agree that both military and civilian sightings have reached what can only be called an epidemic level. Over the last five years, activity has increased by a factor of ten. Frankly, Mr. President, we do not know why. Aside from these sightings, we have had no confirmed communicative contact at this time."

"I—I see," the president managed.

"And what is even more troubling," Stinson added, "is our complete lack of understanding as to whether these are physical craft and beings, or something more...transdimensional in nature."

"Transdimensional?" the president stammered. "I'm trying to follow you here, gentlemen, but you're going to have to meet me halfway. What exactly does that mean—ghosts or something?"

"Not necessarily," Stinson said, leaning forward on the table, "but we may well be dealing with existences originating in another dimension. They certainly manifest themselves in strange ways, according to our three-dimensional perspective. For example, craft are often seen appearing and disappearing, only to reappear almost instantaneously hundreds of miles away. They sometimes make 90-degree turns, while in the Earth's atmosphere, at speeds exceeding a thousand miles per hour. I hardly need to tell you that these movements don't fit with our current understanding of the laws of physics. But more confusing are the vast number and types of crafts observed. There have literally been thousands of variants. Based on this data, we are either being observed by a tremendous number of different types of beings with thousands of different types of craft, or there is some dimensional factor here that we do not yet understand." Stinson took a deep breath. "Frankly, I personally wonder if these are not more spiritual in nature."

5

DR . SATI AM UNNEFER
CAIRO, EGYPT

THE OFFICE WAS ENORMOUS. A large cedar desk occupied the middle of the room, surrounded by bookcases and file cabinets. A conference table in the back against the windows was covered in boxes. Sati gave the file cabinet a final shove, and it slowly scraped across the floor. The cabinets in Zaher's old office smelled musty and had been completely disorganized for a man who ran such a tight ship. Some of the file cabinets had even been placed in front of others, completely blocking off their access. Now that Sati had arranged the office more effectively, he would be able to begin sorting the files, looking for anything of interest and discarding the rest.

Sati stepped back and sat on the desk, wiping the sweat from his brow with a handkerchief. As he stared ahead, thinking about where he should begin, he noticed a rectangular discoloration on the wall that had originally been hidden behind the last cabinet he had moved.

Frowning, he said, "We are going to have to get that painted, Henku."

"Yes, sir." Henku replied. Sati sighed. "Okay. Let's start going through this old green file cabinet," he said. "It looks as if it has been here longer than anything else." Since none of the cabinets were labeled, he decided he would sort through them based on how old they looked. The dust and style of this one were screaming early 1970s.

Sati opened the top drawer with difficulty: a huge brown bag had been jammed inside of it. "I'm certain we aren't going to find anything of great interest," he said, tugging until the drawer finally came free, "but we need to get this office organized."

As expected, the bag contained only specimens from one of the numerous local digs and a paper that detailed where the items had been found. He returned the bag to the drawer as best he could, retrieved an index card, and labeled the file drawer.

As he continued emptying the contents, sifting through them, and labeling the drawers, Sati's mind occasionally wandered from the monotonous work. About halfway through the cabinet that had concealed the wall discoloration, his stomach growled. He glanced at the clock and saw it was long past the time of his usual lunch break. He tried not to be discouraged that they'd only sorted out three and a half of the ten cabinets.

"Henku, let's take a break," he said. "I need some food, especially if we're going to get through all these today."

"Yes, sir. Sounds good to me." Henku wiped the dust from his hands onto his shirt.

Sati leaned back against the wall and stared down at the dust that had fallen from the cabinets and covered his shoes. Out of the corner of his eye, he noticed a small gap between the floor and the wall. He frowned and got down on his knees to examine it.

"Henku! Look at this." They both lay down on the floor and looked through the crack. It ran the full length of the wall and was about half an inch deep.

"I cannot see anything, sir," Henku replied.

"No. Only darkness. But the light seems to go back a ways. This doesn't seem like an ordinary wall." Sati wished he had a flashlight. Standing, he put his ear to the wall, rapping on it lightly. "It sounds hollow," he added.

Sati's stomach growled again, but he ignored it. Rubbing his fingers along the discolored area, he tried to find a finger hold but was disappointed. After deciding that it was probably only a small empty space created by poor construction, he slammed his fist against the wall in frustration. A distinctive *snick* sounded, and the wall sprung open. Sati and Henku both stared at each other. Slowly, Sati pulled back on the door, revealing a dark, recessed cupboard.

"What in the world..." he mumbled.

Cautiously, he opened the door all the way. His eyes traveled across each of the interior shelves. The cupboard had six shelves stuffed full of artifacts, documents, and files. He was surprised to discover that each one was meticulously labeled with excavation-site information such as dates and personnel names.

"What is all this, sir?" Henku whispered, his eyes wide.

"This is what I've been looking for, Henku." A slow smile spread over Sati's face as he reached for a thick file on the shelf marked *Great Pyramid Complex, Giza*. "This is going to be exciting." He nestled the file under his arm. "Let's go. We can look through this over lunch."

They headed out of the building and stopped at one of the street kabob stands. Then they walked to Sati's favorite café for a cup of coffee. Nodding at the man behind the counter, Sati placed their order, then took the cups to an empty table where he and Henku could look through the file.

"Why do you think Zaher hid these files? I don't understand," Henku said nervously.

"Certainly, Henku, there were things he didn't want released to the public, or even to his staff," Sati replied. "I have for a long time suspected Zaher of hiding information from the public."

Sati eagerly removed a leather tie that bound the file and opened it. It seemed to contain many papers requesting further excavation inside the Great Pyramid of Khufu. Glancing over the first request, Sati shook his head and smiled to himself. Of course the request had been rejected: a red stamp proclaimed the refusal across the front. His former boss had regularly rejected first requests, in order to make an acceptance more valuable to the excavators. He continued to scour the papers but found nothing more of real interest. He breathed out heavily in disappointment.

"You know, I have always disagreed with what Zaher told the world about the pyramids," he mused. "According to him, the Great Pyramid was built over a twenty-year period beginning around 2560 BCE. This makes no sense. Don't you agree?"

"I don't know," Henku said. "Why not?"

"Well, to begin with, if that were true, a new block would need to be placed every four minutes, around the clock, for the entirety of those two decades. You know the average block is more than a meter cubed, and weighs around three tons. And this does not even take into account the larger blocks. Have you ever considered that it might be implausible to think that primitive Egyptians working, with even more primitive copper tools, could have cut these blocks, moved them hundreds of miles, and placed them so quickly and so perfectly?"

"N—no," Henku stuttered. "That is what we have always known; that was how our forefathers built the pyramids. What are you saying?"

Sati sighed with exasperation. Had Henku really never thought this?

"Just look at the way the pyramids are built," he insisted. "We could not construct them today without some sort of advanced design software. Each block was meticulously carved to perfectly fit next to the other. You've seen some of the experiments where scientific teams have tried to duplicate the processes with ancient tools—it never seemed to work out right. Not even one block can be cut that way to the exact specifications we find in the pyramids, let alone millions!"

"Sir, I'm confused. If you don't think they were built as we have been taught, what *do* you think?" Henku was visibly worried.

"I've studied the pyramids for a lifetime," Sati replied. "The more I learn, the more I'm convinced they were built by a culture more advanced than primitive Egyptians with primitive tools." This question was ultimately what had led him to seek his position. It was what had helped him remain silent and submissive all those years under Zaher. He wanted to know the truth, and he had long suspected his old employer of concealing part of it.

"But Zaher said—" Henku began.

"Forget about Zaher," Sati interjected firmly, allowing a bit too much spite to seep into his words. "He lied to us all. To me." Seeing the alarm on Henku's face, his voice softened. "I'm sorry, Henku," he said. "It's just that Zaher has always been a very vocal critic of any suggestions that the pyramids were built through ingenuity attributed to anyone but the ancient Egyptians. Why is it wrong for us to question this? For decades, in fact, many have even speculated about intervention from an extraterrestrial race that helped in the construction."

Henku's eyes went wide.

"I'm not saying I believe such a thing," Sati smiled. I just want all the possibilities to be exhausted before we rule them out. Zaher would scoff at anyone making such an assertion. But I will look at any plausible explanation!"

The former antiquities minister infuriated him, but not because Sati believed such a thing. No, he disliked that Zaher, as an academic and as a scientist, would consider no possibilities beyond his own conclusions.

"That is not how true science should operate. You were not supposed to start with a hypothesis and do all that is necessary to maintain that hypothesis. As a scientist, you had to consider any available, relevant information. I have known for a long time of Zaher's suppression or destruction of artifacts in the Egyptian Antiquities office, and at the excavation sites," he went on. "When I asked him about it, he became infuriated. He claimed that he was the expert and I was not to challenge him if I valued my career. For many years I have heard whispers from colleagues and employees claiming they had seen evidence and information disappear when it seemed to indicate that the pyramids were much older than Zaher predicted.

"When experts disagreed with him, saying it was virtually impossible for Egyptians to have been the architects and builders, their reputations were attacked. Frequently they were removed from their position and had any honors stripped from them. I know two of these people, personally. I have no reason to believe they would lie."

"But what would Zaher have to gain in hiding the truth?" Henku asked.

"I don't know," Sati said, shaking his head. "You would think he'd be excited to share some of the stories. One of my colleagues told me a story about finding items of incredible design and unknown writing in a small, hidden chamber deep below the sand between the Sphinx and the Great Pyramid. Someone else began a small and controlled excavation of that spot. But then, suddenly, the dig was scuttled, and no archeologists discussed it. All that emerged were rumors that the tomb of Osiris had been found, and no one believed otherwise."

They sat quietly for some time sorting through the file, most of which seemed to be standard business. Sati set is aside in frustration, and took up the next document. Reading through it, something caught his eye. It was a note from a German engineer named Gantenbrink, a name he recognized, who'd headed a team from Munich that in 2002 explored a hidden 208-foot "air shaft" connected to the Queen's Chamber in the heart of the Great Pyramid.

Sati had not been part of the widely-publicized project, but had been very interested in the mini-robot that Gantenbrink had designed and sent down along the small hidden shaft. As Sati recalled, Gantenbrink had become upset for some reason and abruptly left the project; Zaher, who had taken over the project after Gantenbrink left, had explained that the robot had found a small door at the end of the shaft, but that nothing had been found behind it when they drilled through. Zaher even went as far as to publicly call the German "a reckless treasure hunter."

Picking the papers up again, Sati continued to read. On the next page was a diagram of the shaft, showing its length in meters. Placing the diagram aside, he picked up the next page. What he read there made his hands shake and his eyes widen with excitement.

The next page was a personal communication showing some glyphs and another diagram of the passage, showing a series of two doors. Zaher had written over the top of the communication, "Excavation CANCELED. Further work would likely lead to damage and destruction of tunnels and chambers. Filed 6 June 2011." From the file, it appeared that all communications with the exploration group had ceased after that.

The next page showed a picture of the shaft's interior, taken through the small hole the robot had drilled in the tiny door. Sati leaned in close and peered at the little red markings on the interior. Flipping back through the written transcript, he discovered that behind the door they'd drilled through was indeed another small door in the shaft, as the diagram showed. But this one had what appeared to be two metal bands or levers attached to it. Sati looked closely at the glyphs on this small door. They did not match any Egyptian hieroglyphs, or any artwork he had seen among the works of ancient Egypt.

"Henku! This is the type of thing I was talking about!" He slid the picture over the table, shaking his head in near disbelief. *I need to find a way to get inside this shaft and beyond the door at its other side*, he thought and returned his attention to the photos. Clearly there was a reason Zaher had stopped this excavation; it was high time they resumed it.

As Sati gathered his things, a thin metal jump drive fell out of the folder. He looked at it for a moment before picking it up and placing it in his pocket. He'd have to take a look at it later. For now, he had a new expedition to set in motion.

FATHER MATEO PEREZ
MOUNT GRAHAM OBSERVATORY, ARIZONA

"The Bible is not fundamentally a science book."
—FR . JOSÉ GABRIEL FUNES, FORMER DIRECTOR OF THE VATICAN OBSERVATORY

Father Perez stepped off the plane in Tucson eager to return to the state-of-the-art Vatican telescope. He'd forgotten how stiflingly hot Arizona could be, even in September; moisture seemed to evaporate from his lips. Heat rising from the desert caused the horizon to ripple like waves in the distance. The landscape here seemed so otherworldly and lifeless—perfect for a complex of telescopes that searched the cosmos.

Father Perez had known for years about the rumors and discussions at the facility over reported observations of UFO activity. No one was quite sure what had been going on, but at least it was openly discussed. The Jesuit Order was now in control of the observatory and he was certain he would learn more detailed information soon enough.

In addition to the use of the VATT or Vatican Advanced Technology Telescope, he would also have the ability to access the other two observatories located on the mountain, the Heinrich Hertz Submillimeter Telescope and the LUCIFER, short for Large Binocular Telescope Near-Infrared Utility with Camera and Integral Field Unit for Extragalactic Research. Evidently, though the University of Arizona allowed the Vatican to operate the three telescopes on Mount Graham, it had no qualms about giving the newest one such an ungodly nickname, despite its close affiliation and proximity to VATT.

Father Perez had expected that there would be a lot of new faces at the facility. He was a little alarmed, however, when he discovered that the mountain seemed to have been taken over by men in dark-gray suits and sunglasses. In fact, he didn't see anyone from the Vatican team he recognized. One of the other Jesuit priests assigned to the observatory rushed over to him. He was disheveled, with greasy, short black hair, and thick black-framed glasses that sat on a large, oily nose.

"Father Perez?" the man asked as he approached. "My name is Joseph. Welcome! Or, I—I mean, welcome back. We have some things to show you. Please follow me."

Joseph escorted him into VATT, down a hallway, and into the elevator. Father Perez watched as Joseph pulled a key from inside his shirt and inserted it into a specialized slot under the elevator controls. With one turn, the car descended and all the floor numbers over the doors flashed red. Father Perez's ears popped as the elevator stopped on the third sublevel under the VATT. His escort guided him down a number of short hallways and through a solid blue-steel door.

Inside, an austere-looking man sat alone, surrounded by technical equipment. As he rose from his seat, Father Perez estimated that he was about six foot four. He had a thin frame, and while his thick hair was graying around the sideburns, most of it was jet-black. It was hard to guess his age, but his eyes had the look of one who has seen much. He wore a conservative navy-blue suit with a plain red tie that matched his red zucchetto; his jacket lay across the back of a nearby chair.

"His Eminence, Cardinal Coppa," announced Joseph.

Father Perez's eyes opened in surprise. Most cardinals were over the age of eighty. He wondered what Coppa's position in the Roman Curia was, since he had never heard of him before.

"We're not so formal down here, Mateo," the cardinal said. "Please call me Paul—or Coppa, if you prefer. Our time together will require that we speak openly and honestly with each other. Thank you, Brother Joseph. That will be all for now." Joseph nodded slightly and took his leave.

"I'm afraid you have me at a loss, Your Eminence," Father Perez said once Joseph had gone. "Exactly why am I here? I was told that all would be explained once I arrived."

Coppa ignored the question and instead waved his hand to indicate the room around them. "As you know, *Mateo*," he said, "we are in one of the most advanced observation centers in the civilized world. Many changes have occurred since you were here last. Now we can access every known astronomy database on the planet, including some that are classified, as well as all of the Vatican archives. The information in here is what those agents up top are protecting. No matter how long they stay up there, squirreling around, they can only keep certain information locked up for so long."

His voice faded as he began typing furiously on a keyboard. Then he abruptly turned and pointed to a large screen on the far wall. It displayed what looked to be a very old collection of stone tablets.

"Do you know what that is?" he asked, pointing to the screen.

"Uh—no," Father Perez admitted, glancing at the closed door. "It looks like some sort of ancient writing, no?"

Coppa smiled triumphantly. "Exactly. Any idea as to how old it might be?"

"I'm afraid I really have never been interested in ancient languages or hieroglyphs, Your Eminence—er—Paul," Perez said, shrugging apologetically.

"We estimate it was written around 4000 or 4500 BCE. The language, as I have been told, is a modified form of Sumerian cuneiform." With a few more keystrokes, a larger collection of ancient relics and tablets appeared on the monitor, all containing the same scratches.

Perez nodded, then exhaled heavily. "I'm afraid I'm still rather confused," he said. "I was told that someone here would be able to help me with my assignment and answer my questions. I'm not a translator, so ancient writing isn't going to help me develop any new theological concepts on its own, particularly regarding the Vatican's position on extraterrestrial life. I don't mean to question you; but since I have no background in ancient writings, I'm unclear why you are showing me this." The background hum of the massive computer systems was irritating. Perez struggled to focus.

"A little background will help you make that connection," Coppa continued patiently. "You see, the Cardinal Librarian and Archivist acquired these artifacts some time ago. We call them the Taluk tablets because the author was an ancient Sumerian scribe named Taluk." With a few more taps on the keyboard, two smaller monitors on the wall came to life. Coppa seemed transfixed on the information he was providing. "This documentation contains details about what the Sumerians described as visitors to our planet from the stars," Coppa continued, spreading his hands to emphasize the vastness of his point. "They constitute a record, so to speak, that the Vatican has managed to keep suppressed, along with others, deep within our archives. Furthermore, they refer to three books made of gold, which, roughly translated, are called the *Ascension Testaments*. These sacred golden books are said to contain wisdom and knowledge—real knowledge concerning our creation." Coppa spread his hands as if to emphasize the books' importance.

Perez took a closer look at the monitors. "I'm not meant to presume that by *ascension* you are suggesting Christ's Ascension?" he asked.

"A foretelling of Biblical events?" Coppa shook his head. "No. This tablet tells of a time when man will be given incredible knowledge and wisdom, right before the world is destroyed by a fiery dragon. It specifies that this dragon wreaks havoc on the world and brings great cataclysm and destruction: mountains crumbling, seas coming out of their basins and scouring across the land, night becoming day, fire raining from the sky. It also includes a star map, which you can see here, and which we do not understand yet. But we believe the missing golden texts will help to answer this riddle." He smiled again, his expression standing in stark contrast to the incredible import of what he was saying. "The Taluk tablets, Father Perez, seem to indicate that these golden books were transported to the area now known as Egypt, around 5000 BCE."

PROFESSOR STAN CARUTHERS
PRINCETON UNIVERSITY, NEW JERSEY

Death and life are in the language.

—PROVERBS 18:21

"Listen, James," Robert said over the phone, "before we call Professor Caruthers, let me give you some background. He is a bit of an eccentric. You know the type—rogue mathematical genius, long hair, likes to speak in British slang and colloquialisms when possible. He thinks very highly of himself and his academic abilities, and sometimes enjoys making others feel inferior. Now that I think of it, he's a bit of a dick."

"Great," James said.

"Don't get me wrong—he's brilliant," Robert added hastily. "He has worked on some of the most complex analytical models for Fortune 100 companies and governmental agencies. He is one of the few experts in the world on chaos theory: a very specialized niche of mathematics dealing with predictability in complex systems.

"His office is in Fine Hall. Do you know what that is? Since 1880, it's been home to some of America's most talented mathematical scholars. It had also housed the Institute for Advanced Study, a program known for its pioneering research. The institute's past notable teaching members include Albert Einstein and Robert Oppenheimer."

"Whatever," James interjected. "Let's get this call going."

"Okay, I'm dialing."

"Robert?" Stan answered. "How are you?"

"Doing well, my friend, thanks for asking," Robert said. "I have James on the phone, and he's interested in hearing your thoughts on the file I sent you."

"Damn it, old boy, I wondered why the hell you were sending me that shit. But when I ran a few elementary queries on the data you sent, I saw it almost immediately. I suppose all those years of mathematical analysis, cipher analysis, and crazy thoughts had honed my mind after all." Stan laughed. "I understand your excitement, Robert—you badass, you have to be very proud—I'm not sure how you did it, but it's got to be a first. When do you publish?"

"What do you mean?" Robert asked.

"Your sequence!" Stan said. "The longest DNA strand synthesized to date, to my knowledge, is only a few hundred, maybe a thousand proteins long. How ever you were able to synthesize 50,000 nucleotides, it has got to be revolutionary. I just want some mention in your write-up."

"Why do you think this is my work, and not natural?" Robert asked.

"Right. Don't be such a tosser. Only you would make me spell out your achievement for you! For God's sake, man, who actually synthesizes a nucleotide sequence that large? And who is such a pompous ass that he does it in code—albeit an elementary code? Fortunately, I understand your mathematical limitations—"

"Stan, that's not my code."

"Your synthesized DNA, then," Stan laughed again. "I know it's not your code anyway! It's the Golden Ratio."

"I'm sorry, Stan, but honestly you're losing me," Robert said.

"Rubbish, Robert—stop jacking with me!" Stan sighed. "Did you really pick a sequence to synthesize without knowing its significance? Geesh, I keep forgetting you are a simple gene guy and clearly don't have the appreciation for the beauty of math. The Golden Ratio is a fundamental mathematical principle, and the basis of the Fibonacci sequence. That is the sequence that you used, of course. So I assume you must be somewhat familiar with it."

Robert was silent. James just listened.

"What did you do, a random web search for cool sequences and then use it without reading about it?" Stan finally said. "The significance of the Golden Ratio is that it is the universal proportionality that appears in math, art, economics, biology, astronomy, our bodies . . . really everywhere. Funny you chose this ratio—I was actually fascinated with it as an undergrad."

There was a prolonged moment of silence while Stan waited for Robert to respond.

"Stan," Robert said slowly, "you need to understand something here. I didn't synthesize that protein sequence. We identified it in a DNA specimen we're testing for XNA—the therapeutics project I am working for."

There was an uncomfortable pause. "You're fucking with me," Stan finally said.

"There's more," Robert went on, his voice strained. "I've tested my own and twenty-eight other human subjects' DNA. This same sequence is present in every sample. I think this is probably ubiquitous." James knew from Robert's tone that this was no joke. His voice was strained. He was clearly under stress.

After another long pause, Stan spoke up again. "Frankly, the prospect of identifying this fundamental mathematical principle in the structure of DNA is unbelievable to me," he said. "I'm aware that this simple, elegant rule exists throughout nature. But why would the Fibonacci sequence exist in DNA? Math isn't behind how genes express themselves! Why would the Fibonacci sequence appear in a protein sequence? Why would it repeat identically five times? Unbelievable," he muttered.

"I identified this by chance," Robert insisted. "My intern mistakenly ran an analysis looking for repeating patterns within the same patient's DNA, as opposed to repeating patterns across separate subjects, and that's how we found it. In reviewing the data set, I was the only one who noticed the anomaly. Believe me, I've probably seen more protein strings than anyone on Earth—and I've never seen anything like this. It's like this section was purposefully grafted into the DNA molecule. It occurs in what is known as Human Chromosome 2, generally regarded as the portion of our DNA that makes us human. Had we not made a mistake in the lab, I would never have found it. The proverbial needle in a haystack was just there. It's crazy."

"Well, Robert, the scientific world has to know about this. You need to bring others into this research," Stan said.

Having listened silently up to this point, James now felt it was time to jump in. "No!" he said. "Not yet. We are not going to tell anyone.

We need time to think about this. We need to keep it under wraps until we understand this more."

"I agree." Robert said "Stan, you have to keep quiet on this; I have more tests I want to run."

"Okay, but this is an historic finding," Stan said. "We need to bring others to the table, and soon. I clearly can't help you figure out why this sequence is here, or how it expresses itself. But while you're thinking about that end of it, I'm going to keep looking at this sequence. Years of looking at digital code leads me to believe there is more here—more information hidden in the sequence."

6

KHALID AL HASSAN
THE VATICAN

For nothing is secret, that shall not be made manifest; neither any thing hid, that shall not be known and brought to light.

—LUKE 8:17

THE POPE SAT IN HIS OFFICE behind a small desk. The thick drapes were pulled shut, keeping any sunlight from entering the room. The desk was ornate, a heavy mahogany gilded in gold leaf. The pope's wingback chair was covered in red velour. He was in a casual suit. The room was dimly lit, with dark shadows cast about the room. A single ray of sunlight streamed through the small space between the curtains cutting through the darkness and illuminating the particles of dust moving through it.

A candle burned on the desk, and its slight floral aroma permeated the stale air. Khalid sat on a small couch near the wall.

"Our time grows short, Holy Father." Cardinal Russo said.

The pope held his stare and rubbed his chin. He adjusted his glasses so he could see Cardinal Russo and the two others seated in the corner of the room. He turned his attention to the cardinal.

"Yes. Time is short. But we need to know more. Prophecy only provides us so much. The ancient texts and scientific information in our archives only allow us to guess at timing. Although the scientific information that we have gives us a good estimate, we have to get this right: we need to have correct to-the-minute precision. We need to know—and we need to know now." The pope leaned forward and spoke seriously to Cardinal Russo.

"We must keep our agenda secret. We need to use all of our resources and make our moves now. Do you understand?"

Cardinal Russo nodded, his mouth held in a tight line. "Our intelligence assets are in every power center of the world, Your Eminence," he said, his stress audible. "Those dedicated to the Jesuit Order will provide the information we need, and aid in the control of that information."

The pope sat quietly for a moment. "Prepare for the things spoken of in Revelation," he said finally. "A cataclysm of biblical proportions approaches. The Vatican, led by the Jesuit Order, will rise from the destruction. Our enthronement ceremony so many years ago will not be in vain. Our empire is vast, and we will emerge to bring light to those in the shadows. The world will look to the Vatican in the dark days to come. What was planned so long ago by the founders of the Jesuit Order is at our doorstep. It is time for a new world order to emerge."

Khalid quietly observed the conversation. Beside him sat one of his associates. She was Russian, strikingly beautiful and blonde, and wearing high heels and a tight white dress. Despite her elegant attire, she had a hard, athletic look about her.

The pope turned to Khalid. "The time has come." he said. "We have another task for you and your associates. We have been alerted by our intelligence sources to some information—scientific information—that we need." His voice hardened. "And we need you to get it."

AGENT DEVON STINSON
AIR FORCE ONE

"[Space travel] is the one thing that draws us all together."
—GUY CONSOLMAGNO, DIRECTOR OF THE VATICAN OBSERVATORY

Air Force One shuddered as it climbed to 50,000 feet in the midst of a thunderstorm. Lightning flashed as Agent Stinson's ears popped.

He and NSA Chief Perkings made their way down the narrow hallway to the small private office of the president. The room had a desk, a brown leather couch, and a few chairs. Stinson closed the door and placed his update report on the president's desk, struggling to stay upright as turbulence bounced the aircraft. Rain hammered against the fuselage.

"All right, gentlemen," the president said. "Now, where are we?" He shifted in his seat to address Stinson.

A jolt rocked the cabin, and Stinson sat to the president's left, then paused for a moment to gain his composure. He instinctively looked out the window, only to see the plane was still engulfed in cloud cover. He secretly wished he had a seatbelt on. "Mr. President, we need to take control of a project in Egypt," he said.

"A project in Egypt," President Brooks repeated, a bewildered smile spreading across his face. "Do you want to elaborate on that a little more?"

Perkings leaned in. "The new Egyptian Antiquities Minister seems to have decided that he wants to open up the Great Pyramid," he said. "He has launched a new excavation project to that end."

The president closed his eyes and rubbed the bridge of his nose. "Mr. Perkings, please explain to me why the United States needs to explore the Great Pyramid when we have so many problems here at home right now."

Stinson spoke up first. "Mr. President, if I may, allow me to address this. You see, we have been trying to get into the pyramids for years—all the way back to Kennedy. Under the former Antiquities Minister, Zaher, it was hit or miss—or perhaps I should just say miss. He rarely allowed groups from outside of Egypt to excavate. However, this new guy, Sati Am Unnefer, is different. Our intelligence assets indicate that there is a new planned excavation into a hidden chamber of the Great Pyramid. We have data that suggest there is very pertinent information to Project Aquarius hidden in this chamber that could surface."

This piqued the president's interest. "What information?" he asked eagerly; then his face hardened. "It better be serious. We don't have time for a wild goose chase. Maybe you haven't noticed, but we are currently perhaps the least welcome country in Egypt." He raised an eyebrow and waited for a response.

"Mr. President, a few decades ago an excavation turned up these images," Stinson said. He slid some photos across the table. "This is another piece of the puzzle that Project Aquarius is attempting to solve. These markings are not Egyptian. They're Sumerian cuneiform markings, found inside the pyramid in the shaft leading to this hidden chamber. More specifically, they're inscribed behind a very small sealed door with metal levers deep within the Great Pyramid." The young agent looked at the president intently.

"Mr. President," Mitchell Perkings picked up, "the Sumerian civilization predates the Egyptian by thousands of years. This is direct evidence that the pyramids were built before Egyptian times. This information is being controlled; only a handful of people have access to it. By getting in on the excavation, we would at least be able to remain among that number—and control the information when it is in our best interests to do so."

The president leaned back in his chair and placed his fingertips together in thought. After a minute, he said, "All right. Do it. We will assemble a team of our own archaeologists and scientists. Included in it will be some of our men. You are authorized to do whatever you need to do to get us involved in the way you see fit."

"Thank you, Mr. President," Stinson concluded.

FATHER MATEO PEREZ
MOUNT GRAHAM OBSERVATORY, ARIZONA

"Absence of evidence is not evidence of absence."

—CARL SAGAN

"Again, I hate to disappoint you," Father Perez was saying, "but I do not read Sumerian. A translator would be of more use to you. My expertise is not ancient languages."

He was walking with Coppa outside the observatory complex, following a break for lunch. It was stiflingly hot out, and a haze hung over the mountain. The two men walked along a narrow gravel path through the evergreens. Although it was September, the morning was like a hot summer day. The heat was sweltering, and dust danced around them as they walked. Father Perez rubbed his eyes and squinted in the bright sunlight.

"Mateo, you are wound much tighter than I imagined," Coppa said. "Of course we have several versions of a translation, although this is not an exact science when working with the oldest writing on Earth. And before you raise any more objections, the texts contain verbal references to these star maps. That is your specialty, is it not? Interpreting star maps." Coppa made sure Father Perez realized it was a statement, not a question.

"It is with these maps that we need your immediate assessment." Coppa stopped and turned to an evergreen tree growing by the path. He tore off a small pine branch, pinched it between his fingers, and drew in its scent deeply.

"I am an astronomer, but wasn't I sent here to begin reconciling astrobiology with Church doctrine?" Father Perez asked, turning to look up at the large, open observatory doors, through which the LUCIFER binocular telescope protruded.

Coppa frowned and kicked at the gravel under his feet. "That is true," he said. "Yes. However, there are a few other things that the Holy See has tasked you with as well. Why do you think they sent you halfway around the world to Arizona if your sole charge was doctrine?" He smiled as he followed Father Perez's gaze up to the telescope. "The Vatican has a lot of information. However, you needed to be at a place where you could not only view the information and process it in our mainframe, but also have access to the stars themselves—with the three most advanced telescopes in the world. You must figure out these star maps for His Holiness." With a jerk of his head, Coppa turned and began moving toward the entrance to the facility, motioning for the priest to follow.

They wound down through the bowels of the complex. The temperature dropped consistently as they descended. Soon they found themselves back in the operations room. The annoying hum of all the systems grated on Father Perez's nerves once again.

"Everything you need is in this room," Coppa said. "It has been prepared for you. I am sure the trip has been long, and you will work better in a more relaxed environment. We'll talk again tomorrow after lunch. By then, you should have had the chance to read and digest the materials laid out for you in your chambers. For now, I will tell you no more. I prefer you go into this research free of preconceptions—or perhaps misconceptions." He smiled broadly. "If there's anything you desire, do not hesitate to ring for Joseph to assist you. He has been directed to see to your needs. It was a pleasure meeting you, Mateo," he concluded, extending his hand.

Perez accepted it, immediately noting the subtle strength. "And you—Paul."

As if on cue, the door opened and Joseph entered to escort Perez to his room.

Again, he was led through the lower level, up the elevator, and through more passages. Joseph opened the door to his room, and ushered him inside. It was decorated more nicely than most hotel rooms. A comfortable double bed was in the corner, a small couch was against the wall opposite the large window, and a small table with two chairs was tucked beside a small kitchenette.

"You will find your personal items in the wardrobe," Joseph said.

"The refrigerator is stocked. There are instructions on the table for you to manually plug your laptop into the closed network system." Joseph pointed to the phone. "Call if you need anything. Just hit 0, and I will come and see to your needs."

As Joseph turned to leave, a disturbing question occurred to Father Perez. "Would it be correct to say that I am not free to come and go as I please?" he asked.

Joseph smiled amiably. "I have been directed to see to your needs, Father Perez," he said simply. "All you have to do is use the phone."

"And if I felt in need of a walk, some fresh air?" Perez briefly wondered why it was so difficult to get a straight answer from anyone.

Joseph's expression did not change. "You will find that your room has an open balcony, with a great view of the mountains," he said. "There is also an exercise room at the end of this hallway. If there is anything else, I can bring it to the attention of his Eminence. However, I am certain you noticed the agents in the area outside of VATT. They are very serious about their job, and their job is to ensure that the information we have in *here* does not get out *there*." The young Jesuit pointed toward the window. "For the time being, you must refrain from any sort of communication with anyone outside of the observatory."

"Thank you," Father Perez replied in earnest. "I appreciate the information, and the honesty."

After Joseph left, Father Perez muttered to himself, "Who would I call, anyway?" He stared at the computer as he sat on the bed. In addition to this weight placed on him by the Vatican, it seemed that Coppa had his own ideas about his usefulness. He was not sure if all the discussion about the tablets was from the Vatican or from Coppa's own interests. He would find out soon enough.

Now, when he most wanted to rest in order to prevent the headache that was threatening after a flight halfway around the world, the urgency in Coppa's tone regarding the ancient tablets and star maps made him feel obligated to start his review right away.

With a sigh, Father Perez sat down at the small desk. He considered the dilemma that Christianity and the other Christ-based religions of the world faced in light of an announcement of intelligent life beyond Earth. He himself had always believed in alien life forms, but he had never needed to reconcile that belief with his faith in God; he wondered if it was even possible.

He kept seeing the computer out of the corner of his eye. He struggled to focus on one problem at a time. He had some guidance from the theology documents provided to him before leaving the Vatican. He flipped through a few of these and thought, *How would we expect the religious context of an Earthly savior of mankind—in Jesus—fit for an alien gray for example, if such existed. Were aliens saved? Were they without original sin of man?*

An interesting postulate occurred to him. Surely God would appear to any species of intelligent life in a manner familiar to them; he would arrive in their land, follow their customs in their form and in a way that was familiar and recognizable to them. That was how other religions had been justified by the more liberal Christians; perhaps the new pope could be persuaded to adopt this attitude. Then it would be easy to make the switch to involve alien cultures—God simply appeared to different people in different lands in different ways!

That was it! *There is one God for the entire universe. He appeared to us in Christ through a means we could understand, accept, and follow. He would do the same throughout creation.* This was only a beginning, and obviously did not confront the salvation problem, but it was a start.

Head throbbing, he turned to his laptop. Since he knew that Coppa wanted him to review the star maps, he thought he should capture his thoughts before they fled. He opened a new document and began typing:

> *We witness a multiplicity of lifeforms all over the Earth. Likewise other intelligent beings, brought into creation by the same God, exist throughout the cosmos. We cannot dictate the creative expansiveness of God, nor put limits upon him, and this is consistent with Catholic doctrine.*

* * *

After typing for most of the afternoon, Father Perez finally allowed himself the luxury of a nap just before supper. However, when he awoke, he discovered to his dismay that he had missed the meal and slept through the night. Although he felt he'd made significant progress on the Church's new theological shift, he felt slightly guilty for not even glancing at the materials regarding the tablets and star maps that Coppa had suggested he read.

When Joseph brought him breakfast and reminded him that he was to meet the cardinal at one o'clock, his palms began to sweat. Perez was a fast learner and might be able to come up with something that would look like progress, but he also needed a shower to cleanse himself from the journey and extended nap.

After his shower, the knock came promptly as the priest was fastening the last of the buttons on his suit. Joseph stood on the other side of the door when Perez opened it. As they headed for the elevator, Joseph asked him a question. Father Perez was still groggy.

"I'm sorry, I'm afraid my mind has been wrapped around many things as of late," Father Perez said. "Would you mind repeating what you just asked?"

"Did you sleep well? I know that I always have trouble the first night in a new place . . . different bed and all," Joseph said in a pleasant tone.

"Yes, I slept very well, thank you. How long have you been here?"

"Just a couple of months, working on the VATT. I'm working on my doctorate through Notre Dame University."

Their conversation continued until they reached the lower floor. It was limited to small talk, but Father Perez appreciated the effort all the same. It was a welcome change from his solitude in this maze of confusion.

Once Joseph had deposited Father Perez with Cardinal Coppa in the communication center, he turned and left. Silence again reigned while Coppa finished entering information into his computer, completely engrossed in what he saw there.

"I was just wondering how your summaries were coming," he finally said without turning around.

Father Perez felt like he was back in grade school being chastised by a nun for neglecting to do his homework. Instinctually, he tucked his fingers into fists to protect them from the inevitable ruler.

"I was inspired to write, and I did not want to lose my inspiration," he said. "Since that was the task assigned to me by the Holy Father, I did not feel bad devoting my time yesterday to it. Unfortunately, I have not had time to begin to digest the star map information you provided."

Coppa sat frowning for a few moments before he spoke. "Well, today we are going to give you a little direction. We need the Taluk documents reviewed immediately. I would appreciate it if you would read through the translation and give me a summary as soon as possible." Once he'd finished speaking, he swung himself around to face his monitor again.

Father Mateo resisted sighing aloud as he stepped over to the small desk and computer terminal he had been assigned in the control room. He was now in the heart of MIGO, the Mount Graham International Observatory. The monitor conveniently displayed the Taluk documents and a parallel translation. He forced himself to focus on the work ahead of him. Although he stifled several yawns and occasionally glanced at Coppa, he was able to push through. Over the next hour, in spite of himself, Perez found the information extremely interesting. Finally, he composed the requested summary. With a satisfied smile, he printed his summary and handed to Coppa.

"You have a nonjudgmental style that is easy to read and follow," Coppa said, once he'd read through it.

"I prefer to be as factual as possible. If I remove myself from the material, it helps get rid of any interfering subjectivity," Father Perez smiled.

Coppa swiveled in his chair to greet Perez more appropriately. "I see that," he said. "Go back to the translation. Let's start there. Tell me your first impressions. This time, be subjective."

Father Perez frowned. He was beginning to see why Coppa had been stationed so far from Rome; apparently, he was consumed by this project. Perez turned back to the monitor and reviewed what he had just read.

"It appears that the Sumerian author—assuming he is the author—interacted with gods," he said.

"What gods do they worship?" Coppa asked, in an instructor's tone.

"Let me be a bit more direct," Perez answered. "The Sumerians indicated that they directly communicated with their gods and worked alongside them. Their gods were called the *Annunaki*, meaning *those who from heaven came*, and were described by the Sumerians as real beings. Beings that were not of this world. If this translation is correct, the author is not talking about having some sort of otherworldly spiritual experience. He describes instead a corporeal one. He has physical visitors.

"However, it appears the author worships these beings as if they were his deities or his Creator," he continued. "Along with attesting to seeing them with his own eyes and communicating with them directly, he speaks about their dominion over all things great and small, seen and unseen. He also attests to their ability to travel quickly, even to other worlds."

"How do you feel about these claims?" Coppa interrupted.

"In the archives, I have reviewed similar recordings discovered in other parts of the world, so they are not shocking to me," Father Perez replied. "As an academic, I have studied similar stories from other cultures, including the Mayans and several American Indian tribes. If you are asking for my personal reaction, I already believe there are other life forms out there. I don't know whether they've visited Earth, but I think ancient tales of these encounters appear to be more than writings we have misinterpreted. However, I'm sure many people would disagree."

Coppa pointed to the monitor. "And the second document?"

Perez nodded slightly. "I find this page to be a little less believable. Other cultures and other people have attributed the origins of humanity to celestial beings. But this is the first I have seen that suggests, according to the translation, that we are the product of these alien visitors. If I am reading this correctly, it states that a superior being, seemingly of flesh and blood, had deliberately created man."

"Fair enough," said Coppa. "Let's move on to the third tablet."

Perez could tell Coppa wanted the secrets behind these tablets, and he wanted them now. Clearly, he didn't want to be bothered with pleasantries.

It was apparent Coppa didn't care if he came off as demanding or demeaning. Perez turned to the monitor and took a moment to reread what he had written. "It's the least cryptic of the three," he said. "At some time the visitors will return, or plan to return. Apparently, there is knowledge or important wisdom that has been hidden, and the star maps and accompanying descriptions purport to provide the location of these golden *Ascension Testaments* you referred to yesterday." Perez tapped his chest with two fingers and chuckled. "Of course, if all of this were proven to be true, many believe the entire world's population would panic," he said. "Although I may have too much faith in people, I don't believe every semblance of social structure would come apart."

"Why are your beliefs different?" Coppa prodded.

"I'm speaking from a semi-religious perspective. So for starters, approximately 18 percent of the current world population has no religious conviction. Learning of intelligent extraterrestrial life would not be perceived in terms of their faith, but more likely from a scientific perspective. Frankly, I think for most of today's young people, the revelation of this type of information is something they would see as inevitable, something they have expected. I don't see it as a panic-causing event.

"Secondly, in terms of Catholicism, we provide teachings for perhaps a third of the remainder who do profess a religion. But how many of those truly practice their beliefs outside of christenings, marriages, and funerals? Ultimately, as a Church, we deal with less than a fourth of the world's population: those who show true devotion. Under such circumstances, their first reaction would be to turn to the Church for refuge and guidance, at least psychologically. And we comfort them and explain that this is what was meant all along. As a result, I don't believe it is the conundrum that some world leaders seem to think it—and no,

I don't think whole societies would collapse. I do, however, concede the possibility of a secular knee-jerk reaction."

Coppa acknowledged agreement with a subtle tilt of his head. Father Perez shifted uncomfortably in his seat as he tried to figure out the cardinal. Finally, Coppa began. "Now, I think, is the appropriate moment to tell you why you are here," he said. "As you know, the Holy Father has himself chosen you to join a select team assembled by the Vatican to help us progress on doctrine in the event of an astrobiological discovery. And it is also part of your charge to further investigate this matter by locating these hidden tablets, which these star maps apparently identify."

Father Perez interjected, "The text that accompanies the star map discusses the return of the gods just before upcoming tribulation and cataclysmic events.

"This description seems to parallel the time in the book of Revelation when a great dragon appears in the sky. The star map clearly identifies the constellation of Virgo; it also appears to describe the location of an additional planet or celestial object within our solar system, unless I misinterpreted its meaning."

"Yes. Yes!" Cardinal Coppa clapped his hands in excitement. "Now you see! If these texts *are* true and we find the *Ascension Testaments*, we must assume that the texts describing the coming of these gods and the tribulation are also correct. That is why you must decipher these maps—and quickly."

Father Perez had a sudden moment of clarity. *My God, the Holy See actually believes that these golden books exist,* he thought. *They believe they hold hidden knowledge or wisdom of some kind, and that this star map shows their location. They believe this tale of a coming cataclysm—as if it were real.* He swallowed hard. He knew these were just ancient stories and myths, but he was suddenly nervous: the pope was directly involved.

"You'll be with us for the near future," Coppa was saying. "See if you can decipher these maps. Time is of the essence, Father Perez. Our resources are at your disposal." The cardinal spread his hands.

Father Perez blinked and struggled to keep his breathing even for several moments. "Well, if that's settled, I'll get to work on the maps immediately."

The cardinal smiled. "I emphasize to you that there is an urgency regarding your work here."

"How urgent?" Perez asked.

The cardinal pointed to the tablets "As if the gods' arrival were imminent."

7

KHALID AL HASSAN
PARIS, FRANCE

KHALID HAD JUST ARRIVED and sat in a small hotel room in the 18th Arrondissement of Paris. A single bulb hanging from the ceiling dimly lit the dingy room. A milk crate sat beside the bed, serving as a bedside table. The dank smell of sewage permeated the stale, humid air filtering in through the small window. Khalid hated Paris. He hated the people, and the smell in his room fouled his mood further. The faucet in the bathroom dripped a constant tempo, and the chipped white tile floor looked like it had not been mopped in decades.

Khalid closed the blinds to the window overlooking a small, dark concrete courtyard in the middle of the building, to block out the breaking dawn. He sorted through the bag he had just picked up from one of his contacts to examine the weapons inside. Across the bed, several untraceable prepaid phones were laid side-by-side, identical to the one in his pocket. Each one was labeled with a date. He would cycle through these phones as instructed, using only one number for a specified period of time. He would only call one person with each of these phones.

As Khalid put on his maroon jacket, the phone in its pocket rang. He wondered what motivated his employer. He knew he was a pawn in some political agenda. But he didn't care, as long as he was paid. But he couldn't help wondering anyway—what was this all about?

He answered the phone without saying a word. On the other end, a simple phrase was muttered: "7 Rue Palatine, in the 5th Arrondissement."

Khalid hung up the phone. He grabbed a small backpack from beside the bed and headed out the door onto the streets of Paris.

DR . SOFIA PETRESCU
GENEVA, SWITZERLAND

And great earthquakes shall be in diverse places, and famines, and pestilences; and fearful sights and great signs shall there be from heaven.

—LUKE 21:11

Professor De Vos was late. Sofia sat at a table outside the Cottage Cafe in Geneva. The quaint café, situated on Square des Alps with a great view of the Rhone and the mountains, was far enough away from the U.N. headquarters that Sofia felt comfortable about meeting the professor there. Or mostly comfortable. She was still anxious to be associated with him—and her recent research into the professor's theory had disturbed her greatly.

"I'm so sorry," the professor said, hurrying over to the table. His hair blew wildly in the afternoon breeze as he sat down next to her. Looking around again to see if anyone recognized them, Sofia scooted her chair closer to the table.

"Professor, what have you gotten me into?" She whispered, pulling a graph from under the notepad and handing it to him. "As you know, the magnetosphere protects the earth from solar radiation," she continued, "and the earth acts like a magnet in more ways than one, projecting its magnetic field way out into space like an invisible forcefield enveloping the earth. There is a constant barrage of charged particles, radiation, and solar wind ejected from the sun that impacts this field; if the field didn't exist, everything on earth would be destroyed and the atmosphere would be blasted out into space. Life would cease."

"Yes," the professor said expectantly.

"The magnetosphere is relatively constant, although it fluctuates from time to time due to magnetic changes within the earth itself. However, the changes have been consistently predictable—until recently. Your findings of the pole migration pushed me to dig a little deeper." She leaned in over the chart. "This chart shows the incredible increase in severe magnetic compressions on the magnetosphere over a 22-month period. These compressions are rising at alarming levels. Clearly something is causing the sun to discharge powerful solar winds more frequently, which are impacting the magnetosphere of the earth." She placed another graph on the table in front of the professor. "Now take a look at this chart, which shows a similar increase in the number of near-earth objects, such as asteroids and meteors, that are being discovered. It's as if, at the same time, our protection is weakening, and we are entering an area of space that is riddled with meteors.

"Now this is a graph showing a similar increase in meteorite activity around the earth," she continued, pulling out another paper. "I'm not sure how, but it's possible that all of these are somehow causally related."

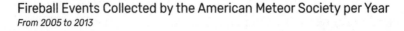

Fireball Events Collected by the American Meteor Society per Year
From 2005 to 2013

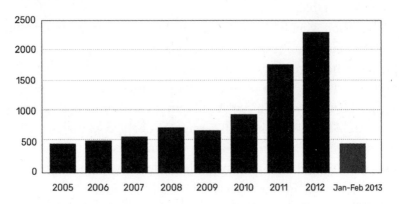

"What do you think could be the cause?" the professor asked.

"I'm not sure. But more disturbingly, I think the entire solar system is being affected."

"How so?"

She frowned. "I have done some digging, and there are few studies that I am aware of that seem to demonstrate that other planets are warming," she said. "There has been no complete study of this phenomenon as it pertains to the rest of the solar system. But looking over many independent studies, it is clear to me that this is occurring. More interestingly, a recent, very thorough study concludes that all the planets' poles have been very recently and rapidly migrating—similar to what we have seen here on Earth. It actually appears that several planets' poles have flipped already."

"How is that possible?"

"I don't know. But the claim is that this phenomenon started with the outermost planets and then moved to the inner planets. Likewise, current data shows that all of the planets are heating up or experiencing atmospheric changes and anomalies—again occurring in the outer planets first." She took a deep breath, again regretting the moment she agreed to look into all this. "It—it just makes no sense to me."

JAMES ANDERSON
PARIS, FRANCE

It had been over a week since Robert's revelation had disrupted James's vacation. Ever since, the constant calls and reviews of data and DNA patterns had been steadily wearing him down.

Today, James's phone had begun vibrating at seven a.m. He had turned the ringer off before passing out on the couch in his flat. Now the repetitive buzzing under his arm slowly brought him into the conscious world; his head throbbed as sunlight flooded in through the living room's sheer curtains. Lying on his side, he peered out at the door and stretched, trying to wake himself. Thoughts of the "anomalies in DNA" that James interpreted as costly business problems, soured his mood instantly. He heard a subtle creaking of the stairs from his apartment hallway—not uncommon, given that he was on the third floor of a seven-story building.

Strange: it sounded as if the person stopped on his level. This got James's attention; his was the only apartment on this floor. The creaking occurred again—right outside his door. He sat quietly listening. He could see a shadow from under the door: someone's feet moving around. Over the muffled buzzing of the phone he heard a quiet scraping on the door—against the lock.

James jerked his head off the pillow. Panic filled his gut. What was going on? The scraping continued, then stopped. A barely audible *click* echoed across the room.

Ever so slowly, the lever-style handle on the front door was turning downward toward the floor.

What in the hell? he thought. He frantically rubbed his eyes holding the door in his gaze but remaining dead silent as he slowly sat upright. Now, very distinctly, he could see the handle of the door moving. With impossible slowness the door began to creak open.

Adrenaline filled James's body. Terror coursed down his spine. His face flushed. His throat tightened, and his heart raced as the world seemed to slow. A thousand thoughts flashed through his mind but before he could think, he screamed, as loud as he could, "HEY!"

In one motion he leaped to the door, slamming it shut violently with his shoulder. He pressed hard against the door, struggling to regain his breath from the force of the impact while he prepared for a confrontation.

Slamming the deadbolt home, he peered out the peephole. He saw a man with short dark hair jumping down the stairs, his maroon jacket waving behind him. James tried to calm himself, he was taking deep breaths in frantic succession. "My God," he huffed.

James hurried over to the couch and grabbed the phone, which had begun to vibrate again. "Hello," he barked, running back over to the door with his phone. He looked back out through the peephole: the hallway was now empty.

"Are you up and moving already?" Robert asked, the sound of a computer keyboard echoing in the background.

"Shit, you're never going to believe what just happened," James said breathlessly. "Some punk just tried to rob my apartment."

"What are you talking about?"

James recounted the story, waiting for his pulse to return to normal.

"That must have been really nerve-wracking," Robert said when he'd finished.

"Yeah." James cleared his throat. "I should probably report it after I get off the phone with you. Anyway, what's up?"

"Did you read the summary I sent you of my last conversation with Dr. Caruthers?"

"Yes. It doesn't make any sense to me. It seems like Stan thinks there is more to this DNA pattern, which I suppose is great for science in general—I'm just worried how it will apply to the business end of things."

"I'm sending you some more information today on the Golden Ratio. I want you to take a look at it. I realize that you're more of a visual type of guy, so I really think these images will help you understand. However, I think we need to formally engage Stan to help with this. I want to bring him on board as a consultant."

"I can't even get my hands around what the hell's going on," James sighed, reminding himself that Robert was a sane individual who wouldn't be dragging him through this without some logical reason. "Can you maybe tell me what we can develop out of this? Will our product benefit from it, or is there some competing product that could? I mean, we can't afford to bring experts in and increase our burn rate just for tangential research."

"Damn it, James! This is bigger than our research!" Robert paused to collect himself before continuing. "Come on, Stan is an old colleague," he said slowly. "I know him. This is right up his alley, plus he owes me one. I think I can get him to consult for free if we cover any expenses." He paused again. "It's not nonsense, James. It should be nonsense, but it isn't."

"Okay, Robert," James released a breath. "I'm happy to bring in another expert at no cost, whoever you recommend. But I want to play this straight, okay? See if you can get Stan to look through all your historical data, too. I would really like a second opinion on your findings. You haven't been getting much sleep, after all."

"Oh, don't worry about that, James. I knew you would agree."

"One more thing. Make sure he signs a nondisclosure agreement before you give him anything more—just in case," James concluded.

"I'll take care of that," Robert laughed. "He'll love the chance to show us how smart he is. I've often wondered if that isn't one of the reasons that he became a teaching professor instead of an independent researcher." Robert suddenly yawned. "I guess I do need to get some sleep."

James glanced at his watch. It was past midnight in Chicago. "Let's just hope that this thing is as big as you say it is," he said.

"Believe me, James," Robert said, yawning again. "This could be the biggest scientific breakthrough since we split the atom. I'm sending you an email right now—I want you to open it and go over the contents. I'll call you when I wake up."

"Okay." James stretched and rubbed his throbbing shoulder. "Great! Talk to you then."

James shook his head and hung up the phone, his head spinning. Turning his attention back to the attempted break-in, he walked back over to the door and opened it. There were some gouge marks on the lock. He contemplated calling the police, then decided against it. This type of crime was common in Paris, after all; and with the classic lack of French administrative efficiency, it would take the cops all day to accomplish nothing.

As he stared at the wooden floor, wondering who else may have walked across its ancient herringbone pattern and contemplating if today was going to be another shitty day, he was drawn to the smell of the freshly baked bread from the boulangerie below. He needed coffee and a cigarette.

Foregoing a shower, he donned a very American baseball cap and headed down the Rue des Cannettes in search of a tabac for another pack of cigarettes.

The chilly morning air helped him to clear his head. After about thirty minutes he found himself back at Place Saint-Sulpice with a croissant, a cup of coffee, and a fresh cigarette dangling from his mouth. He sat on the edge of the fountain, facing north, and watched the people walking by the small shops. Café de la Marie on the corner was already full of people enjoying a coffee and *petit déjeuner.*

He set his coffee down on the limestone fountain base and tore off a piece of his croissant, brushing bits from this shirt. He leisurely looked around at the throngs of people moving through their morning routine.

"What the hell could Robert be on to?" he asked aloud, then self-consciously glanced around to make sure no one heard him. Those passing either seemed not to have heard or were just ignoring him. He scanned the small streets of the square and reached for his coffee.

Just as he was taking a drink, his heart seemed to leap into his throat. In the distance, between passing tourists, he caught the eye of a man glaring at him while talking on a cell phone.

James quickly tried to put the cup down and spilled coffee all down his front. He jumped up, swearing and wiping coffee off of his shirt. When he looked back to the small street where he'd seen the staring man, he had gone.

James's throat tightened. *What the hell?* The man gave him a look expressing pure evil. Could it have been the same guy that tried to break in? Dark complexion, dark hair, tight beard, maroon jacket, jeans, possibly Middle Eastern—James had experienced that glare a few times before in Paris. Among its large Islamic population, there were occasional nasty encounters with someone who despised Americans and Western values. But the guy had certainly taken off in a hurry. It was probably nothing—just a petty thief startled in the act.

James took another sip of coffee, dropped the rest of the croissant on the pavement for the pigeons, and walked back to his flat. *I'm just still jumpy from this morning,* he thought.

DR . SATI AM UNNEFER
CAIRO, EGYPT

The angel took the censer, filled it with fire from the altar, and threw it to the earth . . .

—REVELATION 8:5

"Dr. Unnefer!"

A middle-aged man wearing green cargo shorts and a white, short-sleeved shirt leaned over Sati's desk. His English came with a heavy German accent.

"Professor Kline—so good to finally meet you in person." Sati shook the hand offered to him and motioned to the chair beside his desk. "Have a seat."

"Don't mind if I do," Professor Kline said as he settled into the creaky old wooden seat. Running his fingers through his sandy-brown hair, he continued. "I came immediately upon hearing the news. It's been quite a long flight over here, and the drive from the airport to your office was no easy task either."

Sati could understand why Westerners were not comfortable traveling in Egypt these days. He returned the professor's smile. "Yes, well, many things are in transition right now, as I'm sure you are well aware."

"Indeed, they are." Professor Kline removed his glasses and wiped them with a cloth. "We were very happy to hear that things have changed around your office as well."

"You must be referring to the retirement of Dr. Zaher," Sati said, leaning back in his chair.

"Well, it's more that you have been put in charge of things," Kline said. "Some people don't appreciate efforts to dig up the past around here, not to mention actual archeological research. You seem as anxious as the rest of us to pursue your interest into the genesis of Egyptian antiquities and the pyramids. I think you are the type of man who is looking to fully explore and unlock whatever mysteries the Great Pyramid may hold."

"Of course," Sati said hesitantly. He still wasn't sure he fully trusted this man; news of his decision to once again begin excavation in the Great Pyramid had spread with alarming rapidity through archeological circles. "And I hope you are aware that many other nations have requested to continue the excavation within the pyramid. I had a hard time determining who would be best to lead this particular excavation. But the Germans were naturally my first consideration. After all, they had performed the original exploration of the shafts."

"Ah, yes," Professor Kline said as he put his glasses back on and tucked the cloth back in his pocket. "We were the first to discover the door that leads to the unknown room. A room, as I understand it, that to this date no one understands. Everyone is still asking why this room exists and wondering what purpose it serves. Am I right?"

"Yes, that's correct," Sati said. "And since the German team is familiar with the delicate excavation, I decided the Germans should be brought back to finish the job. And you will be the project lead, of course. However," he added, as he assessed the beaming professor for a moment, wondering how he would react to the forthcoming news, "there is a new wrinkle in our plans. I have been contacted by the United States and have spoken directly to President Brooks, if you can imagine that.

The Americans have offered to fund the entire excavation and allow the Egyptian government to maintain all of any excavated findings and then some. It is a gesture intended to help strengthen our new government's relationship with America and provide some much-needed economic stimulus for Cairo."

"I have no doubt," said Professor Kline, forcing a polite smile and shifting uneasily in his chair. His demeanor took a decidedly defensive posture; his enthusiasm seemed to evaporate.

Sati pushed himself forward and sat up straight. "Let's not play games about this, Professor. I have researched much of your work on the Great Pyramids and Egyptian history in general. While I was very impressed with your theories concerning the Giza complex, I am somewhat surprised that your government would put you forward as a lead archeologist on this project, once again. You and I have many of the same thoughts about the true history of this place and what purpose it served."

"Well, most would think me a little out in left field, but I firmly believe that this pyramid room will help prove my theories correct," Professor Kline said. "I think that those in my government realized this, and also want to solve the puzzle. When they asked if I would head this team and act as a liaison to you, I was honored and felt I couldn't refuse."

"Out in—left field?" Sati inquired.

Professor Kline laughed. "An American expression. It means outside of what most consider the normal."

"Well then, I suppose I would be out in left field as well." The two academics chuckled.

"But seriously," continued Kline, "I can of course work with the U.S. team. I am well aware that there were many other countries vying for this privilege. I appreciate the opportunity to finish what we started, and I assure you, I will do nothing without your approval."

"I appreciate that, Professor Kline," Sati said with a nod, "and that is why I am choosing your team. I need an expert on the inside. That will be you."

"Very good then," Professor Kline replied as he stood up, clearly relieved. "The rest of my team will be ready to begin as soon as you say go, assuming that works for the Americans. If there is nothing further, we will begin our preparations."

"No, I have nothing more to discuss," Sati said. "Until then . . ." He stood up to lead his guest to the door.

Sati watched him as he made his way down the hall. He hoped he had made the right choice with this man, and in partnering with the Americans. They'd given him a very generous offer—but their help was never simply charitable. They expected information. It always seemed to him as if the Americans were staring down their noses at you, waiting for a chance to further their imperialist agenda.

* * *

The next day, Sati was in his office going over the excavation details when suddenly, his door was thrust open, slamming it into the wall. A picture fell, shattering on the floor. Sati leapt to his feet in surprise.

Dr. Zaher stood framed in the doorway. He glared at Sati, entered the room, and slammed the door shut behind him.

"How could you do this?" the retired Antiquities Minister hissed, his finger pointed accusingly at Sati. "How could you betray your country like this? How could you allow the *Americans* to come into our country and pillage our people's greatest work?" Spittle flew from his mouth as he ranted.

Sati stared in shock for a moment, wondering how the news had reached the ears of his predecessor so quickly. Then, seating himself again as calmly as he could, he turned his full attention to his previous employer.

"What are you talking about?" he asked, straightening his shirt. "Have you forgotten that I—we—deal with unearthing the mysteries of ancient Egypt? It is our duty to research the things we find. That is why this office, this position, is here." He spread his arms wide. "It is our duty to find things that will benefit our people and our country."

"We are Egyptians and Muslims, Sati. We have created great things, done great things, built great things!" Zaher's face became flushed. "I don't know what these Americans think they are going to find, or why they are involved in this. But I know all about that German, Kline. He is like the many other fools who have come here thinking they are going to find proof that our people's greatest works were not built by Egyptians, but by some fantasy spacemen or ancient European people. A man like that has no business here, and he especially should not be given a chance to excavate the pyramid. Have you learned nothing from me, Sati?"

Sati narrowed his eyes and lowered his voice. "I have learned much, Dr. Zaher." He stood slowly and began making his way around the desk. "I have learned how you kept many new revelations from being discovered. How you constantly prevented teams from investigating further when their conclusions did not match yours. I even learned how you kept secrets from me!" He glared into Zaher' eyes and motioned toward the wall that had hidden the files he'd found.

Dr. Zaher sat down heavily, seeming to deflate. When he spoke again his words were nearly a whisper, almost as if he were talking to himself.

"I left you with this responsibility because I thought you wanted the same things I wanted," he said, shaking his head with his arms limp in his lap. "Now you are telling me that you are like all the others who came here to desecrate the works of our people and Allah. You will bring on a religious war with these things you are doing, Dr. Unnefer."

Sati uncrossed his arms. "I am not trying to desecrate anyone or anything. Nor do I seek to start a war. I am only trying to find the truth, and I am prepared to accept it—whatever it may be. If this discovery points to a solely Egyptian origin, then so be it. If it does not, so be it. We are not the dictators of history. Our history is what it is. That is what I thought we were here to do: to discover the truth about the past."

There was a long pause. Zaher searched Sati's eyes. "And what if it is not of this earth, whatever you find?" he whispered, his tone suddenly pleading. "Are you willing to shame the Muslim world with such a claim? You, who piously wears his robes? Do you not understand that you will be shaming the great prophet by doing something like that? Is that worth it, Sati?"

Sati sighed as he made his way back around the desk and into his chair. He knew Zaher was right; such a discovery would do much damage to Islam. But he'd spent his whole career trying to uncover proof for his beliefs, and he knew his allegiance to scientific truth was every bit as strong.

"One cannot live in fear of the truth, Dr. Zaher," he said after a long pause. "All these years you were in charge of this office and did that—look at what it got you. Whenever a discovery came about that conflicted with your beliefs, you snuffed it out. Is the world better off for that? Are we not fighting still amongst ourselves? Has cleaving to the notion that *Egyptians built these pyramids* done anything to unify Islam? I have been waiting my whole career for this opportunity. There is no way I can give up this opportunity to finally find the truth. It may upset the imams, and it may not. But in the end, either way, it will be the truth."

Dr. Zaher' face turned a deeper shade of red and tinged almost purple as he slowly stood. "You are a fool, Sati," he growled. "If I had known this sooner, I would not have made you my successor. You were wrong to deceive me, and you have done wrong in deceiving the rest of the Muslim world. You will be judged for your actions." He turned and walked to the door before shouting back over his shoulder: "Especially for collaborating with the Americans! They are a treacherous people that will only bring Egypt, Islam, and yourself to ruin. Watch your back, Sati."

With this last warning, Zaher slammed the door behind him.

8

JAMES ANDERSON
PARIS, FRANCE

WHEN JAMES RETURNED TO HIS APARTMENT, he was surprised to find the door to the building ajar.

"*Bonjour?*" he ventured as he entered the tiled lobby.

"Monsieur Anderson?" a woman's voice called from the other side of the lobby. An elderly lady dressed in an ornate black gown began to stride toward him. Though her face was caked in makeup and heavily lined with wrinkles, Madame Morel still carried herself elegantly, as befitted the beauty she had once been. She wore her long, gray hair piled high on top of her head; on her feet were a pair of fantastically high heels.

"Madame Morel!" James said, kissing his pleasant neighbor on both cheeks. "What a pleasure to see you again."

"Please, James, I've told you for ages—call me Bernadette." The woman gave him a warm smile and batted her eyes. James knew she had been an actress just after World War II and as long as he had known her, she'd shocked, scandalized, and entertained him and his family with vaudeville tales from those difficult years. After a short-lived career as a film actress, and a long marriage to a screenwriter, she now lived alone, a widow of some three years. Still, nothing seemed to stop her and her endless round of social gatherings, soirees, and gossip. She always had something shocking to tell James about the other neighbors; God only knew what she said about him.

"What's the news, Bernadette?" he said, noticing an open toolbox and a selection of screwdrivers by one wall.

"I am sorry, James," she replied, her English thickly accented. "But it seems zat 7 Rue Palatine is starting to crumble beneath our very feet!"

"Why, what happened?"

"Ze electrics, my dear. When I awoke zes morning, I found ze power out. Poof!" She clapped her hands. "I called ze concierge, but he was of no help, as you would expect. So I ring Electrics Centrale. Of course, zey knew nozing about it, but almost immediately one of zer workmen arrived. He informed me zat zey were doing some work on ze lines in ze area. Apparently, 7 Rue Palatine is ze weak link in ze chain. Zey blew our electrics!" Madame Bernadette Morel smiled with a wink.

"Not surprising, with ze way ze concierge keeps the place. He is never available. But ze workman, he is already here. Earlier, he told me zat he would have ze phone and ze power back on by zis afternoon. I have ze utmost confidence in him, if for no other reason zan he arrived so promptly."

"Well, that will make my day a little more difficult." James muttered. To be honest, he had to admit that he almost relished the distraction.

Madame Morel smiled. "Not *difficile* just a little delayed."

"I don't know what the rest of us here would ever do without you," James said, grasping one of Madame Morel's hands and planting a kiss upon it.

"Too kind, monsieur," she laughed. "You are too kind. But where is your delightful family zis visit? I was surprised to find no one in when I knocked at your apartment. You haven't ze children with you?"

Thoughts of his Amy and the rest of his tribe guiltily flashed through James's mind, accompanied by a plummet from his heart. "No, not this time. I'm afraid that me and Kerri, we, er—"

Bernadette Morel pressed her hand to his immediately. "Say no more, James," she said quietly. "I see zat you have something on your mind. When you are ready, come to my apartment. We will share some brandy, and you can tell me all about it."

James half-smiled and nodded his head. "Thank you, Bernadette. You are, as ever, a constant friend."

Madame Morel tutted, walking out the door. "Only to my good friends and neighbors, James. To everyone else, I am an alley cat with her claws out!" She spread her fingers comically as she disappeared.

I'm sure you are! James thought, chuckling to himself.

Just then a bald, stocky man in work coveralls sauntered in through the open front door. Before heading up the stairs, James turned to him and tried in his fragmented French to explain the near break-in he'd experienced earlier. He emphasized that the man must be more cautious about keeping the door closed. The man responded with a nod, and James headed up to his apartment.

After showing, he decided to head to the Ile de la Cite and stop in at one of the excellent cafes along the way to continue to look over the information Robert had sent.

The walk across central Paris was a pleasant one, even if its noise level increased throughout the day. When he was halfway across the Pont St. Louis, his cell phone rang.

"Hey, Robert, what's the news—" James began; but his voice trailed off as his phone suddenly went out. He pulled the phone away from his ear and looked at it with a frown. The line was dead. He looked at the crowd around him; most of them were still enjoying conversations on their phones while they walked.

He dialed Robert's number, only to find the signal light flashing on and off erratically. Perhaps the power outage had affected some of the networks, or maybe there were too many foreign connections going through right now.

Within minutes, he was seated at one of the small, black-painted ironwork tables at a brasserie with the noon sun warming his face. Nursing an espresso, he logged into his email on his laptop.

He noticed several emails from Robert. Opening the most recent, he read:

James,

I've been trying to phone you for the past hour, but I can't seem to get through. I'll keep this short, as I am exhausted and I'm beginning to see double. Stan Caruthers says that he will be available from tomorrow until the end of next week. He said he could do some research from Princeton for a few days and meet with us, if you can get back to the States soon. He said he will put all of his own work on hold for this.

"Well," James grumbled to himself, "there goes my vacation." He ordered lunch and settled in to review the documents Robert had sent and book his flight back.

When he'd finished eating, he smoked a cigarette and watched the tourists flock up to the rear of Notre Dame, squinting upward at the church's magnificent buttresses. His thoughts wandered to his wife and children: the last time he'd been at this café, he was having ice cream with them. Amy had loved running through the gardens under the buttresses and looking at the rose bushes. A stab of guilt ran through him as he thought about his daughter. Even during the divorce, he'd given

Kerri whatever she wanted. He just wanted to get it over with, mainly for the kids' sake—but last August it had almost taken Amy from him.

The tennis coach and Kerri had been out partying in Miami with a group of new friends on the yacht she had taken from James.

Everyone was drinking, and the party that began in the afternoon ended up lasting all day and into the night. For whatever reason, they'd brought the kids along. James detested the fact that his kids were traveling with the tennis coach.

Some drunken dumbass at the party had decided it would be a good idea to get the three Sea-Doos out and run around Biscayne Bay in the dark. James's boys, who were fifteen, thirteen, and ten at the time, hated their mom's new boyfriend and quickly declined the invitation. But five-year-old Amy loved the handsome tennis coach, and he doted on Amy. As the Sea-Doos were being lowered down into the water, she'd begged to ride with him. And, of course, she was way too young to go. Like the damn drunken idiot he was, he took her. They went out far—too far from the boat in rough chop.

They'd raced all over Biscayne Bay that night, until the tennis coach had finally sobered up enough to realize that Amy was no longer seated behind him. Then they'd scoured the bay in terror for an hour as they tried to retrace all of their twists and turns. Even after they'd finally called the Coast Guard, they didn't find Amy until almost seven in the morning, when the sun began to rise. She was alive, but had severe hypothermia and had to spend several days in the ICU and almost two weeks in the hospital.

James knew the experience would haunt his daughter for the rest of her life—that fucking tennis coach. James knew the tennis coach hadn't called the Coast Guard immediately because he was fearful his drunk ass would be arrested. It gave James no consolation knowing that the guy would ultimately be charged for this reckless behavior.

James could not bear to think about his sweet little, baby girl all alone in the dark water— waiting, crying, and screaming to be rescued. He should have been there—not some fucking tennis coach. He felt he'd failed as a father.

Shaking his head, James pulled himself back to the present. He had work to do. After paying his bill, he got up and headed back toward Rue Palatine to pack.

FATHER MATEO PEREZ
MOUNT GRAHAM OBSERVATORY, ARIZONA

". . . if other intelligent beings existed, it is not said that they would have need of redemption. They could remain in full friendship with their Creator."
—FR . JOSÉ GABRIEL FUNES, FORMER DIRECTOR OF THE VATICAN OBSERVATORY

For the past few days, Father Perez had been left to his own devices, and his head hadn't quite stopped spinning. The resources available to him were staggering, and he was painfully aware of how little he'd been able to avail himself of them.

Thankfully, Joseph had become a near constant companion to him, and they had become fast friends. Among other things, they shared a mutual affinity for Amaretto, which had arisen as their daily reprieve from the star maps and Taluk documents.

Today the Sumerian records were still spread out in front of them as they relaxed, and Father Perez frowned over one of them. "Apparently, the best Vatican translation states that the records, these books of gold, were hidden in Orion," he said. "Look here: this reference is clearly to the constellation. But that doesn't make any sense."

"Not unless they'd already solved interstellar travel," Joseph said, chuckling as he sipped his Amaretto.

"More precisely, the records point to the middle star in the belt of Orion, which is Alnilam," Father Perez went on. "There were a lot Sumerian records dealing with Orion, and a lot of the text was dedicated to this middle star. Why?"

Joseph nodded in agreement. "There's certainly more to this riddle."

"But here is where things get even stranger," Father Perez said, point to another document. "The description about Orion stops, and then the text on the tablet begins a story about Ningishzidda, a Sumerian God."

"Strange. What does it say about him?" Joseph asked, refilling their glasses.

"Nothing about stars. The tablet describes his building of a pyramid. It sounds like it is describing the building of the Great Pyramid at Giza. Frankly, this shocks me, according to established historical fact, the Great Pyramid is believed to have been built around 2500 BCE by the Egyptians, not five to ten thousand years ago by the Sumerians—who lived far from Egypt in Mesopotamia. At a minimum, this could change recorded history. It's actually amazingly precise in this description. 'The smooth sides were perfected. It was set with Earth's four corners. Its rising angles and four smooth sides formed a large peak.' The Great Pyramid, no? It's even built at the center of the earth's landmasses, just as that passage said. And then it goes on to describe the pyramid's construction by the gods, with tools of great power."

"You're kidding me," Joseph said. "That is beyond fantastic."

"Isn't it? There are even more passages that describe the building of the Sphinx." Father Perez stopped, an idea nagging at him, it was something he'd read before—something about the pyramid complex…

"Orion!" he shouted, slapping the table and spilling his Amaretto. "Could it be that simple?"

"Could what be?" Joseph asked, alarmed.

"The connection of the three stars in the belt—three pyramids, just like the ones at Giza!" Father Perez leaned forward in excitement. "Could the cuneiform text be referring to the pyramids—The Orion Correlation theory of the 1990s—academics dismissed it as an alternative story in Egyptology, but could it really be true that the pyramids are arranged to match the stars in the belt of Orion?"

Joseph's eyes went wide. "That would mean—" he began.

"That would mean that the golden Ascension Testaments are hidden in the earthly representation of Alnilam, the middle star of Orion's belt!"

"The Great Pyramid!" Joseph exclaimed. "That has to be it. I even remember reading an article by an astronomer that claimed that the pyramids' alignment actually matched the star positions of Orion's belt as they existed over ten thousand years ago, but it was dismissed because that would not have been—"

"—the time the pyramids were built, according to the generally accepted Egyptian history," Father Perez concluded.

JAMES ANDERSON
PARIS, FRANCE

It was nearly mid-afternoon by the time James got back to his apartment. The front door to the building's lobby was still propped wide open. The workman was gone, and there was no sign of anyone.

"You would think the guy could have at least shut the damn door," murmured James, wondering whether he should make a complaint. He'd always felt more secure in Paris than in Chicago or New York, because serious crimes were rare. But there was a lot of petty theft. He figured the workman was having a long lunch and a beer, the notorious afternoon habit of government employees in France. Nobody was ever in a hurry.

When he reached his apartment, he noticed the door was slightly ajar. The hair on the back of his neck prickled as he stopped in his tracks. Once again, adrenaline coursed through him, bringing him to a heightened sense of awareness. *Should I run out of the building and call the police?* he thought. He stood still and listened for several moments, his heartrate accelerating. He took the last few stairs quietly, tip-toeing his way to the landing. He slid around the side of the door and peered through the crack. He lightly pushed the door a bit more open.

From inside, he heard a rustling sound, the muffled scrape of a chair, and whispers.

He looked through the crack in the door. From the hallway, he could just see into the living room. A table had been overturned. Papers were strewn across the floor. The balcony doors were wide open, and the curtains were blowing in the breeze.

What the hell?

Suddenly James caught movement from the corner of his eye as two men emerged into his apartment hallway from his bedroom. Without stopping to think of the risk, James flushed with rage and boldly jumped forward through the door.

"What the fuck is—stop right there!" James grabbed the coat stand and spread his feet in the doorway, ready to fight.

The two men did not react at all but simply stood and looked at James, a bit bemused. They were of average height and build, and their clothing was surprisingly dapper. The first man wore a dark blue suit and had sharp, chiseled features: the second, a balding and slightly overweight man with an unkempt bushy mustache, sported a faded chino suit jacket.

"Ah. Monsieur Anderson?" The first man inquired, his dark eyes peering out from under the brim of his hat. "I am Detective Jacob Bernard of the Serious Crimes Unit. This is my colleague, Detective Durand." The man held out a leather wallet displaying an embossed metal badge, then immediately walked away to survey the apartment.

"Just what the hell is going on here?" James shouted, too shocked and angry to back down.

"We received a call from someone complaining of a disturbance in the building," Detective Bernard said calmly. "When we arrived, we found that yours was the only apartment unattended."

"Unattended? What are you talking about?"

"Well, your flat is in a bit of a state, monsieur. See here," Detective Bernard said, turning James around to show him the damage done to the lock on the door. "The thieves broke in at this point." James stared at the ugly-looking scrape marks around the handle. The wooden frame was deeply dented and splintered. "Crowbars, probably. A good thief can pop out a lock or hinge in a moment with a couple of good crowbars." Detective Bernard shook his head ruefully. "It's a shame to think that despite all of our technology, the older techniques are usually the easiest."

James was amazed that the two men seemed more awed by the crude techniques the thief or thieves used than by the fact that his door and home were ransacked. The fact that he had been robbed was now setting in.

"The electrician!" James finally said. "He left the door open downstairs all day. Do you think he was in on it?"

"Electrician, monsieur?" Detective Bernard asked, retrieving a notebook from one of his pockets and flipping it open. In a few minutes, James told him about the attempted break-in that morning, and how his neighbor had earlier reported a blackout. Detective Bernard nodded sadly while his colleague scuffed his boots as if he was already bored with the crime.

"Ah. That could explain it, monsieur," Detective Bernard said. "If the electrician wasn't behind this himself, he definitely did not prevent it from happening with his carelessness. Maybe that young man from this morning returned, only to find the door open. Personally, I find it ingenious that a crook would be waiting for such opportunities, don't you?"

James certainly did not think it was ingenious, but he could think of several other more appropriate and colorful words to describe the endeavor and the two detectives standing before him. "Have you checked the rest of the floors? Who else was hit?"

"Hit?" Detective Bernard looked confused for a moment. "Oh, you mean, who was robbed? Only you, I'm afraid."

James had to cough to cover an annoyed growl. "Right, well, let me look around and give you an inventory of what they have taken." He tried to step around Detective Bernard, but the detective blocked him with an upraised hand.

"Ah, it's a crime scene now, monsieur," he said. "It looks as if either we arrived too late or the thief must have left through the balcony window as we appeared. There's a lot of disorder, things turned over, drawers pulled out, that kind of thing. I'm afraid that we can't let you interfere with us for the moment. Detective Durand?" The balding, stocky associate was already stepping into the hallway from the washroom, drying his hands with one of James's hand towels. "Would you be so good as to finish with the photographs while I explain police procedure to Monsieur James here?"

Not saying a word, the other detective gave a brisk nod, turned, and vanished into James's bedroom, leaving James with a strong sense of distaste and powerlessness.

Bernard continued, "You see, monsieur, we will need to leave the scene completely undisturbed for the moment, until we can gather all the evidence we need. We'll only need the place for a few hours; by tonight, I am sure that we can return the flat to you."

"What the hell am I supposed to do in the meantime?" James asked.

"Well, it is standard procedure that the Serious Crime Unit takes victims to the station to get an official statement from them. Is there anything particularly valuable, monsieur, that you may have had here? Jewelry? Electronic goods? If you can compile a list of things, we will be sure to check the place for them."

James shook his head in frustration. "Well, I had a couple thousand Euros in traveler's checks in my desk drawer, maybe a silver pen set on the desk, a digital camera on the table…it's mostly things of sentimental value that are important to me." He glanced past the detective. "It looks like they left the TV."

Detective Bernard suppressed a smirk. "You never know what a thief will take. No computer equipment, then? Smartphones, tablets, and such?"

James shook his head. "No, no. I've had those on me the whole time I was out. When am I going to find out if anything is missing? I'm leaving in a couple of days, and I need to pack, close up the apartment, and notify my insurance company about the theft."

"Ah, it shouldn't take long, monsieur. If you'll come with us, I'm sure that we can try to move you quickly through the statement. Just have some faith in the procedure, monsieur. We know what we are doing, and can help you if you let us. It just requires that you give us your complete trust. You must be very honest with us."

Procedure! James thought, not saying anything, but inwardly fuming. He was familiar with French "procedure." There was never a sense of urgency. They passed a couple more policemen in the hallway as they made their way down to the street.

He loved the Parisians, but their socialist society developed the French government into an incredibly slow-moving machine. He was unsure if he were angrier with the French police or with the thief. It appeared both of them were trying to considerably interrupt his plans. He allowed himself to be ushered out of his apartment by Detective Bernard and through the lobby.

As the detective ushered him out of his building, it took all the self-control James could muster to not punch the door. He was a little surprised to see that Detectives Bernard and Durand were not driving regular police cars. Instead, they took him to a large black Renault SUV with tinted windows. There was a small blue police light in the front window and an insignia that said DSGE; other than that, nothing on the exterior indicated that it was a police vehicle.

"No expense spared for the Serious Crimes Unit, huh?" he said, sarcastically.

"Yes, well, the department does like to maintain some discretion with our particular department, Monsieur," Detective Bernard said, opening the door on the rear passenger side for James and sliding in after him.

Detective Bernard got in the driver's seat, and soon they were flying southbound through traffic. The speed was always unsettling to James. Of course, it never caused the native Parisians to blink. The weaving in and out of traffic with an occasional motorcycle between two lanes and barely missing cars on both sides was normal to them. It seemed utter chaos to James. After several minutes, they were on the Périphérique, Paris's beltway, and heading around the east side of the city. This seemed odd to James; he wondered why they were not going to the police station a few blocks from his flat, on Rue des Carmes. He started to feel a bit nervous. Should he have gone with these men so easily? He pushed away the thought, determined not to allow paranoia to stress him out even further.

James was sure all the trouble that had flown his way lately was not doing much for his blood pressure. The delay in being able to deal with

Robert's discovery was becoming more irritating than the robbery itself. He liked to mark things off his list and move on to the next action item. Now, he was having to deal with senseless impediments that prevented him from dealing with the XNA puzzle.

He hoped that Robert was not making a mountain out of a molehill. *What if the anomaly is random? What if it has no other practical uses and we have already spent all this time and money on it?* Robert made it sound as if, with the proper research and application, his team might be onto one of these field-changing discoveries. If that were the case, he was glad he had booked a flight back to the States. He wanted to be right there at XNA with his finger on the pulse of what was happening.

It took them thirty minutes to arrive at their destination through the heavy afternoon traffic. James looked out the window just in time to see a sign reading *141 Boulevard Mortier.* What the hell were they doing all the way out in the 20th Arrondissement?

The SUV pulled into a drive barricaded by solid metal doors. The doors were flanked on either side by two-story, modern-looking buildings with darkly tinted glass. From one of the side doors, a guard appeared. Durand showed his identification. The guard disappeared again, and the metal doors slowly opened.

Inside was a courtyard surrounded by buildings. The surrounding buildings had few windows, and satellite dishes and antennas protruded from every roof. James felt his apprehensions rise and took out his phone to see where they were on the map.

Fast driving and meandering streets made it hard for him to keep his bearings. He had followed as best he could on his iPhone map, but for some reason as they arrived at their destination, the entire block was blurred-out on his app.

Oh, shit, James thought.

＊　＊　＊

Cardinal Russo was alone with the pope in his papal apartment. They sat across from each other in large blue wingback chairs. The wood floor reflected the dim lamps along the wall.

"Many things point to this time, your Holiness," Cardinal Russo said. He opened his Bible. "Luke 21:25: 'There will be signs in the sun, moon, and stars. On the earth, nations will be in anguish and perplexity at the roaring and tossing of the sea.' We know that the ancient Jewish Talmud tells of Jacob's troubles beginning, and of the impending return of the Messiah, in the Hebraic year 5776, corresponding to 2016 AD. According to that tradition, he will announce himself quietly to a few Rabbis. That is next year—the same year that we have the four blood moons, Your Holiness. According to the book of Joel, 'The sun will turn into darkness, and the moon into blood, before the great and terrible day of the Lord comes.' This tetrad is a harbinger, only occurring four times since the crucifixion. All of them have been biblically and historically significant. But this tetrad is unique," Russo said.

"I am aware of these signs," the pope said. "What is more important is that this still lies hidden from most. We have the scientific data under control. However, we need precise confirmation as to timing. That will come from Mount Graham." The pope's face set into a determined expression. "We need certainty. We need to understand those tablets. And now, we learn of this DNA connection. This information must be taken in hand, and quickly. As we know, time is short, my friend."

9

FATHER MATEO PEREZ
MOUNT GRAHAM, ARIZONA

FATHER PEREZ HAD MADE A DETAILED REPORT TO COPPA, who could barely contain himself with excitement. But Perez's own excitement had since faded, giving way to apprehensions. He remembered Coppa's words to him upon his arrival: *If the map about the location of the Ascension Testaments were real, then did that mean the map and text about the coming cataclysm were also real?*

"I've read and reread the tablets that accompany the star map," he told Joseph, as the two of them sat at the small table in his room looking at a stack of papers.

"Have you gotten anywhere with them?" Joseph asked, pouring them both a refill of wine.

"Only to a sense of dread," Perez answered. "These Sumerian tablets are apocalyptic. They describe fire raining down from the heavens, cataclysms of all kinds, and wide destruction of the earth and mankind. They describe the oceans coming out of their basin, the day turning to night, and the earth shaking violently. They are eerily similar to my understanding of the Book of Revelation."

"That seems a stretch," Joseph commented. "I thought Revelation was to be read metaphorically, not literally."

"Well, not according to the Sumerians. These tablets, I believe, portend real events—at least real to whoever wrote them."

"Don't you mean chiseled them?"

Father Perez stared as his friend for a moment, then the two of them burst into laughter. For a moment, Father Perez felt the stress of the work lift from him.

"I don't know," he said finally. "This description of cataclysm accompanies this star map. As best I can tell on this map, this is the constellation Virgo, with some other stars or objects in the background above it. Maybe another earthly reference? Maybe this represents the sun and this the moon, I'm not sure. But that's all there is here. The text just goes through what is to come: the great cataclysm, destruction of mountains, seas rising—all the bad stuff. After that, the gods return, and the tablets finish with a star map. I'm not certain there is anything else to learn from these."

Joseph nodded thoughtfully. "But perhaps there is something to be found in the golden books—if they are real."

"Perhaps," Father Perez said, his brows knitting.

* * *

That night Father Perez lay in his bed, unusually relaxed—the result of Joseph's generosity with the wine after they'd wrapped up for the day. His mind wandered over the strange set of circumstances had led him to this point in his life, the Great Pyramids, and the Sumerian concept of time.

How amazing their chance discovery had been, the father thought. If Joseph had not read about the measurements of the Great Pyramids and alignment of the stars in Orion's belt as they appeared 10,500 years ago before the time of the Egyptians, they might never have verified the connection. *Remarkable*, he thought. Thank goodness Joseph was such a well-read astronomer in his own right, and well versed in the history of "alternative" Egyptology. He wondered about the archeologist who had written the original article, and what had led him to research the alignment of the stars in Orion's belt as they'd appeared 10,500 years ago.

That fit perfectly with the timing of the Sumerian tablets describing the construction of the pyramids. He rolled over and looked at his clock: 1:30 a.m. He needed some sleep. He closed his eyes and began to fade off to sleep.

Time.

Time!

He shot straight up in his bed. *Time—could that be it?* On impulse, he dialed the phone.

"Yes?" Joseph answered in a groggy slurred voice.

"Joseph, it's me."

"What are you doing? It's past midnight. You should be getting some rest."

"I've had a thought—I think there's something to it. Meet me in the control center!"

Hanging up, Father Perez hurriedly dressed and ran out of the room. When Joseph met him in the control room, he was already working frantically at a terminal.

"What is it?" Joseph asked, excitement in his voice despite his obvious fatigue.

"I think I figured it out," Father Perez said. "It struck me when I thought about what you said. That the pyramid alignment matched the Orion belt alignment, but only as it looked 10,500 years ago."

"Yeah. So?"

"So what if this star map was the same thing?"

"I'm not following."

Father Perez pointed to the map, his finger trembling. "What if this map is showing us an alignment at a particular point in time?" he said. "What if this Sumerian account of coming destruction and turmoil is true? What if they were pointing out the date of its occurrence?" He unfolded a large piece of paper on his desk with a picture of the Sumerian star map on it.

"Look. If we assume that this arrangement is Virgo, and that this is the sun, this is the moon, and these other stars are within known nearby constellations, it may correlate to a specific date: the date that this alignment would appear from Earth."

"I guess that's possible," Joseph muttered, his face serious.

"Let's test it."

Over the next few hours, Father Perez ran various computer simulations using the Stellarium, and Joseph created several algorithms, looking for the alignment on the Sumerian star chart to see if such an alignment would occur in the future. Joseph found the alignment fairly quickly; a particular arrangement of stars and planets that occurred only once every ten thousand years. The mathematical brilliance of the Sumerians was proven once again. But Father Perez remained troubled.

"There's only one problem," he said, scratching his chin. "There is no reference to this particular object on the map. It appears to be some object that does not exist in our current understanding of the constellation of Virgo. Strange," he muttered, mostly to himself.

Joseph yelled out from his terminal. "Father, we have something here from my query. I'm not sure, but you'd better have a look." Perez rushed to Joseph's terminal. Joseph had a look of consternation on his face. "If I run a future progression in the Starry Night software, I can match this alignment perfectly," he said. "See, Virgo and the moon are exactly in the same location, as are Jupiter, the sun, the other stars—all of it exactly as they are depicted on the tablet map."

Father Perez took over the terminal. He checked the input. He reran Joseph's numbers. He printed out the alignment. He overlaid it on the copy of the Sumerian Virgo star map; it was a perfect fit.

"There is just one problem," he said, pointing. "Again there is one object on the Sumerian map that does not exist in our software program."

Joseph continued to work on his analysis while Perez studied the maps. Over the hum of the servers and the equipment in the room, Joseph finally said, "Father, you won't believe this. How could the Sumerians have known this? Do you think the date of this alignment is significant?"

"I don't know." Father Perez thought for a moment. "Let me see something. He looked at the data on the screen and jotted down some coordinates before hurrying across the room to the main terminal for the LUCIFER telescope.

The control panel for the telescope looked like the cockpit of a 747, with screens and instruments everywhere. Father Perez punched in the coordinates of the alignment. There was a loud crack, followed by a low hum as the massive binocular telescope's vast motors began to spin. The telescope slowly rotated as the large lenses tracked to the coordinates in the sky entered by Father Perez. Grinding steel squealed and screeched into the cold morning air, and then the telescope came to a shuddering halt.

For several minutes Father Perez scanned the viewing monitor, panning, zooming, and checking the telescope's settings and temperature while reconfirming his coordinates. Finally, an image appeared—fuzzy at first, until Father Perez brought it into focus.

What he saw was an object that should not exist. His stomach flipped. *The star map was right*, he thought.

"Oh my God," Father Perez whispered as he eyes went wide. He zoomed in on the object, applying various spectrum filters to the image to bring the object into better view. Faint and faraway as it was, it was there nonetheless. Father Perez swallowed hard and turned white. A chill ran down his back.

"Joseph," he whispered, "I need you to connect me with the Vatican immediately."

DR . SATI AM UNNEFER
CAIRO, EGYPT

Woe to the inhabitants of the earth and the sea! For the devil has come down to you, having great wrath, because he knows that he has a short time.

—REVELATION 12:12B

Dr. Sati Am Unnefer was a creature of habit, but today he had returned early from lunch without finishing his meal. Henku had not come to work for several days, and today was the wrong day to be without an assistant; equipment deliveries were expected all day, and Sati had little time to supervise them. To make matters worse, on his way out, the restaurant's owner had approached him to personally congratulate him on his promotion, and to discuss the rumors of a new excavation. Clearly, it was impossible to keep anything a secret anymore.

Sati crossed the busy Cairo street to the office building of the Supreme Council of Antiquities. His office was in the middle of a long corridor opposite a courtyard on the first floor, and as he walked down the hallway he looked over a copy of the daily *Al-Ahra*. A prominent article about the excavation was splashed across the front page. *So much for staying under the radar*, he thought.

Sunlight flooded through the courtyard windows that ran the length of the hallway on his left. Offices filled the right side. The sound of his leather sandals echoed lightly off of the terrazzo floor as he walked.

He started going through a mental list of items that needed completing quickly if they were going to start re-excavating the tunnels on schedule. He had to select his local team, order and stage the equipment, and ensure that power was available for the robot and related systems. Feeling a bit overwhelmed, he briefly looked up and saw Henku quickly shuffling down the corridor past his office, peering back over his shoulder. When his assistant didn't stop, Sati was puzzled. But there was something else—something strange in Henku's manner that he couldn't quite place.

"Henku, wait!" he shouted. "Where are you going? Come back here.

Where have you been?" The assistant quickly turned and looked at Sati, his face panicked; then, without a word, he turned and disappeared down the hallway that led to the building's exit.

Sati considered whether to follow him, then decided instead to hurry into his office, where he could hear the phone ringing. He fumbled with his keys for several seconds before realizing that his door was slightly ajar. Had Henku broken into his office?

Anger and a feeling of betrayal welled up inside him. He walked into the office and looked around for anything out of order. Tossing the newspaper on the desk, his foot tangled on something on the floor. What he saw froze him in his tracks.

There beside his desk was a large metal briefcase. His sandal was tangled in a thin wire that was connected to it. Fear caught his breath. His heart nearly stopped, and terror gripped him. The air thickened while he fought to escape as fast as he could.

He turned to run. Time slowed, and he felt as if he could not force his body to move fast enough. It was as if his body was refusing to obey his commands—as if he were moving through thick wet sand.

Sati had only managed a few steps when the detonation occurred.

The office erupted in flame, hurling Sati's body through the air. He flew across the corridor along with shards of wood and a cloud of smoke. He had the distinct, sickening feeling of being lifted off the floor by a massive, moving wall of compressed air and fire.

He inhaled a burning breath of smoke. His body slammed through the window of the courtyard, shattering it into a million glass particles. Sounds grew muffled as his consciousness began to fade. He seemed to feel nothing but the sensation of moving through the air, through glass. It seemed to take forever for him to hit the ground, and when he finally did, everything went black.

FATHER MATEO PEREZ
MOUNT GRAHAM, ARIZONA

Father Perez sat in his room at his table, resting his head in his hands and rubbing his eyes. He could not shake his fear; he'd spent the last several hours thinking about the devastating implications of his finding over and over again.

Joseph's entrance broke through his reverie. "Excuse me, Father Perez, I have scheduled a secure video call with the Vatican," he said, clearly as shaken as Perez. "The pope himself is going to attend. Someone will be here in your room shortly to arrange the connection."

Father Perez gripped his friend's hands. "Joseph, wait," he said. "Before you go, please, listen for a moment. You must promise me something. You must promise me you will keep this quiet until we know more, or at least until I get directions from the Vatican. I know you understand the implications." Perez held his gaze with a serious look.

"I do," Joseph said.

"Not even Coppa is to know."

"I understand, Father." Joseph hesitated for a moment before he walked out, closing the door behind him.

Soon afterward, an assistant arrived and led Father Perez up the elevator to a room that was like a closet. It could barely contained a desk, a chair, and a computer.

"This will give you a secure connection," the assistant told him. Then he typed in the login information. Father Perez then typed his personal password into the Vatican's encrypted video conferencing application.

Father Perez received his second audience with His Holiness Pope Paul. Before embarking on this journey, he would have been awed by the audience and the attention he was receiving. Now, he was too shocked at what he had discovered to think even about himself.

"Father," the pope said in an even tone, "it is nice to see you again. I am most impressed with the assessments of your efforts that I have received from Cardinal Coppa. The writings you prepared were excellent and should suit our new Jesuit doctrine well. The Vatican will release them soon."

"Thank you, Holy Father, but there is something—"

"Father Perez," the pope interrupted, "I think that in the *unlikely* occurrence of any announcement of an extraterrestrial life form, your writings will provide great spiritual guidance. We do the bidding of our Lord, and you, Mateo, will surely be among those rewarded for your service to Him. As you continue with your excellent work, may God and Cardinal Coppa guide your path. Now, my son, what is so urgent?"

Father Perez attempted a half-hearted smile at the compliment. "Holy Father, there is something—that I need to tell you something I have not shared with anyone yet, not even Cardinal Coppa."

"Go on, my son."

"As you know, my research into the Sumerian ancient writings led me to a terrestrial calculation that clearly points to the Great Pyramid as a repository of hidden records, assumed to be the gold Ascension Testaments."

"Yes," the pope confirmed. He leaned back in his chair. "We are very much aware of that, and an excavation is currently underway in the Great Pyramid. Do not fear; our interests are being protected on the site."

"Your Holiness, the star map in those records holds a dark prophecy. It describes the Sumerian gods' return and an apocalyptic time for Earth—a time of great destruction and death. I believe the star map points to a particular point in time, one in the very near future, when the stars and planets will align exactly as depicted in that map."

"Yes—and?"

"Well, I did further calculations and found that the star map did provide an alignment that occurs on a specific point in time. It is this date that the Sumerians described as bringing this great cataclysm to Earth . . ."

"Go on."

"If I'm interpreting it properly, the map alignment is showing us a future date—the date of a celestial alignment that has never happened in human history. That date, Your Holiness, is coming soon."

"Ah, yes," the pope said, his voice betraying his excitement. "Well done, Mateo! Tell no one of this date. Say nothing of it here, and send it only to me using the secure email you have been given. It is good to hear that you solved this riddle! It verifies scientific information we have from other sources that we have previously suppressed. More importantly, it authenticates our findings in the ancient texts here in the Archives. We must hasten our preparations."

This statement struck Father Perez as very strange. How could a date of great cataclysm be good to hear?

"There is more, Your Eminence. The ancient star map showed an object that does not exist within the Virgo constellation. I was able to test my findings through the LUCIFER telescope, and look for that object."

"Go on."

"Well, Holy Father, there *was* something there—something of great concern."

"Father Perez listen to me very carefully," the pope interrupted abruptly. "Say no more. Send your findings through the secure Vatican email system, directly to me. I am aware of what you found. From this moment forward, you are to tell absolutely no one of your findings. You are to report to me alone. This is something that we are aware of, although we did not have a specific date as to when it would be significant. Now we do. It is as we have suspected. No one on Mount Graham, no one at the Vatican, and, at this point, no one on Earth should receive this information without my approval. Do you understand?"

Father Perez was stunned. The pope's tone was almost startlingly urgent, menacing. "Yes, Holy Father," Perez managed.

"Our history deep within the Vatican Archives tells of what comes," the pope was saying. "We have prepared for this for hundreds of years, and now the time is upon us. You are one of only a few on Earth with this powerful knowledge. A great change is coming to the world, and the Vatican will use this information to establish its position of power, following the coming cataclysm."

"What do you mean, Holy Father?" Perez said, a cold sweat breaking out on his brown. *They suspected this? They knew this? And the Vatican has prepared for it? How?* The implications rocked him to his core. He felt this knowledge was now entrusted to him, and his discovery seemed to confirm the timing of this great shift.

"These coming tribulation events will ensure that the Vatican's authority and power cannot be repudiated. The Church will bring light to those seeking solace in the dark days to come."

"Yes. Of course, Holy Father I—I understand," replied Father Perez, the blood rushing to his head.

The pope began to quote from the book of Revelation. "'*And I saw another angel ascending from the east, having the seal of the living God: and he cried with a loud voice to the four angels, to whom it was given to hurt the earth and the sea, saying, hurt not the Earth, neither the sea, nor the trees, till we have sealed the servants of our God in their foreheads.*'"

Perez was struck. His head was spinning.

The Holy Father took his silence as conviction and continued. "*These are they which came out of the great tribulation . . . therefore are they before the throne of God and serve him day and night . . . and he shall dwell among them.* I think it is time for you to join Project Aquarius at the U.N., Father Perez," the pope continued. "We have the information we need. But before you do, first there is someone I want you to meet with. Someone who will provide you some additional visibility into our research in the Secret Archives. I will have my secretary make arrangements."

With that, the call ended. Father Perez sat in the small room in a state of shock, for what seemed an eternity. He was torn as he had never been; he wanted to tell everyone of this threat. But how could he? He had given the pope himself his word as a Jesuit.

Soon the door opened once more, and the assistant entered and escorted Father Perez back to his chambers. Perez sat down at the small table in his room, his head in his hands.

The Vatican knows of this threat and tells no one? The Vatican sees this as part of its destiny? I know of this and can warn no one? The conflict nearly brought him to tears.

A few hours later, there was a small knock at his door.

"Yes," he said weakly.

Joseph entered. "Cardinal Coppa would like a word with you, Father," he said quietly.

Father Perez felt his stomach hit the floor. Slowly, he rose from his chair and followed Joseph through the observatory and back into its bowels. Once they'd reached the control room, Cardinal Coppa turned to greet him.

"I take it you have been working hard, Mateo?" the cardinal said, his smile friendly as always.

"Yes, Your—Paul," Father Perez said.

"His Holiness shared your conversation with me," Coppa went on. "He's pleased with your efforts to this point."

Skeptical, Father Perez kept his acknowledgement to a simple, "Thank you."

Cardinal Coppa paused and assessed Father Perez for a moment. "What were you doing with the LUCIFER early yesterday morning, Father?" he asked, his smile broadening.

"Well, I—I was having trouble sleeping," Father Perez stammered, struggling to articulate a good answer. "I've been immersed in Biblical and Sumerian texts so long, I needed a reprieve. It is a fantastic instrument, and I thought I would take some time to myself and explore its capabilities." Father Perez was amazed he could concoct such a lie so quickly.

Coppa sat up taller in his chair and leaned slightly toward Perez, staring hard at him. But the priest betrayed no expression upon his face.

"As you can imagine," the cardinal finally responded, "yours is a most significant role, Mateo. His Holiness expects you to serve at the Vatican as the Church's mouthpiece on these issues. I have no intentions at this time to recommend otherwise."

An expanse of silence passed between them. Finally, Father Perez cleared his throat and averted his eyes. Mercifully, the door opened.

Joseph stood on the other side, waiting for directions.

Coppa held Father Perez in his gaze. "Joseph, escort Father Perez to his chambers," he said icily. "Help him pack his things. Apparently, Father Perez is going on a trip."

10

JAMES ANDERSON
PARIS, FRANCE

"IF YOU'LL FOLLOW ME, MONSIEUR, we'll get you processed."

Detective Bernard slid out of the SUV. James pulled the door handle on his side and found it locked. Bernard popped his head back into the vehicle.

"You will have to come this way, monsieur," he said. "That door does not open."

"Okay," James said, stringing the word out dubiously. He wondered if he had just entered *The Twilight Zone*.

Inside the building on the left, James discovered a small lobby that looked like what he would imagine any police department might have. A long counter dominated one side of the room. A female officer in uniform staffed it, doing paperwork behind its protective glass window. Only one door led out of the building: the one he was stepping through.

"This way, monsieur," said Detective Durand, indicating the counter.

"*Oui? Qu'est-ce que tu veux?*" asked the pretty female officer who stood barely over five feet tall. Her short black hair was neatly tucked beneath her hat. She gave a cold smile as Detective Bernard rapidly explained their business. James listened, trying to catch the flow of the conversation, but it seemed like mostly numbers—procedural codes of some sort, he assumed.

"*Eh, d'accord . . . Oui . . . Je sais.*" The woman's responses were easy to pick out. When she suddenly switched to English, it caught James a little off-guard. "So, we will need you to sign a declaration and empty out your pockets in order to continue," she said.

"Empty out my pockets?" James said, taken aback. "What are you talking about?"

"Standard procedure, James," Detective Bernard said. "We can't have you walking around the station with dangerous items in your pockets. We will pass through several metal detectors, and there may be dangerous criminals being detained somewhere in the building who could use items you may be carrying against us, or you. We need to control all, eh, visitors' items while they remain in our care. Trust me, this is just a minor technicality."

"Really?" James asked. Although he was very familiar with the laws of the United States, he had never looked into the nuances of French law beyond those necessary from a business point of view. He hesitated to hand over all his electronics, especially the laptop that he was still carrying with him.

The police officer behind the desk gave him a shy smile and nodded. "Standard procedure, monsieur."

James bit down on what he was going to say about all of their *standard procedure* and placed his laptop on the counter, emptying out his pockets on top of it. "I'll want a receipt," he said.

"You'll get a signed notice," the officer said as she wrote down all of the items. "One wallet with ninety-seven Euros, *deux cartes de crédit, un ordinateur . . .*" Her voice was monotone. "*Les clés,* a mobile phone, and—" She stared pointedly at his watch. James opened his mouth and then closed it. He handed her the watch.

A smile broke across her face, "And one Rolex watch! Anything else, monsieur? Keepsakes or valuables?"

"No, it seems that you have just about everything."

Don't worry. We'll keep everything safe until you're done."

"Humph!"

James followed Detective Bernard to the nearest metal detector, through the door on the other side of the room, and into the bowels of the Serious Crimes Unit.

The inside of the building managed to appear much smaller than it actually was. The corridors were barely bigger than James's shoulders, and most of them ended in small yellowing brick T-junctions or sharp turns. Dull blue-green doors sprouted from these drab cinderblock walls, and the dim lighting did nothing to improve the mood. Clearly, the décor had not been updated in decades. James felt as if he were a criminal being escorted to his cell.

"This way, monsieur." Detective Bernard stopped at a door marked "3A" in bold black lettering. He unlocked it to reveal a small interview chamber just ten feet square that could have doubled for a closet. In the center stood a sturdy black metal table surrounded by three gray plastic chairs. Bernard, James, and Durand filed into the room. "If you'll just sit down, we can begin to take your account of what happened," Detective Bernard said.

"I really don't understand why you couldn't have just taken my statement at the apartment. I don't have much to say," James grumbled. By way of answer, Detective Bernard produced a tape recorder and a notebook.

For the next hour, the detectives made James go over every detail of the morning, from the time when he had first been awakened by Robert's call to his arrival back at the apartment.

"So, you have been on the phone to this Robert Matson all day?" Detective Bernard asked.

"No," James said. "I already told you. He sent me some files to look over, relating to our business this morning, and then I was disconnected from him later in the day. We eventually exchanged emails, but I really don't see how this has anything to do with my apartment being burglarized. Nor is my business any of your business." By this time he was tired and irritable, and kept checking his wrist where his watch should have been.

"And what did you and Monsieur Robert discuss?"

"He was calling about a business problem we are having in the U.S. Wait. Why does that even matter? We are talking about a break-in here!"

Detective Bernard smiled patiently. "Just making sure all the facts are covered," he said. "If your mind has been on matters of business all day, then it seems you were distracted. At one of these cafés you've been frequenting, perhaps someone overheard you and followed you home?"

"What are you talking about?" James fumed. "When I got home, my apartment had already been ransacked. If they'd followed me home, they would have done it later."

"So you have not been anywhere else in Paris since you arrived in France?"

"Of course I have been going out, but I haven't been on the phone in public much."

The two detectives exchanged glances, then looked at James as if he were naïve. "What kind of business do you and this Robert do?" Detective Bernard asked.

James eyed the other man suspiciously. "We have invested in a company together."

Detective Bernard looked down at his notebook, wrote something, and then flipped backward a few pages. "Have you noticed anyone suspicious hanging around your apartment?"

"You mean aside from the guy who tried to walk into my apartment this morning? I haven't noticed anyone checking out my place to rob it, if that's what you mean. I would have notified you a long time ago."

"Okay, I'd like you to fill out a complete statement concerning that man immediately. Have you made many enemies in your line of work, Monsieur Anderson? Perhaps there is someone who is not happy with what you and Robert are doing? Perhaps an old business associate or rival?"

"Well, if this has anything to do with my business, it seems the person would be better off ransacking my home in the United States while I'm here. Doesn't it?"

"Have you called home to see if that might be the case?" Detective Durand asked.

For a few seconds James panicked, as he wondered if someone had targeted him and not just the contents of his Paris apartment. But he had a house-sitter; even though he was gone, she would have been in and out of his house every day. If something were amiss at home, she knew how to get in contact with him. And for God's sake, who would want to target him?

"I don't need to call home. I would be notified if something happened there."

"When exactly were you planning on leaving Paris?"

"I've told you this already, too!" James sighed wearily. "My flight leaves on Sunday, at nine in the morning."

"Yes, so our records show. Are you planning on returning to France?" Detective Bernard asked.

"I am leaving the country earlier than I wanted to; however, I have a scheduled meeting that I need to make. I won't return for several months."

"And that meeting is with . . . ?"

"Caruthers. Stan Caruthers of Princeton University. Not that it makes any difference. Why is that relevant, anyway?"

"It all seems rather odd," Detective Bernard mused. "Why are you leaving the country in such a hurry for this meeting if you wanted to stay longer?"

That did it. "I am just about done answering questions that have no bearing on the fact that I was robbed!" James said, not bothering to conceal his anger. "Now you need to—"

"If you will excuse me, monsieur, I just need to go make a phone call," the detective said abruptly.

"What—?" James spluttered, but Detective Bernard had already stood up smoothly and headed for the door.

"Would you like some coffee? I'll go ask the desk agent to get you a cup," Detective Durand said, before following his partner out of the room.

James heard the automatic locks on the door slide into place with a click. In disbelief, he stood and tried the door handle, only to find himself locked in. Slamming his hand against the wall, he shouted, "You call this police procedure? I'd hate to see how you treat criminals!"

He sat down and drummed his fingers on the table. He had never been one for sitting around with no answers and dealing with such inefficiency. The questions the officers had asked him were a waste of time; clearly, nothing he told them would aid in a robbery investigation. Eventually, his frustration overcame him, and he got up and tried the door again. It was still locked.

Never before had he missed his watch so badly. There was no clock on any of the walls. Hours seemed to pass. When he couldn't bear sitting any longer, he began pacing the small room, rolling his shoulders to ease out a cramp. His stomach rumbled, and he realized that he was hungry. With nothing better to do, he began shouting again, "How long have I been in here? And where is my cup of coffee?"

Just as he was about to begin banging one of the chairs against the door and demanding to speak to the American Embassy, he heard a muffled argument and the sound of the door bolts being drawn back.

"—afraid that is out of the question," a voice was saying. "You cannot do this! There are laws that protect the rights of our citizens."

Just then the door opened to reveal a thin woman with a bob of blonde hair and a gray-blue matching jacket and skirt. The woman was strikingly handsome—beautiful, even, in a hard, athletic kind of way. The hint of wrinkles at the edges of her eyes only gave her an air of maturity and control. Hovering behind her, James could see the diminutive form of the female police officer who had been operating the front desk.

"He is in *our* custody," The officer was saying. "Do you understand?"

"And I am revoking that custody. As a consular officer from the American Embassy, I want this American citizen released immediately. By your own admission, he has not been charged with a crime, and will not be charged. He is clearly a victim here. You cannot just go pulling American citizens off the street and holding them against their will when they haven't been placed here on the order of a judge."

James's spirits rose as he watched the new woman glide into the room and smile at him. *Now that is efficiency*, he thought, in awe of how quickly the embassy had become aware of his predicament and leaped into action.

"James?" the woman asked him. James thought he detected the slight twang of some other European accent, something heavier or more guttural. He couldn't decide if it was German, or perhaps Russian.

"Yes?"

"I am Maria Zorin," the woman said. "I work for the American Embassy. We got word of what happened to you from your neighbor, Bernadette Morel. If you would like to get out of this cubicle, you can come with me. I am sure the sergeant here will allow us to collect your things, and you will be free to go."

"I really cannot allow this—" the female police officer began.

"Well, I am afraid that I will have to lodge a formal complaint, perhaps with your president through our diplomat. You have seen my credentials," Ms. Zorin spat at her. "James," she called, and led the way out of the room without waiting to see if he was behind her.

James gave the desk officer a cheery smile and followed his unexpected savior through the maze of corridors and the metal detector into the front lobby.

"But really—this is incredible! Bernadette Morel notified you?" James asked in wonder. "Did she see the officers taking me away?"

"No questions, yet, James. Just collect your things, and let's get out of this place," Ms. Zorin replied as the desk sergeant reluctantly returned to the other side of the counter.

"Yes, ma'am!" James almost chuckled.

"His things?" Ms. Zorin demanded as she stared down at the agent who had taken his inventory. James relished the fact that the flustered sergeant was once again checking off all of the goods that they had confiscated from him.

When they were finally able to step through the door of the building into the courtyard, James was surprised by the sudden fresh chill of evening air that hit him. It was dark, and the streetlights were on.

"Good God! How long was I there?" he asked as Ms. Zorin led him to a large, burgundy car with a distinctive Mercedes badge over its grill and the seal of the United States on its front window. James was impressed. Obviously, the life of an embassy representative had some perks.

"Long enough," she said. "Now get in quickly, please."

James was happy to be out of there, but he did not understand why Ms. Zorin was in such a hurry. She drove toward the front gate, and the doors opened automatically.

"You might want to wear your seat belt," she said, never taking her eyes from the way in front of her. James barely had time to click it before she gunned the engine and squealed the tires into an agonizing turn, rocketing away from the exit.

Ms. Zorin wasted no time speeding toward the boulevard again and weaving through the traffic. James had always thought Parisian drivers were a little over-excitable, but this was ridiculous. He watched as the speedometer began to edge above 60 kilometers per hour. *This woman is crazy*, he thought.

"Uh—Ms. Zorin? Are we going to the embassy?" James asked, feeling a little sick to his stomach with their increasing speed. Ms. Zorin shrugged off her jacket, revealing a light, sleeveless blouse and very toned, almost masculine arms. She spoke assertively as she gripped the steering wheel, firmly maneuvering the vehicle in and out of traffic.

"James, we have no time to bandy words," she said. "You have just been the prisoner of DGSE and DCRI, and now you are not. Be happy you are free from them," Zorin said, her voice steady and level as she flew between a large truck and a car that swerved into their lane. Occasionally, she would glance over her shoulder.

"What? Who in the hell are they? And don't you think that you should watch your speed?" James's voice raised a little, and he shifted in his seat, steadying himself by pressing his arm to the door. Ms. Zorin ignored him, passing so close to another vehicle that James was certain the mirror on his door was going to be knocked off.

"Central Directorate of Interior Intelligence and General Directorate for External Security, respectively," she said. "The first performs human intelligence on French soil: bugging, following people, and searching hotel rooms. The second performs international intelligence operations. You've heard of the Rainbow Warrior incident in the '80s? Or perhaps the rescue of French journalists in Iraq? That would be the DGSE."

"And what the hell would they want with me?" James asked. They came to a stop at a red light, and Ms. Zorin braked hard to avoid colliding with the car in front of them. She reached for something on the side of her seat. "It's not really you they want," she said. "It's the information encrypted on your laptop. We, on the other hand want both—" Suddenly, she produced a stubby six-shot .38 revolver from her seat and powerfully swung it as hard as she could, striking James in the side of the head and knocking him unconscious.

Several minutes later James awoke. Dizziness filled his head, and he had a sharp pain in his temple. Slowly as he came to, a queasy feeling gripped him. He was unable to make sense of the blur of streetlights and dark sky, and his head was leaning against his door. Suddenly he remembered what had happened, and stopped himself from moving.

He could see in the mirror a black SUV with tinted windows,

approaching at high speed. His kidnapper sped into the path of oncoming traffic, overtook a few cars, and slid back into the lane heading out of central Paris. The SUV performed a handbrake turn into the central junction and roared toward them.

The SUV gained ground as Ms. Zorin tried to avoid other cars. Soon it caught up, and slammed into the back of the Mercedes. James was thrown forward and felt the sharp edge of his seatbelt. Maria immediately turned right, going the wrong way down a narrow street, and sped away from the SUV. James nearly vomited.

The SUV tried to turn but slid into parked cars along the street, tearing off at least a couple of passenger doors. Sparks rained down on the road. The world was a sudden whirl of noise and screeching horns as cars peeled off around them, desperately trying to avoid the lunatic drivers swerving across lanes.

"*Derr'mo!*" he heard Ms. Zorin curse as the SUV grazed the corner of her rear bumper. Her Mercedes took out a line of rental bikes and they flew all around the Mercedes, scattering like leaves in the wind. The Mercedes careened into a utility pole on the driver's side and the car suddenly spun out of control into the center of an intersection.

The car came to a rest halfway across the lane of oncoming traffic. Moving as little as possible, James unclipped his seat belt with his right hand and braced himself against the door. This was his chance. He didn't know where the gun was, but the hard impact must have dazed Zorin. He heard her moan and fumble with the stick shift. She desperately tried to restart the engine, and it began to rev hard. This was it. James gathered up his courage for a desperate effort.

Clutching his laptop, James pulled the handle open and drove his shoulder into the passenger door, slamming it open. He pushed his legs against the floor edge to jump with all his might, just as the car began to speed off. He rolled across the pavement, and the world blurred for a horrible instant as James wondered if he would land under the grill of an oncoming car or get shot. He collided with a collection of plastic trash bins on the curb and came to rest lying on his side, still clutching the laptop.

Just then the SUV slammed into the Mercedes again. Zorin's engine gunned wildly, tires squealed, and smoke filled the air around the car. The Mercedes leapt up onto the sidewalk and drove at a frightening speed toward pedestrians, throwing one woman through the plate-glass window of a storefront. The SUV did not follow. The Mercedes drove straight through tables outside of a cafe, throwing chairs, glassware, and umbrellas in all directions. People dove out of the way of the car. The car bounced back onto the road at an intersection and turned down a small street out of sight.

James tried to regain his senses. His ears were ringing; he felt his head spin as he flirted with unconsciousness again. Instinctively, James's hand went to the large welt on the side of his head. His temple felt incredibly tender, but when he surveyed the rest of his body, he was amazed to find that he was mostly all right. He knew that he would probably be black and blue tomorrow, but for now everything worked. Even the laptop appeared to have made it through in one piece.

James stepped through the toppled trash bins and garbage onto the curb. Brushing himself off, he looked up to see Detective Durand standing in front of the SUV.

"Monsieur James, would you be so kind to accompany me back to headquarters?"

James sighed resignedly and followed the agent to his vehicle. As he climbed into the passenger seat, he asked, "Will someone please tell me what in the fuck is going on around here?"

Police cars were arriving at the scene, and Detective Durand rolled down his window to speak in a hurried tone with some officers. He pointed to the road where Ms. Zorin had disappeared, then rolled up his window.

"You deserve some answers, Mr. Anderson," he said in an even tone, as they headed off. "You were the target of a crime—that part is true. But we are not police, Mr. Anderson. We are with French intelligence. We intercepted communications from some of our intelligence sources, indicating that there was going to be a robbery. The target was data contained in a laptop. We believe we intercepted this communication from the Russian Federal Security Service—the newest incarnation of the KGB—although we are not certain. That is why we were at your apartment. Sadly, we arrived too late. We think Ms. Zorin, whom we identified from a surveillance video, is a new agent of their Intelligence Service.

"This appears to be an incident of industrial espionage," the detective continued. "I don't know why, Monsieur Anderson, but the Russians wanted to steal your research. Unfortunately, Ms. Zorin had forged credentials and clearly understood our procedures. Frankly, she made my office look like a bunch of amateurs when she walked out of there with you before I could finish our interview and explain our investigation."

"Why didn't you just tell me this to begin with?" James asked wearily.

"We wanted to ensure there was no illegal activity occurring in Paris that involved you. When we received certain information, our team began monitoring your communications. It appears your biology research is what Ms. Zorin was after."

"What?" James felt violated. "You've been monitoring me? What gave you that right? Did you have a search warrant?"

"Mr. Anderson, when the Russian Federation is involved in activities on our soil, we will take certain liberties. By the way, does the name Father Perez mean anything to you?"

"No," James spat, furious. "I'm agnostic. Go over to Vale De Grace. Maybe you'll find him in the chapel."

Detective Durand nodded opaquely. "Mr. Anderson, I'm not sure what your business is, but the research you are carrying must be very valuable," he said. "I suggest that you leave with that information for the U.S. immediately. I will have you escorted to your apartment and thereafter to the airport."

Through James's disbelief, he immediately thought of Robert.

11

DR . SATI AM UNNEFER
GIZA PLATEAU, EGYPT

"How could it not be left out that life developed elsewhere?"
—FR . JOSÉ GABRIEL FUNES, FORMER DIRECTOR OF THE VATICAN OBSERVATORY

"I HOPE YOU UNDERSTAND that this whole thing is not going to help my reputation here in Egypt," Professor Kline said to Rodney, the American driver of the SUV. Sati, seated next to Professor Kline, looked out the window as they drove in a cloud of dust through the desert.

"That is none of our concern, Professor Kline," Rodney replied unsympathetically. "Our only concern is to help you find whatever is in this hidden room, and to ensure that the relevant information is provided to the United States government."

Sati sighed heavily, looking down in embarrassment at the bandages covering the burns on his hands and the multitude of other wounds he had received in the explosion. He found it hard to believe that two grown men would bicker like this.

"Of course," Professor Kline said sarcastically. "I should have known this was all too good to be true. Am I to understand that I am not running my own excavation?" Dust flew over all sides of their vehicle.

"Gentlemen, please, we have not even begun our work," Sati said. "We need to operate as a team, or I may be forced to reconsider my decisions. Now just calm down."

The convoy of Humvees and utility vans made their way down the sand-ridden road that led to the Great Pyramid complex. When they approached a perimeter checkpoint, they saw hundreds of protestors chanting anti-American slogans and waving banners.

"Looks like this dig is not very popular, Sati," Rodney chided.

"It's just a few zealous locals." Sati tried to make his comment seem casual, but the number of people and their obvious aggravation worried him.

"I'd say this is a dangerous situation," Rodney stated.

After passing through the checkpoint, the caravan pulled up to the Great Pyramid entrance. Sati again checked the bandages on his face and winced in pain. Professor Kline stepped out of the vehicle and carefully adjusted his hat.

"These guys are in a real hurry," Kline said to Sati, motioning toward the Americans that were there to aid in the excavation. They had immediately begun unpacking the heavy tools and equipment from the vans.

"I don't think you could be too early for an event like this," Sati replied. "It was hard for me to sleep these last two days."

"Well, once my crew gets the equipment unloaded, we can get started."

Sati watched as the vehicles emptied. The men worked quickly, extracting the necessary tools and heavy equipment from the vans.

Rodney approached them both. "We should have everything unloaded within 20 minutes," he said.

"So fast!" Sati said with a smile. "You must be just as excited about this as I am."

"The quicker the better," Rodney said sternly. Looking around, he continued, "I know there are many who do not want us here. If possible, we would like to avoid any trouble. You don't mind if I have a few of my men stand guard here do you, Dr. Unnefer?"

Sati chuckled nervously. "Don't worry. The roads may be a little dangerous, but this place is quite secure."

"Just the same." Rodney motioned to a group of eight large, muscular men emerging from the Humvees and vans. They exited with machine guns and took up positions on either side of the convoy as Rodney continued to unpack equipment.

Sati was beginning to regret taking the Americans up on their offer. The American team looked more like the military than archaeologists or specialty contractors. As though he'd heard his thoughts, Professor Kline spoke quietly to him.

"The Americans obviously heard about your little explosion," he said. "Rodney knows this dig isn't popular among some of the conservatives, and he is naturally a little high-strung. Apparently, he used to be in the military, and it seems little of his training has left him. Any idea on who did this to you?" the professor asked, pointing to Sati's wounds.

"Ah, yes. I am pretty sure it was my former assistant. He was very unhappy with me because I challenged the work of our former boss, Dr. Zaher. Unfortunately, the authorities have not been able to find him." Sati laughed nervously. "He just disappeared. It does have me looking over my shoulder quite a bit, to be honest."

"Yes—I meant to ask you how are you feeling?" Kline asked as they walked toward the pyramid.

"I'm fine. Just a mild concussion and many bumps and bruises. But the damage to Egyptian history is immeasurable. The artifacts, papers, and unrecoverable documentation about the Giza Plateau that were in my office are lost forever."

"Better than you being lost," Kline concluded. "Andrew! Max!" he shouted. "Bring some headlamps and come here!"

Professor Kline's crew hurried over with the equipment, and all three followed Sati into the pyramid.

The cool air contrasted sharply with the heat outside. Sound echoed around them as they descended. It took some time for Sati's eyes to adjust.

He led them to the base of the grand gallery and into a side passage to the Queen's Chamber. Sati had always been awestruck with the smoothness of the granite walls and the incredible precision with which the stones where set. He ran his hand alone the seam of a block. The other men searched the walls and easily found the smaller shaft on the south wall.

"We have sent many robots up this shaft over the years, but we have not been able to penetrate the first door," Sati said with excitement.

"You understand, doctor, this time we will have to remove some of the blocks to get to the chamber," Dr. Kline stated.

"If you have not identified another way," Sati said, looking at his sandals, "so be it. However, you must not permanently deface this monument. It must be repaired to its original condition. Otherwise, it will cause problems for both our countries. Everything removed must be taken out with great care, so that it may be reconstructed in its original state as it existed before the excavation."

"If we are careful with these blocks, we can pull them away enough to access the path and make it larger," Professor Kline said. "When we're finished, our crew will set these blocks back in place and repair the damage."

Sati hesitated. The pyramids were sacred to him and to all the people of Egypt. When the country struggled, the pyramids brought tourists in to provide a much-needed boost to their economy. No one would see their defacement as a good thing; frankly many Egyptians wanted the pyramids left alone. They wished all excavation would stop—especially by foreigners. Still, Sati had known from the beginning that this project would create some enemies. He stared at Dr. Kline long and hard, wondering if he would stay to clean up as he had promised. Many in the past had excavated and permanently destroyed portions of the pyramid. Its modern entrance was a direct testament to that.

"I'm sorry, Dr. Unnefer," Kline continued, again sensing his misgivings. "It is the only way to access the chamber. We cannot just send another robot up the tunnel. It could not cut through doors, nor would it be able to recover anything of value."

After a long silence, Sati finally nodded in agreement.

AGENT DEVON STINSON
THE WHITE HOUSE

"Life forms could exist in theory, even without oxygen or hydrogen."
—FR . JOSÉ GABRIEL FUNES, FORMER DIRECTOR OF THE VATICAN OBSERVATORY

Stinson walked with the president through the West Wing of the White House into the main conference room of the 5,000-square foot "Situation Room" complex. The side walls of the room were covered with video monitors, and the back wall had a very large display screen covering the entire wall, where a presentation was already queued up.

"Give me an update on Project Aquarius," the president said as he sat down at the head of the table.

"Yes, sir," said Mitchell Perkings, motioning for Agent Stinson to sit beside him. "Project Aquarius has twenty-two new experts, most working at the NSA. Soon the entire team will assemble under the U.N. Security Council, and the ops center will move to the European Space Agency in Paris.

"Sir, today we received an intercept from Mt. Graham," Perkings continued. "Their research, both with the ancient Sumerian texts and the Sumerian star maps, strongly supports the theory that that the ancient Sumerians hid something in the Great Pyramid of Giza. The head astronomer for the Vatican, Father Perez, reported this directly to the pope, according to our intelligence."

"I presume you are in control of the situation, Mitchell?" the president asked.

"Yes, sir. Our assets are on the ground," Perkings said. "Today, Mr. President, we would like to introduce you to Dr. Charles Enright. He was working for NASA on its Mars project. Dr. Enright will be briefing you today. Doctor?"

A thin man in a gray suit stood up, took a nervous bow, and sat down after adjusting his glasses. The lights in the room dimmed, and Dr. Enright cleared his throat as the screen on the wall began to display images.

"Mr. President, these are the high-resolution data files of our photographs," he said. "Those released to the public are not of this quality, and have been retouched." He cleared his throat again. "I will begin by showing you a photograph that you have likely seen before. This is the original picture of the 'Face' on Mars. This hill is roughly a kilometer and a half square. Its symmetry and shadows are startling, and the photo of it created a media sensation. At the time this photo went public, NASA really did not have a good handle on its information-dissemination protocols. This, of course, is from the Viking orbiter in 1976.

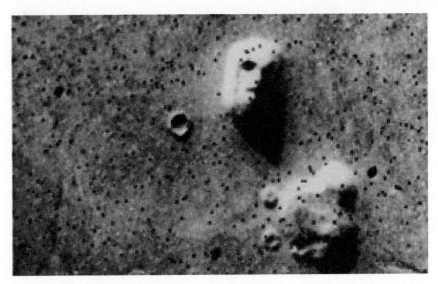

"In later Mars missions, this region was studied in detail. I am now showing you the officially released photographs, which have been obfuscated to reduce the public's excitement and refute findings that this may be an intelligently designed structure.

"These, however," he said, pushing a stack of photographs across the table, "are true recent images. As you can easily identify, this symmetry and organized structure is beyond the randomness associated with geological anomalies. It is clearly what you saw in that first picture: a carved face.

"It bears a remarkable resemblance to the Sphinx and other Egyptian carvings and monuments. If you notice, you can see there are no other surrounding geological formations. The face is positioned in exact alignment on the Mars equator. More interesting than the Face, however, are the structures surrounding and in the vicinity of it."

Dr. Enright projected a wide photo of the entire plain around the face. "Gentlemen, this is Cydonia," he said. "We have identified here what appears to be a large complex of pyramids, similar to what we currently find in Egyptian archaeological digs on the Giza Plateau. This particular structure we call the D&M Pyramid. It was named after the two NASA engineers who discovered it. Like our own Great Pyramid, the D&M Pyramid is aligned on the planet's equatorial spin axis, and is a five-sided pyramid. There are no geomorphological explanations for this kind of structure.

"In this photo, you can see that Cydonia contains a virtual city. It would be comparable to what we had here on Earth during the times of the pharaohs. As of yet, we have no means to date these structures. But based upon erosion, they appear vastly older than what we see in Egypt, and are possibly from the time when Mars might have had a stable atmosphere. As you know, we have rovers in these locations, and a satellite to orbit over this spot and film it multiple times a day. Whoever or whatever built these structures has not been on Mars for a long, long time. Unfortunately, some of this information has leaked into the public domain."

Agent Stinson interrupted. "Sir, this is part of our focus at Project Aquarius," he said. "What Dr. Enright has shared so far is further evidence that intelligent life has built structures on Mars. This is just more over-whelming evidence supporting the conclusion that we are facing an intervention from an alien species."

The president nodded, though he still appeared to be unnerved at such a thought. "Please continue," he said.

"Additionally, we identified anomalies in 1998 on Phobos, one of Mars's moons," Stinson went on. "You are looking at image number SP255103. Very little public attention has been given to this photograph, but those within the Mars surveyor project are very aware of its existence. What you see is a monolith on the surface of Phobos. As I zoom in, you can see it begins to take more of a defined shape.

The emission angle of the photograph was about 19.84 degrees, and as you can see, this monolith is constructed of a highly reflective material. Our geologists didn't recognize the composition, and they couldn't explain its structure naturally."

Dr. Enright picked it up again. "Our analysis concluded that it is not the product of a meteor impact, as there is no crater associated with it. It is certainly not the result of any seismic activity, erosion, or volcanic disturbance, since the moon is not large enough to have a molten core or an atmosphere. What is more unsettling is that this object is the height of a 40-story office building—over 420 feet high."

"Mr. President," Agent Stinson interrupted, "we have ancient structures on Earth that we cannot explain and have long suspected may have otherworldly origins. These recent findings on Mars make the supposition very probable that we are not alone. For years, the NSA has compiled information on sightings and other types of craft contact during programs that include Project Aquarius's predecessors. But as you now know, sightings, radar contacts, and even data-feed intercepts from unidentified craft have escalated dramatically over the last few years. And we don't know why."

"Understood, Agent Stinson," President Brooks said. "Mitchell, we need to find out right now if this presents any clear and present danger. What are we doing in that direction?"

"If you'll pardon me, there's more, sir," Agent Stinson said hesitantly. "Project Aquarius has recently learned of a strange DNA anomaly— potentially one with an alien origin."

"I'm sorry, what?" the president asked. "What exactly do you mean by a DNA anomaly? Some strange alien DNA that was found in what—a human being?"

"Well, actually, sir—yes," Stinson replied.

The president breathed out sharply. "You people are really giving me a lot to think about, you know that?" he said, looking around the room. "And in which human being's DNA, exactly, has this so-called anomaly been found, Agent Stinson?"

Stinson. "Everyone's sir," he said

FATHER MATEO PEREZ
MOUNT GRAHAM, ARIZONA

Father Perez sat in the back of a large suburban as it headed to Phoenix Sky Harbor airport. As it turned out, he was headed to Lima, Peru. The arrangements had been made directly by the pope's assistant.

He knew he should be thinking about the task at hand, but he was too worried about his conversation with the pope to focus. It had been so strange and disconcerting; how could they have known what he would find? And how could they expect him not to raise the alarm? He was most concerned that he was being prevented from warning the world. What he'd seen through the LUCIFER telescope put the vast majority of Earth's population at risk. Was he not duty-bound as a man of God to warn them?

He was sworn to secrecy on the issue, true. But he did not like that at all. "A great change is coming to the world, and the Vatican will be at its pinnacle"—that hadn't sounded like mere religious dogma, but something much more disturbing.

He questioned the Vatican's motives over and over in his mind. He was not cut out for this; he was only at the Vatican to pursue astronomy and his research. He had joined the Jesuit Order because that was his only option in Argentina; he had not embarked on a spiritual quest to align with a sect whose philosophies he found agreeable.

He had known of controversies surrounding the Jesuit Order, even those of which most of the world was unaware. Saverio Ferretti himself had had a checkered past while serving the Vatican in Argentina, prior to becoming pope. He recalled several investigative reports detailing Ferretti's connection to the ruthless dictators and the wave of fascism that overran Argentina. Ferretti had looked the other way during the acts of torture and interrogation, disappearances, and child abductions that had occurred in the so-called Dirty War. When people such as Juan Peron, who'd trained under Mussolini, came to power in Argentina and organized an SS-type, Nazi structure to manage the military, many of them were backed by the Vatican internationally and locally by the Jesuit Order; many said that after World War II, Nazism had simply transferred to Argentina and continued under Jesuit support. Perez also recalled a report of over a hundred and fifty Catholic priests who had been victimized during the Dirty War for refusing to bend to the will of the dictators. They, too, had been thrown in dungeons and tortured. Many leveled blame on Ferretti for doing nothing to stop this abuse, and called him complicit. Reports on Ferretti's connection to these dictators had been blocked and covered up by the Vatican. Father Perez knew the Vatican and the pope were more politically than religiously focused, but prior to this moment, he had never given any credence to these claims.

Several, especially within the Vatican, had raised an eyebrow when Ferretti became the very first pope from the Jesuit Order. Rumors of threats, clandestine deals, and political arm-twisting surrounded the conclave that brought the Order to the pinnacle of Vatican control. Some even said that Pope Benedict, the first pope to abdicate in six hundred years, had been forced to step down.

Again, Perez did not have any first-hand knowledge of this; these were merely rumors, as far as he was concerned. What he could not discount was the historical significance of the Order. The Society of Jesus, the Jesuit Order, had existed in secret for hundreds of years before its formal foundation in 1534. Its original purpose was to be the subversive arm of Vatican intelligence and political and military power. It was the Jesuit Order had taken control of the Inquisition, resulting in the martyrdom of millions. It had been ejected from over 86 countries for its globalist totalitarian agenda, its deception, its spying, and its secret assassinations. When he was exiled at St. Helena, Napoleon had said, "The Jesuits are a military organization, not a religious order. Their chief is a general of an army, not the mere father abbot of a monastery. And the aim of this organization is power—power in its most despotic exercise—absolute power, universal power, power to control the world by the volition of a single man. Jesuitism is the most absolute of despotisms—and at the same time the greatest and most enormous of abuses." He'd also said, "Wherever the Jesuits are admitted, they will be masters, cost what it may; every act, every crime, however atrocious, is a meritorious work, if committed for the interest of the Society of Jesus, or by the order of the general."

During the rise of nationalism in the 18th century, the Jesuit Order was formally dissolved by Vatican decree in 1773. Saint Francis Borgia. the Third Jesuit Superior General, said, "We came in like lambs and will rule like wolves. We shall be expelled like dogs and return like eagles." The order survived, in the shadows, to arise another day. It was rumored to be the secret sect behind the Masonic orders, continuing to operate in secret after its formal dissolution. Now it was again a global order, with the world's largest network of schools and universities, as well as more than twenty-eight colleges and sixty-two high schools in the U.S. alone.

The pope's statements to Perez had brought all of these facts and rumors to mind again for him. He found it was not a topic on which he liked to dwell.

12

PROFESSOR STAN CARUTHERS
PRINCETON UNIVERSITY, NEW JERSEY

"My faith is already full of doubts. And the doubts have nothing to do with what I've learned in science."
—GUY CONSOLMAGNO, DIRECTOR OF THE VATICAN OBSERVATORY

JAMES FELT LIKE SHIT. The stress of this situation was taking its toll on his intestinal tract, and reconstructing the events for Robert on the phone had only done more to upset his already queasy stomach.

Now, waiting for Robert and Stan Caruthers in front of Fine Hall at Princeton, James reflected on the events of the last few days. He regretted not trusting Robert when he'd first called. Perhaps he really had discovered something highly valuable and interesting—clearly, the attempt by the Russians to steal James's laptop meant he must be onto something important. Robert believed they had targeted James's computer to hack his password, which would allow them to log onto the XNA mainframe. The terminals at XNA were hardened with the highest level of OTP encryption. XNA's systems were designed to prevent hacking: the only way in was to have access to a laptop or computer that had authentication software loaded on it, and then hack the user's password.

James checked his watch. It was 4:00 p.m. *Where is Robert?*

"What on earth have you discovered?" James muttered, settling into an uneasy, watchful silence. He sat down on a small bench in the afternoon sun and waited for Robert.

James had felt uneasy traveling back to the U.S. He had scanned nearly everyone he saw on the way, wondering if they were a possible undercover threat from one country or another. He had convinced himself that there had to be one or more members of some secret service among the crowd, but once he boarded the plane his nerves had begun to settle a bit.

The campus was surprisingly well-populated for a summer afternoon. If James had not been so worked up over recent events, he would have loved to spend some time just soaking up the atmosphere. The architecture varied from Colonial and Romanesque to Modern. Fine Hall was unique in itself, because the three-story building had its own tower. After a few minutes, James saw Robert walking toward him through the campus.

"Finally," James chided as he approached.

"Good to see you, too," Robert said, hugging his friend. They went into a building together, rode the elevator to the fifth floor, and walked until they saw Dr. Caruthers's name on a door to the left.

"Enter," said a firm voice after Robert knocked.

What James saw when he entered looked like the hovel of a hoarder, the den of a mad computer scientist. Inside the large wood-paneled room, metal shelving units had been stacked and bolted to each other to house books, papers, and journals. Under these, long work-scarred wooden benches sprouted strange computer equipment that sat and hummed gently. The center of the room was occupied by a broad desk topped by an enormous array of technology, a giant electronic brain with wire neurons flowing from it to no less than three active computers and a laptop, which sat precariously on the edge of another desk. Stacks of papers, threatening to collapse, were defying gravity on several chairs. A man in a buttoned oxford shirt and bowtie sat plugging away at a keyboard behind a few large screens.

"Stan, great to see you! I like what you've done with the place," exclaimed Robert, embracing his old friend.

"Dr. Caruthers, I presume?" James asked, extending his hand.

"Yes! James, is it?" Stan shook his hand warmly. "Good God, man! You look like shit, old boy."

"Thanks. Wait until you hear the story," James said. "I think it's safe to say we are onto something."

"Well, you look like you've spent the past week in that suit, and lost a few rounds to Floyd Mayweather while you were at it. Sit down while I pour some coffee for you," the professor said.

"Thanks." James dislodged some reports from a chair and sat down, regarding the professor as he rather disconcertingly emerged with a large pot of black liquid that he assured James was coffee, and poured it into a recently recovered cup. Stan Caruthers was clearly a proud eccentric, and bore the standard rubric of a rogue mathematical genius: long brown hair, tight beard, blue eyes outlined by horn-rimmed glasses, tweed vest and slacks.

"Robert," Stan said sharply, "I've not slept more than four hours since your data arrived. I have five of my Linux systems running every cipher index on it that I can think of. I wish you had sent this to me sooner— before I sent all my postgraduate researchers off on another project."

Robert moved some books and glasses that were stacked haphazardly on the chair, noticing that one was a philosophical text on Marxism. "Shit, Stan. I know you're liberal—but hell, Marxism? He smiled. "Be careful, James is your consummate capitalist."

Stan ignored him. "Well, I hate to tell you this, but there appears to be more here in the sequence—a lot more."

"What do you mean?" asked Robert.

"This appears to be beyond the simple possibility of the Golden Ratio asserting itself again somewhere in nature."

"You mean there is something more than the one sequence repeating itself?"

"Yes, there is another code here. I'd bet my reputation on it. The repeating Fibonacci sequence in your DNA strand appears to be the equivalent of a marker in a software code. It is designed to help rationalize the deconstruction of the code, and it serves as a primer to help break the cipher."

"You're losing me again," said Robert. "Are you saying there's a second code in the DNA segment?"

"It is likely that there are many levels to this code. There may also be a three-dimensional code created from the protein folding after it's synthesized. I'm not certain if we have any way to model all of these possibilities, let alone attempt solving them, but I'm doing my best to at least decipher the second level," Stan said. "Interestingly, I also calculated measurements of the DNA double helix. It's also precisely in line with phi or the Golden Ratio."

"Incredible," Robert said.

"Here's the interesting thing. If my quick calculations are right, and they always are, one of these DNA cipher patterns theoretically has the potential to store the computer equivalent of four terabytes of information. Clearly, for each layer of code, this is poten-tially doubled. The amount of possible data stored or included in one strand of DNA is incredible. We're talking about the capacity to house the entire Library of Congress." The professor turned to James and said, "Initially, I was shocked that Robert was able to synthesize a DNA strand 50,000 nucleotides long. I believed that he must have discovered a revolutionary new process. When I found out it was a naturally occurring strand, I found that nearly unbelievable."

"Over 6,000 kilodalton long." Robert interjected.

"Listen, James, I just want some mention in whatever Robert publishes here, so don't worry about paying me for this. However, a spot near the top of the list would be appropriate for the amount of work I'm putting into it for you, old chap. Ha!" Stan said, slapping James on the back. James winced in pain as Stan's palm connected with a large bruise. "I've canceled all my plans and found another professor to teach my undergrad classes, so I'm all yours, gents."

James nodded. "We appreciate that. Please, continue."

"Well, within this code is the Golden Ratio," Stan snorted.

"Yes, Robert said something about this. But what is the Golden Ratio? I don't get the significance."

"Stan, can you perhaps give James the truncated version?" Robert asked.

"Are you really that much of a slouch, James?" Stan said, laughing. "What did you major in? Business?"

James wasn't sure he liked this guy, or how to reply to that, so he just waited until Stan chose to continue.

"Before Robert sent me this, I knew that this simple, elegant rule of the Golden Ratio existed throughout nature," Stan said. "I have never seen it overtly appear anywhere, however, as a mathematical code. It is found guiding the way things form naturally. It can be seen in their aesthetics. I found it amazing that it could potentially guide how genes are expressed and what they form.

"For example, consider the Statue of Liberty. You don't look at it and see a bunch of numbers; you see the beauty behind them. With Robert's discovery, we have the opposite. We have a code. We are looking at the numbers and seeing the Statue of Liberty. The Golden Ratio dictates the spiral of petals in a flower or seeds in a sunflower, the shape and proportion of galaxies and hurricanes, and the proportions of the body. All things in nature seem to abide by this rule. All in all, there is only one word to describe it—*amazing*. But frankly, I still don't think it's natural in this case. From Roberts's summation and the offset by two Alu sequences, both he and I believe it's potentially indicative of a splicing or graphing into a DNA molecule."

"And the precision of the protein sequence repetition between the Alu elements appear anomalous within DNA," Robert interrupted. "There is nothing else like it."

James felt like an outside observer barely following along. Stan went into complete detail over the process he'd used to test the code, talking about ciphers and markers and what he thought he should try next—and on and on.

Finally, Stan stared at James waiting for his response. James was frustrated, still feeling nowhere close to finding out what this meant to him and his company. It was time to move this conversation on to the next step.

"Here is the scenario," James began. "We have invested a significant amount of money in XNA's technology and gene therapy. You say that this code may not be natural, but isn't it in all the tested subjects? How are you sure it's not natural? If this ratio is found everywhere in nature, could it not have evolved into its present state? Since I'm not very quali-fied here as far as knowledge about DNA and other things along those lines, I would like you to clear up some of these 'dumb guy' questions. Once I get a little more up to speed, we can see if this is really all that much to get excited about."

"Look, James, this is what I'm talking about," Stan said. "This code looks like it was deliberately grafted into human DNA as a marker, waiting to be discovered. There is potentially data encrypted into this DNA segment Robert identified. Frankly, data could be encrypted into the entire DNA strand itself."

"By whom?" James demanded.

Stan and Robert just looked at each other, neither man ready to answer that question.

James grappled for another explanation. "Based on what you know about evolution, could this have just mutated over time?" he asked.

"Math is my domain—not evolution or DNA, for that matter,"

Stan said. "However, I anticipated that our conversation would go in this direction. It is an important area, but one that is not within my or Robert's expertise.

"Although I reiterate my position that this code is not natural, if I were you, James, I would consult with an evolutionary geneticist or biologist before I do anything else with this. We need to rule out an evolutionary genesis of this code. This could be very time-consuming, as we would need to analyze genetic material from many eras to see if the code is present. However, a discussion with experts in this field would be warranted, and a place to start."

Robert nodded in agreement. "Of course, we know we can manipulate things in the lab. But a sequence this large and odd? Scientists cannot change the original organism's DNA too much, or things go very wrong. Oh, we can take one simple organism's donor DNA, put it into another receiving organism, and make a cell work. But you can imagine the problems that occur with organisms that are more complex."

"Well, then, is it possible those crazy intelligent-design people might be right?" James asked.

Stan interrupted. "No. Science has no place for a god of any kind. Many of us in science are staying away from the ID theory. It is not scientific, per se. You cannot test it. You cannot disprove it. It is based on something supernatural. It breaks all three rules for forming a scientific hypothesis." Stan's voice had begun to raise slightly, but then he paused and chuckled. "Sorry, I get really irritated that those jackasses don't even use real science go around saying that evolution is wrong and creation was just the will of some outside force. That said, though, I don't believe evolution is how this code arrived in the human genome."

James's eyebrow shot up. "Then how did it?"

There was a loud scream from outside. James's heart jumped. Everyone's attention turned to the half-open window of Stan's office. Raised voices could be heard; it sounded like some type of argument.

James immediately became nervous. Tentatively, he stood up and approached the window to look down on the quad. He was just peering over the windowsill, trying to find the source of the commotion, when the window pane shattered into a thousand shards of glass. James dove as fast as he could to the floor, crawling toward a small space between the wall and a bookcase. He covered his head and closed his eyes.

He lay still for a few heart-pounding moments. When looked up, Stan and Robert were still sitting in their chairs, looking at him like he was nuts. Confused, James sat up just in time to see a baseball rolling through the center of the office.

"Are you fucking kidding me?" he asked, standing up and brushing himself off. He grabbed the baseball, walked back to the window, and threw it at the kids below with all his might. "That's the last thing I needed right now."

"Sorry, Professor," one of the kids called from outside.

After a long pause, Stan said, "Are you okay? A bit jumpy are we, sport? I mean, baseballs don't come through my window every day, but that was some reaction."

James felt a bit embarrassed, but pushed on. "So, how do you think this code ended up in our DNA?"

"Frankly, I don't know," said Stan. "I can speculate. But I think it is best to rule out as many causes as we can first. We can begin with evolution."

James felt as if he had just been told he was adopted. "Okay, so I'm still a little lost then," he said. "If you say you don't believe evolution is the origin of this code, and neither is a supernatural biblical type of origin, what are we left with? Aliens?"

"Let's cross that bridge after we talk with an evolutionary geneticist." Stan muttered. "I don't think we should start talking about little green men until we have ruled out other possibilities. I know a guy at UCSF we can speak with, maybe in the next week or so."

James pinched the bridge of his nose and glanced at the clock. "Yeah. Okay. Look, I'm sorry to say this, Stan, but I think we need to speed this up and cut to the chase. You know what happened to me a few days ago in Paris? Who knows who else is after this research?"

"Oh, I'd believe you if you told me the Queen of England wanted a piece of this action!" The professor laughed. "You see, if what Robert says is true, that this code is identical among several—or shall we just take a leap here and say perhaps *all* humans—basically, everyone is going to want in on it."

"Also, that's why I'm worried about bringing more outsiders into the discussion," James reminded him. "This can get out of hand, and we need to keep this information close and confidential."

"I understand," Stan said. "But this is a historic finding. We need to bring other people to the table who can help us. I'm going to keep looking at this sequence. It has me absolutely dumbfounded!"

"It has us all dumbfounded, Dr. Caruthers," said James. "But I need to understand what is so compelling about this finding—and now. I have the Russians and the French aware of our findings already and someone potentially trying to steal them. We can't stall. You tell that UCSF professor of yours we are coming to see him as soon as his schedule allows. Immediately after this meeting, we are returning to Chicago to report to the XNA board concerning your findings, and formulate our action plan."

13

DR . SATI AM UNNEFER
GIZA PLATEAU, EGYPT

A WEEK HAD PASSED since the excavation team had arrived. Sati knew that this would be a long process, but his excitement made him impatient as the first steps were completed.

Once the equipment was in place, the team had removed the large blocks in an effort to reach the door in the shaft. This took tremendous effort and involved hundreds of very large stones. It took much time and effort to brace each stone and pry more away.

Unlike the work of those who first used dynamite and pickaxes to open the gaping hole on the outside, this process was more precise, necessary to preserve the structure. The granite stones lining the Queen's Chamber were peeled back. Although much care was taken with the outer rocks, Sati found himself gritting his teeth as they hacked away and reinforced the passage to the chamber, widening it.

Sati found himself constantly asking the team to be careful, especially when he found some of the stones were damaged, but the workers plodded on, sometimes seemingly without care.

Sati reflected on his surroundings. He found it amazing that the shaft was clearly cut after the construction of the Grand Gallery. He recalled it was only about twelve inches square but ran over two hundred feet long. When the small robot was sent into the tunnel in 1993, the camera on the robot had revealed a small door with copper handles. The robot had drilled through the door and found it to be only six centimeters thick—and behind it was another door. Sati had long felt that something was behind this door. Something of great significance. He did not think these were ventilation shafts, because they did not lead all the way to the outside of the pyramid. The precision of the construction was awe-inspiring. Why would anyone go to such extremes to hide something deep within the pyramid, and construct such a small, precise shaft in the process?

The previous expeditions with the robot had found a small granite ball, a copper hook, and a long cedar rod inside the shaft. Of course, these had been "lost" and thus could not be dated. This was typical of Zaher. Today would begin a new era for the Supreme Council of Antiquities.

The Great Pyramid had been closed to the public, and with the continuing unrest throughout Egypt, tourism was thankfully down as the work progressed. Despite the lack of consideration to detail, and the damage occurring due to the carelessness of the workers, Sati found himself becoming more exhilarated as the work continued and they drew closer to the chamber. They progressed on schedule, and soon they had reached the first door of the shaft.

"Dr. Unnefer," Professor Kline called to him from up the tunnel. "The first door has been opened."

After crawling through the excavated tunnel, Sati was able to enter a small sub-chamber that was tall enough for him stand inside it if he slouched a little. Rodney and Kline stood in the room with Max, one of Kline's men. "Here it is," Kline said. "This door is limestone. Here are the copper handles, although not much is left of them."

He bent down. A small piece of wood was wedged between the stones. "Look here!" he exclaimed. "A wooden rod was clearly used as a lever to move this stone door into place."

Sati looked at the double-helical snake that was carved into the outside of the large door. This was unlike any Egyptian hieroglyph he had ever seen. Faint red markings were on the walls, but they created no discernible form that he could recognize.

"This is very odd," Sati said quietly. "Hieroglyphs have never been found on or in the Great Pyramid, contrary to common misconception."

"I understand that mummies have never been found in the three great pyramids either; they were just assumed to be tombs," Kline mumbled.

"Yes. Dr. Zaher perpetuated this misconception," Sati said, as if talking to himself. "The time of construction of the three Giza pyramids, and what they were used for, is still a matter of complete speculation." He turned to face the men. "Much later, poorly constructed pyramid copies contained carvings, hieroglyphs, and paintings. But as to finding any type of carving in the Great Pyramid, this is a first."

"Just as I figured," Kline said, running his hand along the edge of the door. "They sealed it well." Like Sati, he was practically shaking with excitement.

"Will it be a problem?" Sati asked.

"Let's see." Kline had a large device that he pressed against the door. It had a screen on it like a computer. He moved it from side to side along the door. After a few minutes, he turned to Sati.

"This should be no problem for us. This GPR device has confirmed that this door is quite a bit thicker than the other, so we will have to use laser and water-jet equipment. But that should do the job."

"Okay, just let me finish recording this moment for history, and I will get out of your way," Sati said. He took many pictures and measurements. After about thirty minutes he was done.

Sati wanted to remain where he was and watch as they opened the door. This was what he had been waiting to do for so long. However, he also knew that the workers did not need another body in there, taking up precious space. As soon as he'd finished photographing the chamber, he crawled back down the long pathway.

Soon the crew was running cables up into the shaft. Power lines, data cables, water lines, and air hoses covered the floor. A six-wheel rover with a large industrial Mitsubishi nitrogen laser and top-mounted light appeared in the Queen's Chamber. To Sati it looked like some type of moon rover.

Kline followed with a remote control in his hand as the rover moved up the shaft. Six men had to lift the rover's front wheels so that it could traverse the rise in the floor. Max walked beside Sati into the Queen's Chamber and set up two laptops on a folding table. When he turned on the computers, small screens came up showing the door from the right and left of the shaft. Other screens were brought up that showed a digitized 3-D image of the door, temperature, gauges for the laser, and other measurements. Sati and Kline watched in fascination. "Well, it looks like we are all ready, Dr. Kline," Max said at last.

"Very good," Dr. Kline replied. "Max is an expert when it comes to these industrial lasers. He will have that vault open soon enough." A few of the American team members were in the Queen's Chamber now. Sati looked at them with a bit of apprehension. They were tough, strapping men with serious demeanors.

"Yep, once we get the calculations, we should be in business," Max said as numbers blazed by on the screen. A green light flashed. "All systems are online. We are a go."

"Commence whenever you are ready," Dr. Kline said.

Max brought up another screen that showed the door drawn with a crosshair in the center. He began typing furiously. The edges of the door were outlined on the screen in the pattern the laser would follow. With one final loud tap, a percentage bar appeared.

Sati's eyes focused on the live feed as the meter reached 100 percent. A line of white light streamed from the tip of the laser and sparks flew from it, burning a bit of the stone around the edge of the door.

Beginning at the upper-right corner of the door, the crosshair made its way ever so slowly down the right side.

"How long will this take?" one of the Americans asked. Sati had seen the man hovering around the dig; he always appeared to be assessing the situation, and like Rodney, always seemed to be in a big hurry. Sati was uncertain why he kept questioning Dr. Kline so rudely.

"It will take about six hours to cut around the outside and maybe another two hours to cut down the center," Max replied absently.

The other man grunted in acknowledgement. "I'll be outside," he said, then turned and left as abruptly as he had arrived. Sati doubted anyone would miss him.

"Grumpy," Max chided once the man had disappeared.

Time passed, and Sati watched as the laser rounded the first corner. Soon the laser stopped functioning, halfway across the bottom of the door.

"What happened?" Sati asked.

"Got to let it cool down periodically," Max said pointing to one of the meters on the screen. "Don't want to overheat it. Otherwise, it will take much longer, especially if it breaks down."

They decided to take a break for lunch while they waited for the laser to cool. Sati turned to Kline. "Is that rude man one of your colleagues?" he asked.

"Not quite," Kline said with a smirk. "He showed up the other day. He's apparently part of the American team. One of Rodney's guys."

"I see," Sati said dubiously.

When they returned to the task, Max checked the screens on the laptops and then began typing again. The laser came back to life. It only required one more cool-down before the door was neatly outlined in a thin black cut.

"Now for the center," Max said as he typed again.

He positioned the crosshair over the upper center of the door. With a single keystroke, the laser began its work again. The impatient American returned.

"Are we about in?" the man asked.

"Keep your shirt on," Max chided. "Stuff like this takes precision and time."

The man stood silently behind them and waited with crossed arms for the next thirty minutes without saying a word.

"Voila," Max smiled as the laser stopped.

"Excellent," Professor Kline said. "Now, once that machine is out of the way, let's see if we can't get those doors to move with a little bit of muscle."

Motioning to four of the larger men, Professor Kline ordered, "Grab the crowbars."

"Dynamite would be quicker," the American said under his breath.

"You can't be serious!" Sati said, looking at the American.

"Why are you all standing around? Do what the professor ordered," the American shouted. "Let's get this done."

Max directed the rover out of the tunnel. The four men returned with the crowbars and entered the shaft. After a few minutes, the people in the Queen's Chamber heard a shout.

"I think we got it!"

Professor Kline and Sati made their way up the shaft. The American followed. One half of the stone door was turned sideways, allowing them to enter into the painstakingly concealed room. A floodlight was brought into the chamber. The weight of the historical significance of this moment resonated within Sati; this room had been sealed for millennia, and now they were about to find out why.

They walked in. What they saw seemed to suck the oxygen out of the room. No one spoke. No one moved. Shadows reflected and bounced around the room in utter silence.

There was a large stone-slab altar in the center of the room. It was about six feet long and four feet wide. Laid on top of it in its center were three gilded tomes covered in a fine layer of dust.

Sati approached slowly, barely aware he was holding his breath. Some form of writing was visibly inscribed on top of the books. There was a diagram that looked like stars and the sun and moon, and there was the snake-like icon that they'd seen outside, which ran down the center of the three books. Each tome had one-third of the hieroglyph upon its cover. Other strange markings were on the table—markings Sati had never seen before. *What is this language?* he thought. The sound of someone snapping pictures echoed off the walls.

He noticed something strange. Behind the altar, slumped on the floor in the corner, was a small human skeleton, shrouded in rags. A small clay lamp lay near its outstretched arm.

Sati couldn't believe it. The Great Pyramid was not a tomb; it was not a burial site; it was not a religious monument. It wasn't any of the things that history had speculated it to be. He now knew its purpose.

Dear Allah, he thought, *this pyramid is a vault! Its entire purpose and design is to protect these books.*

It's a library.

AGENT DEVON STINSON
THE WHITE HOUSE

"Well, gentlemen, what do you have for me today?" the president asked.

"Mr. President, please follow me to the Roosevelt Room," Agent Stinson said.

"Of course." The president stood and followed Stinson and Mitchell Perkings out of the Oval Office.

Once in the Roosevelt Room, Agent Stinson closed the doors to make certain that their conversation remained private. "Mr. President, allow me to introduce Einar Randolph, Project Manager for the European Space Agency," he said, gesturing to the man who awaited them there. "He is here to present some startling information on the Mars Express satellite program. This will build upon our prior conversations, and give you some context about what we know of the current Giza excavation plans.

"As you know already the Mars Express contained an orbiting satellite that had every advanced imaging instrument on board, as well as a lander named Beagle 2. Inside Project Aquarius in its earliest formation, team members understood the double meaning behind the name. Beagle was the name of Charles Darwin's ship, used while Darwin was formulating his theories of evolution. Publicly, the ESA's Mars Express was launched for the scientific purposes of sampling Mars's composition and imaging its surface. It returned nice video and images for the ESA to post on its website. However, its primary purpose was to map Mars' mineralogical composition in an effort to further understand its atmospheric makeup and properties, and to gain a better handle on the structures we have observed. Mr. Randolph?"

Einar Randolph looked more like a businessman and less like a physicist in his tailored suit. He stood to address President Brooks.

"Good afternoon, Mr. President. As you know," he began, immediately commanding everyone's attention, "we sent Express to Mars to gather further evidence on the geological surface formations that had intrigued international space agencies for some time. Aside from NASA's 2008 Phoenix mission, which publicly acknowledged that it was analyzing soil samples for organic compounds or perchlorates, we have played down any searches for intelligent life.

"The first geological formation that Mars Express analyzed was the sphinx-like face, and our latest images allow us to see clearly its composition of stone blocks varying between 2 and 10 meters in length. These are not unlike those used in the Giza structures. I'm sure you are aware that the Face is merely one part of a much larger complex of structures.

This plain, known as Cydonia, covers an area of approximately thirty-four square miles. The large structure on the bottom right is the five-sided D&M pyramid. The proximity of these structures suggests that they are all artificial; again, magnification reveals their block construction. What's even more interesting about these structures is that they match the precise star map of the Pleiades, just as the Giza pyramids mirror Orion. They are aligned perfectly, on the exact same geographical latitude on Mars as the pyramids of Giza are on Earth.

"We analyzed these features along with the smaller complex in the lower left, and I think you will be astounded by what we have determined."

"I seem to be getting used to that," President Brooks said with a smile. "Go on, Mr. Randolph."

"There is a clear mathematical arrangement of these massive structures," Mr. Randolph Continued. "The arrangement of the face, the smaller pyramid, and the D&M pyramid are distinctly rectangular. All of these angles, along with the sizes of the various pyramids are mathematically, and geometrically consistent with the Golden Ratio. The D&M Pyramid has bilateral symmetry, with its main axis directly in alignment with the face. From this point, one of the pyramid's axes is 60 degrees from its center, which points directly to the dome structure at the top of the screen. The opposite axis from its center, precisely 60 degrees in the other direction, points directly to the center of the complex of smaller pyramids, nicknamed the City. If you are interested, I have included a mathematical analysis of the structures in your handouts.

"Now, we have found that the Martian pyramids demonstrate astronomical orientations very similar to those identified at Giza. For example, if you were to view the face on Mars from the City during the Martian summer solstice, you would witness the sun rising out of the mouth of the face. The City is also laid out in a clear spiral formation that imitates the Golden Ratio; every structure in it exhibits angles that are mathematically significant. Based on the similarities between these

Martian formations and those found in Egypt, I believe the builders are the same, or at least share a similar origin."

"Astonishing," exclaimed the president.

"Indeed," Mr. Randolph said with a slight smile. "These structures were built for some purpose, Mr. President, and the repetition of the Golden Ratio is intentional, proving their intelligent design and nullifying any argument of natural geological formation."

DR . SATI AM UNNEFER
GIZA PLATEAU, EGYPT

"It appears as if this chamber was designed to be opened," Professor Kline was saying to Sati, "but only when man's technology permitted it. Why else would ancients build such as small room, only accessible through a two hundred-foot shaft one foot square in dimension? This entire pyramid was built to protect this small room and these tablets."

"I don't know, Professor," Sati said, his heart racing. "But this certainly changes history."

No one touched the books, in case they were too fragile after their innumerable years spent hidden away in their chamber. However, both Sati and Kline took pictures of the room and measured everything, and Sati made a few rubbings from the carvings on the table.

"I wonder what these marking are?" Kline mused, examining the walls with his flashlight. "I've never seen this language before. This looks like some form of writing, and a star chart of some sort." He continued to pan his flashlight across the room. As it came to rest on the skeleton, he sighed. "Poor fellow."

Sati had no concern for the walls or the body. His entire focus was on the books. Bending over them, he very gently brushed dust off of the double-helical snake figure carved into the golden text covers. Removing the dust, he peered closely at the books, looking for a way to open them; but the more he studied them, the more solid they seemed.

Sati was puzzling over them when he was interrupted by the sound of boots stomping heavily into the chamber.

"That is quite enough," the American sneered as he stepped into the chamber with two other armed men. They had large padded cases and a handcart with them. They walked up to the table, seized the books, and placed them neatly into the cases.

"What are you doing?" Sati yelled.

Ignoring him, the men set the case on the cart, then turned and began heading down the corridor.

"Wait—no—what are you doing?" Sati yelled, following them to the outer chamber and grabbing one of the men by the arm. The American grabbed Sati's hand and squeezed violently, brining him to his knees. The man shoved Sati away from the cart.

"As I understand your agreement with the president, we have the first opportunity to review any findings," the American snarled. "We need these, and we need them now."

"You deceived me!" Sati screamed, turning to Kline.

"No! I'm not part of this," Kline protested as the man exited through the shaft. "These men are from the U.S. team. They are not mine."

Sati turned to follow the men. "Wait. Wait! You can't do this," he shouted.

Kline grabbed Sati's arm. "Don't be a fool, Sati!" He lowered his voice. "Look at these men. They are military, or CIA. You can't stop them. You brought the Americans into this; you made an agreement with their president. If it's something important enough for them to get involved with, no Doctor of Antiquities is going to stop them."

"I've spent my whole life looking for this. I will not be denied the right to study and examine those tablets," Sati sputtered as he jerked himself from Kline's grip. He hurried down the tight tunnel as quickly as possible, scraping his knuckles, knees, and elbows along the way.

When he emerged from the pyramid he could see the men, now all armed, heading for the long caravan of Humvees. Shielding his eyes from the stark sunlight, he shouted for them to stop. As he approached one of the Humvees, the engine started and it began to move. Unsure of what to do, Sati jumped on the hood and ordered the men to stop.

"Are you serious?" the head agent shouted out of the window, shaking his head. "Get him off!"

The two other men got out of the Hummer and grabbed the Antiquities Minister.

"Please—wait! Where are you going with our artifacts?" Sati shouted, distraught. "You cannot take this away from me. Please, I will help you—I'll do whatever you ask. Please, just let me stay with the texts!"

The men shoved Sati into the sand and drove off.

14

MARIA ZORIN
CHICAGO, ILLINOIS

MARIA ZORIN LANDED IN CHICAGO with a fake passport. Her name was now Sarah Hamilton; she was from Belgium and spoke with a slight French accent. Her blonde hair and blue eyes were startling.

Zorin had been trained by the Federal Security Service of the Russian Federation or FSB, the modern-day version of the KGB. Khalid had employed her for her special skills in counterintelligence and wetwork—otherwise known as assassination. She was no longer bound by the ethics and constraints of FSB oversight. For the last five years under Khalid she had worked exclusively for the Jesuit Order.

As she walked through O'Hare Airport, everyone looked in her direction, dressed professionally in a Halston dress and Ferragamo shoes, she fit right into the corporate scene.

Zorin's instructions were clear: get ahold of one of the computer terminals that had the encrypted client program to access the XNA mainframe. Only a few laptops had the encryption key to access the XNA servers, and even with the laptop, a personal PIN number would need to be entered. There was no other way to access the data. But that wouldn't be a problem for her.

Robert Matson was now back in Chicago, and had been at the XNA headquarters all day. Zorin waited in the parking garage outside the XNA building in her rental car. It was a cold and rainy day in Chicago; she'd had been ready and waiting for hours. She looked in her small Prada handbag, where she had everything she needed: a straight razor, a stun gun that packed a debilitating 21 million volts, and, just in case, a Glock 9mm. She screwed the Gemtech silencer onto the barrel.

Robert exited the XNA headquarters building on his way to the parking garage. She saw that he carried a large bag on his shoulder. Zorin exited her car and stood by the driver's-side door, pretending to look through her purse. When Robert entered the garage, he glanced in her direction and gave a small smile.

"Excuse me, sir," she called out.

"Yes?" Robert replied.

"I seem to be having some car trouble, I can't get the engine to turn over. I'm not sure if it's the battery, or what—it's a rental. I suppose I could call for a tow, but . . ."

"I'll take a look for you. Do you mind?" Robert said, putting his bag on the floor of the garage and opening the driver's side door.

"No, please   here's the key. I'm just not sure what's going on." Zorin had disconnected the distributor cap from the plugs, so she knew it would not turn over.

Robert sat in the driver's seat, put the key into the ignition, and tried to start the car. Zorin looked around the garage to ensure no one was present. She had already disabled the surveillance cameras. Robert kept the door ajar and turned the key. The lights lit up on the dash, but nothing else happened. With the stun gun in her left hand behind her back, Zorin leaned in the open car door.

"What do you think?" she asked.

"Well," Robert began—but before the words left his mouth, Zorin slammed her gloved fist into the side of his head with a devastating blow. Robert reeled into the center of the car. In one smooth movement, Zorin hit him with the stun gun in the abdomen. Robert shook violently.

She slid into the driver's seat, pushing Robert over into the passenger side of the car. Robert's head rolled around, his eyes tracking around wildly. Zorin hit him again with the stun gun. He was out.

AGENT DEVON STINSON
FORT MEADE, MARYLAND

It was a rainy day at Fort Meade. The president's limousine approached the black building of NSA headquarters.

Agent Stinson waited at the entrance with an umbrella. "Mr. President, welcome to the NSA," he said.

"Thank you, Stinson. I'm sure there's a good reason that this particular briefing on has to take place here?"

"Of course, sir." They walked through the lobby to a secure elevator. Once inside, Stinson continued. "Today, Mr. President, the information gets a little more sensitive."

The president looked at him with concern. "You're kidding me."

"No, sir."

They entered a secure conference room. It had no windows, and was very sparsely decorated. The room was uncomfortably cold. A small pot of coffee had been placed on the table along the wall, but it offered little consolation for the temperature. Soon the door opened, and Mitchell

Perkings entered with another gentleman following him.

The man had a thick, bushy moustache straight out of the '70s. His balding head was encircled with a rim of graying brown hair, which looked a bit out of sorts on him. He was an older man, likely in his sixties. His pocket was full of pens, and his trousers, slightly too short for his build combined with his white shirt and small red tie gave him a comical appearance.

"Mr. President," Agent Stinson said, "I'd like to introduce William Clodfelter, our liaison within NASA. He reports directly to the NSA. Bill here has the background information on all the U.S. government projects that researched the UFO phenomena. He also has foreign files that were shared by our international partners."

Stinson turned to Mr. Clodfelter, who licked his lips nervously and cleared his throat as he stood. Instead of beginning his presentation or even going to the head of the table, he grabbed his briefcase, approached the credenza against the wall, and poured a cup of coffee. Reaching for the cream, he tipped his cup over, spilling his coffee everywhere.

The president exchanged a look with Stinson.

Mr. Clodfelter jumped, apologized at least ten times, and cleaned up his mess. Eventually, he wandered over to the empty chair at the other end of the table, strategically placing himself as far as possible from the others seated around the table. However, he still did not say a word. Dabbing the coffee from his fingers, he stared at his briefcase lying on the table in front of him and idly fidgeted with the clasps.

The president broke the silence. "Well, Bill, where do you want to begin?"

Clodfelter looked up, his expression pained. "You'll have to forgive my appearance," he said. "I was working late last night when I was collected and brought here to join you." He inhaled deeply as he positioned himself on the edge of his chair. "I want you to know that what I am about to share with you may be a surprise. For the last twenty-five years, I have personally struggled with this information.

"I understand that Agent Stinson provided you with a history of

Project Aquarius, so I'll try not to duplicate the facts. As you probably know, we are aware that the earth has been observed by an extraterrestrial presence for a long time. In fact, the NSA first confirmed this in 1964. Up until '64, we really only had intermittent direct contact, oddly enough. Of course, since then we have had an innumerable number of radar contacts, pilot accounts, and visual sightings. Globally, according to our research, similar accounts go back as far as recorded history allows." He exhaled loudly. "If we were to add it up since the first recorded NSA confirmation, we would have more than 150,000 accounts in the last sixty years alone. Now, this number excludes most civilian sightings and those reports that were not corroborated. Most of the real accounts are from experienced pilots and military personnel. They tend to relate very specific encounters at close range. Obviously, we don't have time to review all of these in this meeting, although I have personally examined them—well, most of them, anyway."

"Yeah, I know there is a lot of UFO junk out there," the president said. "I've seen the History Channel—the Roswell stuff. I prefer to keep an open mind, though. Are you trying to tell me the premise of those shows is true?"

"Well, yes and no," Clodfelter said. "Some of that information may be accurate. We occasionally lose information that turns up later in some sort of media. However, beyond the simple question each of those programs attempts to answer—whether there is life in outer space—those shows are mainly disjointed accounts of little green men, and speculations. We would classify most of those accounts as possible sightings and exclude them from our data."

"And what of your files?" the president inquired.

"The official reports I am referring to are much more specific, and contain corresponding testimony that was corroborated by two or more individuals. Much of our evidence has supporting radar confirmation, video evidence, and, less frequently, communication intercepts that are mostly data feeds. What is becoming very disturbing to the NSA is the fact that the frequency of these confirmed sightings is increasing, as I know you have been made aware. Up until five years ago, the frequency of sightings and types of sightings were very consistent. Then something changed." Clodfelter moved his eyes away from his suitcase and scanned the room. "Our most credible sightings and evidence came from within NASA itself, through the encounters of our astronauts.

"There is a lot that the public does not know with regard to our space exploration. Nearly every space mission to date has recorded some form of a UFO sighting. Most of these are at a distance and indistinct; some are stationary, some move at high speeds. A few seemed to track our spacecraft, but they are all verified through multiple witnesses and film. We have hours of documentation."

"Bill," the president interrupted, "if so many sightings have occurred, why haven't any of the astronauts said anything?"

"Our astronauts, like those from other countries, keep this information above-top-secret, or Cosmic Top Secret, which this project is considered as well," Clodfelter countered. "All astronauts are under strict confidentiality agreements and recognize the importance their silence has for our national and international security. If you want particulars, a breach of confidentiality would be the equivalent of treason. We have always had staff that leaked this or that to the public, but as a general rule our astronauts have remained loyal to the cause.

"Our first confirmed sightings were with the Gemini. After the first sighting during our Gemini IV mission, official communication code protocols were put in place. We had an astronaut mutter a seemingly innocuous word that would alert Mission Control to switch to a secure frequency. Astronauts also began to be subjected to U.S. military security regulations, and all photographic, video, and radio communications were screened and sanitized by the NSA before release. These sightings became so routine that, prior to vehicle launch, we incorporated a top-secret NSA directive into each astronaut's training protocol.

"Oh, there were some remarkable slips in the beginning," Clodfelter chuckled uncomfortably. "For example, I am sure you are all familiar with the Apollo 11 landing on July 20, 1969. Since we had never traveled to such distances and we were charting new territory, we pre-pared for several possible contingencies. One of those was to switch from analogue to digital communication code if we received the signal from an astronaut. Once the code word was given, both command and the astronauts would simultaneously switch to the secure communication frequency. This prevented HAM radio operators from monitoring the communication on analogue channels. Armstrong was on the moon and following protocol to inspect the LEM upon landing for any structural issues, debris, or any other anomalies that may need to be dealt with prior to the command module's, ascent burn from the moon's surface—that's when this was recorded."

Clodfelter turned back to his briefcase and opened it. He pulled out a laptop and connected it to a cable from under the side of the table. The screen flickered to life on the opposite wall. While waiting for the computer and screen to boot up, he walked to the door and dimmed the lights. Returning to his laptop, he continued, "Mr. President, this is a video that was taken of the craft seen by Buzz Aldrin and Neil Armstrong on that first lunar landing, from the surface of the moon."

Stinson could tell the president was captivated. The film began with the astronauts looking outside the LEM window.

"This is unbelievable," came Aldrin's voice. "Frankly, it's quite frightening. All we can do is sit and wait. We do not know what they want. They have not moved. These craft have been present now for approximately seven hours."

The quality of the film was surprisingly good, considering the technology of the era in which it was shot and the age of the film itself. However, there was a considerable amount of reflection from the sun on the LEM window that obfuscated the craft in the distance. The five ships varied in size and appeared to be several miles away.

The film ended abruptly, but a few moments later, it resumed.

This time, Aldrin was carrying a camera and walking on the surface of the moon. He zoomed in to slightly magnify the objects in the distance. The spacecraft were long and cylindrical, sloping on the ends. It was difficult to discern from the film how large they were, or how far away. Not much detail could be gathered from the images because the objects appeared white in the sun's reflection and emitted some sort of light—but they all appeared to be metallic and very smooth.

Just as it had the first time he'd seen this film, Agent Stinson felt a rush of fear overcome him. The hair on his neck raised. It was like being in a room and sensing an evil presence, or perhaps being in a dark place and having the sensation that something ominous was watching or approaching. Even with all the resources of the NSA, it was shocking to him that this information could have been concealed for so long. Judging by the look on the president's face, his reaction was similar.

The president rubbed his face in a frustrated manner as the film ended, then sat quietly for a few minutes. "I've always believed there was life out there somewhere," he said finally. "It was impractical to believe otherwise. I have even secretly hoped I would see it someday. However, being shown clear evidence of this—this long-term, persistent observation is deeply disturbing. Agent Stinson," he continued, "it seems like a good time for a break."

"Of course, Mr. President," Stinson said, noticing that the president's hands were shaking. He knew the hardest part was to come. "But Mr. President, there is more," he said gently. "And I want you to begin to prepare yourself. What you have learned so far is startling—yes. But it is nothing compared to what you will learn next. We just intercepted a communication from Mount Graham to the Vatican on this very subject. It is something only a few people on this planet know. Something that means mass devastation."

MARIA ZORIN
CHICAGO, ILLINOIS

Zorin punched Robert squarely in the mouth as he began to regain consciousness. Blood ran from his split lip as he slowly lifted his head.

They were in an abandoned warehouse. The only light was from a small bulb on a table before Zorin, and a few small cracks of light slipping through large industrial doors at the far ends of the building. The smell was acrid, a chemical smell. There was water in pools across the cracked concrete floor.

"Where am I?" Robert asked. "Who are you?" He slowly regained his senses and looked around, taking account of his situation. He was bound by steel wire to two large support beams. His arms were stretched out wide, and his wrists bound tightly. He hung from the wires, and they bit deeply into his wrists. His hands were turning purple. His legs were bound at the ankle, each to a beam, spreading his legs wide.

"I'll ask the questions here," Zorin said in a sinister tone.

"I don't understand," Robert began. Zorin punched him in the face again. His nose made a sickening crack. Robert's head snapped backward, and blood flowed down his face.

"I only have one question for you," Zorin demanded, "and your life depends on it. Give me the password to the terminal. Now."

Robert struggled against the wires, shaking violently and pulling at each wire as they tore into his skin. "Help me, someone!" he screamed at the top of his lungs, over and over. He looked around frantically for some means of escape.

"Scream all you like," Zorin cackled. Then, as loud as she could, she yelled, "I have Robert Matson here! Does anyone hear me? Please come help him!" She punched Robert in the stomach and he made a terrible guttural sound as he fought for air. Zorin opened the computer terminal on the small table and opened the login client for the XNA server. "Give me the code."

"But I don't understand," he panted. "What is this all about?"

Zorin hit him with the stun gun in the center of the chest, and Robert screamed. Drool ran from his mouth and his eyes spun in their sockets.

He struggled for a breath.

She slowly walked up to him and put her face an inch away from his. She grabbed him by the hair and held the stun gun up to the side of this face. "I don't think you understand the serious nature of your situation here," she whispered. She licked his cheek. Robert tried to pull away and she tore his shirt front open, exposing his bare chest. Buttons flew across the floor, and the sound of them bouncing echoed around them. She walked over to her purse and pulled out the straight razor. This was her favorite part. The light flashed across the blade.

Robert's eyes shot wide as she approached. She pushed herself up against him, her mouth against his ear. Robert stiffened in terror.

"You will give me that password," she whispered. She bit his ear. Robert heard the crunch as her teeth cut through the cartilage. Robert screamed, his voice beginning to fail him from the force of his pleas. She held the razor against Robert's cheek.

Robert choked out, "P– p– p– please my family . . ."

She laid the blade against his cheek and pressed down. A small trickle of blood ran down his face. Zorin pressed her thumb into the cut and smeared the blood across Robert's face, then licked the blood off of her thumb. She was excited now, her heart racing. She stood in front of Robert, smiling. Placing the razor against his right shoulder, Zorin pressed it down just enough to break the skin.

"Help me!" Robert yelled, thrashing violently against his restraints.

Zorin began moving the blade downward. Robert screamed with pain and terror. The sound of his wail echoed throughout the warehouse. She slowly traced a small, thin cut from his upper-right shoulder across his body, cutting slowly as he fought to move and escape the blade. His body shuddered. She continued down his abdomen—and he writhed in anguish. Slowly, she continued to his waist. A bloodcurdling scream exploded from Robert's lips, emanating from his core.

Zorin smiled.

FATHER MATEO PEREZ
CUSCO, PERU

"We are like a bridge, a small bridge, between the world of science and the Church."

—POPE JOHN XXIII

Father Perez stepped off the airplane onto the tarmac in Cusco, Peru. The sun was shining. It was a clear day, and the temperature was very comfortable.

He made his way to his hotel, a small boutique in the center of town. This was going to be a very short trip, but the pope had insisted that he meet Enzo Viviano before continuing on to meet his colleagues with the U.N.'s Project Aquarius. Enzo was the Prefect of Vatican Secret Archives, which meant he probably knew more about the Archives than anyone alive. Father Perez was intrigued because he was also the Head of the Pontifical Academy of Sciences and a member of the Pontifical Committee for Historical Sciences.

The pope had been perfectly clear, saying, "Listen to all that Bishop Viviano has learned, but say nothing of the revelations from Mount Graham. Now we know what approaches, and when it comes. I need you to learn what you can of what cataclysm it brings upon its arrival. What destruction and effects can we expect? Ancient histories, references, and prophesies may speak of this."

Father Perez was still personally torn by his commitment to remain silent. He knew that if people were going to have any chance of survival, they would need to be evacuated from the coasts—and that would take a lot of time.

He met the bishop outside of a small café on a hilly street. *Jack's Café—not very Peruvian,* he thought.

"Nice to meet you, Father Perez," the bishop said, taking his hand. "Please come inside." The small café was very quaint, and the food smelled great. Father Perez felt the rumble of his stomach. "Best sandwiches in Cusco," Bishop Viviano insisted.

The bishop took a seat at a small bistro table near the open door. "You have come a long way, Father," he said.

"Please call me Mateo."

Bishop Viviano smiled warmly. "And of course, call me Enzo. Too small a town for such formalities." They both laughed.

The bishop took a sip of coffee that he must have ordered before Father Perez's arrival. "His Holiness has informed me that you are engaged in writings concerning possible positions for the Church to take, should we ever find or experience an extraterrestrial intelligence. Sounds very interesting."

"Yes. Of course the Church must be prepared for this contingency, although many believe it is unlikely."

"And you, Mateo?" Bishop Viviano asked pointedly, watching Father Perez intently.

"Well, who knows," Perez said, smiling. "Maybe secretly I wish for such a discovery, but in my lifetime it is probably unlikely."

"Well, I hope the events of my current research, as directed by His Holiness, never come to pass," the bishop sighed. "The pope has asked that I inform you about my research into the end times. Or more specifically, what ancient cultures' histories, stories, and prophecies say of end times. As you know, most civilizations and nearly all religions—both present and past—have end-time prophecies. You and I are, of course, familiar with the biblical predictions of the tribulation in Revelation, but you would be surprised, I think, to know I have come to realize how startlingly similar these prophecies are across the world, in their description of this."

Their lunch arrived, and the bishop continued. "I have worked closely with the Pontifical Commission for Sacred Archaeology, and they have helped direct my research. As you can imagine, much of the information to be gathered is contained in artifacts, ancient writings, and carvings. That's why you had to track me down here in Cusco. I'm currently looking into the Incan culture's end-times prophecies, and working with experts at Machu Picchu and the museums here." He paused. "But before we get into that, how about a little quid pro quo. I'm fascinated with space and the potential for alien life. Tell me what you think on this topic."

Father Perez smiled. "Well, we always think that we know everything at any point in time," he said. "Yesterday we thought there were hundreds of billions of stars in the universe. Just this year we found new evidence suggesting there are over 300 billion stars in our own Milky Way alone, which is just one of a hundred billion galaxies. Can you imagine?"

"Makes Earth seem small."

"Yes, and with the vastness of the universe and the new things we learn each day, I do expect that we will soon not only discover life on other planets, but intelligent life."

The bishop raised a skeptical eyebrow. "Maybe."

Father Perez paused momentarily and continued. "Many scientists now believe life is very common in the universe. We have found dense clouds of organic matter in nebulae. The ingredients and circumstances for the creation of life are not so remote as we once thought. Consider all the places here on Earth we once thought were uninhabitable, but now know that they contain life: boiling hot springs, volcanic steam vents. Some life on Earth doesn't even need oxygen to survive."

"Here in Peru, some believe there are structures built by advanced intelligence—from some other place in the universe," Bishop Viviano said, letting his statement hang in the air. "For instance, the Nazca Lines of Peru. One particular line is perfectly straight for nine miles, in a complex of figures extending across an area thirty-seven by fifteen miles. Why would ancient man build such a structure? Another form is laid out in a perfect trapezoid. Pre-Incan civilization had no means for such precise surveying over such vast distances. The locals say they were built for their gods to see, and with their help."

"Archeologists scrap around for answers to these questions," Father Perez challenged. "It is taboo to suggest that they had help. Most want us to believe these were just remarkable people—ancient Einsteins. But maybe they did have help."

"I'm certain they did." The bishop paused for a moment. "The Mayan, Incan, and Aztec cultures had a calendar that provided measurements of the equinoxes and lunar movements. The ancients also corrected their calculations for variance in the earth's rotation. How is this possible? How could they know the precise moment when the earth had reached its equinox without some . . . help? And try this on for size: the Gate of the Sun, which I've recently seen, is at Tiahuanaco, just across the Peruvian boarder there in Bolivia," he said pointing to the south. "It was ten feet high, almost twenty feet wide, and carved out of a single block of stone weighing over ten tons. Carved into the Gate of the Sun is the story of a golden spaceship descending from the stars. A woman named Oryana with four fingers arrived to be the Great Mother of the Earth. The story says that she helped create man. Then she returned to the stars."

"I've not heard of that story before," said Father Perez, his interest piqued.

"My research has found another common thread, Mateo. All ancient cultures have a story about cataclysmic end-times, but also similar stories of creation and interaction with the gods, their perceived creators. For example, on the other side of the planet, the Sumerians, a civilization that is possibly 15,000 years old, told a very similar story to that of the Peruvians. They claim their gods came from the stars, created man, and interacted with him on Earth. That story is repeated across multiple cultures."

"It's not impossible that ancient cultures interacted with visitors from other stars," Father Perez interjected.

"Maybe," Bishop Viviano said. "Each story has these gods giving man incredible information, and teaching and advancing human society. The Sumerians had calculations for the rotation of the moon around the earth to within 0.4 seconds of our present-day calculation, using incredibly accurate numbers that contained up to fifteen digits." He stared at Father Perez. "Amazing, no? This information certainly came from somewhere else." The bishop looked down at his coffee, and a serious expression came over his face. "Why and how were the Sumerians so advanced in mathematics? Why would the oldest civilization on Earth need a number so big? We have no use for such a number in today's sciences, except for very high-level, precision calculations. The Greeks, Romans, and other early Western cultures never used numbers this large. The Sumerians knew we had multiple planets in the solar system circling the sun, thousands of years before Ptolemy and Copernicus.

"Likewise, the Mayans also made incredible calculations using advanced mathematics, calendars, and astronomy. They were aware of and believed in heliocentricity—even going so far as to calculate the year cycle of Venus. They calculated the exact time of the earth year at 365.2420 days. The Sumerians knew about Uranus and Neptune, which are not visible without a telescope, two thousand years ago." He paused and smiled, seeming to weigh how this information was impacting Father Perez. "They, too, told us that the gods came down from the Pleiades with great ships and weapons, instructed men in sciences, arts, customs, and laws, and then boarded great ships and returned to the stars. This is a consistent theme in ancient civilizations, not only in South America and Mesopotamia, but also across Asia, North America, Europe, and Africa. Why would so many ancient peoples tell of visitors in strange craft descending from the heavens to create them and instruct them in the sciences, war, and other aspects of culture? The worldwide population in 3000 BCE was only about twenty million—the population of the state of New York today. These people were distributed all over the world in small groups, giving birth to the beginnings of civilization. How did they all end up telling the same story of visitors from the stars?"

"It does seem incredible," Father Perez replied.

"Egypt, too, is riddled with vast structures paying homage to the gods from the stars along the Nile," the bishop added, almost to himself. "They're positioned so they mirror the constellations: Andromeda, Pegasus, Altair Achernar, Canopus, Canis Major, and Orion."

Suddenly he looked up, fixing Father Perez's gaze intently. "But I'm running on. Doesn't this all sound rather familiar to you Father?"

Father Perez was startled. "Familiar in what way?" he asked.

"Gods from the stars, teaching man of technology and weapons—doesn't it sound eerily familiar to the story of the Watchers in Genesis 6:1 and the Books of Enoch?"

This struck Father Perez very odd. "How do you mean?" Father Perez asked.

The bishop laughed. "Perhaps your focus on the sciences has dulled your memory of the religious texts?" he teased. "Two hundred angels rebelled against God and were cast from heaven and descended to Mount Herman—the Fallen. Their leader was Lucifer—the God of Light. They took wives and had children with the daughters of man. They gave man technology, taught them in magical knowledge, how to make weapons of war, taught them about astrology and the secrets of the stars." He looked upward a moment, the light seeming to catch his eyes as he turned them again on Father Perez. "Maybe your aliens are the Fallen, who were given dominion over the earth." he said.

15

JAMES ANDERSON
CHICAGO, ILLINOIS

It is the glory of God to conceal a thing: but the honor of kings is to search out a matter.

—PROVERBS 25:2

"WHERE ARE YOU?" James's secretary Catherine sounded distraught, like she had been crying.

"I'm home. Why?" James asked, his tension rising.

"It's Robert . . . he's dead."

The words hit James like a punch in the stomach. For an instant his head swam, unable to comprehend what he'd heard. "What—what are you talking about? What happened?" he stammered.

"He was killed, James. The police are here at the office. They asked me to call you and see if you could come to the office to give them a statement."

James sat stunned, his mind completely overwhelmed. When Catherine spoke again, it was as though an eternity had passed.

"Here, they want to talk to you," she said.

"Mr. Anderson," a voice came on the other end.

"Yes," James muttered, still unable to believe what he was hearing.

"This is Sergeant Mallory. I'm very sorry about your colleague Mr. Matson, but we have some questions for you. Would you mind coming into the office for a bit? We are trying to get as many statements as possible for our investigation."

"What happened?"

"I can explain more when you come down."

When James arrived, there were several police cars in front of the building. Inside the office, the mood was somber. Many people were talking quietly in small groups. A few were crying at their desks. Everyone who saw him gave him a sympathetic look.

Catherine was waiting for him at the entrance. She wrapped her arms around James and sobbed. James couldn't help himself and wept too.

Catherine led him into the conference room, where a policeman was sitting in a chair.

"Mr. Anderson. I'm Sergeant Mallory," he said. "Thanks for coming down. I know this is difficult. Please have a seat." Catherine left them alone in the room.

"What happened, Sergeant? Please," James whispered.

Sergeant Mallory pulled his chair up close to James and leaned forward, exhaling. "Your friend was murdered, Mr. Anderson."

"How?"

"It may be hard for you to hear this—but he was shot point-blank in the forehead. He was found about six hours ago in an abandoned warehouse on the south side."

"Oh my God," James breathed in horror. "His wife, Susanna, does she know?"

"Yes. We just sent an officer to their home. She knows now." James buried his head in his hands.

"Mr. Anderson, your assistant told me about what happened in Paris," Sergeant Mallory said. "That you think someone was after data from your servers here at XNA."

"Yes, that's right." James choked back tears, trying to think clearly.

"Well, I think this was another attempt to steal that information. Your IT department tells me there were over twenty attempts to log into the servers between 10:00 p.m. the night before last and 5:00 a.m. yesterday morning. All attempts were with the incorrect password until just after 5:00 a.m., when a specific password was entered that locked the system down. Your IT department tells me that you have a kill code that you can input to lock the servers down from outside data access." Sgt. Mallory questioned.

"Yes, that's right," James mumbled. "Why would there have been so many attempts to log into the system? I don't understand."

"Mr. Anderson," Sergeant Mallory said, pausing for a moment and looking directly at James with a sympathetic expression, "this may be hard for you to hear, but Mr. Matson was tortured. And very brutally." At this, James began to sob. He held his hands to his face. "My guess is that Robert gave them false passwords as long as he could hold out. Then when he locked the system down, they—they killed him."

"I can't believe this. This is my fault. Robert was working for me. This is my fault," James stuttered, almost unintelligibly. He sobbed for a long time. Finally, decisively, he got up and grabbed a napkin from the credenza along the wall and blew his nose. He looked hard at the sergeant.

"Do you know who did this?" he asked.

"No, Mr. Anderson. We don't have much to go on. But there is more." He paused for a moment. "There were strange carvings on Robert's body, occult-like symbols. An upside-down cross. Does this make any sense to you?"

"You have to be kidding me," James wailed, his temper rising. "Who fucking did this to him? We have to find these people!"

"We are working on it, believe me. I'm very sorry for your loss." Sergeant Mallory stood up. "The media is asking for a statement. I'm going to make sure that we tell them that all outside terminals have been eliminated and the XNA facility is locked down. We want to discourage any more attempts to breach your security. I also have approval to keep a uniformed officer on premises until we get to the bottom of this." He put his hand on James's shoulder. "I'll call you if I have more. Please, if you think of anything that could be helpful, Catherine has my direct number."

* * *

The week went by at an excruciatingly slow pace. Trying to cope with Robert's loss was unbearable, especially alone. James's kids had been very supportive; he couldn't have gotten through this without them.

He could barely bring himself to go to the funeral; even there, James couldn't look at Robert's widow in the eye. He knew Susanna blamed him, although she said otherwise. He blamed himself. Guilt consumed him. He thought he was having a nervous breakdown.

What had he done to his best friend? What had he gotten Robert and himself into? Who was trying to steal their information, and why was it worth murder?

But he was a man of action, and as the days slowly went by, James's sadness and sense of loss transformed into anger and resolve. He was determined to find out what this was all about. Why had Robert been killed? What was so valuable about his DNA code? He owed it to Robert to find the answers.

James ran his fingers through his hair. Had his pride betrayed him again? He had wanted to give Robert the opportunity to be successful, and he felt an inner sense of satisfaction that XNA Pharma was growing into a valuable company. What had they stumbled onto that had led to the death of his best friend? His anger swelled. He had to find out who'd killed Robert, and why.

FATHER MATEO PEREZ
CUSCO, PERU

And the serpent cast out of his mouth water as a flood after the woman, that he might cause her to be carried away by the flood.

—REVELATION 12:15

Father Perez walked slowly beside Bishop Viviano through the Museo Inka, the Museum in Cusco dedicated to Incan culture. It was a short walk from where they'd had lunch.

"I apologize, Mateo, if you thought my tone was rude at the café," the bishop said. "It's just that something behind all of these stories feels ominous to me."

"No, not at all," Father Perez said, though he was still a bit unnerved.

"On to the end-times findings," the bishop said, stopping in front of a stone carving. "Experts believe that the Incan civilization began as the Mayan ended. But little is known about them. Further north, my research has found that the Mayan and Aztec civilizations, with their famous calendars, had end-times prophecies that tell of the beginning of a new age—a new world. There is some disagreement among experts, but it appears these prophesies anticipate a cataclysmic destruction of the earth during that time of change."

"You mean the 2012 calendar date?" Father Perez asked.

"Well yes, and no. Experts disagree on the calendar end date. Some think it was 2012, others as far out as 2025. I imagine by the time I leave here, the Incan story will be similar.

"The Hopi claim that the world will end in a catastrophic manner, preceded by a sign of the blue star Kachina in the sky," the bishop went on. "This is similar to the story told in the Zohar, the Jewish religious text of the Kabbalah priests that was hidden for nine hundred years. It explains that a burning star will arise in the east. Seven stars travel around this star, making war with each other. These seven will go around the middle star three times a day for seventy days, and all the people of the world will see it."

Father Perez stopped dead in his tracks, struck by the image. "That is incredible," he said.

"Yes. They believe this star will precede the arrival of the Messiah," Bishop Viviano said, assessing the father's reaction.

The bishop went on to enumerate a number of other descriptions of end-times prophecies from cultures around the world as they walked. They then sat in the late afternoon sun at a small outdoor café. There was a chill in the air as the sun began to set behind the mountains.

"The Chinese have a similar ancient description of an event, one that they believe will occur again: an account of two suns that fought in the sky, causing the mountains to crumble. They ran to the sea, and the sea rose like the mountains before them.

"I also find it interesting that in many recorded histories there was a story or myth recounting a day when the sun stood still. This story of the long day—or long night, depending on the culture—was retold in Babylon, in Egypt, among Native American tribes, in Norse mythology, and among the Incas. Hebrew, Indian, and Chinese legends also mentioned the sun standing still in the sky. Does that mean something to you, Mateo?"

"Not particularly. These myths are interesting, but make no sense scientifically," said Father Perez, clearing his throat.

Bishop Viviano frowned at this answer. "These stories of end times also recount similar occurrences in their histories, as if they are events they expect to repeat," he said. "Each story tells of a day of the death of hundreds of thousands of men and animals from upheaval in the earth's ground, forests burning, waves reaching to the sky, and floods and strong winds that cause devastating destruction."

"It's possible, I suppose," Father Perez ventured, "that there was a global catastrophe common to these groups of people. But the sun appearing to stop in the sky is so dramatic! I'm not sure what celestial event could have given them the illusion that the earth had stopped rotating. You would need to entertain far-fetched notions that a major earthquake or asteroid somehow changed the rotation of the earth to give a reason for this."

"I suppose so," Bishop Viviano said. "But you, Mateo, know individually each of these stories in isolation seems far-fetched; but collectively, they may have captured evidence of some global cyclical cataclysm." He smiled bleakly. "One that all those ancient peoples expect to return—and soon."

MARIA ZORIN
SAN FRANCISCO, CALIFORNIA

Maria Zorin, or Sarah Hamilton, had been thwarted. It would not happen again. The California sun was hot, and she rolled up the window in her rental car and turned on the A/C.

She sat across the street from the private-jet hangar in a Ford Focus. She was in the parking lot of the private jet hangar, Fixed-Base Operator (FBO), looking at the Citation through high-powered military-grade binoculars. She had been given the flight plan and tail number for the jet when the flight plan had been filed two days ago, and she was able to get to San Francisco a day before the Citation to prepare.

Today, she had tracked the jet's progress by entering its tale number into the Plane Finder app, watching it all the way into San Francisco International. She watched as two men left the jet, got into a car, and drove off. She could see that one had a briefcase; and she was certain it held the laptop she was after. She looked down at the Ruger .45-caliber pistol in her lap. She preferred her MP-443 Grach 9mm, but she had to work with what she could get quickly here in the States. It was matte black. The clip held seven rounds in addition to the round that was chambered. In the pocket of her leather jacket was another clip. *More than enough for the job*, she thought.

She laid the binoculars beside her on the seat. She grabbed her purse from the floor and pulled out the Gemtech Blackside .45ACP suppressor and screwed it onto the gun. The silencer was nearly as long as the gun, exceeding six inches. Its lightweight construction was perfect for her; it kept the heavy gun in balance in her hand.

She fished through her purse again, pulled out one of the burner phones she had been given, and dialed the preprogrammed number.

"I'm at the hangar waiting for the package to return to the FBO," she said when a voice answered. "They just left. I'll be waiting for them."

"Make sure you get that package," the voice replied. "Use any means or force necessary. We will have you out immediately on the next flight. Just confirm when you have it."

"There are two pilots at the—oh, shit." Zorin looked up as three black SUVs driving into the FBO caught her attention.

"Is there a problem?"

"There is. Damn it!" She watched several men walk into the hangar. She crouched down and looked through the binoculars again. "I'll call back." She slid the gun into the breast pocket of her jacket and hung up the phone.

JAMES ANDERSON
UNIVERSITY OF CALIFORNIA, SAN FRANCISCO

"You know, Stan, I don't usually get an inquiry from a mathematician and a venture capitalist," Dr. Michael Peterson said with a very nervous giggle. "Add to that the fact you wanted to come out to San Francisco to meet so quickly—this is all a little unusual."

Dr. Peterson was an evolutionary geneticist at the University of California, San Francisco. He rarely ventured far from his laboratory on campus; his appearance showed it. He was a large, round man who looked a bit unhealthy and uncomfortable in his own skin. His hair, exceedingly thin, was styled in a painfully ridiculous comb-over. His head was covered in liver spots, and he wore thick bifocals. Conversation with something other than a microscope was apparently a bit outside his repertoire.

James and Stan had flown out to California that morning on James's small business jet. James was tense, and a headache was forming at the base of his skull. He ignored the pain and collected himself to focus on the meeting. Guilt and a sense of the tremendous debt he owed Robert forced him on.

"Dr. Peterson, I know this all sounds a bit strange, but as I explained on the phone, we have a specific interest in the evolutionary effects upon DNA. Stan thought you could help us," he said.

"Well, I don't understand," Dr. Peterson muttered. "The field is very broad and there has been much work, and of course, there are some areas that are still theoretical." He rambled on for a few minutes, mostly reiterating that "our work is about precision, and as you know, very technical."

"Here is the scenario," James interrupted when he couldn't bear the meandering thought process of the professor any longer. "We have invested a significant amount of money in a DNA technology, and we need to know how DNA has changed through evolution."

"But why would a venture capitalist and a mathematician care?" asked Dr. Peterson, clearly skeptical.

"We are in the midst of raising capital. A potential investor is worried that DNA can evolve and thereby invalidate our DNA therapeutic delivery mechanism. You see, his willingness to invest is conditioned on his satisfaction with various due-diligence questions and requests being satisfied. This appears to be his last stumbling block prior to authorizing the investment. We just need to complete the request as quickly as possible."

Stan looked at James, impressed with his sudden and passable fairy tale.

After a long pause, Professor Peterson shrugged, "Well, I can appreciate the urgency that financial pressures can pose. I know how many times I've fought tooth and nail to secure grants for continued research. I recall one occasion—"

"So," James interrupted, "since I'm probably the least qualified here concerning evolution, genes, DNA, and things of that nature, let me begin with some basic questions. Then we can get more elegant with inquiries from Stan here. What can you tell us about the evolutionary effects on human DNA specifically?"

"Well, ha-ha, much, I suppose," Dr. Peterson chuckled. "We can see various slight changes within a species in the fossil record. As you know, we can't access the DNA, but we can identify any anatomical changes that may have occurred over time."

James and Stan traded frustrated glances.

"I'm sure you are aware of the Darwinian theories," the professor insisted, his eyes narrowing. "I mean, everyone has to learn those in grade school. Do they not? If we didn't—"

"Yes, man came from apes," interjected James.

"Well, yes, that's the proliferate view. We see various species that differ slightly and that is the preponderance of the evidence for evolution. Many of my colleagues would string me up for saying this, but it's still just a theory and not law—although it is the dominant and accepted theory."

"Just a theory?" James asked.

"And a very difficult theory to prove, I might add," said the professor, waving his finger. "Yes, on one hand, we do have many particular examples of evolutionary changes within a species, or more specifically stated, mutations within a species. However, we have no *actual* observable evidence of evolutionary changes progressing from one species to a completely different species. We have the fossil record that seems to suggest such a process, but no direct evidence of this genetic migration. For example, we do not have a complete evolutionary species morphology of even one animal transforming over time into another. And when you look at humanoids, there really is nothing: just a few vastly different hominoid species separated over great distances of time. I know this sounds like I'm a creationist, which I'm not. I'm just more comfortable than many of my peers in identifying the holes in our field of research. I believe science is stronger when we admit our difficult problems and collaborate to find their answers."

James was a bit perplexed. "But we all learned in high school that we evolved from apes," he said, holding his arms open and looking around for validation. "Right? I wasn't sleeping in class the day they taught that. You know—the drawing showing a monkey progressing from all fours to upright walking and finally to present-day man."

"Well—well, now," corrected the professor, "what you learned was the dominant scientific theory of the day. Today, we believe all hominoids and monkeys evolved from a common ancestor. But there are still very large gaps—and I mean millions and millions of years—to fill, in order to complete the evolutionary cycle to *Homo sapiens*, or between any hominoid. You know, some paleontologists would state that in all practicality, we have reached the end of the fossil record. Some believe we found what there is to find regarding human evolution—and all the evidence we have in the world of human evolution could fit in the corner of this office."

Looking around the room, James saw that he was not the only one feeling like an idiot. Stan was clearly perplexed.

Unfazed, the professor continued. "Really, the more we research environmental impacts on a species where one would expect to find evolution in process, the more we find mutations—but more importantly, entropy is more prevalent," he said. "That is, there is a loss of diversity in nature. We now know that once an organism changes too much from its parents genetically, it dies. This is where I focus my research.

"There have been decades of experiments on fruit flies, for example. We can produce hundreds of deformities and anomalies among them; we can introduce various environmental conditions and stimuli, trying to force evolution. But nothing at all that we produce ever resembles another species. Now consider: the population of *Homo erectus* was very small when present-day *Homo sapiens* arrived on the scene. We estimate that the worldwide population of *Homo sapiens* in 3000 BCE was only about twenty million—"

James interrupted. "Are you telling me that the Bible was right? That there was some form of creation or intelligent design?" He was surprised to find that the idea rather comforted him; raised a Christian,

James had always thought that some type of creation was in play, even if things also evolved over time.

"Of course not," Stan interjected. "Don't insult the professor's intelligence. Belief in creation is for the masses, and has nothing to do with science. Some form of evolution is the accepted science. Right, Professor?"

Professor Peterson continued on as if Stan hadn't spoken. "But you see, in modern times we have witnessed the birth and death of tens of billions of people on the planet," he said. "If evolution were active, we should have seen glaring examples of it manifesting itself in present-day biology. It would stand to reason that we would see many more species evolving into existence, what with the exponential growth in population. Yet have seen none. So how does evolutionary science deal with this? Very embarrassingly, scientists simply conclude that humans have stopped evolving."

Drawing on the apparent confusion he had caused, the professor turned to Stan, "Yes, the dominant scientific theory is evolution, and it is likely correct. However, there is no beacon of evidence, no significant ancestral chain, to help us conclude that evolution is correct and move it beyond theory. We just have fragments of information to *suggest* a progression—we have no certainty of it. A horse is closely related to a rhino, though they have vastly different eyes, neurological systems, and organ structures. Under the theory of evolution, we should find in the fossil record a continuum of morphology from horse to rhino, complete with changes in the different complex structures they share. But we don't. We just have horses and rhinos. Similarly, the evolution from a transitional species into modern man is theorized to have occurred over a roughly thirty-five-million-year period. However, we have no transitional species evidencing this from about thirty-two to twenty-two million years ago, meaning we have one species and then *Homo erectus*, with nothing in between. This is generally known as the hominoid gap. There is no physical evidence of this divergence.

"Most findings claiming to have identified the missing link have been academically challenged and criticized. They have been scientifically invalidated, or disappeared before peers could examine the sole specimen. And when you consider the mental capabilities or intelligence exhibited across the evolutionary timeline, we have even less information."

"What do you mean?" asked Stan.

"Well, I'm not an anthropologist, and this question is probably best answered by one of those, but we have roughly thirty-five million years of primate fossils. *Homo sapiens* as we know him—or us—appeared basically out of nowhere, in numbers, only about fifty thousand years ago. The earliest evidence of him dates back a few hundred thousand years. In my circles this is called the Great Leap Forward, whereby out of nowhere suddenly there was modern man with our current state of intelligence. Suddenly we had incredible skills, abilities, communication, and even more remarkably, the development of culture." Dr. Peterson smiled at his listeners, seeming hardly as awkward as when he'd begun. "Hence, the proverbial search for the missing link continues," he concluded.

DR . SOFIA PETRESCU
ESA, PARIS, FRANCE

Reviewing Jonas De Vos's findings, Sofia Petrescu found herself performing a surprising about-face. His reputation had been slaughtered—but why? His postulates were well thought-out and documented with real evidence.

Several independently published studies corroborated his research, and seemed to suggest that climate change was the direct result of solar activity. So, what was all the hysteria about? Why was it so important for the U.N. to take control over climate change? And why wasn't anyone in the U.N. scientific crowd talking about these findings, or trying to correlate the changes observed on Earth with those on other planets?

Dr. DeVos's opinion that climate change was all about control. That did ring true. In its Agenda 21 documents, the U.N. had positioned itself as the global arbiter of truth in this arena. But the U.N.'s solution was technocratic and authoritarian; it dictated that no country alone had the right to object to its decisions under Agenda 21. Under those terms, Dr. De Vos's postulate was true: they could control and direct development of the world population and the use of its resources under a global taxation authority, without granting any opportunity for legal resistance.

What Sofia found particularly upsetting was a study she found where 31,000 scientists had signed a petition, known as the OISM Petition, stating that there was no convincing scientific evidence that human release of carbon dioxide would cause the heating of the earth's atmosphere. The petition was not reported on by any major news agencies, and the few who did comment on it mostly dismissed the scientists as "climate-change deniers."

What is going on here? Sofia wondered. *There are changes occurring on Earth and throughout our solar system—there is no denying that. But the U.N. just wants us to accept that it's caused by man-made CO_2 and to stop asking questions.*

She looked out the window, amazed at her own indignation. *But it's not so strange*, she thought. *I'm a scientist.*

I need to find out what is causing all of these changes.

JAMES ANDERSON
UNIVERSITY OF CALIFORNIA, SAN FRANCISCO

James could sense that the professor was feeling more at ease himself. He'd probably had not had such an engaged audience in his entire career.

"The Great Leap Forward is basically this: as if out of nowhere, we find ourselves as modern men with abstract thinking, planning, and artistic expression. Hominoids go from basic cave dwellers to modern man wearing jewelry, living in complex communities, and using specialized techniques in hunting and agriculture. We also see specification into trades such as building, teaching, and writing.

"The theory of evolution comes from Darwin's great writings and observations while on his way around the world on his expeditions aboard the HMS Beagle," Dr. Peterson continued. "It's my belief, and I think many would agree with me, that our real basis for a continued grasp on Darwin's theory is our very real and visible ability to view the passing on of genetic information to our offspring through the reproductive process. In essence, we believe we have microevolution occurring before our eyes: my traits and my wife's are visible in our children. It's a theory that fits our cultural demand for answers. But the actual evolution of one species into another species is an entirely different matter, and has never been completely documented for any life form.

"One must ask, if we evolve, do we leave behind a different human species that we are evolving from? Why don't we see a multitude of different hominoid species? Evolution today cannot provide a satisfactory explanation for this or for our origin, *but* any academic risks his career if he tries to publish anything contrary to it. Don't get me wrong; I'm not saying we were put here through creationism. I'm simply saying—as a research professor and from a scientist's perspective, using the scientific method—the theory is weak. Here, let me read you Darwin's own words to scientists of the future." He fumbled over to his bookshelf behind his desk, and thumbed through a book riddled with Post-It notes. "Here it is, *On the Origin of Species*," he said. He cleared his throat and read "'If it could be demonstrated that any complex organ existed, which could not possibly have been formed by numerous, successive, slight modifications, my theory would absolutely break down.'" He laughed and pointed at the seated onlookers. "See? Even Darwin understood the fragility of his postulate, and how little would be required to disprove it. Now, with Darwin's own perspective, with the value of hindsight, with the great progress in technology, and with the fossil record thoroughly explored by countless scientists, the theory must fail under Darwin's own test. We need to start from scratch. In short, we have learned that *On the Origin of Species* was wrong!"

"Basically, Darwin says humans are so complex that we need to see slow successive changes in the entire human system, organs, molecular biology, biochemistry, and genetics over a great period of time.

Otherwise the theory is invalid. Under his own litmus test, we have disproven the theory." He closed the book with a bit of pomp and walked back to his desk.

"So, Mr. Anderson, in my view, evolution poses no risk to your DNA therapy, nor to your business."

James blinked, having forgotten briefly of the pretense they had given for the meeting. "Well, that is great news. Thank you, Professor," he smiled. "If you don't mind, personally, I'd just like to know what you think." He eyed Stan, knowing that he was risking another smart-ass retort. "Are you saying the pretext of creationism makes sense to you? Adam and Eve?"

The professor giggled, clearly enjoying the controversy he'd stirred up. "No, no," he said, shaking his head. "We know the earth is billions of years old, and man is hundreds of thousands of years old, not a few thousand. But from the evidence before me, it seems more practical to say that one day modern man just showed up." His eyes sparkled behind his bifocals. "How this occurred, I don't know."

16

JAMES ANDERSON
SAN FRANCISCO INTERNATIONAL AIRPORT

"Any entity—no matter how many tentacles it has—has a soul."
—GUY CONSOLMAGNO, DIRECTOR OF THE VATICAN OBSERVATORY

JAMES AND STAN WERE DISCUSSING THEIR MEETING with Dr. Peterson as they walked toward the entrance of FBO, the private jet hangar, for their return flight. To their surprise, they found eight very official-looking men standing near James's jet, all wearing dark, well-tailored suits. Two more men were in black military gear with machine guns, standing at either side of the entrance to the jet. As James approached the plane apprehensively, he noticed that the pilots were being questioned by a man in a suit in the corner of the hangar.

What the hell? James thought, a knot beginning to form in his stomach.

"Mr. Anderson," one of the men in suits said as he approached. It was not a question.

"What are you doing with my pilots?" exclaimed James, with a nervous tremor in his voice.

"Sir, could you and Mr. Caruthers follow me, please." The man walked toward James's jet and continued up its stairs.

"Well, why don't you first tell me who you are, and what I can do for you?" blurted James, both defensive and perplexed. "I'm not comfortable entering my own jet with someone I don't know, particularly while it's surrounded by men with guns whom I also don't know, and while my pilots are clearly being interrogated. Hey! You need a warrant to enter my plane!"

Stan had not moved a muscle. The silence that followed was intense.

It became apparent as they looked about that the hangar was empty. There were no FBO staff within sight. The man slowly retreated back down the stairway.

"Sir, I am Agent David Lopez with the National Security Administration." He flipped out his credentials as if it were a formality and quickly returned them to his pocket. James thought about demanding to scrutinize the badge, but Lopez continued without concern. "The Marines at the entrance of the plane are here for your protection, I assure you. I'm sure you can appreciate that after your Paris encounter and the death of your associate Robert Matson. We'll talk more after takeoff."

"What the hell is going on here?" muttered Stan.

"I will explain more inside your aircraft. Gentlemen, please," said Agent Lopez, pointing the way.

Reluctantly, they followed Lopez into the Citation. There was another dark suited man already sitting in the back of the plane.

James began to say something, but stopped himself as the thought of Robert's horrific murder flashed through his mind.

The man in the back of the plane held up his hand as if to silence them. He opened a small black case and took out what looked like a suction cup attached to a small electronic device, and stuck it to the window of the Citation. He pushed a button on the device, and a very low hum filled the cabin of the aircraft.

"Now, Mr. Anderson, we can talk," he said, as Agent Lopez closed the cabin door. The sound of white noise was all around them. It almost sounded as if they were in flight. Behind this was a deeper pulsing sound, almost unnoticeable.

"What are you attaching to my jet?" demanded James.

"No need to worry," the man replied. "This device prevents any eavesdropping. It's an acoustic electromagnetic generator. It is scrambling and muting our conversation while creating a sonic barrier around the aircraft. In effect, we just went stealth." The man leaned forward. "I am Agent Devon Stinson, and like my colleague here," he said, pointing to Mr. Lopez, "I work for the National Security Administration. Please, have a seat."

Lopez remained standing at the front of the aircraft as they sat.

"From this point forward, all of your research and all communications are considered classified—above-top-secret. We want you to know that these are your responsibilities and the expectations associated with your confidentiality in this matter." He handed each of them what looked like a lengthy legal confidentiality agreement. James flipped quickly through his to the end; it was lacking the signature lines.

"What are you talking about?" he said. "This is preposterous. You can't simply classify our work. It's owned by XNA Pharmaceuticals, a private company. We own the intellectual property."

"Mr. Anderson," interrupted Agent Stinson, "please. We are the NSA. I have a FISA warrant right here. We have been following your project for nearly three months now: every land and cell conversation, all of your text messages, the incident in Paris. We have all of your emails and copies of your server files. The federal government has a priority interest in XNA Pharma and your research concerning the

DNA pattern you identified."

"How did you even know what we were working on? Who leaked the information to you?" James demanded.

"Dr. Caruthers is a government asset," said Agent Stinson without pause.

"I'm a what?" stuttered Stan.

"You have been a consultant with the Central Intelligence Agency on a few artificial intelligence matters, Dr. Caruthers," continued Stinson.

"What are you talking about?" Stan shouted, bewildered. "that was three years ago! And I was working for a software company as a consultant, not for the CIA directly." Now James was really pissed about bringing this pompous math jackass into the XNA project—though he could tell that Stan was alarmed to learn he had been under constant surveillance.

"Dr. Caruthers, the U.S. government has a vested interest in anyone who has provided services to them, especially those who work indirectly with the government with various contractors on national security matters," Agent Stinson explained. "Your work was a matter of National Security, after all—so whether you want to be or not, you are a security asset."

James thought of all the moments in his life when it would have been outrageous and intrusive to have someone constantly listening—and watching. His anger grew. Stan seemed to recoil at the same thought.

"Gentlemen, we are going to make our way to Fort Meade, where you will be briefed," Agent Stinson went on, oblivious to their fury. "More of your questions will be answered there. We are taking you, your jet, and your servers into custody as an emergency safety precaution. We have a federal warrant, which you are free to peruse during the trip." From his jacket, he pulled out a federal court order and handed it to James.

"When?" asked James.

"Right now," answered Stinson. He nodded to Lopez. "Bring the pilots back onboard. We're taking off immediately. Once we touch down, a car will be awaiting so that we can proceed directly from the airport to NSA headquarters."

James couldn't believe what he was hearing. He felt like a puppet on a string. "We absolutely will not!" he protested, panic rising in his throat. "We have meetings tomorrow in Chicago, and our families will need—"

"—nothing from you right now," Agent Stinson said mildly.

JAMES ANDERSON
NSA HEADQUARTERS, FORT MEADE, MARYLAND

". . . if we consider earthly creatures as 'brother' and 'sister,' why cannot we also speak of an 'extraterrestrial brother?'"

—FR . JOSÉ GABRIEL FUNES, FORMER DIRECTOR OF THE VATICAN OBSERVATORY

After they touched down in Washington, DC, James and Stan found themselves being led to a large black passenger van with three rows of seats. Once inside, they were told they were waiting for others. James sat calmly in the first row in the back of the van, studying his hands in his lap until the door opened and a man entered who, by his outfit, appeared to be a priest.

Strange, thought James.

The priest immediately seated himself in the front passenger seat, without a look or word to the others. As soon as the door closed, James took out his iPhone and began dialing a number. He glanced up at the priest, wondering what in the hell he was doing here. *Shit, he looks excited and happy to be here*, he thought. *Asshole.*

The office answered, and James spoke in a hushed tone, occasionally glancing at the priest.

"Look, I have to see to some obligations for the next few days, so . . . No, this is very important...Yep. Uh, a government contract, but that's all I can say. Like all of them, there is an NDA involved—No, no, no, no! Look, I've got to let you go. Call Serena. She has the necessary paperwork. Yeah, I'll make sure she gets the numbers...Right... Uh–huh...Bye."

"Bloody hell. It's about damn time," grumbled Stan, who was now sitting in the far back row of the van. "What do you think they would do to us if they caught you calling people? All you business types care about is your bank accounts."

"I'm sure they *are* listening. Seriously, it's the NSA," James replied. He'd had enough of Stan and his ego.

At this point, the priest tried to politely interrupt and introduce himself. "Hi there. I'm Father Mateo Perez."

James paid him no attention. "Look, Stan. I never imagined this research would cause this much trouble. I mean, it's a biological molecule. What does the government know about biology, for God's sake?" James said loudly, casting an uneasy glance at Father Perez.

Stan slammed his elbow into the seat. "I don't see why a molecule is all that important to the government either, damn it," he answered bitterly. "I didn't sign up for this NSA shit. I'm a professor. I'm not some soulless corporate leech who wants to see if he can still get money out of a deal gone south—"

James tensed and clenched his fists. "Look here, pal—I work over eighty hours a week to earn my paycheck. I pay my taxes on time and give to charity, so don't—"

"And there it is. It's *still* about the money to you. Really, you are a worthless son of a—"

"Stan! Get hold of yourself," James demanded.

The door opened just then, and a man in traditional Muslim garb holding a black hard-sided plastic case to his chest squeezed his way into the van.

"Who the hell are you?" Stan swore at the new addition to the group.

"Ah, yes, my apologies," the man said. "I'm Dr. Sati Am Unnefer."

"And why the bloody hell have you been invited to this party?" Stan spat.

"I, um, am the Egyptian Antiquities Minister," he responded humbly, as he put one of his hands into his chest pocket, reassuring himself that its contents were still present.

Silence fell on the vehicle for a moment as the five men studied one another carefully.

"Well, I'm James, and Stan is the one with the attitude problem in the back." James turned to the priest again. "I don't believe we have the pleasure of your name, sir."

"Father Mateo Perez, thank you for asking," the priest said, as if it were the first time he had announced it.

James could not place the thick accent. "Why would the NSA want a priest and an antiquities minister?" he asked.

"I wanted to come," Sati replied. "In fact, I demanded to follow these artifacts." He glanced at the case.

James and Stan looked at the man incredulously.

"You wanted to come?" scoffed Stan. "Who would want to be kidnapped by the NSA?"

"This is my life's work. What I have in this pack will alter our view of history," Sati said, hugging the case tightly. "Would you just watch your Secret Service agents drive away with your life's work before you even had a chance to look at it? That is what I was faced with."

"I understand," James said, his voice clear and bold.

"Are you here because you want to be, too, priest?" Stan snarled.

"Uh no," Father Perez chuckled. "Actually, I'm on official Vatican business. There is a briefing here, apparently, prior to my continuing on to Paris. I am an astronomer, normally. However, like any priest, I must do as the pope bids. His ways are not always ours," he added, looking nervously at the others.

Stan snorted. "Yes. Fine. As long as you don't try to convert me."

Father Perez cracked a half smile. "Believe me, I will do nothing to try to convert you."

Agent Lopez climbed into the driver's seat of the vehicle. Agent Stinson entered the back and sat next to James. "Gentlemen, let's do without the chitchat until we are safe at headquarters," he said.

They drove from BWI airport twenty minutes to Fort Meade, Maryland. The van parked in an expansive parking lot, a large portion of which was filled even at this late hour of the evening. Two huge connected rectangular-shaped buildings, one taller than the other and both as black as obsidian, rose from its center. The newcomers were shepherded toward the ominous-looking structure, and a sense of foreboding settled over them. The buildings appeared to absorb the light around them. For James, they looked like the monolith from the movie *2001: A Space Odyssey*: intimidating and solitary.

"Welcome to the NSA," Agent Stinson said, handing them all badges. Inside, the marble flooring was offset by walls covered in insignias and seals of the United States, the NSA, the Central Security Service, and other governmental agencies. Honorary lists with photos accentuated the walls, and a security desk stood alone in the center of the space.

Stan and James exchanged wide-eyed glances as they followed Stinson deep within the building, passing through several security checkpoints and secured corridors without stopping. Finally, they were ushered into a small conference room lit with a very bright fluorescent light.

After everyone took a seat at the table, Agent Stinson said, "Gentlemen, I understand your frustration, and I know it is late. However, very soon you will understand that you are at the center of a global security issue. One that demands your skills, ingenuity, and continued research, as well as your unwavering secrecy." He looked around the room, ensuring his words were having their intended impact. "We need all of you for continued research on a global security issue. Mr. Anderson, your journey ends here. You will be briefed today in regard to the NSA's sequester of the XNA technology. This project involves highly technical information of a scientific nature. Your company will be compensated for the time associated with the use of your research at XNA, and that research will be held confidential and proprietary. I'm having the documents assembled right now. An agent will go over the agreement with you and instruct you as to your and your company's obligations to this issue of national security. I'll have my assistant come and collect you so you can review the documents. We can discuss this in more detail later this evening—"

"Bullshit! I'm not leaving!" James said, with more emphasis than he'd intended. "I'm staying here with my scientific data and intellectual property. You tell me that there is some issue of national security; you kidnap me and Stan, hijack my jet, and steal my company's research when I have invested tens of millions of dollars into it; and now you want to continue with our research and kick me out. Are you out of your mind?"

"Mr. Anderson, calm down. I'm sure once I explain, you will understand—"

"To hell with *I'll understand*. I'll have my counsel on this within five minutes of leaving here. You can't just take my property and research. I'll blow this up in the blink of an eye in the press and in court unless you tell me what the hell is going on here."

Agent Stinson regarded him with a cold eye. "Mr. Anderson, we are the NSA. There is no real choice here. Please come with me, and we can discuss this privately."

"I'm not going anywhere without my intellectual property," James repeated, "and the same goes for Stan. I want answers, and I want them now. You can't threaten me that I have no choice. I know my rights. I know what we're onto with this research, and I have copies of all the data. I'll have this information published immediately. I'm not letting you lock down my company on some bullshit allegation of national security."

Just then the conference room doors opened, and a tall, serious man walked to the head of the table. Stinson immediately rose and said, "Sir." The man looked at James. "Mr. Anderson, I understand your concerns. Can you please come with me for five minutes where we can talk personally?"

It was clear he had observed the entire exchange from outside the room. Everyone looked at James. This caught James off-guard a bit. The man carried himself with the air of authority, his demeanor calm and collected.

"Who are you and why should I go anywhere with you without my attorney?" James said, conscious that his voice was now a little less commanding.

"I'm Mitchell Perkings, Director of the NSA," the man said firmly.

Everyone in the room became wide-eyed. The seriousness of the situation seemed to suddenly hit James. He slowly stood up and followed the director into a small adjacent conference room. The director pointed to a chair and sat beside James.

"I understand your reaction, Mr. Anderson," he said. "I do. But we really need your cooperation on this." He held James's glare.

In a more even tone, James replied, "I'm not relinquishing anything until I find out what's going on. This is our intellectual property, and I'm not just handing my data and research over to you and going home quietly. You need to understand—our chief scientist, my best friend, was killed because of this research. I'm not going anywhere."

The director studied James for a long time. He leaned back in his chair and inhaled deeply in contemplation for what seemed an eternity.

"Look, we need full cooperation," he finally said. "Understand this: You were not the chief scientist on the XNA project, and you add little here from an ongoing research perspective, which is what we need right now. You are way out of your league." He paused for a moment. "However, you are a chemical engineer with project-management experience. It's possible your deep knowledge of XNA, the history of its research, and your understanding of the findings could add some value. So I'm going to let you stay. But only as a courtesy and a convenience to me. Do you understand?"

James did not answer.

"Frankly, I want this information completely compartmentalized," Perkings went on. "It serves my interest to keep you within arm's reach and to ensure that no information about your findings gets out until I deem it appropriate. For this reason, I will allow you to continue with Project Aquarius." The director sat forward on his chair and leaned in close to James. "But you will cooperate. Not one word of this will go beyond these walls—no more talk of lawyers or press. Are we clear? Or I'll lock your ass up so fast your head will spin, and I'll park you in a cell where no one will know where you are until we figure out what in the hell we are dealing with here." He paused for a long moment.

Swallowing hard and trying not to betray the fear he felt, James nodded.

The director stood up, smiled, and shook his hand. "Besides, who knows?" he added pleasantly. "You may even add value."

James wasn't sure the director actually believed that. But he was grateful to not be on his way home.

He followed Perkings back to the main conference room. Agent Stinson stopped mid-sentence when they walked in, a puzzled look on his face.

James looked at him and said, "I'm staying." As he retook his seat, Stan looked at him with astonishment. James tried to smirk with a triumphant expression, projecting the impression that he'd negotiated his ability to stay. But he knew that was far from the truth. Deep down he had a nervous, sick feeling in his gut.

The director sat in the back of the room. "Continue, Agent Stinson," he said.

Stinson cleared his throat. "Make no mistake" he continued, "this is the single most daunting security concern we have ever faced. The United States and our partner nations will do anything to ensure that absolute secrecy is maintained. Nothing you have learned thus far, including in your own findings, nor anything you are going to learn from here forward can be shared outside of these walls.

"From this moment forward, you are all members of Project Aquarius. This will be your home for the time being, until we have the full international team assembled. At that time we will be moving to another location: Paris's European Space Agency headquarters.

"We do not mean to make you uncomfortable, but we need to make sure that you are not tempted to break our secrecy protocols. You will be allowed a short period of time after this meeting to call those whom you need to call who might miss you. You are to tell your families, friends, and business associates that you are consulting for the NSA regarding a hacking threat that concerns your domain of expertise. You will inform them that the matter is of eminent national security. Your presence will be required until the project is complete, which may take weeks to months."

The team shared exasperated looks.

"Months?" muttered Stan.

"We have drafted our standard consulting agreements," Stinson said, setting a contract before each of the men. He looked at James. "Mr. Anderson, your company will be directly contracted and compensated very handsomely for use of your research and the consulting services you will be providing. Professor, your university has already been notified of your required immediate absence," he said.

Everyone shifted uncomfortably and looked around, waiting for the others to react.

"Please be aware that in a few moments, when you make the calls necessary to modify any other commitments you may have over the next few weeks, we will be monitoring you. You will notice a delay between your communication and the person's response on the other end of the line. Should you say anything we deem inappropriate, the call will be disconnected.

"You will continue working with Project Aquarius until we deem that we have accomplished the goals of the project—at least as they pertain to your collective expertise. We have much to discuss, and a lot of information to equip you with. However, it is now 10:30 p.m., and it has already been a long day for most of you."

"Yeah, I spent the week sorting out important algorithms, had a meeting with a businessman, was kidnapped by the NSA, and had a flight on a hijacked jet to Washington," Stan interjected. "I would say that's more than enough."

As much as Stan had gotten on his nerves, James knew he could not have said it any better. "Dr. Caruthers," said Stinson, clearly losing his patience, "we can reengage in our banter tomorrow. I think you will change your point of reference once you hear what we have to say."

After everyone signed the documents—and there were a few more attempts by Stan to get more information on their situation—they were escorted to a hotel not far from the main NSA campus. It looked like a typical hotel on the outside, though James thought it odd that they entered a side entrance instead of passing through the main lobby.

"Everyone in," Stinson said, motioning to the freight elevator. Once they were all inside he entered a code on the keypad, and they began moving up. When they emerged, they were on the top floor. There was a small desk with a man and woman in military uniform standing beside it. Beside the desk was a locked, sliding-glass door that closed off the hallway.

"They will be checking in for the night," Stinson told the uniformed pair. "They are allowed to make calls for the next hour."

"I couldn't possibly notify everyone in the next hour," James groused. "I run a business. They are used to me constantly checking in."

Stinson inhaled deeply and frowned. "Two hours—and that is all, Mr. Anderson," he said.

"How cliché," James muttered when he noticed the man at the front desk was armed, with his hand resting on his gun.

"Brilliant," Stan said, looking around at the rest of the group. "This is literally unbelievable. I mean, seriously, even if you told this story to someone, who would believe it?"

"You have food in your room," Agent Stinson continued. "We will have fresh clothes delivered first thing in the morning. You will find that the bathrooms have all the necessary toiletries. I will collect you at 7:30 a.m."

"You know my size?" asked Stan.

"Of course," Agent Stinson replied simply.

Before leaving he added, "Please remember that all your communications will be monitored, and please limit your conversations. Also, you should avoid wandering around at night." With that, he bid them goodbye and left.

"You will find your rooms down the corridor," the woman spoke as the door slid open. "If you need anything, feel free to dial zero. An operator will assist you."

Each of them received what looked like a hotel keycard with a number on it as they walked past the desk and through the door.

Once the last of them entered the hallway, the glass door slid shut. Stan immediately jumped. James glanced backward at the door, but Father Perez, who had been accustomed to captivity, and Sati, who still clutched his black case, were unconcerned and continued to their rooms.

"Jesus," Stan said. "What the fuck is going on here? Now we're prisoners of our own government? I don't have time for this shit. I'm a fucking mathematics professor."

"Relax," said James. "There is clearly something of significance going on here. I'm sure we'll have a better understanding tomorrow."

"Well then, while you sorry bastards entertain yourselves with musings on 'something of significance,' I'm ordering up some beer," said Stan as he stomped off to his room, his long hair waving as he turned.

James was relieved to find that his suite had two bedrooms and a large living and dining area with a kitchenette. There was even a small buffet set out on the dining table, with more food than he could possibly eat. He smirked, wondering what Stan would do when he discovered he already had some cold beers waiting for him. He threw himself into one of the chairs, setting his laptop on the table.

A few minutes later, after he had downed a beer in an attempt to relax, he felt his head clear. Splitting them into their own suites had been a godsend. He hoped he wouldn't be working in close proximity with Stan tomorrow.

He pulled his cell phone from his pocket and pulled up "Home." *Here we go*, he thought. He knew the kids were waiting for his return, and he was already overdue. Kerri had dropped the kids off at his house with the nanny, Sonja, an older woman who had been indispensable to James since the divorce.

"Sonja, hi. It's me," he said when she picked up.

"Hi, how are you? The kids have been asking when you are coming home. Is everything okay?"

"Everything's fine but something has come up. And now I'm in DC on business."

"DC? I thought you were in California."

"Yeah, It's kind of a business emergency, if you will. So, here's the deal, I'm going to be stuck here for the next couple weeks."

"Oh, no. The kids are going to be so disappointed," Sonja said.

"I know, yeah. I'll have to call Kerri and make arrangements. Until then, I'll need you to take care of them for me."

"Well, of course."

"You know you can call my mother too. She'll help you out if you need it." He felt a deep stab of guilt. "Who's still up? I'd like to talk to them if they're nearby."

"Only Allen is still awake."

"Great, I'll talk to him," James said. Allen was his oldest, and they had always had a bit of a strained relationship. Probably because James had been gone so much when Allen was younger.

"Hey, Dad. What's up?" Allen said, a yawn in his voice.

"Hey, pal. Are you guys having a good time?"

"Yeah. They're all in bed. When are you going to be home?"

"Well, I have some bad news. Really crappy news. I'm stuck in DC on an emergency. I'm not going to be back in town for a couple weeks. We're going to have to reschedule our plans. So I'm going to have to call your mom and make arrangements to have you guys picked up again."

"Paris for two weeks and now this?" Allen flared out. "You said you were going to do something fun with us, like go to the beach. This is bullshit."

"Hey, don't say that," James began. The phone disconnected.

Crap, thought James, *that went well.* Guilt weighed heavily upon him.

After leaving a few business voicemails, he tried to find something to eat and opened his third beer. He felt even more alone than he had in Paris. Even if he hadn't called and rearranged his schedule, he wondered if anyone would have noticed or cared, other than his kids. *Shit.*

It's always something. He knew all the kids were going to be upset. He missed them so badly already that his heart ached. Not being able to tell them the real reason he was here only made it worse.

Depression suddenly weighing down on him he walked toward the bedroom with the king-sized bed and closed the door.

A few minutes later there was a heavy knock on James's door. It was Stan, a sandwich in one hand and a pillowcase full of beers in another.

"What are you doing here? They told us to stay in our rooms," James said in an irritated manner when he answered the door.

"Poppycock," Stan said, stepping past him through the doorway. "They have us locked in so tight, what's the big deal? After all, they said they needed us. So, I'm not sitting and drinking beer in my room alone. I'm not rude, though, so I brought my own." He raised his clinking pillowcase and stepped through the door. "Honestly, I wish I could thank Robert for getting me involved with this bullshit. I'd tell him this is more than I bargained for. I was just trying to help you out—and now I'm stuck here as a prisoner with Mr. Capitalist." He flailed his arms about, casting crumbs and bits of lettuce from his sandwich around the room.

"You know, Stan, sometimes you can really be a dick," James said in disgust. "Robert was killed for this shit. Just relax. Nobody asked for this. Hey, don't forget, you're the government asset here! Shit—I'm just as frustrated." He walked over to the ice bucket to grab a beer for himself.

After a few minutes of silence, he continued. "You know, you really need to step back for a minute, man. Stop reacting and think. I know you're good at that. We already knew we were onto something extraordinary. My guess is that the NSA knows more than we can imagine. I'm actually very interested in hearing what's to come tomorrow. Who knows? Maybe they can shed some light on our discoveries."

Stan finished his sandwich and thoughtfully removed two more beers for himself from his pillowcase, popped the tops, and sat down heavily in the chair next to James. "Ehh, you're probably right," he said. "I know you're right. I just don't like being told what to do, where to go, when to use the loo."

There was a long pause and some tension in the room seemed to ease. "So did you make your calls, Mr. Jet Boy?" He smirked, pointing at James with his beer. "Family and all, I assume?"

James felt uncomfortable. "Ah. Yes. The kids," James said uncomfortably.

"No wife?" said Stan, rummaging in his pillowcase for a bag of potato chips.

"Try this on for size," James spat. "Four kids, married for nearly two decades, and she decided to fuck the tennis coach." Immediately he wished he hadn't said it. But it stopped Stan in his tracks.

"Shit," Stan said, his smile vanishing. "Sorry, mate." He handed James a beer and the two men drank in silence.

* * *

At 7:30 sharp the next morning, James was fumbling with the hotel-grade, one-cup coffeemaker when Agent Stinson knocked at the door and let himself into his suite.

"I hope you slept well. We have a long day planned," Stinson said. "You have about thirty minutes to meet me in the hallway." With that, he was gone before James could say anything to him.

There was another knock. James waited a few moments, expecting the agent to let himself in again, but after the second knock, he went to open the door. Stan slowly stumbled into the room.

"We ready? Let's get this over with. Do you have any Advil in here?" he said, pushing past James.

"I haven't even had my coffee yet," James said, closing the door as Stan made himself at home on the couch.

"Detestable habit. You should really switch to tea," replied Stan. "Did you know I have a gym in one spare room and an office in the other? This is fucking amazing. I can't believe they spend our tax dollars on this. The ham-and-egg omelet was actually pretty good," he yawned.

"Breakfast?" James asked.

"Yeah, you know, room service." Stan smiled.

James raised his eyebrows and went to the phone to dial. Stan snorted in disgust.

They hurried out to the hall shortly after James finished eating, and found Agent Stinson, Father Perez, and Sati already waiting.

"Well, if I had known you guys were throwing a party, we would have all come," Stinson said, frowning at them. "Let's go."

Back at the complex, they wound themselves through NSA headquarters once again. This time, James took careful mental notes on everything he saw. The building was even more daunting and prison-like after a good night's sleep.

They were ushered through more security checkpoints. Today, they exited the elevator on the top floor of the building and walked down a long hallway to a door with another security device. Stinson placed his palm on the pad beside the door, and after the pad beeped, he typed in a code.

"Fucking James Bond," Stan muttered. James smirked in spite of himself.

"Okay, guys, this will be one of the rooms where you will be working," Stinson aid. "You each need to place your palm here and have it scanned. And remember, as long as you're visiting, always wear those red-striped cards." The cards had a large yellow "V" printed on them.

After everyone's hands were scanned, they entered the room. It was very large and filled with computer servers, file cabinets, and dark, one-way tinted glass that overlooked the parking lot. Several other people, including Agent Lopez, were already hard at work in cubicles on the side of the room.

"Gentlemen," Stinson said, over the hum of the servers, "this will be your office and lab until further notice. All of the NSA resources for Project Aquarius are at hand." He waved his arm around the room. "Agent Lopez and I are at your disposal to ensure that you have all the equipment, resources, and expert advice that you may need to continue your research here. The XNA Company servers have been replicated here, so your work is on that terminal." He pointed to a bank of servers in the corner. "We have team members analyzing the sequence as we speak. All the necessary equipment, including a DNA sequencer, are provided for continued research with our team of biochemists, although our main focus is on the code identified by Dr. Matson and what the hell it is. If there are other items, resources, or personnel that would aid in your research or the expediency of your results, they will be provided.

"Father Perez, the Vatican is now a partner of Project Aquarius. Based upon our cooperation with the Holy See, you will have access to any information or database you need. You will find a reproduction of your Mount Graham files on this terminal.

"And Dr. Unnefer, you have a team over there and the table space to do your work on the tablets. Also, we have appointed one of our men as your assistant. He is an expert in hieroglyphs, and originally from Egypt as well." The man glared at Sati coldly. He was older than Sati, short but fit with graying short hair. His brow was heavily lined.

Stinson exited the room with everyone in tow. He led them further down the hallway, stopping outside a large conference room and motioning for them to follow him inside. Once inside, James was surprised with the quality of the furnishings. The conference table was solid walnut and there was a matching credenza along the wall. The chairs were Herman Miller Aeron chairs. The computer system and audio/video system were all state-of-the-art. The entire back wall of the conference room was an LCD screen running from floor to ceiling.

"More of my tax dollars at work," James grumbled to himself.

"Let's get started, gentlemen," said Agent Stinson. Everyone took a seat, with the exception of James. He walked over to the credenza and poured himself a cup of coffee, making sure to take his time.

"Would anyone else like some?" James asked after he had taken a sip.

"Oh, why not?" Stan sighed. "This looks like it might take awhile."

Sati declined. James noticed he was still clutching his case, and wondered if he had slept with it.

Despite his air of confidence, James had not slept well. He hoped the dark shadows under his eyes didn't betray him. He set his coffee down and took a seat.

Once they were settled, Agent Stinson passed out a small binder to each of them.

"Gentlemen, this is a brief overview of what each of you have discovered," Stinson stated. "Please take a moment to review it, and then we will discuss it together. I'll be back in thirty minutes."

They each read the ten-page binder, forming their own opinions about what was mentioned. When Stinson finally came back to the room, the tone of the meeting had changed dramatically: everyone was talking loudly and excitedly asking questions of one another.

"Yes. The excavation revealed three books of gold," Sati was saying. As Stinson entered, his eyes flashed over at the agent and his grip on the case tightened. "They are inscribed with hieroglyphs unknown to Egyptology on their covers and evidence an advanced construction and technology. I invited the Americans into the excavation. And how was I repaid? They tried to steal these from me." He said, squeezing the case. "Had I not threatened the president directly that I would go public with a claim that an Islamic artifact had been found during the excavation and stolen by the Americans, I would likely not be here with these books that rightfully belong to Egypt's people."

"Seems to be a lot of that going around," James muttered.

"What's the meaning of the hieroglyphs on these books, doctor?" Stan asked.

"We do not know, but some of the markings we have identified as ancient Sumerian," Sati stated. "These markings roughly translate into the word *Wisdom*."

"Let's see the books," James said.

Sati hesitated for a moment and surveyed the others. Then, very carefully, he unpacked the books and placed them on the table where everyone could scrutinize their perfect form and dimensions. They appeared to be solid gold, but were much lighter anyone than expected.

James was awestruck. He remained quiet, observing as the others all began speaking at once. *Why would the NSA be bringing this group of researchers together?* he wondered.

As the last of them finished looking at the books and sat back in their seats, Agent Stinson addressed them.

"The presence of the anomaly in the DNA code is difficult to comprehend," he said. "We understand that the question of why or how it got there is of utmost importance, so this is what we seek to answer first.

"Here is what we have, gentlemen. The first civilization on Earth, the Sumerians, encoded the location of these gold books on ancient stone tablets that they described as the Ascension Testaments. These stone tablets, I'm told by Father Perez, speak about the creation of man, and therefore may open up more information on this DNA anomaly."

"What are these markings on the tablets?" Stan asked.

"They appear to be some kind of star chart," Sati said.

"What do you think about that, Father?" Stinson asked, Father Perez.

"Yes, it appears to be some sort of star chart," the priest said. "This chart matches charts from ancient Sumerian tablets within the Vatican archives. We have determined that this is Virgo, with Jupiter and Mars here. We believe this is the sun, and this the moon." He paused for a moment.

"What do you mean by Virgo?" James asked. "The constellation?"

"The constellation of the zodiac, yes."

"You mean like the Virgin Mary?" James asked.

"Correct. Anyway, this star map and these ancient stone tablets tell tales of great cataclysms. It is something my fellow Catholics interpret as Armageddon."

Everyone sat quietly, absorbing what the priest had said.

James sensed that there was more to the story; it looked to him as if Perez wanted to say more but had decided against it.

"Look at this, gentlemen." Stinson stood and organized the gold books in a row. A sound like two magnets attracting each other occurred as each book connected to the next. Down the middle of all three books was now a single large glyph, made up of two snakes twisted around each other.

"Oh my God," James said, realization hitting him. "The snakes on the books are twisted like a strand of DNA."

"Right. Which brings us back to our principal enigma." Stinson walked over to the LCD wall and touched one of the file images projected on it. On the screen, DNA microarray imaging software launched, and the sequence that Robert had identified appeared. "It is our opinion, both within Project Aquarius and among a few NSA cryptologists who have analyzed the sequence, that this is statistically impossible as a biological anomaly. In their view, it cannot be a natural occurrence. A random DNA mutation would not have found its way into every human's chromosomes with this unique pattern. We believe that these books and the DNA pattern are connected, and may provide information on the origin of mankind."

"Well," Stan interjected, "even incidents with relatively small probabilities can occur, but I agree that it was most likely deliberately inserted into our DNA—but it could be a random insertion. Goodness knows we have seen very odd things when we've studied nature."

"And what do you mean by that, professor?" asked Stinson.

"Agent Stinson, I'm really not interested in wasting my time while you play coy. The bottom line is that this is either random or something that was engineered by an intelligent source. You called on us to work this out for you; my input is that we need every scientist in the world to see this data, and soon. I say we share this, so the work can be corroborated and expanded."

"Professor, you have just given two possible answers to this riddle. One is that it is just random. What would be the point of exciting the entire scientific community—or worse, the general public—about a random occurrence?"

"The scientific community thrives on collaboration," Stan countered. "Excitement over the questions this sequence presents is precisely what we need."

"That may be the case. If this is simply a naturally occurring phenomena, then the scientific community is more than welcome to have the information. However, should your second hypothesis hold true—that it has been intentionally placed into our DNA structure—think of the incredible impact on society. It would challenge our fundamental views of life as we know it. Everything here, including those books, supports this conclusion."

Agent Stinson held Stan's gaze. "Do you seriously expect us to just present this information publicly? It would be socially irresponsible. Surely you must acknowledge that you cannot just make the statement that everyone has some form of a foreign marker in their DNA. What would you say about it? 'Well, it may be nothing, folks, but it could have been put there by a god or an alien creator.' You would disrupt civilization on Earth irreparably in an instant.

"Until we understand what we are dealing with, *and* decide that the world is ready for whatever information we find, it will remain above-top-secret in its classification. After the President of the United States and the member nations of Project Aquarius have been fully briefed, no public comment will occur. Now, Dr. Caruthers, we have more important items to cover today. Sitting here and arguing about something that isn't a real choice is a waste of our time."

"I don't see disruption as bad," Stan shot back. "It encourages growth. I also don't see why it isn't a choice. Isn't America a democracy?" demanded Stan. "You cannot restrain the truth. People have a right to know about this, and should know, damn it! This isn't Plato's Republic here. We shouldn't be holding back this information."

"You're sounding a bit like a reasonable libertarian here, Stan," James chimed in. "Mind you don't betray Karl Marx, now."

Stan threw him a glare.

"Professor Caruthers is on step forty. I am trying to prepare you for step one," Stinson told them. "If any of this information gets out before we fully understand what we are dealing with, immediate turmoil will ensue. Financial markets could collapse, fundamental religious tenets would be challenged, and many other institutions could be threatened with invalidation and violence. We—"

"World War III could break out," Sati said softly.

They all turned and stared at the Egyptologist. He was staring out the window into the sky. Suddenly, he realized everyone was looking at him and flushed.

"The bottom line," Stinson continued, "is that we have an obligation to fully understand these matters *first*. Let the people who were elected to lead the nations of the world decide if and when this information is provided to their people."

"I understand the need to verify a hypothesis first—probably more than you do!" challenged Stan. "I'm not suggesting we go running to *TIME* magazine with the latest gossip, or even our assumptions. I just believe that if scientifically verifiable evidence is obtained, we should provide it to the scientific community in peer-reviewed journals for validation and further research."

Stinson pursed his lips, clearly, he was fighting the urge to throttle Dr. Caruthers. There was a long pause while he attempted to regain his composure.

James glowered at Stan, "Stan, shut the hell up and let's get on with this," he said.

"That isn't necessary, Mr. Anderson," Stinson said in a soft voice. "Professor Caruthers, you mistakenly believe this is an issue open for discussion. It is not. I don't have the luxury, or the burden, of making this decision, nor is it open for your interpretation. You can continue arguing with me as long as you like, but for every minute you continue, you will be keeping this information from the others for that much longer in the end. We will proceed exactly as I explained last night. You will not breathe a word of this finding to anyone outside of this room. If there is any breach of this policy," he added, and paused again, sternly looking at each of them in the eye, "you will not like the ramifications." The conviction in his tone ended the argument. The seriousness of this threat was palpable. It startled more than Dr. Caruthers. Stinson began to pace. "I'm going to resume now," he said, his tone decisive. "I am the lead on Project Aquarius inside the NSA. As some of you know, there are counterparts from several nations' security organizations that basically occupy the same role I do. This particular NOC, or network operations center, is not the only one. There are five additional locations across the globe..."

17

POPE PAUL VII
THE VATICAN

"Very soon we will not have to deny our Christian faith, but there is infor-mation coming from another world, and once it is confirmed it is going to require a re-reading of the Gospel as we know it."

—FR . GIUSEPPE TANZELLI – NITTI, JESUIT PRIEST

AS HE HAD BEEN INSTRUCTED, Father Perez contacted the pope when he had joined the Project Aquarius team. He informed the pope about the findings regarding the golden books and the DNA anomaly. "It appears, your Eminence, they know very little of either. I think there is a lot of research to be done before we have any answers."

"I understand," the pope replied. "Unfortunately, we don't have much time. Father Perez, you need to understand that things far bigger than you or I are playing out here. These things have been spoken of in prophecy. These findings were recorded in ancient scriptures. Remember your oath to me, to the order: you cannot share with anyone at the NSA or within Project Aquarius what we know."

"I understand," Father Perez muttered, reluctantly. "I can tell you, Holy Father, that they know of the star map, but not its significance. It does not appear to be a focus of the team's research at this time."

"Good. Do what you can to keep it that way. We need these books and the information regarding the DNA findings. We need to know what information they hold; it's information that the Vatican must control. Keep me informed of their progress, Father Perez. Your service will be rewarded."

The pope hung up the phone. He dialed another phone number. "It is time. I have a job for you," he said.

DR . SATI AM UNNEFER
FORT MEADE, MARYLAND

For the stars of heaven and the constellations thereof shall not give their light: the sun shall be darkened in his going forth, and the moon shall not cause her light to shine.

—ISAIAH 13:10

Back at the hotel, Sati sipped a glass of water. James, Stan, and Father Perez awaited an explanation for the invitation to his suite this evening, but it had been long in coming.

Sati sighed. In some ways, Dr. Zaher had been correct. He was sure his country would receive none of the benefits of this information, and that it would eventually come back to haunt him. As it had so many times, his hand went into his pocket to finger the mysterious metal drive he'd found in the hidden files. He had seen the pictures on this drive, but he would say nothing. Sati did not feel he could trust anyone associated with the U.S. side of this investigation; they'd already tried to run off with these relics.

When he finally spoke, it was with delicacy. "I just felt we should get to know each other better," he said. "We will be working together for a while. It seems that you two know each other, but Father Perez and I are alone. Also, it seems I have been further singled out and given an assistant. I think that was the person who was supposed to do my job."

"What are you talking about?" Stan said. "If you are going to stand here and talk some sort of sentimental garbage, the least you could do is offer us some beer."

Sati was a bit startled. "I am Muslim. We do not drink."

"Too bad for you." Stan walked over to the phone and pressed the now all-too-familiar number zero. "Yes, we want a case of Samuel Adams," he said into the phone. "Please note: we are supporting the American economy with this order." He hung up the phone.

"I know I don't belong," Sati said sadly.

"Well, then, drink some beer and get it over with. It should be here soon."

Sati sighed.

"Professor!" Father Perez chided. "I'm sure the young man is simply overwhelmed. It can happen to anyone. In fact, I'd wager that even *you* have found yourself in over your head on at least one occasion."

"Oh, stuff it, priest—"

There was a knock on the door, and Stan went to get it.

"That guy is a real ass sometimes," James said to Sati under his breath. "I think this is all too much for him. If truth be told, I think he has been an ass his whole life, but he is the best in his field. And the situation is not exactly helping his attitude." James walked over to the table with Stan to grab some food.

"I think they are going to kill me," Sati said quietly, looking at Father Perez.

"Now, then, you don't have to drink with them," Father Perez said good-naturedly. "Soon they will be too far gone to remember. And Stan may be a rather rude gentleman, but I think he just hasn't spent much time with people."

"I am not talking about them—I am talking about those who tried to blow me up." Sati tilted his head toward the door. "Those books—someone wants them badly, and they're willing to kill me to get them. I'm probably safest here. For whatever reason, I feel I can trust you, because we are all facing the same ordeal."

The priest raised his eyebrows.

"Even my assistant today, who is Egyptian, chided me on allowing the Americans to steal the artifacts of our homeland. He discussed the coming Islamic caliphate and said I have betrayed Islam. I feel I have enemies all around me." He leaned over to Father Perez. "If something—happens, I want you to find out what this is." He pulled the flash drive out and showed it quickly to the priest before returning it to his pocket.

"What is that?" Father Perez asked.

"I don't know. But I have reason to believe it relates to all this. There are photographs of tablets with more Sumerian markings found inside the Great Pyramid. I found all of it hidden, by Zaher. I'm keeping this to myself for now. I need leverage with these Americans." Sati looked down at his hands. "I don't feel like I owe them anything. I do not want the Americans to run off with what I have, as they did with the tablets. I want to find out what these golden books say before giving them this. This may be the one bargaining chip I have to get the golden books and other stolen artifacts back to Egypt where they belong. After what I have been through, I do not trust any Americans. You don't have to stay with me." He looked sadly at Father Perez. "Go drink beer with them if you want."

Father Perez shook his head. "Just an occasional amaretto for me," he laughed. "I think we are going to work well together."

Sati smiled for the first time since the texts had been recovered.

FATHER MATEO PEREZ
FORT MEADE, MARYLAND

Speaking with the pope had done nothing to put Father Perez at ease with his commitment to the Vatican. Each conversation seemed to further cement in his mind that something was wrong. *If the Vatican has knowledge of a cataclysm and could release that information and potentially save millions of lives—or at least give them a chance—what is to gain by keeping it secret?* The riddle vexed him. It was as if the Vatican, the pope, or the Jesuit Order were attempting to use this information to their advantage, to seek dominion on the other side of this tribulation to come.

Father Perez's mind drifted back to the history of the Order that he had read about years ago but never thought applicable until today. When they were expelled from many of the civilized nations on the planet, they just went underground, continuing their work in secret Samuel Morse had even stated, "The Jesuits are a secret society—a sort of Masonic order—with super-added features of revolution odiousness and a thousand times more dangerous." Abraham Lincoln had said that the American Civil War "would never have been possible without the sinister influence of the Jesuits." John Adams, too, had expressed his hatred of the order, saying, "The Jesuit Order's restoration in 1814 by Pope Pius VII is indeed a step toward darkness, cruelty, despotism, and death . . . If ever there was a body of men who merited eternal damnation on earth and in hell, it is this Society of Ignatius de Loyola."

Perez knew that the Jesuit Order had been closely aligned with the fascist movement of the early 20th century. The Order had backed Hitler, who'd modeled his SS regime after the Order's founding principles. It was even suspected that Jesuit priest Father Bernhardt Stempfle had penned *Mein Kampf* for Hitler.

Father Perez recalled the strange oath he had taken for the Jesuit Order. At the time he'd chalked it up to tradition, but some of the recitations now sounded particularly nefarious: ". . . all information for the benefit of your order as a faithful soldier of the pope . . . to take sides with the combatants and to act secretly with your brother Jesuit."

He felt as if he were being used—not for his academic abilities, but to keep secrets for the sole benefit of the order for some unseen future conquest or rise to power.

The pope's recent comments echoed the dark historic descriptions that had been given to the Jesuits by so many world leaders. Father Perez knew that the pope was on the verge of a schism; with his incredible doctrinal changes, one could understand why. He had called for a one-world government, a one-world monetary system; he was forcing global migration to eradicate nation-states. The thought exhausted Perez; as a priest, he was not in the game of politics, and he certainly did not appreciate being one of its pawns.

A cataclysm to come; a tribulation. It brought to mind another strange piece in the puzzle: another seemingly ridiculous historical note—ridiculous, at least, until now. He recalled that the Prophecy of St. Malachy, penned more than 600 years ago, contained visions prophesying that the biblical Judgment would begin during the reign of the 112th pope. The prophecy had precisely described each pope—leading up to the last. Pope Paul was the 112th.

It had gained much media attention several years ago, especially when lightning struck St. Peter's Basilica at the moment Pope Benedict resigned; no pope had resigned in over six hundred years. *And with that bolt of lightning the 112th pope was ushered in,* Perez thought. The prophecy concluded that the final pope would "feed his flock amid many tribulations, after which the seven-hilled city will be destroyed, and the dreadful Judge will judge the people."

Father Perez could no longer discount prophecies like this one. He knew what was to come.

MARIA ZORIN
FORT MEADE, MARYLAND

No one noticed the small drone that flew over the northwest gate off Patuxent Freeway. Maria Zorin had just arrived in Fort Meade,

Maryland and soon connected with the small cell operating in DC arranged by Khalid. She had to get this right. No more failures. She knew what happened to people who failed.

Khalid had been feeding her intel and connecting her with his associates as she moved across the U.S. He was disappointed with the high-profile murder of Dr. Matson; no information was gained. "You get me the XNA data or those golden books. We need them now," he demanded.

Khalid had explained his plan to Zorin in detail; his team was assembled and ready to execute the instructions. It was a bold plan—and dangerous. Despite being the epicenter of American intelligence and information gathering, it was fairly simple to obtain forged delivery credentials. And although the building was shrouded in many levels of security, the parking lot was not: it was encircled by a single chain-link fence. That was as far as they needed to go.

Zorin maneuvered the drone around the outer perimeter of the parking lot. Its tiny frame had been outfitted with a camera that was streaming video to a white van parked at the Shell station beside the National Cryptologic Museum. This section of Fort Meade had heavy civilian and visitor traffic. No one bothered to question a van in the parking lot behind a gas station.

The trees obfuscated the drone as it cleared the gates. It carefully recorded the current layout of all the parked cars, and where security was stationed today. The two Arab men with her had spent the last three days at the Marriott Courtyard less than two miles from the NSA compound, preparing for today.

Once they had recorded all they needed, Zorin nodded. "That should do it," she said. "Let's get back to the hotel to map this out. If all goes according to plan, we are going to just grab the package. If this doesn't work, we will need to be prepared to get out quickly and meet up with the transfer vehicles."

Outside the Courtyard, she checked all the equipment in the van, ensuring the weapons were loaded and functioning properly. She barked at one of the men, "Get over here and check the mountings on this tripod. They do not look secure."

An M2 Browning .50-caliber machine gun had been bolted to the floor of the van with half-inch stainless-steel bolts. As the men retrieved a tool to tighten the bolts, she loaded the ammo belt into the gun and chambered a round. All was set.

JAMES ANDERSON
FORT MEADE, MARYLAND

For the past several days the team had been working inside of NSA headquarters. Their charge was to attempt to decrypt the DNA code and learn what they could about the tablets. As they understood it, they would be assembling with a larger team soon; for now, the pace of work was breakneck. Stinson continually pressured them for results—but so far, there had been little progress.

James had found their in-depth briefings on Project Aquarius fascinating. Ruins on Mars, a vast database of UFO contacts, an escalation in their presence on Earth—it was terrifying and exhilarating at the same time. He coveted more information on these topics, wondering what connection they had to these tablets and to the DNA found inside of him, his children—everyone. There was a bigger puzzle here to solve.

"Gentlemen, you are nearly complete with your briefings," Stinson told them when they'd assembled for the day. "I know it is a lot of information to absorb. But we wanted to outfit you with as much knowledge as we could in effort to connect all of these dots. And when you assemble with the rest of Project Aquarius, you will be on equal footing as far as background information goes.

"Today I want to introduce you to someone within the program. William Clodfelter is with NASA. He will provide more information regarding the UFO phenomenon. Bill—"

"Good morning," the strange newcomer said stiffly. As though on cue, Agent Stinson retreated from the room. "The information I'm going to provide today is only known by a small group of people on this planet. Today you are going to learn about the Gemini and Apollo missions—and the observed presence of extraterrestrial craft."

The presentation continued for an hour. At the conclusion, James's palms were sweating. He excused himself to the restroom. For several minutes he stared in the mirror. It was one thing to hear of UFO sightings, but learning that his childhood had heroes observed craft on the moon put the phenomenon in a much more real context—a threatening context.

When James returned to the room, he noticed that Stan was absent. He sat down quietly and waited with the others until Stan finally stormed through the door.

"How is it possible?" Stan said, his voice almost pleading. "These landings were televised. Thousands of people heard the audio. How could something this big have been covered up?"

Mr. Clodfelter paused and licked his lips. "As I said, we switched to secret frequencies immediately," he said. "At the time, the public didn't even know the digital sub-channels existed. The Soviets were listening, of course, but they were just as willing as we were to cover it up. Their astronauts had also experienced unusual things when beyond our atmosphere. We didn't openly share our information with them, but we were willing to reach an agreement about what was done with any information each of us found out from the other. Preventing unwanted public reactions and panic became our common cause."

"But there had to be leaks," Stan challenged.

"Yes, there were some things that made it into the public arena. For this incident, with the help of the NSA, we modified all the audio broadcasts before we released them to the public. By stripping out any information or code dialogue associated with our sightings, we were able to keep the public in the dark. The NSA revised everything—even then they had the technology to properly modify the audio. However, it became common knowledge that they'd made a mistake. They forgot about the time delay that would occur. Even NASA initially missed this, so once they went live, several physicists began to question them."

"What do you mean by time delay?" asked James.

"Well, radio waves travel at the speed of light, or around 300,000 kilometers per second. The distance from the earth to the moon is around 384,404 kilometers. This means that if I radio, 'Come in Apollo' from Mission Control, the transmission will reach the surface of the moon 1.258 seconds after I actually said it. Now, say that Apollo immediately answered, which is unlikely—there would be another 1.258-second delay in the audio for the response to reach the earth. In the audio tape, a complete communication would have a gap between question and answer of at least 2.51 seconds. The audio that was released to the public initially only had a gap of 1.07 seconds, like in a normal conversation here on Earth or radio conversations between Earth-based transmitters and receivers. We totally missed it." Clodfelter sighed. "Last year, some smart-ass from Purdue University identified this problem and posted it on his blog. Luckily, it didn't garner much attention, and we are now trying to contain the information. We gathered as much of the original audio as we could. But it's still out there. Honestly, those who possess originally released audio could prove it was a fraud. I mean, it really is a danger." Mr. Clodfelter opened his briefcase again and dug out a folder before continuing.

"The problem is that, as more of our staff gets older and retires, more information is released," he said. "Now, some of our own astronauts are starting to switch loyalties. Since a few of them have begun to believe that the public has the right to know, they have been telling the accounts of their own experiences. They have done this despite their security and confidentiality obligations, and in the face of very direct threats from the CIA. Some of these people I worked with for years, including my old friend Maurice Chatelain, who was Chief of NASA Communications Systems. He was a good guy, but once he went public with information about an alien presence on the moon, the CIA had no choice but to discredit him. This dossier," he said, waving the small file folder, "is the account of all the leaks."

James thought Clodfelter seemed almost repentant as he tossed the file on the table. It was clear that the discoveries were profound for him.

On one hand, he seemed to hold those leaking information as brave men, willing to ruin themselves to come forward; on the other, he felt the pain of not being able to keep these men in the fold of secrecy.

James felt his initial fear slowly morphing into wonder. He was used to making decisions based on available information that may or may not be correct, and had spent years reading between the lines of financial statements, past performance statistics and the misinformation businesses put out in efforts to get buyers to sink more money into them than what they were worth. In this case, it was clear to him that they were in the presence of game-changing facts. Stan, he could tell, was approaching the experience very differently; his analytical mind was clearly challenging the new reality from every angle. James knew it would take more objective, testable evidence to make Stan accept the things they'd heard, and the contrast to his own mood fascinated him.

James continued to look around the table, reading the other members of the group the NSA had chosen to toss together. Sati acted as if he was receiving confirmation for something he had believed his whole life. Father Perez looked bored, but perhaps he was just doing his best to retain a meditative façade.

Clodfelter finally cleared his throat and continued. "After Armstrong, Collins, and Aldrin returned, we interviewed each of them separately to discern their impressions," he said. "All three said they'd felt threatened. Our astronauts believed the crafts they saw were warning us to stay off of the moon.

"The problem was that we had already been building rockets and training astronauts for nine more Apollo missions. What could we do? We had to continue the missions. Apollo 18, 19, and 20 were all scrapped within six months of Armstrong's first step. But we had to continue with the missions that were already underway. We did not want people questioning why we had wasted all the time and money to get to the moon, only to abandon all the later missions. Imagine how the public would have reacted if we'd failed to finish those well-publicized flights!

"So we carried on. Each trip became more and more dangerous.

When Apollo 13 was about to land, we believe the craft was intentionally disabled. We thought we were done there. We canceled the next launch and told the public we needed to learn what went wrong, as if we didn't know." Clodfelter snorted. "The outcry was so great, though, that we were put under pressure to launch again. We tried to avoid the ships as best we could when planning landing sites. We plotted missions to avoid areas where previous encounters had occurred, and tiptoed through until we launched Apollo 17. This time, the warnings were more aggressive; the craft followed the module and emitted painful bursts of light that our astronauts saw even if they closed their eyes. It was worse on the moon, and it conveniently slacked on the way home. It was clear we were not wanted there.

"I think this speaks to the urgency of our situation, gentlemen," he concluded. "We are now seeing an increase of activity and a presence on Earth—tenfold—that we have every reason to believe is hostile to us."

Everyone around the table stared at him in awe.

"Surely you must have wondered why, in all these years, we have not returned to the moon?" he said, one eyebrow rising. "Why we try to keep our astronauts as close to Earth as possible? I mean, we have had the International Space Station in orbit since 1998. None of you ever wondered why we were orbiting our own planet instead of the moon?" Bill shook his head and grumbled. "The public is nothing but cattle, it seems. Well, gentlemen, we have the technology. Shit, we could have had a moon base of our own thirty years ago. In fact, some people think that was why the Soviets launched Salyut in the '70s—they were going to orbit the moon and use it to build a base there. But they were not welcome either, and they knew they couldn't go up against the technology that was already there.

"We developed our Star Wars program in response to this perceived threat, not because of the Russians. The Russians deployed a similar defense system. We each used nuclear defense as a cover story, but in reality that was when we started collaborating with the Russians."

"But Star Wars was Reagan's thing," James interjected. "I thought we gave that up a long time ago. If we felt that threatened, why didn't we continue with the program?"

"We never gave it up. It's still out there," Clodfelter said. "Only it's gone through several upgrades as we have gained more technology. Each time, we would change its name to something a little less noticeable and a little less newsworthy. This is where part of the five trillion dollars the Pentagon is missing went. Perhaps you heard about that on the news."

Stan still looked frustrated. "How can so many astronauts have this type of information and word not get out? Are we as a nation threatening them and their families?"

Bill held his glare for an instant, then responded in a measured tone. "Well, we have stressed that this is an issue of national security. Yes, I guess you could call them threats. The bottom line here, Professor Caruthers, is that we are attempting to prevent mass hysteria. We need to learn more about the situation first. Your DNA finding and these books only raise the stakes.

"That being said, we have done a terrible job containing this information. In my opinion, we should have been more forceful with what you call our threats. As it stands, we have had several staff and astronauts come forward with this information." He began to walk around the table. "Christopher Kraft, former director of the Johnson Space Center, told the media in recent years that during the Apollo 11 mission 'there were other spaceships on the moon.' Can you believe it? The director! I mean, this guy created NASA's Mission Control operations and was the flight director on all the Mercury missions, for God's sake." Clodfelter rubbed his forehead. "It's amazing his claims have not caused a sensation. No one really paid attention or believed him, I guess.

"Likewise, our celebrity astronauts, Buzz Aldrin and Neil Armstrong, have caused problems. Armstrong, on several occasions, stated in private conversations after a cocktail or two that he'd witnessed spacecraft on the moon watching the astronauts' movements Unfortunately, he went further and relayed, to his listeners, his belief that the and others had been 'warned off' the moon. You see, the race to the moon was initially a very real proxy for the Cold War; we wanted to gain a military advantage and secure the moon. Apollo was a military expedition.

"One such conversation was with a U.S. senator, who called and gave us hell for not releasing this information. Armstrong frightened the senator, apparently describing the ships as 'huge and menacing . . . superior in technology and size to ours.' We had to have Nixon and Director Gayler meet with the senator to calm him down and keep him quiet.

"Aldrin continues to tell anyone who will listen that he has observed very large craft. In fact, nearly every astronaut has commented publicly on seeing craft.

"Over the years we contained some information from our presidents: Ford, Carter, and Clinton all inquired into the UFO phenomenon. We gave them very little. But Brooks, he has been fully briefed and apprised of the current situation. It was necessary, due to the escalating events. He about soiled himself."

James smirked.

Clodfelter sighed and sat back down in front of his computer. "After Apollo 17, we realized that we clearly needed more information," he said. "Were we being threatened? Were there security risks to the earth? We wanted to know more. We knew we couldn't risk the lives of more astronauts without first having some answers, and we wanted to avoid any more highly publicized missions to the moon.

"So in 1974, NASA launched a secret NSA satellite, equipped with state-of-the-art cameras, infrared and multispectral sensors—you name it, that satellite was meant to observe it. As it approached the dark side of the moon, the satellite was lost. It simply disappeared.

"Now we believe there is a threat there—a constant extra-terrestrial presence. How does this correlate with the evidence you have found? Could there be a seminal event foretold in these ancient tablets? These texts that tell of the return of man's creator, these Sumerian gods, and of a great coming cataclysm to befall earth and man-kind are disturbing, to say the least. We need to understand this enigma, now. Could these 'gods' be coming back? Could they be seeking dominion over man? Did they create this mark in our DNA—and what does it mean?"

"If you had so much trouble with the moon, why were you sending a satellite into lunar orbit?" inquired Father Perez.

After a deep breath, Mr. Clodfelter paused and gave them a sardonic smile. "Are you ready for part two?" he asked. He waiting a moment, smiling, then went on. "There are artificial structures on the dark side of the moon," he said simply.

"Bullshit!" replied Stan, throwing his hands up. "First you say there are a bunch of fucking UFOs whipping around, and now you're telling me there's an alien base on the moon?"

"I did not say a base," replied Clodfelter very matter-of-factly. "However, there are structures of some type on the moon's further side."

He opened a folder and slid a group of photographs over to Stan. These were images of the lunar surface taken from orbit. They seemed to show some large wall-type structures and other large excavated areas.

"Here are some of the photographs from the Apollo missions," Clodfelter said. "They are not geological anomalies, nor are they impact craters. Our researchers have concluded these are intelligently and architecturally designed structures."

"What are they?" asked Sati.

"These photographs and many others like them seem to be of some form of mining operation on the moon. That is our best guess. Look at this," he said, sliding over another photograph. It was a large, foreign-looking structure with what looked like steeples. We call this 'The Castle.'"

"That's no geological formation," James breathed.

"No," replied Clodfelter. "This photograph is from the Apollo 11 Service Module in lunar orbit. We used every technique we could to enhance and zoom in on the structure. This is as good as we could get. Our satellite was supposed to take higher-resolution photographs of areas of interest, but, of course, it was lost. Apollo witnessed lights which seemed to be fixed on the surface, emanating possibly from these structures."

"What do you mean by 'the dark side of the moon?'" inquired Sati.

The question apparently caught Clodfelter a bit off guard. Plainly he had forgotten the mixed company in the room.

"The same side of the moon faces the earth all the time," he explained. "Hence, each side is in approximately two weeks of sunlight and two weeks of darkness. Unlike with the side that faces us, we have very little information as to what is on the dark side or far side of the moon. In fact, 40 percent of the moon's surface area has only been viewed a few times. Nearly all photos of the dark side are classified, aside from the few official photos and maps we have released, and none of those are very recent. We have identified approximately fifty different artifact locations, most of which are from photographs taken during the Apollo missions. There are some very small structures on the side facing earth, but they are extraordinarily difficult to see from orbit.

"The NSA has the authority to review all NASA photographs and film prior to public release. On many occasions, the NSA has released these photographs with minor touch-ups. However, if anyone actually looked at the photos from a forensic perspective with today's technology, they would probably laugh. They are smudged and very amateurish."

At this point, Agent Stinson walked back into the room and looked around. "Where are we, Bill?" he asked.

"Somewhere past disbelief and in the midst of shock, if I had to guess," grumbled Clodfelter. "We are basically done."

It had been a long day of briefing. James was tired and ready for a drink. The team quietly discussed what they'd heard as they walked out of the NSA building. Their black Suburban sat parked and waiting to take them back to the hotel. Sati, as always, held the case with the tablets close to his chest. His assistant Hassan followed them out, talking to Sati in a quiet tone.

Suddenly, as they made their way across the parking lot, sirens began going off throughout the facility and the parking lot. Alarm lights flashed on the light poles. An announcement echoed through a speaker system across the parking lot and NSA campus: "Emergency lockdown.

Stay where you are until further notice. A security breach is in progress."

"Bloody hell," Stan said, looking around nervously.

Screeching tires could be heard coming towards them from a line of parked cars from their right. James moved to one side trying to see between cars.

Bang! Bang! Bang! A series of gunshots rang out.

James dove to the ground as fast as he could. He looked behind him to see Sati's assistant Hassan lurch forward and plow into Sati, grabbing the case with the golden books. Hassan wrestled Sati to the ground and pulled the case away, then he began to run in the direction of the oncoming vehicle.

Stinson came running out of the building lobby and looked at James.

"There!" James shouted, pointing to where Hassan had run.

Stinson's pistol quickly came to eye level and they heard two shots ring out. James got to his knees to peer through the window of the parked car he was hiding behind. A white van sat in the middle of the parking lot. A man slid the van door open and stood behind a large machine gun mounted to the floor inside the vehicle.

"Oh shit!" James yelled.

From behind the van, a military-style pickup truck came to a halt about one hundred yards from the van behind a row of cars. The man in the van opened fire on the truck. The shots were continuous, coming at an unbelievable rate. James peered through the window to see flashes of flame flying from the barrel of the huge gun. Bullets tore through steel and glass, creating a huge line of destruction in their wake as the weapon swept toward the truck, vaporizing glass. Chunks of asphalt flew into the air as the bullets traced a line up and through the truck.

A stream of bullets riddled across the row of parked cars. Glass exploded into dust. James felt trapped. He had nowhere to run.

A man jumped from the NSA pickup truck and rolled to the ground as bullets continued to slam into the hood. With a terrific concussion, the truck exploded in a ball of fire, flipped over with a thunderous sound, and burst into flame.

A blonde woman appeared with a machine gun in the van and began screaming and waving her hands violently, motioning for Hassan to run toward her. James could not make out what she said. Shots came from the direction of the burning pickup truck, and the woman in the van dove out of view in the back of the van as small black bullet holes appeared in the van's white paint. She reappeared briefly and threw something toward the pickup truck.

Oh my God, James thought as he ducked under the window. An explosion erupted in the direction of the man returning fire. The smell of sulfur was overpowering.

Black smoke began to fill the parking lot as gas, oil, tires, and plastic smoldered. The acrid smoke rolled over James and he coughed and struggled for air. He had to move. He slowly crawled along the row of parked cars, peering between tires and trying to find his bearings. He made it to an area of the parking lot where the smoke began to clear, and again peered through the car windows to see that the grenade had destroyed several vehicles between the pickup truck and the van, dividing the two vehicles with a huge wall of black smoke and flame.

The woman in the van began screaming and waving again to Hassan, who had resumed running toward the van.

Now shots were coming from behind James. He jumped and spun in the direction of the oncoming gunfire, crouching as low as he could. Two military personnel were running out of the building with automatic rifles, firing at Hassan as he ran. Hassan's arms were flailing as he pushed forward with all his might. Suddenly he toppled to the ground, just short of the blonde woman's outstretched arm. He jerked wildly as his body was impacted by multiple shots and the case fell, skidding across the ground. Blood spread across Hassan's clothing on his back, and soon the pavement was covered in a dark pool.

Two Humvees smashed through several vehicles, trapping the van. The woman in the van began shooting at the Humvees, leveling her rifle at their windshields. James heard the dull impact of each round against armored plate.

Suddenly, shots came from what seemed like all directions as NSA security and military personnel approached the scene. Then suddenly, there was silence. Slowly the security personnel approached the van.

"Clear," James heard one of the men say. Two others approached the open van door, looked inside and repeated, "Clear."

Even from here, James could see that Hassan was lying dead on the ground. The case that held the Ascension Testaments lay beside his body. Out of the van door hung the lifeless body of the woman, her blonde hair draping down to the asphalt.

AGENT DEVON STINSON
THE WHITE HOUSE

"Gentlemen, please follow me," Agent Stinson commanded.

He led Stan and James out of the NSA conference room and into the elevator. They descended to the ground floor and followed him through the crowd of employees exiting the building. James looked at his watch. It was 5:30 p.m. He secretly wished he could go home, too, although the gravity of the situation he found himself in after yesterday's attack. had him enthralled.

They all got into a large SUV, and drove to a helipad located on NSA grounds, and pulled up to large Sikorsky Sea King helicopter.

As they exited the SUV, James turned to Stinson. "Okay, where are we going?" he demanded.

"The White House," replied Stinson.

When they arrived, the president was sitting behind his desk in the Oval Office. His normally broad smile was conspicuously absent. When the team entered, he rose to greet them and motioned for them to be seated.

"Gentlemen, I have been fully briefed on your incredible findings, and it appears we have enemies of the state trying to acquire this information as well," he said. "Mr. Anderson, to your group we apologize, but we needed to take immediate action to protect the information that you discovered. I understand that you feel a bit like a hostage. I need your help, and your country needs your help." He looked hard at James and Stan. "Project Aquarius is now an international effort. The U.N. has determined that the team will be formally assembled and operate out of the European Space Agency's headquarters. In recent years, the ESA has been the repository of all Project Aquarius data, especially since it was internationalized under the U.N. Security Council.

"At this moment, gentlemen, Project Aquarius is facing the most profound questions in history. Who placed these tablets in the Great Pyramid, and what can we learn about the DNA anomaly Dr. Matson identified? Is there information or a hidden code in this sequence— *wisdom*, as it says? How does this information relate to this approaching apocalyptic time foretold in the Sumerian tablets, and what devastation may come to the earth? And most frighteningly, are these the reasons we have witnessed a massive increase in the presence of UFO activity? Was this DNA code put there by an alien race? Or man's creator?

"In light of the recent attack, I have to acknowledge the situation personally, and reach out to you for help. I'm asking for your continued participation as a part of the team—part of my team. The United States will protect your findings and your intellectual property, and compensate each of you very well. But more importantly, this is a mission to protect mankind. I can't force your hand here, but I need to ask you, as free Americans, whether you are each personally committed to this project, to me, and to your country." The president sat and waited for their response.

"Mr. President, if XNA will be compensated in a way acceptable to our shareholders and if we will have the ability to retain and protect our intellectual property, my company and I are fully committed to this issue of national security," James said.

President Brooks nodded and smiled. "You have my word. You will also have increased security, of course, in light of the very public events at NSA. We will continue to work to find out who is behind these attempts to take the XNA data—and who is responsible for Dr. Matson's death."

After a long silence, Stan responded too. "Oh, bloody hell," he said, more than a little angst in his voice. "I'm in too, of course."

"That settles it," concluded the president. His famous smile returned as he turned to James.

"Mr. Anderson, you may be pleased to learn that the ESA is located in Paris," he said. "As I understand it, you are pretty familiar with the city—and with the French Secret Service." He gave James a knowing smile.

18

JAMES ANDERSON
ESA, PARIS, FRANCE

JAMES HATED THE BUILDING. It reminded him of a mausoleum.

ESA headquarters was located in the 15th Arrondissement, not far from the Eiffel Tower and the École Militaire so the location wasn't bad. But the building was straight out of the '70s. It looked like a large white tiled steamship covered in flags. The internal offices were claustrophobic and smelled musty, although the conference rooms were large and well-situated.

The first two weeks at ESA headquarters involved many discussions and presentations from various team members. Stan had presented the XNA sequence finding; Father Perez and Dr. Unnefer gave an overview of the Sumerian records and the excavation of the golden books. Many other new team members gave reports from their own areas of expertise. The international team was comprised of nearly sixty members, including astronomers, physicists, biologists, mathematicians, and linguists, and the dominant theme of conversation concerned the possible origination of the Golden Ratio within human DNA. There was a fearful tension that hung over the group, as no one present could make any sense of the star chart and its foretelling of an impending destruction to come.

Much dialogue also centered on the DNA sequence and the possibility that it had been deliberately placed. A team had been assembled around a sequence analyzer at ESA, and had reviewed countless samples of non-human DNA; they confirmed that the code sequence did not appear in any of those samples. Additionally, they had gathered and tested DNA samples from all over the world, and only the DNA from *Homo sapiens* had the marker—including the Golden Ratio sequence.

The team collaborated very openly. They were on an urgent quest that was unlike anything any one of them had previously experienced. The atmosphere around the place was at once exhilarating and unnerving. Even Agent Stinson had relaxed his harsh demeanor, and was now viewed as the group's moderator——no longer the imposing and intimidating government jailer keeping them captive. Everyone on the team understood the importance of the work they were conducting and the sensitivity of the information they harbored.

They constantly discussed the significance of the golden tomes and the DNA sequence having been discovered simultaneously. Some argued the timing was important and beyond chance. Others felt it was merely another odd coincidence.

Stan and James listened to the lead scientist review his findings from the DNA sequencer. "I looked at the mathematical ratios associated with DNA's components, and it appears that the proteins T-A-C-G are also found in the 1.618 golden ratio. This is in addition to the already known fact that the dual helix and grooves of its structure form a Golden Section spiral. I have examined thousands of nucleotide pairs so far, and the ratio remains the same from strand to strand, regardless of which human sample I use."

Stan turned to James. "What I think is strange here is that this is very similar to a digital code," he commented. "DNA and the entire structure of the genome is almost identical to the binary language of computers, and the more I work on this, the more I realize that DNA is the ultimate hard-drive. If you were a god or an alien race involved in our creation, how else would you ensure information was captured for eternity? Carve it in stone? Leave it on a papyrus scroll? No—you would embed it in the fabric of your creation. It's the ultimate time capsule: one strand of DNA could hold the equivalent of 750 terabytes of data. Think about that." He beamed. "I think this is the key to something far bigger."

"Stan, you're starting to sound like the priest," James laughed.

"I don't know. Maybe the Golden Ratio holds the key to cracking this code," Stan mused.

JAMES ANDERSON
PARIS, FRANCE

Having children, and the responsibilities that came along with them, did not mix well with ancient prophecies of apocalyptic events. James had not been sleeping well; he wanted to talk to Sati about the golden books some more, and he needed to get out of that damn office building for awhile.

"Stan, Sati, I need a drink," he said, puffing on a cigarette. "Period."

With a security detail in tow, the three men left the ESA and stopped in Le Violon Dingue on Rue de la Montagne. It was a pub run by one of James's long-time friends, Irish-transplant Killian. James and Stan had a few pints; Sati tagged along and had a Coke.

Killian had been working in the bar business since James first met him when he was in boarding school. He enjoyed a good lager and the occasional shot of Jameson's and always had his own mug close at hand, even while he worked.

Killian whispered in James's ear between gulps of his pint. "Whatcha doin' hang'in whit dis group?" he chucked. "A bit stiff, even for you."

"Uh—it's a work thing. And yes, stiff is the word of the day."

"A shot'll do you good," Killian chortled. "Hell, I'll even do one witcha. In fact, it's on the house if you can get your buddy in the dress over there to do one too."

"Just give me a pint and don't be an ass," James smirked. "I'll be over at that table in the corner. And turn that damn music down a bit, for God's sake—there's no one in here anyway!"

"Fine, have it your way, old man. I'll drink your share," Killian said, raising his mug in salute.

After they tipped Killian for the beers that had been free as usual, they headed up Rue Valette to The Bertold. James had stumbled across this small, quaint restaurant years ago, and was always drawn back by its incredible osso buco. Today the place was lively, with people talking loudly and great music filtering throughout the space.

Perched at the top of a low hill, the restaurant commanded a terrific view of the street and all the nightlife traveling along it, and the food was fantastic. Stan and Sati were not disappointed. They sat outside on the small terrace, their security detail at another table. The evening air was cool. James leaned back, sipped his wine, and lit a cigarette, reveling in the bit of relaxation that had crept into the conversation.

Just after the crème brûlée arrived, a reporter, who had apparently zeroed in on the unusual activity at the ESA and followed them, approached their table. One of the security detail stood and blocked her approach.

"Dr. Unnefer? How are you? I'm Marie Baudin with Le Figaro." She did not wait for Sati's response. "What have you been doing at the ESA? What's with all of the activity?"

Sati stared at James and Stan. He said nothing and looked very uncomfortable. Everyone stared back at the reporter.

"Who are these other scientists?" the reporter went on, unfazed. "What value is your work with antiquities and mummies to a space agency?"

"Can't we have five fucking minutes to relax?" James mumbled to the others.

Just then, the waiter came outside with a basket of bread and a pitcher of wine. He could tell that his guests were being harassed, and frowned at the reporter's small recorder being held in the faces of the three men.

"Sors d'ici! Au revoir!" he said, shoving her back. One of the security officers took over, and began to walk the reporter down the hill.

The reporter snapped a few quick photos, then disappeared quickly. On edge now, James scanned the street for any other reporters that might want a quote. He looked over at the two bars across the street, where several patrons drank at tables outside and others stood by the door smoking.

Then something caught his eye. In the alley between the two bars, a man stood leaning against the stone building in the shadows. The man's eyes locked on James's and the man held his gaze. James sat straight up, the hair on his neck raised, and his face flushed.

Was it the same guy he'd seen at his apartment?

"What the fuck!" he whispered. Abruptly the man turned and walked down the alley, talking on his phone.

James jumped up from the table, nearly knocking it over. "Come with me!" he yelled to the security officer seated near him. Pushing chairs out of his way, he ran across the street, dodging a taxi that was turning the corner. He nearly slipped. Ahead of him, he saw the man turn and run. The man ran through the busy alleyway and pushed past a group of people, scattering them. They yelled and cursed as he ran past. James was too far behind; he knew he would not catch him. He came to a stop and watched the man disappear.

He walked back to the table, breathing heavily and sweating.

"What was that?" Stan demanded.

James turned to the security officer. "Did you get a good look at him?" he panted, out of breath.

"No, he was moving too fast."

"Dammit!" James aid, slamming his hand on the table. "I've seen that guy before. I think he may be the one who robbed me. Maybe he's working with whoever is trying to steal our damn data. I need to tell Stinson in the morning." Sitting with his hands on his knees he took a deep breath, trying to regain himself. "Shit, I'm out of shape."

* * *

The next morning, their picture appeared in *Le Figaro*. It was buried in the Politics section, but Sati was identified by name.

"Oh, shit, what do we do about this?" James asked, handing the paper to Agent Stinson. The editorial read:

Why is the Egyptian Antiquities Minister at the ESA?

More questions for the Hollande Administration: The Minister of Egyptian Antiquities is meeting with the world's top scientists at the ESA. There has been a noticeable increase of activity lately at the headquarters. Has the agency lost sight of its primary mission—to explore space—or are they finding new ways to fund expeditions that have been denied? What is the ESA doing given that no new missions of any significance are scheduled? One has to wonder why nothing has been posted on the ESA website to explain all the new faces of scientists and experts. There isn't even a current convention that might attract such an odd crowd.

The piece continued, with a lot of speculation and ridicule, but nothing coming close to the true purpose of the mission. As a story it was more of a hit piece on President Francois Hollande. Still, it was more light than what they wanted shone on the project.

"I'll take care of this," Stinson replied. "DSGE can certainly get control over the local press. Really, I can't believe they missed this."

DR. SOFIA PETRESCU
ESA, PARIS, FRANCE

So God created man in his own image, in the image of God created he him; male and female created he them.

—GENESIS 1:27

Over the past three weeks, James had been paying particular attention to Dr. Sofia Petrescu, the Romanian astrophysicist assigned to Project Aquarius. Actually, he was pretty certain most of the men there had been. It was hard to resist the desire to constantly look at her; she was tall, fit, blonde and had an incredible body. In James's view she was also a badass, never fearful to go toe-to-toe with anyone on the team in a debate. Stan also stood in awe of her, saying she was one of the greatest quantum physicists in the world. He even used the term "genius"—a word he usually reserved for himself.

Listening to her speak, James learned about the battle between the relativity theorists and the quantum theorists. The paradigm of the former apparently worked very well for calculating and explaining the very large, such as the movement of planets, the solar system, and galaxies. Quantum physics, on the other hand, allowed for better calculations of the very small, such as subatomic particles, molecules, and photons. However, no one had married the two in a single theory.

When Sofia learned that the Golden Ratio was expressed in the DNA sequence, she was mesmerized.

"There is beauty here," she'd said, almost emotionally. "I cannot believe it. I always thought that the Golden Ratio was a fundamental physical law, something we never really understood, that nevertheless defines the structure of our universe. I wondered if such symmetry existed in the quantum world. And now, I know that it does! I have long recognized that planetary orbits and the structure of galaxies obey the Golden Ratio, but this confirmation that even DNA obeys the constant gives me hope. Perhaps it is the Golden Ratio that will unite quantum and relative physics."

Okay, James had thought, *maybe she is both too hot and too smart. Romania has definitely cornered the market on beautiful astrophysicists, short skirts, and tailored button-down blouses. I haven't seen any of the other scientists wearing clothes like that, but then I guess most of the other astrophysicists around here are men.*

However, aside from the spirited conversation surrounding the committee discussions of Project Aquarius, Dr. Petrescu kept largely to herself. During downtime, at breaks and after hours, she was always buried in an academic paper or text, and did not socialize as many of the other members did.

James had had enough. *For God's sake*, he thought to himself, *if no one is going to talk with her—I am.* He certainly wasn't sure he could measure up to the expectations of a hot young astrophysicist; after Kerri, his pride had been bruised. She would probably think he was an idiot anyway. But he felt he had nothing to lose, and that was a feeling that worked wonders. One day after lunch, he approached the table where she was sitting, alone as usual.

"Dr. Petrescu? May I have a seat?"

She looked up from her *Annual Review of Astronomy and Astrophysics* and smiled. "Of course, Mr. Anderson," she said. "How can I help you?"

That's good news, he thought—*she knows my name.*

"Although I primarily focus on business and management, I have a little bit of an engineering background," he said, taking a seat across from her. "However, this physics stuff is very much out of my comfort zone. I'm having a difficult time understanding the way the Golden Ratio could connect relative and quantum physics. I'd also really like to know your thoughts about this astronomical map foretelling of devastation and death. It has me pretty nervous. I guess I wouldn't mind knowing what you think about quite a few things. He laughed self-consciously. "Do you think you could explain a few of these things to me?"

"Well," she began hesitantly, "on the quantum-physics front, that would take quite some time, and my lunch break only lasts another ten minutes. I'm not sure you want to hear about the fractal origin of self-organization in wave systems in the universe, or Unified Theory in general. And anyway, we would need to get you up to speed first on fractal fields, and how those apply to infinite nondestructive compression."

Suddenly James wished he had kept quiet. "What—what kind of compression?" he managed.

She smiled at him. "You know," she chuckled. "That gravity thing."

"Oh shit," James mumbled. "Well, I'm willing to try...I mean, it doesn't have to be right now. Do you have plans this evening? We could meet for a drink at the Bonaparte for *cinq à sept*."

"*Cinq à sept?*"

"Five to seven. Sort of the Parisian happy hour."

Sofia laughed. "I don't mix business and pleasure, Mr. Anderson. It tends to make things too messy."

"This isn't pleasure. Believe me, you will find nothing pleasurable about teaching me the basic tenets of physics." He smiled back at her, not ready to give up just yet. "This is work in an outside location. Relaxed work, without the confines of twenty-minute lunch breaks."

She hesitated, smiling and looking down at her journal. "Come on," he persisted coyly. "If you find it too pleasurable, you can always leave. Do it for mankind, for God's sake—even the world, if these tablets are correct. Besides," he added, "you'll have the protection of your security detail."

"All right, Mr. Anderson," she finally agreed with a sly smile. "But bring a notebook so you can take notes."

JAMES ANDERSON
PARISIAN NIGHTS

Over the following weeks, James enjoyed spending time with Sofia. Although the relationship moved very slowly, their coffees and end-of-day drinks became more and more frequent, and progressively less focused on physics. Spending time with her helped ease the pain James felt in missing his kids, too: although he talked with them every couple of days, it was not the same as being with them.

He discovered that although Sofia was very academic, once you got beyond the façade of science she was likable and even funny, with a dry sense of humor. However, when discussing anything personal, she retreated to academic conversations, politics, or French history. During physics presentations she was anything but shy, her intelligence was clearly a cover she'd learned to hide behind.

James soon gleaned that she'd had a difficult childhood, and had learned early to retreat into academia. Her grandmother had accepted the burden to raise her, but was strict and hard on her. They'd lived on a fixed income that was meager when it supported two, and from an early age, Sofia understood that education was her only way to rise above her situation.

James didn't ask, but he got the impression Sofia had not made much time for relationships if her life. She didn't mention any significant relationships, just friends she had made in school. But even so he found Sofia to be very engaging when he sparked a debate on world politics or broached a subject close to her heart—just not too close.

Late one afternoon, they were walking along the Seine River near the St. Michel metro stop when James realized he must have asked too personal a question.

"Why do you Americans think you can go around the world, stealing the resources of other sovereign nations and polluting them without any accountability?" she ranted, steering away from her childhood.

James sighed and shifted his focus to the crowd, thick with tourists and Parisians making their way home. Large masses of people were clamoring toward the stairs to the Metro stop, or waiting to cross the busy street; people filled the cafés, and taxis zipped in every direction through the chaos. The massive city felt as if it were overflowing: the sun had just touched the westernmost point of the horizon and reflected off the Palais du Justice. James could feel the frustration rising inside him—the inferiority he felt during every day's ESA meetings, the constant walls Sofia built to prevent him from getting closer to her, the continuous

Big Brother security looking over his shoulder.

Sofia raised her voice just as James stepped out of the swiftly flowing crowd to linger at a Bouquiniste with some interesting old books on display.

"You really should be ashamed of yourself for allowing the financial elite in America to control the global economy," she was saying. "Why can't you just leave third-world countries alone? You create unrest and turmoil by deposing rightful leaders, and for what purpose—to gain more money for that same elite? They just pillage the resources and leave the cleanup for the impoverished native population."

At that moment, James's eyes shifted from the books to Sofia's burgundy lips. In that moment, for whatever reason, he could see only one way to relieve all his pent-up pressure. In one swift motion, James ran his hands up through the sides of her hair and pulled her lips to his.

Sofia stiffened on contact, and for a brief moment James thought she might flee. Desperately he deepened the kiss, allowing one hand to fall to her waist as he pulled her close. After what James felt was an eternity, she relaxed—and he felt that spark that he had thought was long lost to him.

The city continued to move around them. No one stopped. No one stared. No one noticed. Romance was just part of Paris, and James was thankful for it.

FATHER MATEO PEREZ
THE VATICAN

"As a multiplicity of creatures exist on earth, so there could be other beings, also intelligent, created by God."
—FR . JOSÉ GABRIEL FUNES, FORMER DIRECTOR OF THE VATICAN OBSERVATORY

The Vatican operator patched Father Perez through to the pope.

Obedient as he was being, Father Perez was not looking forward to another conversation with the Holy Father. He wrung his hands in his lap. These interactions made him so nervous, he was nearly sick. Ironically, his nervousness no longer stemmed from an audience with the pope but from what may be asked of him and how his conscience would be tested.

"Holy Father, I'm troubled," he blurted when they were connected. "I know what destruction comes. I know what this apocalyptic day means. You know the cause, too; you know what is coming. How can you remain silent? How can you tell me to remain silent, knowing what it means to mankind?"

"It is a burden you and I must both tolerate," the pope said coldly.

"I'm an astronomer, Holy Father. I cannot be responsible for this, for not telling—or warning—anyone. There is much we could do, things that would save people. Think of these good people here working with me on this problem. I feel that I must tell them."

"No! You cannot, and you must not. Remember your vow of obedience!" The fierceness of the pope's voice startled Father Perez. "This day has been long coming, Father Perez. The church is prepared for it. You cannot stop these events; you cannot change the future. It has been written in the heavens. This is the fate of mankind. Take heart, my friend. There will be rebuilding, and at its center, the Vatican will rise. We will bring light to those suffering; we will become the light-bearers in the darkness. We will lead mankind." There was a long pause. "What news do you have from Project Aquarius?"

His hands were shaking. He felt sick to his stomach.

Deep down he questioned the pope's motives, but he felt bound to his oath. *Should he continue to betray his conscience, the innocent people of the world—and his project team associates?*

Duty overcame Father Perez's inner turmoil. "Yes, Holy Father," he said. "There is something. I think that Dr. Unnefer has additional information that he is hiding. He has a USB flash drive with information on it, information that relates to the Sumerian tablets—information he is holding back as leverage. He wants to ensure that the Ascension Testaments are returned to Egypt."

"Mateo, we need that information. It could be the key to this code."

"He will not part with it. I have become quite close to him." Father Perez considered whether he wanted to continue, but finally did. "Dr. Unnefer has told me that if something happens to him—he wants me to have the files, to help solve this mystery."

"I see." The pope was clearly disappointed.

"I'll do what I can to gain his confidence and get access to the information."

"Good. You do that, Mateo. Time is of the essence."

Father Perez hung up the phone, unimaginably conflicted by the knowledge that he harbored.

"Why me?" he muttered into the air.

Father Perez thought to himself for a long time, rubbing his forehead with both hands. He struggled with his oath, with his loyalty to the Vatican and to the Jesuit Order, and with the moral obligation he felt to his friends and to mankind; it was a paradox he could not extricate himself from. He could not betray his oath, but he could not sleep if this day came and he told no one.

What if other members of the project found the information themselves? he thought to himself as he stared up at the wall. *What if they independently discovered the impending destruction that awaited man? I would be absolved from my burden.*

After much thought, he decided a few breadcrumbs to help people along a path would not be a violation of his oath to the pope.

19

It is I who created the letters . . . it is I who made the Earth and created the Adam upon it.

—ISAIAH 45:11

JAMES FOUND HIMSELF SITTING in the midst of more and more meetings where the focus was on purely scientific detail. In the back of his mind, he knew that only concentrating on these aspects of the puzzle was a mistake. His forte had always been his ability to take seemingly disparate pieces of information from a multitude of sources and connect them in a meaningful way; and when he did that now, he realized there were some glaring gaps in the overall picture.

James believed there was more information from the ancient records that would be useful. However, it seemed that the academics had already dismissed this information as useless to their task. One afternoon, following a discussion on code-breaking, James decided he could no longer sit quietly. He wanted to help, and there was only one area where he thought he could.

"Agent Stinson," James begain, "frankly, I think the team is missing a large piece of the puzzle. The brief discussions we have had concerning ancient history have only covered generalized information. You guys all knock your heads together trying to figure out codes and delve deeper into the materials that were used to create our DNA, but did you ever think that the answer to the code might be somewhere in our history? Maybe we need to do more examining of ancient texts on the creation story, and see if one of them points us to the code key."

Father Perez was seated in a nearby chair and looked on as the two talked, paying close attention.

"James, if the ancients had any more information to offer, we would have heard it from someone by now," Stinson said. "We don't have time to chase our tails on this. We have to focus on the DNA code, in the hope that we can crack it somehow and learn something. That is our focus. Now, if you'll excuse me, I have to talk with Mr. Appleton before he leaves." Agent Stinson turned and walked off.

James turned away, frustrated at having been rebuffed so forcefully.

"You know, James," Father Perez murmured as he caught up with James, "that presentation was interesting to listen to this morning." The priest's eyes scanned the room as he spoke. As soon as Stinson was out of earshot, his voice dropped to almost a whisper, and he stepped close to James.

"James, I agree things are missing from this sideshow," he said. "I was sent here as an observer for the Vatican, but I have something for you. And I will trust you in this confidence. There is a bigger picture that needs to be displayed—before it is too late. There are things that the Church has known for centuries. I can tell you no more." With that,

Father Perez smiled and firmly shook James's hand, leaving behind a slip of paper.

"This man will help you find the answers you seek," he added, his voice barely discernible. "Just keep it to yourself until you are alone. Forgive me that I cannot be more directly helpful."

James casually placed his hand in his pocket as Perez walked away, mingling with others on his way to the refreshment table for a cup of coffee.

* * *

As soon as James was back in his apartment at Saint-Sulpice, he reached into his pocked for the paper. Opening it, he found a single name printed in fine block handwriting: "Zecharia Sitchin."

James wondered how one name could answer all his questions about ancient civilizations, and how it fit into their investigation. He also wondered what information the Vatican had locked in its bowels that Father Perez was forbidden to share. Sitting down with his laptop, James lit a cigarette, poured himself a glass of Bordeaux, and Googled "Zecharia Sitchin."

Sitchin, as it turned out, was an Azerbaijani immigrant who'd spent his entire life studying the Sumerian culture, that pre-dated the Egyptian and Babylonian cultures by millennia. This piqued James's interest. The Sumerians were at the epicenter of this riddle and the cuneiform tablets. Sitchin was one of the few scholars in the world who could translate ancient Sumerian cuneiform, the oldest written language on Earth. Apparently he could translate a multitude of ancient languages. The more James read, the more interested he became—and he was disappointed to find that Mr. Sitchin died in 2010. However, his former protege and assistant, Klaus Jurgen, still lived in New York.

As James closed the lid of his laptop and retired to his room, he decided he would do what he could to contact Jurgen as soon as possible.

PROFESSOR STAN CARUTHERS
ESA, PARIS, FRANCE

"We spent weeks trying to identify a way to open the books before it became evident that they weren't really books at all," Stan explained to James. "The tablets are blank except for the intertwined snakes on the outside and a few cuneiform markings that our experts translated as *knowledge or wisdom*. But here's the interesting finding. The three books connect with a small channel on the long edge of each one. The channel has a magnetic property that holds each tablet in place, which baffles us, because gold lacks magnetic qualities. When they're connected, the twisted snake glyph is complete.

"Multiple X-ray fluorescence or XRF tests verified that the books are gold. We know that gold is an excellent insulator from X-rays, so the team was unable to look inside them that way. Short of drilling holes through them, which of course was flat-out rejected, we had few options. But due to their calculated densities, we knew they were not solid gold. This led the team to believe," Stan concluded, "that there was something with less mass inside of the books."

"It's here," someone exclaimed, rushing into the room. Two lab technicians wheeled a large cart past the others.

"That's it?" asked Stan. "It looks pretty small."

"Powerful things can come in small packages," one of them responded.

"What is that?" James asked.

Stan ripped the packing tape off the large box and retrieved what looked to James like a medical terminal of some sort. The box it came in was at least three times bigger than the device. James decided it must be a delicate instrument to need so much protection.

"This, my boy," Stan said as he unpacked the small device, "is a three-dimensional ultrasonic testing terminal. It's the latest and greatest form of gold-bar verification. This is one of a handful of available machines, and it cost taxpayers an arm and a leg to get it on loan from the University of Nevada. It was designed to find tungsten in gold bars."

"What do you mean?" asked James.

"Well, in lieu of a metallurgy lesson, I'll give you the economic explanation—which you will be able to follow. Tungsten has nearly the exact mass of gold. However, it costs about $1 per ounce. Gold is obviously a little higher than that."

"Let me guess," James said. "Fraudsters are plating tungsten bars with gold and selling them as 24-karat solid bricks."

"Seems like a profitable venture," said Stan.

"Yeah, if you want to go to jail once the gold is melted for use," James laughed.

It only took a few minutes for Stan to set up the device. James thought it looked like a standard ultrasound machine you would see in any hospital; however, multiple instruments could be connected to it. One looked like a sharp probe and one was flat. There were even four panels that could be set up on all sides of an object for three-dimensional visualization.

Stan used the simplest instrument, which looked like a large pen, to squirt gel over the gold books. The screen fluttered, and multiple graphs came to life on the terminal. After several tense moments, with more and more onlookers gathering around them, one of the technicians hovered over one of the golden books while Stan watched the terminals.

"Wait. Right there. No, back up—there," Stan directed. "See? The phased-array image clearly shows a discontinuity." The room, as a whole, gasped.

"What the hell does that mean?" James asked loudly.

Sofia, now standing at James's side, gently placed her hand on his arm. "It means there is something inside," she said.

"Without precise calculations, it looks as if there's something almost in the exact middle of the book," Stan said. "Turn it over and scan from the bottom. Let's see what you get. There," he said. "See, I was right. It's the same on this side. Whatever it is, it's in the center of the book—perhaps it's something made of another type of metal with a higher melting point, so the gold can be melted away from it. We'll have to complete additional scans and analysis to try and discover what it is. My team will report our findings, of course, in the morning."

JAMES ANDERSON
PARIS, FRANCE

"[If extraterrestrials were sinners,] Jesus has been incarnated once, for everyone. The incarnation is a unique and unrepeatable event. I am therefore sure that they, in some way, would have the possibility to enjoy God's mercy, as it has been for us men."

—FR . JOSÉ GABRIEL FUNES, FORMER DIRECTOR OF THE VATICAN OBSERVATORY

James turned the lights on in his flat and closed the door behind Sofia. He couldn't believe she'd agreed to come up for a drink. He grabbed an open bottle of Bordeaux and poured two glasses.

"Look, Sofia, I convinced Stinson to let me leave for a week. I mean, we have been at this for over month. And I'm not really adding any technical value."

Sofia held his stare.

"It's just, I haven't seen my kids, and frankly, this entire thing about Armageddon and all that crap has me terrified. I want to be with them for a bit."

"I understand, James," Sofia said, retreating over to the window ledge. "We will find out what this is all about. We just need more time."

"Yeah, well, if these Sumerians and their 'gods' are right, we may not have much time. I also believe there is more to this story here. I know you don't think that information on these ancient civilizations will help us with the challenges we face. But I do. That is one area of this project where I can add value: I'm not a physicist or genetics PhD, but I can check the validity of the historical information."

"James, first of all, you're being too hard on yourself," she said. "You should go and see your kids. Come back as soon as you can."

James sensed a bit of disappointment in her voice. *Maybe she'll miss me,* he thought.

"There is one more thing," he added. "I have made arrangements to meet someone before I return here. An expert on Sumerian culture."

"Good! Maybe you'll learn something helpful."

"Well, I was thinking, maybe you could meet me in New York to talk with him, too." James handed her the glass of wine, hoping she wouldn't outright reject the idea.

"Are you crazy?" she laughed. She turned back to the window. "How could I do that, James? I can't imagine Stinson would approve."

"Well, we're not in jail here," James said, walking over to the couch and fidgeting idly with a newspaper lying there. "And I'm only talking for a day or two. We may learn something, and I could show you around New York." He turned and smiled at her. "Come on, think about it—you should come for a couple days. We deserve a break—you more than anyone. Who knows, it may be the last fun trip you have the opportunity to go on, with the coming destruction and all."

There was a long pause: This was a good sign, as far as James was concerned.

"I don't know," Sofia said, smiling.

She turned her back to James and looked down at the square below. The fountain was cast in a violet hue as the setting sun dipped behind the buildings across the square. The sound of gently flowing water from the fountain softly echoed in the room. A scattering of stars was slowly becoming visible in the clear evening sky.

James watched Sofia as she gazed out the window. She was beautiful. Her lavender turtleneck and black leggings accentuated her curves. A light breeze jostled the curtains, catching a loose strand of her hair. After taking a deep breath, she turned back to him.

"I feel I have a lot to contribute to the project by working on the analysis I'm doing here, James," she said.

James took another sip from his glass to boost his confidence, and walked over to her. "Still, you never know; it could be interesting. If nothing else, it won't be a complete waste of time. You will be with me."

He placed his hand on her shoulder and gazed into her eyes. His breath caught in his throat. He pushed the stray lock of hair from her forehead and secured it behind her ear. Her eyes dropped to the floor.

"You do know that you're beautiful, right?" he felt compelled to ask.

She bit her lip, and he realized that incredibly, somewhere in there she didn't. Slowly, gently, he raised her chin. "Sofia, you are not only the most intelligent person I know, but also the most attractive woman I know," he said. Her eyes met his, questioning for a moment, and then he slowly kissed her.

He had not kissed her since the day in the street. After it had happened, he'd gone home feeling like a schoolboy who had stolen his first kiss. But she didn't mention it afterward, and James hadn't been confident she wanted more. Now he had his confidence back. They were not standing in the street. This time, they were alone in his apartment.

Meeting his enthusiasm, she deepened the kiss. Her hand rested on his chest, and she clenched it slightly as if begging him not to stop. He returned her passion, running his fingers through her hair. His hands slid down her back, and his lips traced a pattern on her neck.

"Sofia," he whispered in her ear, "if you want me to stop, I understand—just tell me now." Her mouth twitched upward in a little half-smile, and James immediately reclaimed her lips.

PROFESSOR STAN CARUTHERS
ESA, PARIS, FRANCE

Immediately after the tribulation of those days shall the sun be darkened, and the moon shall not give her light, and the stars shall fall from heaven, and the powers of the heavens shall be shaken.

—MATTHEW 24:29

"The material inside these books is very different from the gold that surrounds it. After many tests from several angles, we deduced that the object contained within the gold was two millimeters thick. It runs nearly the entire length and width of the books, with dimensions just short of 304.80 by 254 millimeters."

The room was full but silent as Stan glanced up from the lectern. Nearly every member of Project Aquarius was present, sixty people in all.

"So we have a wide, very thin object—similar to a piece of paper," Stan continued. "However, when we changed to the multiple transducer array, we nearly fell on the floor."

On the screen, a three-dimensional image appeared.

"As you can see from this digital reproduction of the data we gathered, the object's dimensions are minute. However, further imaging revealed that the center is not one object, but a stack of several extremely thin layers."

A close-up of the blue line representing the object in the book appeared, emphasizing what looked like thin layers stacked together. Everyone in the room began murmuring.

"Yes," Stan said, raising his hands to regain everyone's attention. "We have what appear to be thin metal layers, not more than 50 nanometers thick. Our testing cannot provide any better resolution."

"Are they connected?" one of the physicists asked.

"I wish I could tell you. The best I can postulate is that we have between twenty and thirty very thin, I guess we will call them *pages*, sandwiched together in the center the gold books. That is all the information we have about them at this point. However, we found something else interesting, I believe.

"As you know," Stan continued, "the books can be connected down their spine. We discovered during our testing that these stacks of 'pages,' are positioned within 10 nanometers from the edges of the connecting spines, although they are further away from the non-connecting edges. It appears they somehow link to each other, forming one long sheet of material when the books themselves are connected."

Everyone began speaking at once.

"What is that?"

"Clearly a highly technical design."

"Unbelievable."

"Professor Caruthers, have you determined what the material in the middle of the book is comprised of?" Sofia asked.

"Well, using the XRF, we tried to penetrate the gold on the edges and see what this film or paper is made of. The results seem to indicate it is titanium dioxide."

The crowd began to murmur again, but something tickled James's memory. He stared at the words on the screen, "titanium dioxide," and its chemical formula, TiO2. Without realizing it, he stood. He continued to look at the screen, and he muttered to himself under his breath.

"It's a memristor," he said.

"What's that, James?" asked Stan.

The rest of the room fell silent, aware that James had worked on many high-tech projects in his past business dealings.

"It's a memristor!" James exclaimed louder. He looked around the room to see if anyone was following him; the others returned nothing but blank stares.

Stan also looked around the room for an explanation. Everyone was at a loss.

"James, what exactly is a memristor?" Stan asked in frustration.

James felt a bit uncertain of himself. He'd considered investing in a business that was involved in creating them, but he knew only a little about the technology behind it. His knowledge on memristors only went deep enough to understand their market potential. He was uncertain if he could explain them to a room of highly educated people who would demand more depth.

"Well, what caught my attention was that the center is layered titanium dioxide," James said, a little uncertainly now. "I've heard of layered titanium dioxide being used in manufacturing mechanical devices once before, and that was at Hewlett-Packard Labs. They were working on memristors. Memristor is short for *memory resistor*. It's a resistor that changes its state based on the voltage supplied to it, then stays in that state until changed again by a different voltage. It's the theoretical fourth-base element in integrated circuits." Seeing confused looks among some of the scientists, James paused to explain. "I learned from a scientist at HP that in addition to the resistor, capacitor, and inductor, there is a theoretical fourth-base component of electrical circuits, written about since the 1970s. Several companies were working on these, and Stan Williams finally built one at HP in 2008. They're the next step in memory devices. Memristors are basically a type of resistive memory that is nonvolatile. Although voltage changes the physical state of the array, the array stays static. In this case, wrapping it in gold would prevent any electrical or magnetic corruption to the array." He exhaled loudly and concluded, "The gold books are a memory-storage device."

* * *

The Grande Mosquée de Paris was busy today. Built in the 1920s, the structure was a beautiful Moorish architectural creation with a 33-meter minaret, visible from all over the Latin Quarter. The green tile roof and walkways reflected the bright afternoon sunlight.

Khalid walked through the white columns surrounding the courtyard. There were many people in the café of La Grande Mosquée, but he did not talk to anyone—nor did he care about the elegant architecture, the white and green mosaic tiles, the minaret, the cedar arches. He was not here for prayer, or for the famous hot peppermint tea.

He passed several people wandering throughout the mosque. Khalid stood near a marble column for a moment, pretending to read the paper. *There*—he saw who he was looking for.

Khalid walked toward the restroom off the main corridor. The other man followed him as he had been instructed. The two walked into the small restroom off of the main corridor. Once inside, neither said a word. Khalid looked in each stall to ensure they were alone, then locked the door. Still silent, Khalid walked over to the trash can, pulled out the trash bag, and set it on the floor. Using the light from his phone, he peered down inside the can.

There on the bottom was something wrapped in a piece of dark cloth. Khalid reached down and pulled it out, then unwrapped a 9-millimeter Glock pistol and two full magazines of hollow-point ammunition.

Silently he handed the gun to the other man, along with a small piece of paper with the name and address of a restaurant on it. The man looked at the paper, then tore it up, put it in one of the toilets, and flushed it. He shoved the gun in the rear waistband of his jeans, making sure it was covered by his shirt.

Nodding in approval, Khalid unlocked the door, and the two walked out of the bathroom and off in separate directions.

20

JAMES ANDERSON
MANHATTAN, NEW YORK

And God said, Let us make man in our image, after our likeness; and let them have dominion over the fish of the sea, and over the fowl of the air, and over the cattle, and over all the earth, and over every creeping thing that creepeth upon the earth.

—GENESIS 1:26

"I'M SO GLAD I WAS ABLE TO SEE THE KIDS," James told Sofia, when she'd met him in New York. He was thrilled she'd agreed to meet him here; even in light of the intensity and importance of their work, their relationship added electricity to his daily outlook.

"How was it? I'm sure they were happy to have you to themselves for a whole week." Sofia laughed lightly, looking out the window as their car passed one opulent Upper East Side building after another. "Even if it was with a security detail."

"Yeah, it was great," James smiled back. "After getting past the first few hours of my oldest punishing me for having been gone so long, we all got along. Maybe with all this in the back of my mind, the little things that usually drove me crazy just didn't seem to matter: socks on the floor, leaving the cereal bowl out. I rented a house on the beach, and it was just me and them. It was fantastic."

"I'm so glad," Sofia said. "It wouldn't do to have you distracted. Hey, looks like we're here."

Their security officer opened the door for them, then escorted them into the building of Zecharia Sitchin's former assistant. A nurse opened the door after buzzing them up to the apartment.

"Mr. Jurgen is expecting you," she said. "He is very excited to have you here. I've not seen him with this much energy in weeks." The nurse smiled. She was young, and dressed in white scrubs, as if she had been working at the hospital that day.

As they walked into the apartment, they noticed that all the drapes were drawn. The whole apartment was dark and stuffy; the air was as stale as that of a hospital or retirement home. James hated the smell of hospitals and was immediately uncomfortable.

Overstuffed bookshelves decorated almost every wall, and books, papers, and magazines were piled in stacks everywhere. It looked like nothing had changed in the apartment for fifty years, other than the addition of more clutter; the décor was clearly from the 1960s. James eyed an Eames chair that he was certain was original. *Funny*, he thought; *the furniture in this place may slowly make it back into style.*

The nurse showed them into Mr. Jurgen's bedroom, which had been transformed into a hospital room containing a hospital bed, oxygen tanks, monitoring equipment, and an IV pump. Clearly, the man had only recently returned home from a lengthy hospital stay. Based on the medical equipment, it must have been something quite serious.

Mr. Jurgen smiled and did his best to sit up as they entered. "Welcome," he said, directing them to sit in the chairs placed beside his bed.

They found him to be a sweet man, soft-spoken with a thick German accent, and very patient. James was struck by the thoughtful deliberation of his comments; he never blurted anything out, but first weighed each statement's impact.

The premise of the meeting, as far as Mr. Jurgen knew, was the recent excavation in Egypt at the Great Pyramid. There had been much speculation in archeological circles that those working on the dig had found something important, though what it was, no one knew. In keeping with this pretense, James and Sofia had told him that they were representatives from the State Department and wanted an audience with him to understand more about Sumerian culture. After they'd spoken casually for an hour or so, and Jurgen had described a few aspects of his research to them, James explained in detail about the golden books with the writing on them and the twisted serpent.

"Our translators believe the cuneiform writing says *wisdom*," he concluded.

Mr. Jurgen was mesmerized. "And the twisted serpents likely stand for the Sumerian god of fertility, Ningishzidda," he stated.

It was clear the elderly scholar was excited. James decided to back up for a moment, to see what information he might gather as to why Father Perez had put him onto this man's scent. "Mr. Jurgen, maybe we should start at the beginning here," he said. "If you don't mind, please tell us a little bit about how you came to be one of the world's foremost experts on Sumerian culture."

"Ha! Well, I don't know about that, James," Jurgen laughed. "I am a German-born man, although I grew up most of my life in Palestine. From a young age, I wanted to become, and did become, a biblical scholar. I began studying the Old Testament in detail in its original Hebrew with Zecharia Sitchin. We learned that what was being taught was wrong or at least not accurate because of mistakes and misunderstandings in the translations.

"You see, many teachers and scholars rely on what *others say* the words mean. They never bother to learn the root languages themselves in order to see what the original writings are actually saying to us!" he exclaimed.

"I can think of no other area of study where this could be more important than with the Bible. As scholars translate it from this language to that, it has lost a lot of its original meaning. I studied the original languages, and I can tell you that much of the Bible comes directly from the Sumerian cuneiform texts—or more specifically, tablets. If you believe in the Bible, you must believe in its source materials. And we have many. Some of the Sumerian artifacts and stories are engraved in reverse on hematite drums, so they could be rolled across the clay to create bas-relief images. It is fascinating how they did this thousands of years before Gutenberg even thought of his press. Over one million cuneiform texts have been found in Mesopotamia," Jurgen continued. "Even though these are the oldest known human writings on Earth, few academics had made it a priority to translate any of them. Thousands remain unread and inaccessible, locked up in basements of the British Museum and elsewhere."

"Why aren't more scholars or universities or even religious groups trying to read them?" James interjected. "From what we have learned, these ancient people had a wealth of advanced knowledge. These tablets could hold a vital key to history!"

Mr. Jurgen looked over at the window as if lost in thought, "I don't know, James . . . I just don't know. Not only do they keep these writings locked up, but they also do not encourage people to learn how to decode them. Aside from me, fewer than two hundred people in the world can translate cuneiform. I think some part of the government knows, however."

"Why do you say so?" James asked.

"I find it strange, the pretense that got us into the Iraq war; I find it stranger still that the base we established in Iraq encompassed the oldest Sumerian city on Earth, Ur—where Abraham was born. My sources tell me that during the war, the military excavated a massive number of artifacts from the ancient city." He looked at James. "The Sumerian culture gave mankind the first of almost everything: the first writing, the first government, even the first Farmer's Almanac. The first schools appeared there, teaching medicine, zoology, botany, math, language, poetry. Even all the major religions stemmed from the foundational stories written by the Sumerians. They provide us with the first philosophical understanding of an ultimate creator. From a technology perspective they gave us the plow, the potter's wheel, paved streets, kilns, looms, bricks, mirrors, beads, cemeteries, even breaking the circle into 360 degrees.

"Understand, scholars and archeologist who research this area all believe that this culture appears with shocking abruptness—from city planning to advances like the first legal system."

"The cultural big bang?" James interjected.

"Exactly. I personally believe that the Sumerians were the first people we should classify as *Homo sapiens*. In my studies, I have found many stories stating that the Annunaki created them."

"What are the Annunaki?" James asked.

"In the Sumerian language, it roughly translates to 'those who from heaven came.'"

There was a long pause. James looked at Sofia.

"The first writings on Earth say that man was created by 'those who from heaven came?'" James asked.

"Yes," Mr. Jurgen nodded. "According to the texts, and Mr. Sitchin's translations, the Annunaki came to Earth in search of gold 450,000 years ago. They needed the gold for use on their planet, Nibiru. Nibiru seems to be a planet we have yet to identify. According to them, it orbits on an elongated elliptical path around our sun." Jurgen laughed aloud at the look on Sofia's face. James recognized that look well enough; she frequently expressed disbelief when speakers at the ESA brought up alien-creation theories. "Of course, it sounds preposterous until you have studied it for a lifetime as I have." He became serious. "I know you are a woman of science. How would you react if I told you that the Sumerian texts state that Saturn's Titan has water? What if I said that the texts proclaim that Neptune and Uranus are icy planets, and accurately describe their color and position in the solar system?"

"I would say that is impossible," Sofia replied. "We just learned those things through modern instrumentation in the last century or so."

Jurgen nodded. "Of course, as you know, Uranus and Neptune are not visible without a telescope," he continued. "We discovered them in 1781 and 1846, respectively. We are just now learning about their ice composition, since Voyager passed them. However, our first civilization on Earth wrote about these things and much more. These are the things the Sumerians say they learned from the Annunaki."

Sofia frowned.

"Hard to believe, I know! But it's true," Jurgen laughed. They accurately stated that there are twelve major bodies to our solar system, counting the sun, moon, and their planet Nibiru, and described them in the correct order. This is from a civilization living more than six thousand years ago! They also precisely calculated the distances between the planets and their orbits around the sun—which means that the first civilization beat Copernicus to the punch by several thousand years. The main difference between their astronomical records and ours concerns the planet they called Nibiru."

"Where is this planet Nibiru, if it is part of our solar system?" Sofia said, unable to contain herself. "We should have found it decades ago."

Mr. Jurgen held up both of his hands in defense. "The Sumerians tell us that Nibiru—which is called the planet of the crossing and is symbolized by the cross—is in a very elongated elliptical orbit lasting 3,600 years. Based on their writings, Sitchin made this sketch of the planet and its orbit." He fumbled with a book he had on a nightstand. Taking his time, he finally found the page he wanted. He gave the book to James and Sofia.

"This is the home of the creators of man, and likely your golden books," he said, smiling.

Just then, the nurse came back in. "I'm so sorry to interrupt," she said, "but Mr. Jurgen needs some rest, and to take his medicine."

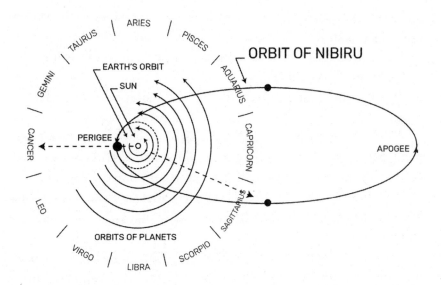

It was true, Jurgen had tired noticeably during their conversation; they'd been speaking for just under two hours. They all agreed Mr. Jurgen would rest while James and Sofia had lunch. They would reconvene after a few hours if he felt up to more conversation.

Back out on the streets of New York, Sofia's frustration came out. "I find this interesting, but unbelievable," she said. "My entire career has been spent studying the solar system, our galaxy, and this universe. If there was another planet in our system, we would have known about it for decades. I just don't find this even plausible."

They took the subway to Gramercy, where James introduced Sofia to Pete's Pub. They sat in his favorite spot, a small round table near the door that was secluded, then ordered a few of Pete's own beers and discussed the day's illuminations over appetizers.

Talking over the music and loud patrons at the bar, they concluded that even if the claims regarding an additional planet were far-fetched, something was very intriguing about the accurate descriptions of planets and other information that was not discovered by modern science until thousands of years later.

"Jurgen and Sitchin have been speaking to Universities and researchers around the country, and selling books," Sofia said. "Why have no mainstream archeologists or other scientists picked up on this work? How do we know it is credible?"

"I'm not sure," James answered. "He is certainly well-learned on the topic."

When they returned to the flat, James was relieved to see that Jurgen had regained his energy. Although the nurse had kept them away until late in the afternoon, James was excited to continue the dialogue.

"Mr. Jurgen, when we left off you were about to tell us more about what the Sumerians say about the origin of mankind," he reminded the elderly scholar.

"Ah, yes," Jurgen said, remembering. "Did you know that Genesis is a direct excerpt from the Sumerian texts? You have to go back to the original texts, however, to learn this. You see, over time the translations and meanings got changed a bit, but the basic story of Genesis is what the Sumerians tell us."

"What are the differences?" James asked.

"The Sumerian texts state that the Annunaki, those who from heaven came, created man in '*their*' image. It is plural, just as it is in the original Hebrew account of Genesis. Ironically, modern Biblical scholars overlook this, or attribute it only to the holy trinity. The cuneiform text goes on to state that the Annunaki settled in Sumer or modern Iraq. They tell us that they created man as a worker to mine gold. They called their creation the *Ad-am*, and they created it in the part of Sumer they called *Ed-en*. The original word 'Adam' in the Sumerian texts, long before the writings of the Old Testament, literally means *Earthling*."

"Why did they need gold?" asked Sofia. "It seems a petty thing for an advanced race to be seeking wealth on other planets."

"No," interjected Mr. Jurgen, "their purpose was scientific. The Sumerians recorded that the Annunaki surveyed the planets and recognized Earth to be the only planet in the solar system to have gold. They came to find enough atomic gold to repair their atmosphere."

"I don't understand," Sofia replied.

"The writings indicate that they had a problem not unlike our ozone hole, or global warming. They explain that the Annunaki were able to particularize gold into their atmosphere to protect their planet from harmful radiation."

"They mined gold on Earth and took it back to their planet? And this is written in the first writings we have on Earth?" James asked incredulously.

"Yes. In their accounts, they describe going from Earth to Mars. They had a spaceport there that was larger, so they could transport the gold to their home planet in larger vessels. They wrote that it was also easier for them to leave the solar system from Mars than it would have been from the earth."

James looked at Sofia, wondering what she thought of all this. "Mars? Now you're telling me that the Sumerians' tablets told tales of the Annunaki having gone to Mars?"

"We believe we have found one of their structures that would have supported whatever transport they used, in Baalbek, Lebanon," Jurgen nodded. "The Trilithon stones. No one can provide an explanation to this day about the stones in this ancient city, which may be the oldest structure on Earth. They're the largest cut stones in history, but they appear from the dawn of man. They are bigger than a semi-trailer—fourteen feet tall and wide and sixty-eight feet long. After these people cut the stones, they somehow moved them over a mile to build a great structure; the stones were placed on the upper level. The Sumerians referred to this place as some sort of spaceport or launch pad. We have no modern technology that would make this construction easy. The cuneiform text indicates that it was from here that the gods came and went from Earth." One of Sofia's eyebrows shot up, but she remained silent.

"The Sumerians also have a much more detailed and complete account of the Great Flood."

"Noah's flood?" James asked.

"Yes, that flood. Although, to the Sumerians, he was known as

Atrahasis. Scientists found evidence for this flood all over the world. The Sumerian texts go into great detail about the cause of the flood and the creation of an ark, and describe how the Annunaki—or the Nephilim or Fallen, as the Hebrew text called them—had inhabited Earth and began taking human wives. They found human women beautiful, because we were made in their image."

"So after they had made Adam or man, they took some of the women for wives?" James asked, incredulous.

"Yes. Read your Bible, Mr. Anderson. It is all there," Jurgen replied. "After the flood, the process began again. And many of the Sumerian texts are very detailed direct accounts of the ancient bloodlines of the Annunaki, both before and after the flood. Many of those who were half-Annunaki and half-human became the high priests and royal lines that persevere even today.

"Humans perceived the Annunaki as gods. That is why ancient cultures refer to the Creators and gods in the plural. The Annunaki found a primitive species of man, *Homo erectus*, on Earth, and genetically modified him with their own DNA. This is why we see millions of years of *Homo erectus* and other hominids, but modern man arrives on the planet only about fifty thousand years ago in his present form rather suddenly. There is no evidence of slow evolution."

James immediately thought about the DNA sequence they'd discovered—only in *Homo sapiens*. This eerily explained that anomaly. A chill ran down his spine.

"So these ancient texts talk about DNA and bioengineering?" Sofia asked, exasperated.

"Well, yes," Jurgen said, "hard to believe as it is. They describe taking the sperm from *Homo erectus* and mixing it with the eggs of an Annunaki woman in many iterative experiments of *in vitro* fertilization. They talk about their first attempts as failures because they wanted Adam to be able to procreate. This is the story of Adam and Eve in its original."

"So why aren't there any Annunaki here, then?" Sofia asked, clearly exasperated.

Jurgen laughed. "Who says there aren't?"

"Huh?" asked James.

"Well, they say they created us in their image! How do we know? According to the Sumerian accounts, the Annunaki live for thousands of years. One Annunaki ruled Earth for the period of precession of one age of the twelve zodiac signs, or approximately two thousand years. There were twelve ruling Annunaki; hence, each one ruled for one cycle of the Great Year. The Great Year is the time it took for the twelve Zodiac constellations to complete a cycle, or about 24,000 years.

"Twelve, in fact, apparently was the base of mathematics for the Annunaki. Have you ever wondered why all of our time, counting, and measurements began in bases of twelve, and why many of them still are? According to the Sumerians, the Annunaki gave us the twelve constellations of the Zodiac, twelve hours of the day and night, twelve months, the dozen, twelve inches in a foot—all based on the twelve high elders of the Annunaki that ruled their people. This is how the number twelve became sacred to mankind, too; I would go so far as to say it's the basis for the twelve tribes of Israel and the twelve apostles.

"You see they lived much longer than we do, as did their offspring. This is why some of the great men of the Old Testament lived hundreds of years—Methuselah, Seth, and others. When they designed Adam, they made him so he would not live beyond 120 years. At the same time, according to the Sumerian tablets, the Annunaki living on Earth began to age much faster because of our short 365-day solar cycle. Apparently, our planet affected them to the point where they could no longer return to their home planet, Nibiru, or they would die. So, according to the accounts of the Sumerians, they never left."

"Well," Sofia interjected, "if there were another planet, we must presume that it is a large planet, large enough to sustain life, in our solar system. Even on an elliptical orbit, we would see massive disruption to the solar system if it passed by the sun. Why haven't we found it? Where is it?"

"As far as where the planet is, I think it has been found," Jurgen said simply. "You should look into the work of Dr. Robert Harrington from the U.S. Naval Observatory: I think he has found it, and there is actually a video recording of him meeting with Mr. Sitchin online. The reason, however, that it has taken us so long to discover it is because of that elliptical orbit. The Sumerians stated in their records that it took 3,600 of our Earth years for it to complete one orbit. As it draws closer to Earth, it wreaks havoc on our planet. When it is distant, though, it is difficult for us to detect. The Sumerians claim this was the cause of the great flood, and many other of the cultures and religions around the world talk about it too: the Red and Blue Kachina, a visitor planet in China, Wormwood, the great destroyer. These are references to Nibiru. The Sumerians themselves called Nibiru the Red Dragon. Of course, Revelation 12:3 also says, 'and there appeared another wonder in heaven; and behold, a great red dragon.'"

Just then, the nurse returned.

"I'm so sorry to interrupt, but Mr. Jurgen needs to wrap up for the evening."

Jurgen tsked. "You may be my nurse," he chided her. "but you aren't my mother! These people need my help."

"It's okay," James replied. "We've learned a lot today that will aid our research. Thank you."

"Well, I won't keep you then," Jurgen said. "The books of Zecharia Sitchin may help answer any additional questions you might have. And remember that you can always come back and visit another time."

Back outside Sofia was agitated, almost angry. "I don't buy it, James," she said. "He may be well read, but that doesn't mean he is credible. An object large enough to sustain life would likely rival the earth. We would have found it by now. And it couldn't exist on an elliptical orbit, as Mr. Jurgen believes, because it would be a frozen block of ice when it moved out of the center of the solar system, and then it would heat up as it approached the sun. I mean, the surface temperature of the outer planets is something like 33 Kelvin. That's minus 240 Celsius! I can't imagine the temperature of such an object, but it would garner virtually no light from the sun. It certainly couldn't support any life."

"Maybe there is another explanation," James said.

"Everything alive requires light. The bottom line is, he is wrong, James. Trust me. It makes no sense within the laws of physics."

"Well, you have to agree that there's an interesting relationship between the DNA sequence and his story," James insisted, surprised at her vehemence.

"There are definitely some interesting aspects of the story," Sofia agreed. "But there's too much of it that just doesn't make sense."

POPE PAUL VII
THE VATICAN

"I don't expect to convert anybody here. I don't expect to convert any aliens."
—GUY CONSOLMAGNO, DIRECTOR OF THE VATICAN OBSERVATORY

"Holy Father, there are still no breakthroughs on the DNA sequence," Father Perez told the pope in their next communication. "The team has contacted an expert in the field with regard to the tablets. They are learning more about the threat, and it is only a matter of time before they learn what we already know."

"They must not find out!" the pope said, clearly agitated. "Not yet. The timing is not right. Do what you can to slow down their research, Mateo. We must take action to prevent this from being known before the right time."

"I . . . I'm not sure there is anything I can do," Father Perez said tentatively. "I will keep you apprised as to the team's findings. Perhaps they will uncover the DNA portion before they come close to the rest."

"What about the information that the Minister of Antiquities is holding back? Have you gained access to it yet?"

"No, Holy Father. Not yet."

* * *

In the heart of St. Michel on Rue Xavier Privas, on the left bank of Paris, below a couscous restaurant in an ancient cellar, Khalid sat at a small makeshift worktable. The rounded cellar smelled of mildew and hundreds of years of age. Lamps were set on the floor around the room. The rough-cut, hand-hewn stones formed a perfectly arched cavern, as in many ancient Parisian basements.

Sweat beaded on Khalid's forehead. His trained, calloused hands shook momentarily in fear. After quickly rubbing his bearded chin in frustration, he calmed himself. He glanced at the clock before refocusing on the task at hand, then twisted a pair of wires and soldered them to a small circuit board, trying not to think about the minutes ticking away. A small plume of smoke rose from the device as he finished.

Carefully, he attached a detonator cap to the wires. Then he connected the wires to a capacitor and a cell phone. The circuitry had to be precise before he moved on to the final phase of the build.

Very gently and as slowly as he could, he pushed the detonator into the block of plastic explosive. Then, without breathing, he loaded the plastic and the electronic assembly into a shoe box. He checked the power on the phone and taped the box shut.

21

DR. SATI AM UNNEFER
PARIS, FRANCE

Behold a great, fiery red dragon, having seven heads and ten horns, and seven diadems upon his heads.

—REVELATION 12:3

FATHER PEREZ AND SATI were spending a great deal of time together. Father Perez was fascinated by the Great Pyramids, and never tired of learning more about them. For his part, Sati seemed comfortable confiding in Father Perez. They discussed religion, politics, and history.

Today they sat at their usual spots in the café La Place, regulars now. The proprietor waved to them as they sat down. He obviously enjoyed having them there, and had grown accustomed to driving off any journalists who came along to bother them.

There was a new waiter on the terrace today, a man with a Middle Eastern look. Sati wondered where their usual waiter was. He wasn't sure he liked this man; he had a hard look about him.

"We don't know how old the Great Pyramid of Khufu is," Sati said, in response to Father Perez's question. "In fact, the records of ancient Egypt were all written after the pyramids were constructed. They explain everything about the ancient culture of the Egyptians, from agriculture to lovemaking—but none of them contain contemporary explanations as to how the construction occurred, or who directed it. Of course, we haven't done much to investigate it either," he added. "Dr. Zaher intentionally stifled this information. The more I learn about the DNA code and this Sumerian information, the more it confirms for me that we must have experienced visitors from somewhere else in our universe in ancient times, and they helped build these immense structures."

"I'd have to agree the evidence is starting to point that way for me, as well," Father Perez commented.

"Why would a simple people choose to work with material of such scale?" Sati went on. "Wouldn't a smaller stone block have been easier? And even on this scale, the fact that the Great Pyramid is less than half an inch off of perfect center over its thirteen-acre base is just too unbelievable. No modern building can match that accuracy. I always knew something was wrong with attributing the pyramids to ancient Egyptians. They had no written records, no plans, no advanced mathematics, no sophisticated technology. We're supposed to believe they cut giant, two-ton blocks of limestone with a simple copper ax? Copper doesn't even cut granite or limestone! But they supposedly did it—and then moved the blocks across the land for miles, before depositing it so precisely, mortar wasn't needed! That is more sophisticated than even modern capabilities allow."

"It seems to me that the fault would lie with other archaeologists," Father Perez replied. "Why haven't they challenged this?"

The waiter brought tea and set it nervously down in front of Sati.

Sati stared directly into his eyes and assessed him.

He faltered for a moment. Did the man recognize him? His unease ebbed as the waiter moved on to other tables.

"Dr. Zaher never allowed anyone to challenge it," Sati continued. "And, as time has taken its toll, and more and more people steal from the pyramids, we lose sight of some of the grandeur. You know, they were covered in flat polished stone, with seams that were less than one-seventh of an inch wide. Can you believe that? And Zaher never questioned it—never allowed it to bequestioned. It would have given them a smooth, reflective surface. Since the stones were stolen, people no longer think about it, or how tightly the blocks would have needed to fit together to create that illusion."

"That is amazing," Father Perez said. He lowered his voice, looking past Sati to where their waiter was wiping down a table. "I think the waiter forgot my sandwich. He is definitely not as good as our usual."

"Yes, I agree," Sati replied. "Often, people are not observant." He gave a wry smile. "Father, what would you say if I told you that the Great Pyramid does not have four faces, but eight?"

Father Perez frowned. "Surely you are joking with me, Sati. I may not study Egyptology, but I have seen pictures of the pyramids."

"Ah, but that's just it. You didn't study them, and so you missed the important details, just as others have. Each of the four wide faces of the Great Pyramid at Giza are subtly divided, precisely down the middle. It's remarkable that you can only see the eight sides from above during the equinox, when the sun casts a shadow across its face."

"That is fantastic. So why do you think the pyramids were built?" asked Perez.

"I think the facts point to an advanced race. We could not have done these things as primitive humans. Huge granite boxes are found near the Great Pyramid, polished to within a one-thousandth of an inch of being perfectly flat. We found dozens of these in an antechamber. Ancient Egyptians could not have carved this granite using crude copper tools, and then polished them to a mirror-like surface. But there they are—and, as another fact that might interest you, those granite boxes are all built to the exact dimensions of the Ark of the Covenant as it was described in your Bible."

The afternoon was growing late. The sun was approaching the rooftops of Paris in the west, and it already cast most of the street in late afternoon shadows. People were everywhere, and the café was full of Parisians enjoying a drink after work. The two men ordered their usual evening libations: a small carafe of Bordeaux for Father Perez, an espresso for Sati.

They did not notice the man watching them from across the street— the one who had watched them here several times before, standing in the shadows with his hands in the pockets of his maroon jacket.

As they talked, their waiter returned to the table. But this time he was no longer wearing his apron. He was dressed casually in jeans, with his white shirttails untucked.

That is strange, Father Perez thought.

The man did not say a word, but he stared directly at Sati. Father Perez forced a smile. People occasionally recognized Sati, particularly Egyptians.

This man, however, did not return Father Perez's smile.

Sati's face paled as the man continued to glare. He slowly put down his cup, rattling its saucer. Father Perez shifted uncomfortably and tried to think of something to say. An awkward silence hung in the air.

Finally, the man spoke. "Dr. Sati Am Unnefer?" he said in a raspy voice.

"Yes," Sati said under his breath, the word seeming to fall from him involuntarily.

In one smooth motion, the man pulled a small gun out of his jacket. The matte-black finish of the pistol seemed to absorb the sunlight as he moved the gun to eye level, pointing it at Sati.

Before Father Perez could grasp what he was seeing the gun went off. Flame and smoke emanated from the barrel and the report sounded as the bullet slammed into Sati's chest.

Sati's eyes shot wide as he looked at the man in disbelief. The man turned his gaze to Perez and held it there for what seemed like an eternity.

Father Perez watched his eyes, and terror filled his being as the man slowly shifted the gun toward Father Perez.

The gun was now pointed directly at the priest's head. He couldn't breathe—couldn't move.

Then, unbelievably slowly, the man lowered the gun. He gave Father Perez a slight smirk, and then ran into the crowd, where tables were already toppling as people scattered in all directions. The shooter took off and disappeared into the crowd. Blind with panic, a young girl ran directly into the path of a car and was struck.

Father Perez sat at the table, gasping in disbelief. *Why had he escaped death?* Father Perez felt as if reality had abandoned him. Before he knew what was happening, Father Perez found himself on his knees in a pool of blood, holding his friend's head in his lap. He tried to stop the bleeding with the tablecloth. Sati coughed as Father Perez stared in shock at the impossible amount of blood coming from the small hole in his robes.

Sati tried to speak, but could not. Father Perez was beside himself; all his knowledge of last rites, all the comforting verses and prayers, had left him. "It'll be okay," he said, trying to prevent Sati from coughing up more blood. "Hold on. Help is coming."

There was terror in Sati's eyes. With his last bit of strength, he fumbled in the pocket of his robe and pulled out the small USB drive. Grasping at Father Perez, he managed to put it into the priest's hand.

When Father Perez closed his fingers around the drive, peace washed over Sati's face. He closed his eyes and exhaled his last breath.

AFTERSHOCK

*My people are destroyed for lack of knowledge: because thou hast rejected
knowledge, I will also reject thee, that thou shalt be no priest to me:
seeing thou hast forgotten the law of thy God, I will also forget thy children.*

—HOSEA 4 : 6

Losing Sati was traumatic for everyone. Father Perez was the most disturbed, and took several days off from the project, lighting a candle for Sati and praying in his room.

No one knew for sure if the assassin had targeted Sati individually, or if it had to do with his association with the ESA project. The authorities assumed that Sati was targeted in Paris, as he had been in Cairo, because he had allowed the Americans to excavate the Great Pyramid.

However, many of the others feared for their lives, and Agent Stinson had all team members placed on a supervised and guarded lockdown. A few days after the shooting, Stinson held a security briefing in the large lecture hall for all Project Aquarius members.

"As everyone knows, our good friend and colleague, Dr. Sati Am Unnefer, was tragically murdered by a gunman, just around the corner," he told them. "This is a huge loss for the Egyptian people and to our team. In our view, however, this incident does not in any way indicate that other team members will be targeted. Intelligence chatter intercepted by DSGE and other agencies confirms this, and I want to assure you that after a multi-governmental investigation, we have concluded that this was an isolated incident, perpetrated by fundamentalist Islamic extremists who were directly targeting Dr. Unnefer."

"Doesn't this all seem related?" James interrupted. "I mean, there have been attacks against me, too. And what about that attack at the NSA? These aren't random shootings. Someone is targeting Project Aquarius."

"We don't think so, James. You were the target of a corporate- espionage attempt to steal data. Sati's assistant was a hardliner; several radical Muslim groups in Egypt feel that Sati betrayed their faith and their people. They feel that he had sold out their culture to the Great Satan.

There are many who wanted retribution. We believe the same group was responsible for the attack at NSA. Here is what we have so far on Sati's death. An Egyptian Islamic sect known as the Hashashin had been targeting Dr. Unnefer for his progressive views. The Hashashin are a secret, ancient Muslim sect formed, in the eleventh or twelfth century, who vehemently defend the Muslim religion. They are assassins—in fact, the word comes from their name. We believe that they killed Dr. Unnefer because of some public statements he made that were seen as contrary to the Muslim faith, and because of his excavation of the Pyramid. Additionally, we have connected his assistant in Cairo, the one responsible for the bombing of his office, with this sect. We don't think there is any connection to be made to the greater team."

Something stirred within Father Perez. *The Hashashin—where have I heard that name before?*

James pressed the issue. "Agent Stinson, how do you know that this man or this group will not return and target others?" he asked, looking over at Sofia. "After all, if Sati was doing something that these fundamentalists found offensive, the rest of us could certainly be accused of the same."

Stinson ignored him. "Based upon video surveillance at the scene obtained by DGSE, we were able to identify the murderer as Mohamed Abdallah of Jordan," he said, crossing his arms, resolutely. "Three days ago he came to Paris on a flight directly from Cairo. This was confirmed by French border control at Charles de Gaulle. Unfortunately, DGSE also confirmed that he left from Orly Airport less than two hours after the shooting before he could be apprehended. This was very well planned and orchestrated. By the time we had an ID on him, he had already landed in Egypt and disappeared. But we have assets on the ground looking for him now. We'll do everything we can to find him."

* * *

The meeting ended, and everyone milled out of the conference room. Everyone but Father Perez, who remained behind, sat in contemplation. Something fluttered through his memory about the Hashashin;

he struggled to place where he had heard that name before.

In a flood of realization, it came back to him.

When he had joined the Jesuit Order, he had prepared himself by reading official Catholic accounts of the Order, as well as some accounts that were outside of the Vatican's purview. There had always been rumors of Jesuit assassinations and a secret alliance with the Hashashin, but these were never spoken of openly. In fact, recent assassinations, such as that of Jill Dando for her work on anti-Jesuit productions and Juan José Gerardi for his publications connecting the Guatemalan Civil War and the Jesuits, had received little attention. Clearly not as much attention as the failed assassinations such as the attempt on John Paul II's life. Although in that case, the news tracked down the killer, they did not continue investigating the trail that many speculate would have taken them to the stronghold of the Jesuit Order.

There were deep rumors and apparent secret ties between the Jesuit Order and the Hashashin. When anyone within the Church attempted to research the subject, they were met first with silence and then threatened. Father Perez had heard that people who continued to focus on the issue often disappeared.

Perez's own interest had never rested in the political matters of this world; as long as he was left alone in his observatory, he had always been content. Yet ever since Cardinal Russo had shattered his peaceful existence, that had begun to change; he'd begun to question his previous indifference. How much of the history of his Order was rumor, and how much of it was suppressed fact?

THE GROUP OF FRIENDS
PARIS, FRANCE

And as he sat upon the mount of Olives, the disciples came unto him privately, saying, Tell us, when shall these things be? and what shall be the sign of thy coming, and of the end of the world?

—MATTHEW 24:3

James, Stan, Sofia, and Father Perez sat at a small table at the Papillon in the 5th Arrondissement. This tiny restaurant on Rue Mouffetard gave them the privacy they needed to talk and mourn their friend, whose absence was vivid. Their security detail sat near them, ever vigilant.

"Here's the drawing Jurgen gave us of the planet Nibiru and its 3,600-year elliptical cycle, created by Zecharia Sitchin," James said, opening the sketch on the table between them. "Jurgen believes this planet would cross the Earth's path, based upon the Sumerian records."

Sofia exhaled deeply. "I know what you want, James," she said. "I'll look into it and see if there is any evidence of such an object. Just don't be disappointed when there is nothing out there."

"Clearly nothing is there," Stan chortled.

"Look," James said, looking around at all of them. "Robert is dead. Sati is dead. Someone wants Project Aquarius's information about the books and the DNA sequence. The longer these mysteries remain unsolved, the longer we are all in danger and the longer it will be until we can go home." He looked at the others. "We have to look into every lead we have."

Father Perez stared blankly at the wall. "Who will advocate for the artifacts and ensure they are returned to the Egyptian people now?" he asked.

"Sati would want us to solve this mystery," James insisted. "What if these Sumerian gods, the Annunaki, are behind the memristor in the golden books and the DNA code?"

"The idea's preposterous," Stan exclaimed. It was obvious that this avenue of evidence was beginning to scare him.

"It's not, Stan. Look at Mars, look at the Great Pyramid, look at the Sumerian records."

"The only thing keeping me from walking out of here are these damn gold books with their sophisticated engineering," Stan said. His features softened. "But you may be right, anyway. Let's do it. Let's look into this map of Sitchin's."

Father Perez looked down at his hands and exhaled deeply.

JAMES ANDERSON
PARIS, FRANCE

And another angel came out from the altar, which had power over fire; and cried with a loud cry to him that had the sharp sickle, saying, Thrust in thy sharp sickle, and gather the clusters of the vine of the earth; for her grapes are fully ripe.

—REVELATION 14:18

"You know," James continued that evening, as Sofia walked with him to his flat, "we're are wrong. We have thousands of religions, thousands of stories, thousands of gods, all of which proclaim themselves as the only correct version. By default, they're all wrong."

It was late evening. The cool air was invigorating as they walked from the Papillon to James's apartment. As they approached Saint-Sulpice, the two agents assigned to protect James and Sofia stopped them outside the building. Thankful as he was for the added security, James let out a frustrated sigh.

"Sorry, sir, you know the routine," one of the agents said, as the other one went inside. "It'll only take a minute."

James playfully captured Sofia in his arms. "This sure makes having a drink with you more difficult."

She smiled back at him. "Who said I'm thirsty, Mr. Anderson?"

"Oh, back to Mr. Anderson, are we?"

Before she could answer, a tremendous blast threw them to the ground as the building erupted.

The ground shook like an earthquake. The concussion drove glass and flames from the windows of James's apartment and debris rained around them. Alarms from parked cars began blaring everywhere. The tree abutting the building erupted into an inferno, its green leaves transforming into roiling black smoke instantly. Screaming people fled the square in all directions; an elderly man was struck by falling stones and fell to the ground, and someone struggled to help him up.

"Move! Now!" The agent lifted them to their feet and dragged them down the street. "Code one at Saint-Sulpice! Explosion in James Anderson's flat. Priority one response!" he bellowed into his walkie-talkie.

"10-4, 342," came the response. "Pickup in three minutes. Rendezvous point two."

Suddenly, before James could make sense of what was happening a small blue delivery van pulled out of the alley that ran behind his apartment building. Its windows were tinted; its tires squealed as it came to a stop about fifty yards away. Slowly its window lowered, and James saw something emerging from it.

Almost immediately, automatic gunfire erupted from the window. The agent threw them both to the ground and covered them with his body as he fumbled for his gun to return fire. Machine-gun fire riddled the side of the building beside them, sending small fragments of limestone flying around them and biting into their skin. The dust mixed with the smoke from the burning building, covering them in a thick haze. The sound was deafening.

As the van screeched past, a bullet caught the agent in the hip. He cried out, grabbing his leg, then struggled to pull them up from the ground and shove them forward. Blood was already pooling on the cobblestones.

"Go! Run to the car—" he growled through clenched teeth, struggling to stand. "Get to that corner." He pointed ahead of them, then fell back to his knees. James hesitated, wanting to help him. "Now!" the agent screamed. "Don't stop! No matter what—just run your ass off!"

James grabbed Sofia's hand, nearly jerking her from her feet, and they began to run. James's lungs burned with the caustic smoke from the fire; he felt as if he would retch. He couldn't run fast enough.

Before they could get more than a hundred yards, they heard the return of the squealing tires. More gunfire rang out.

James pulled Sofia into a large doorway, and they peered around the corner. The agent had risen to his feet and emptied his magazine into the approaching van. As he fired the last bullet, the van screeched to a halt.

The agent dropped the empty clip and reached for a spare. He was visibly shaking from loss of blood. A man stepped out of the van with an automatic rifle aimed at him. As the agent struggled to raise his gun, the man with the rifle opened fire. The agent's body shuddered with each shot fired, and a mist of blood filled the air behind him. It was finished before the agent's pistol hit the ground.

James pulled Sofia to his body, covering her mouth to stifle a scream. He hoped their attackers hadn't seen them. Peering out from the planters beside the door, he watched as the door of the van closed with the assassin inside. It reversed slowly, then crept forward toward the fountain. It continued down Rue Palentine, perpendicular to the street they were on. They were in the clear—for now.

"Let's go," he whispered, as soon as the van was out of sight. He ran as fast as he could, pulling Sofia behind him to Rue de Vaugirard in front of the Luxembourg garden. James was thankful all the one-way streets in the area would prevent the van from returning too quickly.

"Do you know where we're supposed to meet the car?" Sofia asked.

"I think right here," James replied. He looked around: no sign of the car.

The seconds ticked by like hours.

"Shit!" James swore, near panic. "We may be safer if we keep moving on foot."

He grabbed Sofia's hand and they ran behind an odd corner in front of the Hotel Luxembourg Parc. There was a small green space in front of the hotel. They squatted behind a little hedgerow that ran along the sidewalk. The gunfire had cleared people from most of the surrounding streets. A couple in the lobby looked out the window, clearly wondering what Sofia and James were doing.

James peered out between the bases of the bushes. He could see the street just a few feet away from where they lay. He struggled to hear anything other than the pounding of his heartbeat in his ears. There was very little traffic on the road other than a taxi that passed ten feet from their position. A bus approached from much further down the street.

Then he saw it. The van approached slowly, coming straight

toward them.

"Don't move," James whispered. The grass and branches from the hedge pressed into them as they tried to make themselves even flatter to the ground. Both of them held their breath. James could hear arguing from inside the van.

The van was right in front of them and had slowed almost to the point of stopping. James's heart skipped a beat. *Should we run?* he thought. His instinct to escape was overwhelming; he heard sirens in the distance and concentrated on their sound to steady his mind.

The van crept past them and turned the corner. James sucked in a breath, then jumped up and peered around the building. The van continued down Rue de Vaugirard.

"Oh my God," Sofia said breathlessly behind him. "There," she said suddenly, pointing. A black Mercedes approached from the other direction and stopped in the middle of the road the moment the driver saw them.

"How do we know it's safe?" James said, holding her back.

"Mr. Anderson! Ms. Petrescu!" shouted the main in the car. "Over here. Quickly." He motioned them forward.

"Well, he's not shooting," Sofia said.

They exchanged a tense look before running to the car. As soon as they reached it, they dove into the back seat and the driver took off at top speed.

Sofia curled up on James's shoulder and sobbed. James stroked her hair, his bewilderment catching up to him. Why had they been targeted? They had nothing to do with Egypt or its Antiquities Department. He shook his head darkly.

"Stinson was wrong," He muttered. "The team is the target."

22

And there shall be signs in the sun, and in the moon, and in the stars; and upon the earth distress of nations, with perplexity; the sea and the waves roaring.

—LUKE 21:25

"YOUR HOLINESS, we still know nothing about the DNA," Father Perez reported. "There are some avenues of hope that the research will break it at some point soon, but there has been little progress."

"Have you reviewed the information that Dr. Unnefer gave you?" the pope asked.

"Yes," said Father Perez anxiously. "I'm looking into it now. I should have a report on it soon."

"Good. How tragic an end for Dr. Unnefer," the pope said.

"Yes. It was deeply upsetting. And Holy Father . . . that leads me to ask you . . . again: don't you believe it is time to tell the Project Aquarius team of our findings from Mount Graham? Perhaps they need to know the urgency we face," Father Perez searched for a rationale. "It may compel them to work faster to solve this DNA code?"

"Absolutely not," the pope said firmly. "No one is to know. You need to take every possible precautionary measure to prevent this information leaking to them. It is for the Vatican and the Vatican alone to use this information. We must prepare the church first. Only after this event will we have the power to bring salvation to millions and unify the world under the Vatican. We are keeping this quiet. But while we're on the topic, Mateo, I'm afraid I have some rather bad news."

"Yes?"

"It is about your young assistant, Joseph. Do you remember him and the help he gave you at Mount Graham?"

"Of course. What is it?" Father Perez asked, a knot forming in his stomach.

"It appears that he had sent an unsecured message to his mother by email, alluding to your finding and its cataclysmic meaning."

"Oh no!" Father Perez couldn't believe it. "Why would Joseph do that?"

"Out of love and fear for his family I'm sure," the pope replied. "Of course, we had to chastise him for this breach of security. Cardinal Russo spoke with him to ensure his understanding of the Jesuit oath." The pope slowed his speech down as he went on. "I'm sorry to tell you this, Mateo, especially over the phone, but poor Joseph must have been deeply distraught over his dereliction of duty. Chastisement can create an overwhelming sense of failure in those who rebel against their oath." He paused.

Perez felt the racing of his heart. "What happened to Joseph, Your Holiness?" he breathed.

"He was found hanging outside of the LUCIFER telescope housing.

He had apparently hanged himself with an extension cord."

Father Perez was speechless. He could not believe what he was hearing. The young, vibrant astrophysics student was dead? A wave of immense sadness, frustration, and guilt washed over him. Was it his fault for involving Joseph in this finding?

"It is all very tragic and very sad—and odd," the pope went on. "He was found hanging sixty feet up in the air from the telescope housing. How he got up that high, no one knows. He was barefoot and wearing a white cassock."

Perez was speechless. Tears welled up in his eyes. One sob escaped his throat.

"But, Father Perez," the pope finally continued, "at least we can take solace in the fact that our information is safe. We can honor Joseph, knowing his contribution to our research will be continued with the work you are doing for the Church, and that it will benefit our holy work of salvation in the coming dark days."

Was this a threat? A chill ran down Father Perez's back.

DR. PETRESCU'S RESEARCH

And God blessed them, and God said unto them, be fruitful, and multiply, and replenish the earth, and subdue it: and have dominion over the fish of the sea, and over the fowl of the air, and over every living thing that moveth upon the earth.

—GENESIS 1: 28

After a week of being confined to the Le Relais Saint Germain hotel, James wished some level of normalcy would return to their lives. The French police had apprehended six men in conjunction with the bombing. Agent Stinson assured them all that this was only a small cell operating in Paris; but even with the near-constant supervision and security detail, James felt very uncomfortable moving about in public. Miraculously, none of his neighbors had been hurt in the blast;

Madame Morel had even been out of town. Stinson was apologetic, and gave several excuses for the lapse in intelligence. What else could he say?

The night of the bombing, the authorities apprehended the van on the Périphérique as it tried to flee the city. They arrested two men, whose phones were recovered. Several days later, they arrested three others at a small flat in the Latin Quarter, after scrubbing phone records. Stinson conceded that the Hashashin were behind the crime, and that there might be a greater threat to all Project members.

Each team member was limited to a minimal amount of move-ment in public, even with their assigned security detail. The French news media had been told that the attackers had been ISIS extremists targeting westerners. For the most part, the press bought off on that line, especially in light of the recent rise in radical Islamic terrorism and the Paris attacks.

Sofia had rented a small flat in the Marais, a neighborhood James loved. A marsh in ancient times, the Marais had been drained and donated to the religious orders; it was where the Order of the Temple, the Knights Templar, built a Maison du Temple in 1240. Now it was a hip area and the center of the Jewish community, with its famous Rue des Rosiers as its main pedestrian thoroughfare. Fantastic shops, restaurants, history, and youth combined to make it electric, especially on Sundays. However, today all of this was lost on James.

He approached Sofia's building and the doorman let him up to her apartment. The guard in the hallway knew him on sight, and let him pass through as well. He pushed the front door open and found Sofia sitting in the middle of the living room floor, legs crossed, still in her pajamas.

"Hey," James said. "What are you doing? It's 1:00 p.m. Why weren't you at the ESA today? I tried to call you twice."

"I'm sorry," she said, continuing to scan the paper in her hand. James glanced at the disorganized piles of paper scattered around her on the floor and wondered if she needed to see the ESA psychologist. The printer was spitting out more paper. Two computers were open in front of her. And James could see deep concern in her eyes, which were framed by dark circles.

"We need to talk," Sofia said.

She didn't get up, but instead began rifling through the papers immediately to her left. Now James could tell she had not slept, despite being in pajamas. He looked over in the corner of the studio by the window and saw the bed still made, with her purse, coat, and more papers covering it.

Suddenly, Sofia stood up and handed him a sheet of paper.

"Yes," James said as he glanced at the image. "This is the picture from Sitchin's book."

"No. It's not," she said, walking across the room to a series of neatly stacked piles along the wall. Out of this paper chaos, she had apparently reserved the organized piles along the wall for the serious stuff. She grabbed a stack, fished through its contents for a moment, and then pulled out a stapled document.

She returned to James and handed the document to him.

He read aloud. "The Location of Planet X by Dr. R. S. Harrington, October 1988." He looked up at Sofia, confused.

"Dr. Harrington was Chief Astronomer at the Naval Observatory. He was in an elite class of astronomers," she said. James scanned through a few pages of the document as she continued. "He was working to determine the cause of a perturbation in the outer planets' orbits."

James stared blankly at the document before him. It contained pages of astrophysics jargon that clearly went beyond his education. Sofia dropped her paper-filled hand to her side, letting out a sigh of frustration.

"So, imagine a planet going around the sun in a smooth orbit," she said. "Now, imagine at a point in the orbit, the planet is pulled outward just a bit, and its rate of travel changes. That is a perturbation. A perturbation tells us there is another gravitational force acting on a planet's orbit. That's how we found Neptune. Uranus's orbit had a small bump outward, due to Neptune's gravitational force. From this, we could calculate the exact location—then when we turned our telescopes to that location, there it was. However, after Neptune was tracked, a perturbation was noticed in its orbit too. So we simply repeated the process, and that's how we found Pluto.

"However, Harrington did the calculations based on the masses of Pluto and Neptune, and discovered that Pluto alone could not account for the perturbations of Neptune's orbit. At that point, he knew there was another object out there. As we continued to develop better telescopes, we decided it was likely that small planetoids were causing the perturbation. Not surprisingly, we found many of these, but they were tiny and smaller than our moon.

"Dr. Harrington noticed other very subtle perturbations in all the planets' orbits, and calculated that a very massive gravitational force was acting on all of them from one precise point in space. From this, he calculated the location of this mass. That is reflected in the picture I handed you. He believed this object was in a highly elliptical orbit, 30 degrees below the ecliptic plane approaching Earth from Sagittarius. You noticed that it's identical to Sitchin's drawing. Harrington also believed it may have an orbital cycle of about 3,600 years."

Her voice had risen throughout her explanation, but now, they stood in silence looking at each other for a moment.

"What the hell?" James said, excited. "So you found confirmation that the Sumerian texts are correct? Why did you stay home today? We need to tell the others right away."

"Wait," Sofia interjected. "There's more."

She shuffled through the papers in her hand and gave him another stack of documents that were stapled together. James looked deeply into her eyes, loving her even more for all the work she had done.

"So," she continued, "Dr. Harrington, one of the most experienced astronomers alive at the time, was so convinced of his calculations, he had a special telescope commissioned and organized an expedition to New Zealand. Only from there could they observe something in deep space if its orbit were below the orbital plane of the earth and the other planets. This was his life's work. He planned for years to go on this expedition." She paused, biting her lip.

"Well?" James demanded.

"Dr. Harrington died mysteriously before he returned to the U.S.," she said staring at James. "Although he must have made his observations, none of his findings were ever published."

"What do you mean?"

"Let me read from his obituary," she said, looking down at one of the papers in her hand. "'In his final years, Dr. Harrington lost interest in the search for Planet X . . . Bob became quite skeptical about the existence of any other large planets.' James, he died right after the exhibition he'd planned to test his theory. No one could believe he'd died so suddenly.

"Apparently even his longtime friend and colleague, Dr. Tom Van Flandern, affirmed Harrington's findings prior to his death. However, shortly afterward, Van Flandern reversed his comments and went radio silent. No one has heard from him since." Sofia's face was white. "Things are not adding up here. Something is not right." She let the accusation hang.

"But why would anyone care if someone found another planet? Isn't that interesting scientifically?"

"I don't know, James, but it is very strange. I want to know why it is that Dr. Harrington's information—based on modern scientific research and calculations—matches the predictions of the ancient Sumerians. I want to know where his research is. I want to know why someone published a lie in his obituary. I want to know why he died so suddenly of poisoning. I want to know why his colleague changed his story and then disappeared."

Once he was sure Sofia had calmed down and was not planning on jumping into the Seine, James convinced her to join him at ESA later. "I'll arrange with Stinson for us to stay late," he said.

"Okay. I need to look into this more. I have some other findings that concern me, deeply. But—" she paused and exhaled. "I don't want to raise concern unless I'm right. Give me some time. I need to do some additional research and make a few calls to some colleagues."

* * *

That evening at the ESA, James gathered with his friends in a small conference room. Stan and Father Perez needed to hear what Sofia had found. She gave them the version James had heard earlier.

When she'd finished, Stan confronted her. "Look, Sofia, honestly—think about it. If this planet is out there, we would know about it. If this thing were coming toward us, it would be one of the greatest findings in astronomy. Why would someone keep it hidden? Plus, what about all the amateur astronomers? Surely some of them would have noticed it and posted it on the internet. You just couldn't keep something that big hidden from society.

"And you think the circumstances surrounding Harrington's death are strange? Who would kill an astronomer to keep the discovery of a new planet from being announced? Why would that be such a big deal? We have found several of these new planetoids or dwarf planets—whatever they call them," Stan added. "And of course, Sitchin is wrong about the possibility of any planet that far out supporting life. These are ice balls in space. No life is out there."

"Look, I'm in your camp," Sofia said. "I'm just telling you something here is bothering me. Some things aren't adding up."

Father Perez leaned over to James. "Look, James, I don't think there is any reason for me to be here. I'm not valuable to this conversation—after all, I was sent here by the Vatican merely to observe as a nonparticipating U.N. representative. I think I have been straying from my initial objective too frequently as of late." He swallowed rather loudly and glanced quickly to the side before excusing himself.

James frowned as he watched him go. For the guy who'd helped him find Sitchin, Father Perez was sure acting strangely. *What could have him so nervous?* James wondered.

JAMES ANDERSON
PARIS, FRANCE

*And I saw when the Lamb opened one of the seals, and I heard as it were
the noise of thunder, one of the four beasts saying, 'Come and see.'*

—REVELATION 6:1

James had convinced Sofia to walk, with their security of course, to the
Musée d'Orsay and talk. It was clear she needed to get away from her
research and the ESA.

"You are sweet to force me to take a break. I know what you're doing,
and I appreciate it," she smiled. James paid the admission for Sofia and
himself, as well as for the two security guards walking with them, and
the four of them entered.

"I'm glad for the chance to talk to you alone," she said quietly. "The
information on Harrington and his findings has me really nervous. I
clearly can't talk to anyone at the ESA about it—I don't even really feel
comfortable bringing up the issue there."

"I understand. Well, we can talk here and enjoy some of the masters
as we walk."

As nervous as she was, once they were in the museum she relaxed
noticeably. She talked freely of the masterworks they saw, and James
was amazed at her depth of knowledge: she seemed to know everything
about Van Gogh, Cezanne, Monet, Gauguin.

They had walked for about forty minutes, James figured they should
probably be getting back to the ESA. As they wandered through the main
gallery, James looked around the massive expanse, his eyes taking in the
beauty of the architecture. It had once been a train station, he recalled.

It was then that James saw him.

Up on the balcony, an Arab man was staring down at them. As soon
as James made eye contact with the man, he moved, walking quickly
out of view. James couldn't be sure, but it looked like the face he had
seen so many times.

James's heart rate accelerated. He didn't want to scare Sofia, and he fought the desire to run. But it had to be him—James was sure of it. He was coming for them.

"Shit," James muttered. He grabbed Sofia's hand; his look let her know something was wrong. He whispered to his security detail, "Look, I think we are being followed. I think I've seen this guy several times before."

"Which one is he?" one guard asked, scanning the crowd.

"He's an Arab-looking guy—he's gone," James said. "We have to get out of here now."

"Oui, Monsieur Anderson," replied one of the guards. "I know a back door that exits on Rue de Lille. Let's avoid the main entrance."

They began moving quickly. Both security guards had their hands on their guns, inside of their jackets. They jogged through the halls of the museum toward the exit. As they wound through a narrow hallway, one of the men tapped James on the shoulder.

"You and Sofia walk ahead a bit, with Michael, to the exit," he said. "It is just down this hallway. I'm going to wait here at this turn to see if he's still following us."

James continued through the narrow hallway, with Sofia and the other security guard following closely. James rounded a corner and ran straight into the chest of the Arab man. James screamed "Help!"

Michael immediately jumped between them and leveled his gun at the man's head. "On the ground, now!" he shouted.

The Arab man let out a shocked scream. "Wait—don't shoot!" He quickly laid face down on the ground. "What have I done? Please—don't hurt me!" he cried.

"Who are you? Tell me right now!" Michael demanded.

"I don't understand," the man muttered.

"Why are you following me?" James demanded. Furious thoughts of Robert, Sati, and his destroyed apartment flashed through his mind.

"I . . . I . . . was trying to give you back . . . this . . . your wallet," the man pleaded. At once, Michael and James looked to his outstretched hand, where he clutched a wallet.

James was stunned. "What do you mean give me my wallet?"

"You left it at the ticket counter. When . . . when you paid me, Monsieur. I saw your picture on your ID in your wallet, and came to find you . . . to give it back. I'm sorry—I don't know what I did wrong."

James bent down and grabbed the man, pulling him up and shoving him against the wall. He took a hard look at the man. Then the realization set in.

"Oh my God. I'm so sorry," he said, his hands shaking. "We thought you were someone else. Please forgive us."

ESA, LATE NIGHT

And I beheld when he had opened the sixth seal, and, lo, there was a great earthquake, and the sun became black as sackcloth of hair, and the moon became as blood.

—REVELATION 6:12

Stinson had arranged for ongoing access to ESA headquarters after hours. In fact, he was more than happy for them to meet on the property. Not only were they easier to guard there, but it also kept them out of public places where media could potentially overhear their discussions.

The security guard at the front desk checked James, Stan, and Father Perez in individually as they returned from dinner. Everyone sat close around the small table, which was just big enough to accommodate them. Although Father Perez continued to act as though he wished he were somewhere else, Stan and James were engaged in a lively discussion about the latest attempts at opening the secrets of the golden books.

"So when the books are connected, we can measure a very subtle magnetic field, which we're now analyzing." Stan was saying when Sofia walked into the room, a large stack of paper on top of the laptop she was carrying. She was clearly agitated; she said nothing but went right to work, setting up a small projector and connecting her computer to it. She avoided eye contact with the others, even James. Once she had everything settled, she faced them.

"Well," she said, "it turns out Dr. Harrington and Sitchin were correct."

Stan raised his eyebrows, pushed back a bit from the table, and crossed his arms, ready to refute the evidence. He and James exchanged glances.

"However, I don't think it's a planet," Sofia continued.

"Clearly, both Sitchin and Harrington had been discussing a planet in their research," Stan countered, crossing his arms. "What are you saying now?"

"Since the 1980s, when Dr. Harrington was alive, we have performed more accurate observations using satellites, and more detailed calculations with computers," Sofia said. "To have a gravitational impact big enough to cause the perturbations that he measured in the orbits of the planets, it is more likely that this object is a brown dwarf. I used more recent data and redid those calculations, no fewer than ten times. That's what I think we are dealing with—a brown dwarf." She looked deadly serious, almost as if she were about to cry.

"Sorry, Sofia," James said. "You have to teach the new kid again. What is a brown dwarf?"

"A brown dwarf is a smaller version of a star. Its mass wasn't large enough to initiate hydrogen fusion, so it radiates very little or no light, or it radiates outside of the visible spectrum, although it may produce a lot of heat and have a large gravitational force." She anticipated James's next question. "And yes, these can hold planets and planetoids in orbit, as we believe many do. This could fit Jurgen and Sitchin's narrative."

James looked over at Father Perez. The priest's head was buried in his hands. James wondered why both of the astronomers were so upset. This had to mean something very bad.

"Since the early 1900s, we've known that some stars were binary, meaning they were rotating around each other in pairs," Sofia went on. "These were usually of similar size and mass, and maintained a fairly consistent orbit, with a constant distance between the two stars. We observed these type of stars for years, though it was always assumed that the occurrence is very rare. However, around 1995, we realized we were wrong—really wrong. We discovered that nearly half of all stars in the galaxy were in a binary relationship.

"This fact was startling to astronomers. Then, in 2005, there was another shock to the astronomical world. Up until that point in time, we had only been looking in the visible-light spectrum for binary observations. When we utilized an infrared telescope, such as those on the IRAS and WISE satellites, we found that *well over* 90 percent of all stars are binary."

"Holy shit," Stan muttered.

"The vast majority of binary stars include a star like our sun. In these cases, the other is almost always a brown dwarf. These brown dwarfs are only visible within the infrared spectrum, are cool compared to our sun, and are much, much smaller: about thirteen times the size of Jupiter would be a good reference on average.

"We now know that, statistically, most stars have a smaller companion star as part of their system. These companion stars orbit their main star, but due to their gravitational and mass differences, the dwarf star moves in an elliptical orbit. In other words, the orbits of binary brown dwarf stars look just like Sitchin's and Harrington's drawings. At their perigee, they are very close to their larger companion, like our planets. In their apogee, they may be hundreds of billions of miles from the star.

"I looked at perturbation measurements over a period of ten years, for all of the planets. As time goes forward, the perturbations are increasing in amplitude, getting stronger. This object is getting closer. How close, I don't know. It could still be hundreds of years off. But it is heading our way. It all depends on how big it is."

Everyone was speechless for a moment.

"So it's possible Sitchin's interpretations of the cuneiform writings may be correct?" James asked hesitantly. "Including what he wrote about the Annunaki and all?

"Well, hold on," Sofia said, her tone defensive. "Let's not get ahead of ourselves. We don't know there is a planet or planets around this object. And even if there were, it is very unlikely they could harbor life."

"Oh my God," Stan said, shaking his head. "Does anyone else know about this?"

"I think we have to assume so," Sofia said, "thought I believe we would have heard about it if it were only a planet. After all, as you mentioned, we recently identified many other planetoids in the outer regions of the solar system. However, the discovery of a brown dwarf so close to Earth is unheard of. I think some people in very high positions must know; maybe they don't want the public to panic. The IRAS and WISE telescopes had to have surveyed this."

"Panic? Why should people panic because a dwarf star is found?" asked James, confused.

Sofia let out a long breath and sat down heavily in her chair. "I don't know how to put this . . . well, take our moon, for instance," she said, "it has a very small mass. However, it is big enough for its gravity to cause a bulge in our oceans. The oceans on the side of the earth that faces the moon can experience tidal swells of more than nine feet."

"Yeah, that's what makes the tides," James stated.

"Right," she said. "So if the sun has a binary companion, the gravitational effects upon us at its passage would be about a thousand times stronger than the moon's. This would be catastrophic. The tidal swell alone could be six hundred feet high, maybe even twice that."

"A massive moving wall of water washing over the globe," Stan said quietly.

"A flood of biblical proportions," Father Perez said, looking down at the floor.

Everyone stared at him for a moment, stunned.

Stan turned to Sofia. "Could this be what caused the great flood recounted by so many ancient civilizations?"

"That would be one of its real geophysical effects, yes," Sofia answered. "Based on my calculations, this things is already moving very fast. And it should accelerate as it approaches the sun. Its passing could occur very quickly, within a matter of weeks or months from when it first becomes visible."

Stan leaned forward in his chair and looked hard at her. "So this star causes a great flood that repeats once every 3,600 years, and that lasts—what—forty days and forty nights?"

James shook his head in disbelief. "How could this be covered up?" he wondered aloud. "Why would this be hidden from the public?"

"What could we do, James? There is nowhere to go—nowhere to hide," Sofia said grimly. "We have no way to prepare for such a calamity. Knowing the truth would just cause massive social unrest, rioting, panic."

"This is all connected . . . all connected," Stan mutterer, his face turning white. "The golden books with the cuneiform writing, the apocalyptic warning, the pyramids, Sitchin, the Annunaki, this brown dwarf—there is something connecting it all. We need more people working on this."

"What if Sofia is right? What if someone, or several someones, are deliberately hiding it?" James challenged. "What then? I mean, it sounds like someone killed Dr. Harrington over this."

"There's more," Sofia said, rubbing her forehead. "Dr. De Vos was right. Climate change is a cover-up."

"What?" James asked.

"This brown dwarf's proximity is what's causing climate change on Earth," Sofia said. "It has nothing to do with man. It has everything to do with increased seismic activity, massively increasing volcanism on Earth, movement of our poles and migration of the polar centers—all caused by our binary companion, in an electromagnetic relationship with our sun. I believe we are very near the perihelion of our binary brown dwarf. It is quickly approaching. I have found a systematic shift of all of the planets' magnetic poles—all the planets are being affected. And all the planets are experiencing unprecedented changes in their atmospheres: Pluto is warming and its atmospheric pressure is increasing, Venus's atmospheric oxygen content is rising dramatically, Mars's polar ice caps are melting, Jupiter's atmospheric temperature has increased eighteen degrees and its storm system has changed. Neptune and Uranus are also exhibiting incredible changes in their atmosphere. We know all these things are occuring, but they are usually only looked at in isolation. The binary star is the common causal link.

"In fact, I know I'm correct, because these changes began occurring with the outermost planets first, and the pattern is working its way toward Earth. Jupiter is the most recent to experience a pole flip. We could be experiencing the same thing soon. The sun itself has shown an increase in its electromagnetic field: more than 200 percent in the last one hundred years. This is all more evidence of an electromagnetic connection between the planets and the sun's binary companion."

"Incredible," Stan muttered.

"Throughout history, astrophysicists have been trying to figure out why there is a subtle procession of the zodiac across the sky that changes by about fifty-three arc seconds per year," Sofia explained. "Basically, every year a constellation changes its alignment with Earth ever so slightly. Copernicus first calculated this phenomenon based upon the earth's interaction with the sun and the moon.

"Basically, it was believed that the gravitational relationship between the earth, sun, and moon caused this deviation. However, over the years scientists noticed that a simple calculation was insufficient to describe the motion. So we added more variables to it. Every ten years or so, we completely recreate the calculation. When I factored in the assumed gravitational force from the brown dwarf, I balanced the equation—perfectly. This explains why the rate of procession is accelerating: it naturally accelerates as the gravitational force upon the earth and the sun from our binary companion increases as it gets closer. The procession is moving faster and faster all the time, now; only an inbound gravitational anomaly can account for it."

"Sofia, can you prove this?" Stan interrupted. "Is it something you can show the team? I mean, do you have actual calculations, measurements, images, statements? If everyone on the team is aware of the significance of this and its reality, the higher-ups won't be able to sit on it. As they say, there is safety in numbers."

"I know it's there. But short of tapping into the WISE or an IRAS satellite, I cannot provide you an image." She contemplated the situation for a moment. "However, I do have some friends and colleagues I could reach out to. I can try to get some corroboration."

"We'll need that. We need to go to the full team with as much sound evidence and verifiable information as we can," Stan said.

"I'll do my best," Sofia said melancholically.

"And until we have that proof, we tell no one," James concluded.

* * *

Cardinal Russo strolled into the papal offices. A large upside-down cross, representing the crucifixion of Saint Peter, sat on the pope's desk beside a small vase of flowers. Pope Paul was intently reading something there, and Cardinal Russo waited, standing before the desk. His eyes roamed over shelves behind the pope that were packed with books, artifacts, and pictures.

"Yes," the pope said, looking up from his reading.

"Our efforts are failing, Holy Father." Cardinal Russo said. "We cannot control the information. It is just days away from being widely distributed."

The pope groaned. "Is there nothing more we can do? The DNA has not been decoded, and that is something we need first."

"With all due respect, Your Holiness, there will be time to continue work on the DNA code later. Once the information is out on the findings concerning our second sun—chaos will ensue."

"You are correct, of course," the pope sighed after a long pause. "The appearance of the sign of the son of man is upon us. I suppose we have enough information. It begins." The pope nodded resolutely. "Do what needs to be done."

Father Russo nodded and walked out of the office.

23

JAMES ANDERSON
PARIS, FRANCE

And I looked, and behold a pale horse: and his name that sat on him was Death, and Hell followed with him. And power was given unto them over the fourth part of the earth, to kill with sword, and with hunger, and with death, and with the beasts of the earth.

—REVELATION 6:8

JAMES FOUND HIMSELF WANDERING through St. Germain, absorbed in thought. Though he walked with two security guards, he felt utterly alone.

He wound down the back streets near Place Buci trying to forget about Sofia's revelations and the implications they stirred up. In the crowded evening streets, lined with tables and chairs full of Parisians drinking and laughing, he felt like he could simply disappear. He stopped at the Bonaparte and lit a cigarette.

Looking across the square at the church of St. Germain, he wondered what Sofia's discovery meant, spiritually speaking. He had always been a spiritual man, though he'd never believed that every word in the Bible was literally true. Still, he believed that some sort of higher being had spiritually induced the messages, the ethics, and the intent of the Bible's parables and stories, and felt deeply that this life was not all there was.

He stared at St. Germain, as it glowed softly in the nearby streetlamps. The builders had laid its first stone around the sixth century, in a grassy field outside of the main walls of Paris. He often wished he could peer back in time and see what it was like in those days. He could almost imagine the people walking from the city to attend the small church out in the field.

St. Germain had withstood the conquering Romans and many failed governments, and it still bore the wounds of the Nazi occupation. It had been bombed, shot, and burned, and yet it still stood—as testimony to the pervasiveness of man's faith in the Almighty. Would his team's discovery, this project, be the thing that tore that faith down along with all that represented it? He could not stand the thought.

What would it do to man's faith in Jesus? How would the Christian conception of life and man's purpose fit into all of it? He found it deeply ironic that this coming star, the bringer of Armageddon, was discussed in the Bible. And how, he wondered, could it have been kept secret for long?

For that to happen, not only would the person or people keeping it quiet have to have eyes and ears all over the world to detect and stifle whatever information was discovered, but they also would have to have the power to pass the information on to successors in order to keep the data quiet for at least two thousand years. Only certain empires had enjoyed power that pervasive; only certain religious orders had endured for so long.

The Vatican! James suddenly thought.

Perez!

James frowned. It was hard to believe, but it had to be true. Father

Perez had given him the name of Sitchin. He had led James on this journey.

But why did he share that information with me if his job is to protect it? The thought hit him like a ton of bricks. His mind now questioned all of the attacks on him and his team in a new light. *Is he allowing us to discover the truth—while knowing that the Vatican is trying to stifle it?* James couldn't reconcile himself to the implications. It was too overwhelming. He looked around at all the people milling about in the streets, sitting in the cafes, peering into shops, kissing on benches, walking their dogs, getting into taxis—all of them oblivious to the approaching danger. Maybe that was better than knowing.

He slid five Euros under the ashtray as he stood up. His hands were shaking, but he forced his body to move across the café to the sidewalk and out into the street. His thoughts flew from scientific implications to emotions, from rational thought to deep personal turmoil. He walked on, not realizing where he was going.

When he finally stopped, he looked up and saw that he had inadvertently walked back to his flat. The black hole in the building that had once been his apartment was boarded over. Soot from the fire covered the building. He walked over to Saint-Sulpice, where the door was open for an evening service. When he approached the massive structure he looked up at the spires, crushed out his cigarette, and slowly walked through the entrance.

As soon as he stepped inside, he felt like an unwelcome guest. Many men had walked across the threshold; great men were buried in the chapels. He ran his hand over a stone column before sitting in a chair near the back and bowing his head. Before he realized it, he was on his knees, quietly sobbing into his hands. He didn't know if it was the weight of the project and all that he had been through, or the fear of the impact their research would have on himself, his children, Sofia, this church, his fellow man.

He felt exposed—completely vulnerable. It was as if he were watching himself as a middle-aged man, walking solitarily in the world;

the burden of his knowledge was one of such magnitude. He felt old and helpless; he wished he could go back in time to his home, his wife, and his children, and be again unaware of all that he now knew.

After several minutes, he stood and slowly walked out of the church, not bothering to wipe the tears from his face. The few people entering stared at him, sympathy in their eyes. They probably thought he'd lost a loved one. An elderly woman reached out and took his hand. She looked deeply into his eyes with pity. If she only knew that he was crying for her, for his children, for everyone.

THE FIND

Here is Wisdom. Let him that hath understanding count the number of the Beast, for it is the number of a man; and his number is six hundred and three score and six.

—REVELATION 13:18

There was a flurry of activity around the ESA. People ran down the halls while others shouted. *This is uncharacteristic of the tempo around here,* James thought on entering, as a man rushing ahead of him careened into a mail cart, sending papers flying everywhere.

"James!" Sofia yelled from the other end of the hall. She hurried toward him and grabbed his arm. "They did it. We are in!"

Without saying a word, James hurried with her to the lab. People packed the room. Stan sat at a computer next to a technician, talking to three scientists standing around him.

"A few days ago, we were experimenting with power—cycling the device," he said. "Right now, we are at 60 milliamps at three volts for three milliseconds, which is similar to a modern flash memory device. This is the level where we noticed that we were receiving data. The device appears to be gated, because we are getting indications of a massive number of switches, both on and off."

"What does that mean?" someone asked.

"Well, very simply, it's binary code—the system of using binary numbers zero and one to represent a letter or digit or other character—so we see ones and zeros, ons and offs. Except, I can tell you, it's odd. We see some repeating within the patterns of the switches from on to off."

"Can you explain that for those of us who aren't computer scientists?" James asked.

"There is data here," Stan said. "When we power the device, we are receiving data. The data repeats in sequence. We have identified a binary code series that indicates that the data is a set of numbers."

"What do you mean? The data inside is just numbers?" James asked.

"They are very specific numbers, James—meaningful numbers." Stan looked down at his lap. "These numbers are a code. Each one refers to letters."

"I don't understand," James interjected.

Everyone in the room was silent. They were all listening intently. Stan ran his fingers through his hair. "Something came to me when I first saw these numbers. You see, the world's first codes were written in the ancient languages. It has been around so long that I should have seen it earlier. We don't know why, but many ancient languages, such as Hebrew, Aramaic, and Greek, have numbers associated with letters in their alphabets. No one knows why or how this came to be. It was always just that way. I never thought about it myself, because I didn't care. But now I know."

"I'm still confused," James said frustrated. Glancing around the room, he could tell others were lost, too.

"The data from the golden books is giving us numbers," Stan said simply. "I took a cue from you, and I applied the mathematical numbers that are associated with the Sumerian language. And I got a message, a message that repeated seventy times. The golden books are a memory device that is giving us a message in the ancient Sumerian language."

"You've got to be kidding me. This is fantastic. What's the message?"

The room was dead-still. At least thirty people had now crammed into the small lab; no one moved. The silence was overwhelming.

"The code, according to our Sumerian translator, has two components," Stan said. "Individually, each number corresponds to a Sumerian word; roughly translated it means:

"*Those who from Heaven Came to Earth (the Annunaki).*

"*Anu is their Supreme God and ruler.*

"*The God who teaches wisdom.*

"When the numbers are read together, they have another interpretation: *Here is Wisdom.*"

"Do we know that's correct?" asked James.

"We do," Stan said. "These numerical interpretations come directly from Zecharia Sitchin's own work, according to our expert." He gave James a knowing look.

The room erupted in conversation. Many argued that beyond a doubt, this constituted direct evidence that ancient man had interacted with an extraterrestrial intelligence. Comments and questions flew around the room in excited and frightened tones.

Does this mean the Sumerians and the Annunaki built the pyramids? They hid this code in the Great Pyramid for us to find when we had the technology to excavate it. Why? Will they return? How does this relate to the DNA sequence? This will turn world religions on their heads. History will have to be completely rewritten.

Stan had a concerned look on his face, and he slowly walked away from the crowd. "James, can I talk with you for a moment?" he asked.

"Stan, this validates extraterrestrial intelligence," James said. "The Annunaki, just as the ancient Sumerians recorded, were from the heavens—and they were here!"

Stan grabbed James by the arm. "Come with me," he insisted. "Sofia, you too." On the way out, he motioned to Father Perez. "Father, we need to speak, in private," he whispered.

Once outside the lab Stan led them down the hallway. "Stan, what is this all about?" James asked.

"Just a minute, please." Stan's demeanor was more serious than James had ever witnessed; it shook James more than what they had just learned.

They walked into an empty office, and Stan shut the door.

"There is more. A lot more."

"What is it?" James demanded.

"We've also cracked the DNA code, James. But I needed to talk to you three first," Stan said, looking at each one of them intently.

"Why would you not tell the entire room? This is groundbreaking—"

"Stop!" Stan demanded. The room was silent as they waited for him to speak. James's heart began to race.

"I applied the same numerical references to the DNA sequence," Stan said finally. "I broke the sequence down based upon codons, by a numerical value of three; as you know, each nucleotide, C, G, T, and A binds in threes. That's when I found the same code, the same words repeating seventy times, just like they do in the golden books, in the DNA fragment identified by Robert. It said the same thing in the DNA sequence; the main code says '*Here is Wisdom.*' Who or whatever made these golden books put this code in our DNA. And I think it's fair to assume, as I have said all along, that an immeasurable amount of information is likely hidden in the larger DNA molecule that is yet to be deciphered."

"Does this mean they created man? Maybe new laws of physics, new formulas, and new approaches to universal energy?" Sofia began, excitedly.

Stan ignored her. "You all need to know what the numerical references are, and we need to—we need to discuss what we are going to do about it," he stammered, clearly trying to maintain his composure.

Sofia, James, and Father Perez all looked at one another, concern apparent on every brow.

Stan continued. "Here are the codes," he said, "the numbers associated with the words.

"600 means *the Annunaki, those who from Heaven came to Earth.*

"60 means *Anu, their supreme God and ruler.*

"6 means *the God who teaches wisdom.*

"Together, it adds up to 666—which means, '*Here is Wisdom.*'"

DR. SOFIA PETRESCU
PARIS, FRANCE

Then the earth shook and trembled; the foundations also of the hills moved and were shaken, because he was wroth.

—PSALM 18:7

Sofia crossed Boulevard Saint Germain to Le Relais Odeon with her guards in tow. She could see James waving to her from the entrance while Stan stood talking to a security officer next to him. James led her through the bar to the back of the restaurant. There were a few tables outside the restaurant in an old alleyway behind it, Cour de Commerce. It was said this was the place where the Guillotine was invented. For the information she was going to disclose, Sofia thought it ironic.

They had all agreed to tell no one anything more about the deeper implications of the DNA code until they were prepared to disclose their report concerning the brown dwarf. They would do it all at once, and stick to safety in numbers. Once they made the report, more than fifty scientists would have the information they had.

Father Perez greeted her from the table with a grim smile. Sofia was much more composed today; the information had hit her hard. James ordered a bottle of Bordeaux as their guards positioned themselves at nearby tables.

Sofia looked around her. "It appears that the most dangerous profession on Earth right now is being an astronomer—especially a deep-space astronomer focused on stars, brown dwarfs, and the infrared spectrum," she said. "Scientists have been disappearing and dying in unbelievable numbers. A simple Google search turned up thirty to forty mysterious deaths. Someone wants all knowledge of this brown dwarf silenced and controlled."

"Damn it," Stan said, rubbing his face and draining his wine glass. "Now we are potentially in that group."

"Some information did come out into the public domain," Sofia continued. "But it was quickly hushed. Immediately after Dr.

Harrington's death there was suddenly total silence on the issue. It is as if everyone in astronomy agreed to stop looking for this perturbation force. I have a colleague from UCSC helping me search journal databases; I had to tell him I was looking for the source of this perturbation, but he keeps to himself and would not share something so trivial. I decided to check news archives as well, for any mention of unusual astronomical anomalies. This is a photocopy of an article from the *Washington Post* in 1983. It is an interesting report about the IRAS, the Infrared Astronomical Satellite:

> A heavenly body possibly as large as the giant planet Jupiter and possibly so close to Earth that it would be part of this solar system has been found . . . by an orbiting telescope aboard the U.S. Infrared Astronomical Satellite. So mysterious is the object that astronomers do not know if it is a planet, a giant comet, a nearby 'protostar' that never got hot enough to become a star. . . .

Sofia pushed a couple of other articles across the table. She read aloud, "'A Mystery Revolves Around the Sun,'" posted on MSNBC on October 7, 1999:

> Two teams of researchers have proposed the existence of an unseen planet or a failed star circling the sun at a distance of more than 2 trillion miles, far beyond the orbits of the nine known planets . . . A planetary scientist at Britain's Open University speculates that the object could be a planet larger than Jupiter.

"This article is from *Discovery News*:

> *Large Object Discovered Orbiting Sun.* The discovery of a large reddish chunk of something orbiting in Pluto's neighborhood has reignited the idea that there may be more than nine planets in the solar system.

"This is from *Newsweek*, June 28, 1982:

> A dark companion could produce the unforeseen force that seems to tug at Uranus and Neptune, speeding them up at one point in their orbits and holding them back as they pass. . . . the best bet is a dark star orbiting at least 50 billion miles beyond Pluto. . . it is most likely either a brown dwarf—a lightweight star that never attained the critical mass needed to ignite—or else a neutron star, the remains of a normal sun that burned out and collapsed. . . . To resolve the question NASA is sending Pioneers 10 and 11 . . .

"Between what I have found, Dr. Harrington's work, and these public announcements," she concluded, "we have viable evidence substantiating that a brown dwarf was discovered. This information was publicized before they clamped down on the information—before the cover-up got started. Frankly, it was probably released before the implications were fully understood. The cover-up is further substantiated by the fact that these stories were removed from their sources' public sites shortly after their release. They are hard to find now without searching an archive."

"So it's really out there," Stan stated.

* * *

"I appreciate the update, Father Perez," the pope said. "It appears that we soon may have an answer to these gold books. Who could have imagined this? What an incredible message. Wisdom—locked up in our DNA. Genesis written into our very being."

"Holy Father, this is deeply disturbing—is it not?" Father Perez said. "There's a direct reference to Revelation 13 in the technology found in the Great Pyramid. And in the DNA segment there is reference to the number 666! The Church must be prepared to respond to this; how are we going to handle this information? It will strike fear into every Christian worldwide."

There was a long pause before the pope spoke.

"Father Perez, we can deal with this information; there are interpretations around this passage. And we can manage the giving of wisdom."

"But Your Eminence, we must—"

"We will handle this information. How to interpret it is not your concern." In the forced silence that followed, the pope cleared his throat. "Mateo, do you have anything else?"

Father Perez could barely collect his thoughts. "Yes, Holy Father, yes," he stuttered. "There is a small research group here at the ESA that has been focusing on finding a binary companion to the sun. It has been identified. They know. In the next day or two they will report their findings to the entire Project Aquarius team."

There was a long silence. "Is there nothing you can do?" the pope asked quietly.

The question hung in the air, almost an accusation. "There is nothing I can do, Holy Father. I believe their research is nearing completion. They plan to file a report with Project Aquarius and the U.N. Security Council by the end of the week."

"You have done all you can do, Father Perez. Your work is complete. Thank you for your service to the Holy See."

The pope hung up, then dialed a prepaid phone in Paris. The recipient picked up, but said nothing.

"The time has come," the pope said into the silence.

DR. SOFIA PETRESCU'S RESEARCH

And the heaven departed as a scroll when it is rolled together; and every mountain and island were moved out of their places.

—REVELATION 6:14

"I think we have the last evidence we'll need to complete our report," Sofia said. "Just follow me here—I'll try to keep it simple.

"A binary companion's gravitational interaction with the sun would accompany a continuously increasing electromagnetic interaction with the sun and the earth. The difference is that the earth is orbiting the sun, and is not in any direct orbital relationship with this object. This means that if we say that the sun is at one point and the binary object at another, and draw a line between them, the earth will be in direct line of the sun and its binary companion twice a year. At those times, both gravitational and electromagnetic forces from the binary companions would act in opposition on the earth with the most strength.

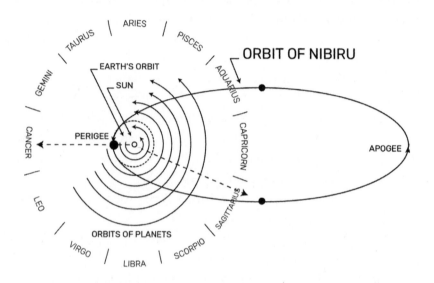

"That means that we can prove definitively that this companion exists if we can observe the most gravitational and magnetic disturbances here at two points in our orbital year: once when the earth is between the brown dwarf and the sun, and once when we are behind the sun but the brown dwarf, the sun, and earth are in alignment." She pointed at an image on her computer screen. When I analyzed the last ten years of data, I found that there is roughly a 188-day cycle of magnetosphere compression. It changes by a few days each year—something that we would expect if the binary companion has an elliptical orbit and is approaching its perigee.

"This got me thinking. If we align with it every 188 days, what other geophysical evidence supports this hypothesis? Not surprisingly, I discovered that this alignment causes a huge increase in the number of earthquakes right around the end of the cycle, every 188 days.

"The computers here gave me access to some direct NASA data on Earth's magnetosphere. I logged into the Geostationary Operational Environmental Satellite, available through the Community Coordinated Modeling Center to find historical readings of solar-wind impact on the earth's magnetosphere and ionosphere. Look at this." She brought up a new slide on-screen.

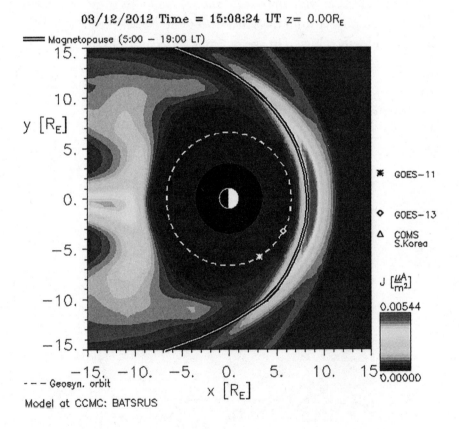

"This first slide is before the hypothetical alignment. As you can see, the earth is in the middle, signified by the black dot. The white dotted line represents the satellite orbits, and the magnetosphere is the shaded area. You can see that the solar wind from the sun is impacting the magnetosphere from the right. The right edge creates what is called the bow shock, with the magnetosphere being swept behind the earth from the solar wind.

"As the day progresses, and we get close to alignment, you can see this start to change. We see a flattening of the magnetosphere in the area where the sun's solar wind impacts it, and what appears to be some form of solar wind impact from the other direction." She clicked through to the next slide, showing an image radically different from the first.

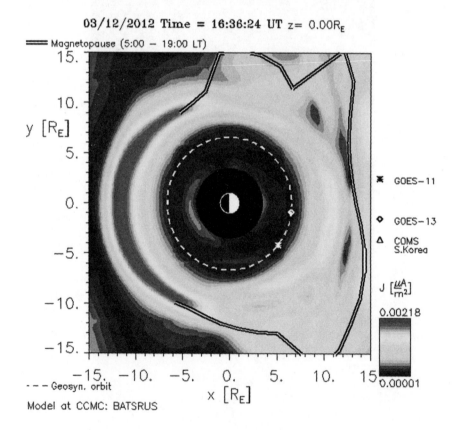

"Now, this next one is truly terrifying," she said, clicking again. "You can see that at the point of alignment, the bow shock has totally flipped to the other side of the earth. There is only one explanation for this: we are receiving a massive amount of solar radiation from the *opposite* direction from the sun. Something is creating an incredible disturbance, and it's coming from the wrong direction. In fact, as you see in this final slide, the event is so intense that it flips the tail of the magnetosphere toward the sun instead of away from it."

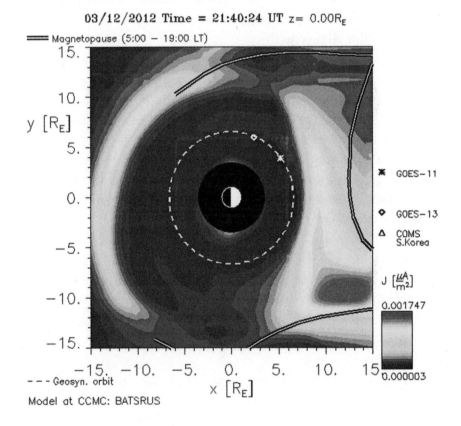

"My God!" Stan burst out. "This is conclusive!"

"I believe it is," Sofia said. "In my judgment, this means this object is inside of the heliosphere, so it's close. The heliosphere is similar to the magnetosphere of the earth, but is generated by the sun. It protects the entire inner solar system from interstellar radiation," she explained.

"What does that mean, exactly?" James asked.

"I believe this object has moved at least inside of the heliosphere, but because it doesn't emit any light, it won't be visible until it's very close to Earth."

"Why hasn't anyone seen this before?" Stan demanded. "Between the earthquakes, the magnetosphere compression, and the acceleration of all the natural disasters, someone should have noticed. Why hasn't anyone put this all together?"

"There are two answers to that, Stan," Sofia answered, a little curtly. "One, each area of science is highly specialized and completely disconnected. It would be highly unlikely for a scientist to look at the big picture and connect the dots, so to speak. The seismologist looks at his particular field of information and comes up with theories based on the anomalies he sees. Then the volcanologist looks at what she sees, or those researching greenhouse gas increases look only at their information. Nobody is in the business of looking at large, disparate data sets across disciplines and trying to find a common thread.

"The other answer, as I have said before, is that we are *not* the only ones to determine this. There is deliberate suppression of information."

"Well, what the fuck do we do?" James interjected, now standing. "I've got kids, damn it. What do we do? And who do we tell? We have to warn people. We have to find a safe place to go. If nothing else, people deserve to know—to prepare themselves spiritually and be with their families before the end."

Father Perez cleared his throat and spoke in a soft tone. "Calm down, James. Just take a moment to think. If Sofia is correct, there is nowhere to go. There is nothing we can do. If this is a brown dwarf and it passes by our sun, it will have an enormous impact on the earth. A wall of water will follow its path and wash across our planet. When that is combined with the geographical pole shift and magnetosphere reversal, there will be nowhere safe to go."

"We have to tell someone. Right now." James was getting angry.

Sofia inhaled deeply. "James, haven't you been listening? I think they already know. *Someone* knows this: the powers that be, the elite. They have already made the decision to hide this. Remember the dead astronomers."

"We need to present this report immediately," Stan said nervously. "As long as we are the only ones with this information, we are at risk. We need to gather any final scientific facts and submit a comprehensive report to the U.N."

"I've requested more data from NASA." Sofia slid a piece of paper across the table to the team. "I received this when I requested additional magnetosphere historical data from the NASA Modeling because I noticed they omitted certain date ranges from the online database. Specifically, they were dates that correlated with my 188-day cycle."

James read her letter aloud:

Dr. Petrescu,

Archived images for the dates you have selected have been omitted from the record pursuant to a joint Homeland Security / NASA directive. Corrected imagery for the anomalous frames in question have not been cleared for public dissemination and are likely to remain unavailable. Please find the official release concerning this matter below.

RELEASE: 05-432

NASA SIGNS TECHNOLOGY AGREEMENT WITH HOMELAND SECURITY

NASA and the Department of Homeland Security signed a memorandum of understanding today to collaborate and coordinate on appropriate research and development projects.

The agreement allows the Science and Technology Division and

NASA to apply joint expertise and technologies to improve national and homeland security and develop complex systems designed to protect the nation . . .

"What the hell?" James fumed. "What does the Department of Homeland Security have to do with NASA?"

"That release is posted directly on NASA's website. They are not hiding their alignment with DHS," Sofia stated.

"Dead fucking astronomers," Stan whispered.

* * *

"How are ya, James?" Killian shouted as James walked in the door of Le Violon Dingue. In the past James had spent a lot of fun nights there, but he was not here for fun tonight.

"Oh, man, you look like shit,: Killian said. "Whacha be having today? The usual?" He waited for James to nod, then brought a shot of Jagermeister to him. Killian always was a subtle guy. He offered a drink to James's security detail, who politely declined.

James slammed the drink down. "You have no idea how awful today has been," he said miserably.

"Whatcha ya doing taking on this consultin' gig? Surely you know that's the reason for your troubles," Killian stated.

"Well, perhaps you're right, but now isn't the time for a career change," James said, fumbling for his reply.

"Shit. If it's that bad," a voice said from the back room, "better pour three Jamesons." Sean walked out of the back room and toward James with a smile. Sean had been friends with Killian growing up, and kept him on the straight and narrow while managing the financial end of the business. He was also one of the oldest friends James had in Paris.

Sean swung onto the stool next to James as Killian passed two full mugs of beer and two shots of Jameson's to them. "I need a cigarette," James exhaled.

"Gigi, we'll be heading out front now," Sean yelled to another bartender. Le Violon Dingue had a few tables out front, although you had to keep your voice down out there or the neighbors living over the bar would call the police immediately. James, Sean, and Killian elbowed through the crowded patio and sat at a small bistro table.

"I haven't seen you look like this since all that business with your old lady," Sean said.

At first, Killian and Sean were able to make small talk and joke in a way that kept James's mind off everything. However, as the night progressed, they each had to get back to work. James took advantage of the humor when offered, drank several more beers, and inhaled nearly an entire pack of Camel Lights.

The bar closed around 1:00 a.m. James decided to walk back to his rental flat. Ignoring his security detail, he pretended he was alone. He loved Paris at this time of the night, but tonight it did nothing to break his somber mood. He wandered down Boulevard Saint-Germain past the Metro Café, where he saw a bum stumble against the large tree in front of the café. He wound his way through the Latin Quarter, still bustling with people. Paris never slept. There was always something going on, and no matter what time you called an end to the night, you always felt like you were missing something. This time, James knew that feeling was right.

A couple of hours later, James found himself back in his rental. He lit a cigarette and turned on his computer.

24

TURMOIL

"I HAVE FOUND A TON of anecdotal information that corroborates Sofia's findings," James began. "If nothing else, there is a strong indication that the highest levels of a few governments know what is going on, and are preparing for it.

"My strategy was to look for anomalous spending. If someone knows something, I figured, we should be able to find it in the spending. After a lot of digging, I found it. In just the last year, it has been announced that both the CIA headquarters in Langley, Virginia, and the NSA headquarters in Maryland are being moved to Denver. Even NASA is moving to Dayton, Ohio. Decades of infrastructure and equipment are integrated into these facilities, but the government is fleeing the coastline. I'm sure these are not cost-saving moves.

"Americans are not the only ones to jump on this trend. The British moved their most prized National Archives to a salt mine in Winsford. Likewise, Russia, China, and other countries are building underground complexes—some of them quite large.

Whistleblowers have come out and provided concrete evidence of the structures in all of these countries. I believe they are quietly preparing for the passing of this brown dwarf. A tremendous amount of information has come out about the Denver Airport and the massive underground complex constructed underneath it; based on records I have found, this construction project was the largest earthworks project in this century, even bigger than the Panama Canal. Additional facilities of similar magnitude have been identified in the Ozarks."

"Who gets access to these protective locations?" Stan asked.

"If you have to ask, you don't have a ticket," Sofia answered.

"That seems like the right answer, from what I can tell," James said. "China has built twelve brand-new cities, each capable of providing homes for over two million people. The media refers to them as China's 'ghost' cities because, despite their vastness, they are empty. Like the construction by the U.S. and Russia, they were built in the center of China, far from any coastline. They contain universities, malls, offices, parks, highways, apartments, and anything else a typical city would have; China spent hundreds of billions of dollars building them over the last ten years. A similar city was constructed in Kazakhstan. Maybe when they cannot control the information—when people see this thing coming—they are going to move as many people as they can to these interior locations."

"Away from the wall of water," Stan muttered.

"Yes. At the same time, there has been a race to create seed vaults.

351

These facilities store specimens of nearly every fruit, vegetable, flower, tree, and other plants that exist on Earth. Countries deposit seeds from their native vegetation into these banks; each country is also developing duplicate vaults of their own. The main vault is above the Arctic circle, one thousand feet underground in solid granite in Svalbard, Norway. This international effort to store every type of seed on the planet is the back-up for individual countries' vaults. They are planning for massive devastation, ensuring they can repopulate the earth with plants.

"A little closer to home for me are the anomalies occurring on governmental purchases," James went on. "All available MREs, or military-grade storable food, have been bought by the Department of Homeland Security. 1.6 billion rounds of hollow-point ammunition were also on the purchase lists. Why does the DHS, which only operates within the borders of the U.S., need 1.6 billion rounds of hollow-point rounds? Hollow-points aren't used for target practice; in fact, several congressmen made a stink about this, because we used less than 50 million each year during the heat of the Iraq war. 1.6 billion rounds is enough ammunition to sustain a thirty-year constant war—within our borders. They are preparing for mass chaos. I guess when they can no longer maintain secrecy, they plan to control the population through force and martial law.

"FEMA has also purchased millions of low-cost plastic coffins, and they are stacked up in various locations in the United States: Georgia, Texas, Indiana. The patent on these, number US5425163A claims that these can each hold two to three bodies.

"If there is going to be a wave of water racing across the globe, another great flood, earthquakes, and a possible pole shift, all of these things make sense," James said. "If you look at them as isolated events, they do not. They know this second sun is coming. Our leaders know what it will do to the earth, and they are preparing."

"How can we possibly say anything to anyone?" Stan said. "They are preparing, while keeping as tight a lid on this as possible. I'm sure their reasons are to protect only the select few."

"They don't want anyone poking around and stumbling across this either," James agreed. "I found evidence of that, too. Across the world, for instance, all infrared telescopes are being decommissioned. In fact, the few infrared telescopes left in working order, whether on Earth or on a satellite, are now in the direct possession or control of either the U.S. government—" James turned and looked directly at Father Perez, "—or the Vatican."

Perez shifted uncomfortably and turned a bit red. James educated the group on the VATT and LUCIFER telescopes on Mount Graham in Arizona.

"Well?" James asked pointedly.

"James, as I have told you before, I have nothing to offer," Father Perez said, shrugging. "These telescopes are for research only. I have been there, and can tell you there is nothing to learn from them."

"Frankly, I don't like it," James snapped. "It's not hard to wonder how much the Vatican is involved in government conspiracies. I wonder if the good Father knows more than he has told us?" He glared at Father Perez. "Come on Father, you're the one who informed me about Sitchin. Are you going to sit there and just act like you don't know anything, to protect your precious church? What for?"

"James, get off it," Stan interjected, slamming his hand on the table. "The man said he doesn't have anything to offer. Don't start accusing your friends of lying and hiding information. If we can't stick together, we won't get anywhere."

James exhaled deeply. "I'm sorry, Mateo," he said, his tone softer. "It's been a long day—a long week. I didn't mean to accuse you."

Father Perez weakly nodded his head.

"We have to move quickly," Sofia said. "Maybe we can give people a chance to survive, if they can prepare. Clearly, those elites in the know have made the decision to abandon the populace. No one can count on the government for protection; they aren't looking out for us. If we don't expose this, and now, we are no better than they are. Our families, friends, and every stranger on this planet deserve the truth." She shook her head. "We just don't know how fast this object is moving yet—we won't know when this is going to occur. It would really help if we could report on the timing of the event. But short of access to an infrared telescope, we cannot pinpoint the date it will be closest to Earth. We aren't going to get any direct observations of the thing—until it's too late."

DESOLATION

The great day of his wrath has come, and who shall be able to stand?
—REVELATION 6:17

Father Perez wandered the streets. A dark mood had settled over him as he struggled with his inner demons. He knew too much. He felt as if he were betraying his closest friends and possibly the world.

Today, he also felt as if he were betraying himself. Yes, the Church had provided him with his education and his livelihood, but he viewed himself as a scientist, not a priest. He was not one to delve too deeply into the philosophy of religion, creation, and spirituality; even the bits of doctrine the pope assigned him to write were challenging and foreign.

It began to rain—softly at first, but soon the sky opened. Thunder rumbled and shook the ground. As large drops poured down, he looked up and let them hit his face. Lightning flashed at him in rebuke.

Something stirred deep within him. Perhaps the feeling was some innate connection with an ultimate force, something spiritual? He was suddenly ashamed.

He crossed Rue Monge and headed toward Eglise St. Medard. The church had a small square beside it where playing children and gossiping mothers usually loitered. Today, it was abandoned. Only a few pigeons scurried around, looking for a meal. He sat down on a green bench. Water ran down his face and soaked into his clothing.

Father Perez looked up at the church and the gray sky surrounding it. Slowly, without realizing what he was doing, he unclasped the clerical collar from his shirt and held it with his fingertips. It slipped from his loose grasp and fell into the mud at his feet.

He'd had time to consider all that had occurred—all that he had been told by the Vatican. And a dark picture had emerged. Had they killed Joseph to keep this under wraps? Was he himself responsible for that poor boy's death? He had told the pope about Sati's USB drive, and that Sati wanted Father Perez to have it if something happened to him. Was he also responsible for Sati's death?

Anger welled deep within him. Resentment. Shame. He could not now be responsible for millions more lives by remaining silent. Could he? He knew that if he betrayed the Vatican, the popes' directive, he would be turning his back on everything that he knew. Everything that defined him was associated with the church. But he knew it meant nothing next to the sense of personal duty he felt toward the masses of people he could save.

Falling to his hands and knees, Father Perez pounded his fists into the wet ground. He collapsed in tears—of anguish, of loss, of fear. And for the first time in his life, he truly prayed. It was not a formal prayer like the many he'd learned or recited countless times. His prayer arose from deep within his heart and soul. He prayed for guidance. He prayed for forgiveness. He prayed for strength.

Emotion overcame him, and he wept.

JAMES ANDERSON
PARIS, FRANCE

"This excess of objects with unexpected orbital parameters makes us believe that some invisible forces are altering the distribution of the ETNOs."
—CARLOS DE LA FUENTE MARCOS

James called his children, as he did just about every other night. It was becoming more and more painful to carry on a light conversation with them. But he knew he had to put up the façade, not show his deep sense of fear, depression and concern.

"I'm so happy, honey. It's always fun to have a new dress."

"And I'm going to wear it for the school musical next week. Are you coming?" Amy asked in an excited tone.

James stifled a sob. "Sweetie, like I've told you, I'm here in Paris on very important business, but Daddy will be home soon. Make sure Mommy sends me a video. I'm so proud." James couldn't stand it. The sweet innocence of his little girl, so happy and carefree, clashed inside him with the horror of what he knew was to come. "Amy, I love you," he said, overcome with emotion. "Please hug your brothers for me."

"Okay, Daddy. When are you coming home?"

He didn't have an answer for that. "Look Amy, Daddy is working very hard to take care of you and your brothers. I'm not sure exactly when, but soon."

"I miss you, Daddy."

James could hear that she was trying to be brave and do all she could to keep from crying. "I know . . . I miss you, too."

He hung up with a sick feeling in his stomach. *What the fuck am I doing here? I'm not needed here. They can do this shit without me. Time is too precious now for anything else but being with my family.*

He ran his fingers through his hair in frustration. Pouring himself some Bordeaux into a water glass, he walked out on the balcony, leaned on the railing, and rubbed his temple.

What the hell is this all about? There was something deeply disturbing about all these disconnected facts. The strange DNA code, tied somehow to this golden artifact found in the Great Pyramid—neither the artifact nor the code should exist. Yet it couldn't be coincidence that they'd been discovered at the same time. And with some kind of a star map, too—though that was the aspect he understood the least.

If he could only figure this riddle out he could go home for good. He might even retire—especially if the end of the world was near, as those damn Sumerian tablets seemed to predict. He pushed on his stomach, trying to relieve the heartburn that was getting worse by the minute.

James walked back inside, frustration and confusion clamoring within him. When he could bear it no longer, James did something he rarely did. He sat down on the small couch in his room, set his glass of wine on the table, and slowly folded his hands to pray.

He'd never been a particularly religious man. Yes, he had gone to church as a kid; his parents had forced him to. He believed in a god—whatever that meant. Occasionally, he even took his kids to church himself, because he thought it was important for their development and the right thing to do. Prayer was a different matter altogether; he'd never really considered where he fit into the consciousness of a Creator. He barely had time to deal with day-to-day issues, much less universal ones. Besides, he knew there were no answers there—just more questions. He was a bit embarrassed to admit it to himself; he generally only prayed when he was scared, when someone was sick, or when he needed something. He prayed when it was convenient to him—a thought that, whenever he acknowledged it, made him feel a bit selfish.

Yet still, the urgency of the moment compelled him to clear his mind and ask for help from a higher power. He looked up at the ceiling.

"God, if you are really there . . . help me through this," he said. "What is this all about? I've lost my marriage; my relationship with my kids is terrible. Now the world's ending, and it's all I can think about. Help me find a way through this. Help me figure this out for Robert. For Sofia. Help me get back to my family."

He slugged down the wine, got up, and gazed out into the street below. His knuckles turned white as he gripped the iron railing; he needed something to hold onto, something real. The ancient wood floor creaked under his weight as he walked back over to the couch and collapsed in frustration.

He looked at the table beside the bed and saw a small reflection of light—something gold, glinting from the streetlight. *What is that?* There on the table was a very small book, stacked beside tourist guides and magazines. It had been so long since someone had opened it that it was covered in dust.

"The Bible," he said as he stood and walked over to grab it from the shelf. "Well, this is something that foretold the end, anyway."

Opening the book, he refilled his glass of wine. *How ironic*, he thought, *they put Revelation at the end.*

As he started reading, he found his mind skipping through the letters to the churches. *Blah, blah, blah . . . do good or get punished . . . just like I remember it.* Around chapter six, it began to get very confusing. *Yep, here is the crazy shit. What is it talking about—144,000 sealed up? I don't get any of this gibberish.* With a yawn, he kept skimming forward until he saw:

> *They had as king over them the angel of the Abyss, whose name in Hebrew is Abaddon and in Greek is Apollyon (that is, Destroyer).*

How eerie, he thought, *Revelation 9:11—does that really have anything to do with 9/11?* He paused for a moment, then reread the chapter about the opening of the Abyss and the rise of the Antichrist. A chill ran down his neck.

Pressing forward, he came across more gibberish.

"How do people read this?" he asked out loud. "Seals," he said, flipping the page. "Trumpets, witnesses, scrolls. None of this makes any sense." He set the Bible open on the couch next to him and reached for his wine. In between sips, he glanced at the open book. His brain was swirling with horsemen and censers—whatever those were. He was definitely having nightmares tonight.

His eyes began to glaze over. He was doing everything he could to keep from nodding off. *One more chapter and that's it,* he thought, glancing at his watch. It was nearly midnight. *Shit, I've got to get some sleep.* Returning to the book, began reading in the center of the page:

> *A great sign appeared in heaven: a woman clothed with the sun, with the moon under her feet and a crown of twelve stars on her head. She was pregnant and cried out in pain as she was about to give birth.*

He sat bolt upright on the edge of the couch, his eyes growing wide. His glass fell to the floor and shattered; he barely registered the sound.

He read the words again to make sure he hadn't dreamed them.

"It's the star map!" he said aloud.

He grabbed his phone and called Sofia. It rang and rang. He thought it was about to go to voicemail. "Come on. Pick up," he said anxiously after the fourth ring.

"Hello?" Sofia's voice was groggy on the other end.

"Sofia," he said, excitement rising in his voice, "I think I've figured something out."

JUPITER

And they worshiped the dragon which gave power unto the beast: and they worshiped the beast, saying, 'who is able to make war with him?'

—REVELATION 13:4

James was at ESA headquarters all morning, but he hadn't seen Sofia when his phone rang.

"James, come down here to the lab," she said. "You are going to find this amazing. Frankly, I don't know what to think, but this alignment is incredible."

James swiftly walked down the hallway to the computer lab. Sofia was busy working at a terminal.

"We have access to the most powerful and precise astronomical databases on the planet here," she said, "and they're backing up your theory. Look what I found."

On the screen appeared a telescope image of Virgo with some other unknown objects. "Watch this." She overlaid an image of the Sumerian star map over it, then she smiled at him. "An exact match. See this object between the legs of Virgo?"

"Yes."

"That's is Jupiter. At this particular juncture, Jupiter goes into retrograde motion."

"What does that mean?"

"The simple explanation is this: the earth passes Jupiter in its orbit just like you might pass a slower car on the highway. During this time, Jupiter will appear to slow down, stop, and actually go backward from our view on Earth."

James was confused. "Okay, so what is the significance of that?"

"Well, nothing on its own. We observe retrograde motion of the planets all the time. But this particular event is peculiar, in that Jupiter will exhibit retrograde motion *within* Virgo. Specifically, we will see Jupiter doing this between the legs of Virgo. That is what is shown in the Sumerian tablet: Jupiter will appear to stay in Virgo for exactly nine months. This matches the description in that passage of Revelation that you point out to me:

A great sign appeared in heaven: a woman clothed with the sun, with the moon under her feet and a crown of twelve stars on her head. She was pregnant and cried out in pain as she was about to give birth.

"It is an incredible coincidence that Jupiter will appear to be in the womb of Virgo for the exact gestation period for a human," Sofia added. "This exact alignment only happens once in human history. Jupiter will exit Virgo on September 23, 2017—and the alignment will not happen again for another ten thousand years."

"That is incredible!" James could not contain his bewilderment. "So the Bible lays out this astronomical alignment—which only happens once in history—and the Sumerians leave us an apocalyptic message with a star map pointing to this specific date?"

"There's more," she said, her, her voice trailing off into a whisper as she looked around the room.

"Shit, hold on! I don't know if I want to hear it."

"James, there is something very wrong here. This alignment works perfectly, except for this object. See this?" she said, pointing to the ancient Sumerian star map.

"Yes."

"This object does not exist in the known databases for Virgo. When I went into NASA's SkyView database and entered the coordinates 13h 50m 44.0s -8 13' 59.7, look at what I found." She laid a photograph down in front of James.

"I'm not sure what I'm looking at—" James said.

"How could you be?" she laughed bitterly. "It has been deliberately obfuscated—blocked out. The SkyView program is a complete astronomical survey of the sky. Astronomers use it for reference. This very tiny portion of the sky's image has been deliberately blacked out. I then went onto Stellarium, a software program that has also compiled full images of the sky, then Google Sky, and Microsoft WorldWide Telescope. This exact place was blacked out in all of them. No one would ever find this tiny blacked-out section of the sky image unless they looked very deliberately at this precise coordinate, like I did. This coordinate is exactly where the Sumerian star map pointed."

"What does it mean? Who is hiding this?" James asked.

"Whoever it is, they're hiding our companion star," Sofia said. "This is the answer for everything; it connects everything. It fits with the Sumerian tablet; there is an object on that tablet that does not exist in our records. That object is blacked out on NASA's systems. On September 23, 2017, our companion star will be in our sky at these coordinates. I think it's the object that was described in Revelation. Remember the passage you found? It continues:

> *Then another sign appeared in heaven: an enormous red dragon with seven heads and ten horns and seven crowns on its heads. Its tail swept a third of the stars out of the sky and flung them to the earth. The dragon stood in front of the woman who was about to give birth, so that it might devour her child the moment he was born. She gave birth to a son, a male child, who "would rule all the nations with an iron scepter. And her child was snatched up to God and to his throne.*

"Our binary star is the Red Dragon from Revelation. It is the destroyer." She shrugged hopelessly. "And it's just about here."

ESA

And when these things begin to come to pass, then look up, and lift up your heads; for your redemption draweth nigh.

—LUKE 21:28

Stan, Sofia, and Father Perez sat in the small conference room at the ESA. This was their final overview of the report. They would give their presentation on the binary star tomorrow. It was late, 9:00 Sunday evening, and they were emotionally exhausted.

"Where the hell is he? James is never late," Stan said. The lights in the room flickered suddenly. "What was that?"

James stormed into the room and slammed the door. He was disheveled, and his face was beet-red. No one had ever seen him like this before. He slammed his fist on the table and pointed at Father Perez.

"You!" he shouted, throwing a stack of papers at the priest. "Fucking tell us what you know right now, you son of a bitch!"

The others sat momentarily silent in shock.

"James, what—?" Stan sputtered.

"Shut up. Just shut up!" James turned his attention back to the priest. "Tell me, now. Tell me what you know."

Father Perez looked down at his hands folded in his lap and nervously rubbed his thumbs together. No one had even noticed that he wasn't wearing his clerical collar. His expression was void and perplexed. His mouth moved as he struggled to formulate his thoughts into words.

James snatched back the papers he had thrown at the priest with a wild look in his eye.

"Don't all conspiracy theorists blame the Vatican?" he ranted. "It's so fucking cliché. But that statement about the dead astronomers got under my skin. I decided to do a little digging. I discovered a few interesting statements by our priest here, and those of other Vatican officials to the public."

Father Perez continued to stare at his hands.

"Should I tell everyone about Father Malachi Brendan Martin?" There was no answer. "He was a fellow Jesuit priest with our Father over there. He was a professor of paleontology at the Vatican Biblical Institute, an advisor to multiple popes. But he broke ranks, didn't he, Father Perez?" James's gaze locked on the sad, pensive priest. "Father Martin was a critic of his fellow Jesuits and their obsession with power in the Vatican. But mostly, he was a critic of the Vatican's decision to not reveal the Fatima Prophecy. Although the church had released statements concerning the prophecy, most believed the third part remained concealed. When the press questioned Pope John Paul II on this prophecy, he said to a German newspaper:

It should be sufficient for all Christians to know this: If there is a message in which it is written that the oceans will flood whole areas of the Earth and that from one moment to the next millions of people will perish, truly the publication of such a message is no longer something to be so much desired.

"Father Martin was, of course, upset by this stance. In his view, the people deserved to know what the future had in store for them, and the real nature of the prophecy.

"What frustrates me more is what Father Malachi Martin said in an interview regarding the LUCIFER observatory—the same observatory from which you recently joined our team, Father. Father Martin apparently fell to his death down a long flight of stairs—a tragic fall initiated by a push, I'm sure!" James glared at Father Perez. "Just before that he gave an interview to a national radio talk show and stated that the reason for the Vatican's LUCIFER Observatory was 'to obtain knowledge of what is going on in space and of what is approaching us.' Father Martin went on to state that what they were observing had to do with secret revelations held by the Vatican."

He let the statement hang. The room was silent.

"You know. You know—don't you, Father?" James seethed. "You know because you have seen it. Your pope knows, and that is why you are here. You have seen this brown dwarf approaching, and that is why you are so fucking silent in our meetings. You know, and you told no one."

Father Perez held James's gaze as the room held its breath. He rubbed his hands over his face in consternation. When he finally spoke, his voice sounded lifeless, resigned to despair.

"What you have found, this alignment, is known as the Great Sign," he said. "It signifies the beginning of Jacob's troubles, a seven-year tribulation period spoken of in the Bible. It is the only sign called the Great Sign. According to Revelation, it is to herald the coming of the Messiah. Virgo is the virgin, and Jupiter is the symbol of the messiah being born. And it is occurring on September 23, 2017—during the Feast of Trumpets—the Jewish high holy day in the Bible."

Stan scoffed. "You can't be serious," he said.

"Whatever your beliefs, I can tell you this: the Vatican and the Jesuits are taking this very seriously—more seriously than you can possibly imagine. There are multiple prophecies that the Vatican is acting on. This is just one.

"The Red Dragon is our binary companion. According to Revelation, as you saw in the Virgo alignment, the dragon is waiting to devour Jupiter, the messiah of the Bible. Jupiter is known as the king planet, representing Christ. The alignment means that the tribulation is beginning; the only astronomical alignment that matches Revelation, it came after four blood moons, known as a tetrad, that took place on the Hebrew feast days. These were the harbingers of the tribulation spoken of in the Bible; tetrads are very rare and are always biblically significant. The Bible says the stars, sun, and moon are signs of appointed times: as in the time of the birth of the Messiah, so it is in the time of his return. This sign is the beginning of the seven years of tribulation. The Bible says the first three and a half years will be a time of peace, but suffering from famine and drought will increase. The Great Sign heralds the beginning of the Messianic process. Even the Jewish Zohar foretells the Messianic period beginning with the appearance of a new star, which was to appear in the Hebrew year of 5777—our year 2017."

The building alarm's chirped once, then stopped. Everyone stopped talking and looked at each other. James stood and opened the conference-room door to look down the hall, but saw nothing.

"In short James, you are right," Father Perez said. "I have seen our companion star. And, yes, it is approaching the earth. The alignment date of September 23, 2017, is accurate." The room sat in shocked silence. "This is the beginning of the dark times. Our binary star will cross Earth's orbit three and a half years later, on March 23, 2021, ushering in what is known as the Great Tribulation—a period of unimaginable destruction on Earth.

"Father Martin knew this, and he had more strength than I. He did what he could to warn the people without openly alarming them. But,

I—I was torn between my oath to my pope and to the Vatican, and my duty to do what was right by my fellow man and by my Creator. But in my defense, James, you know I tried to help. That is why I sent you to research Sitchin. And it is why you need to take this." The priest slid a USB drive across the table to James. James took the device and slipped it into his jacket pocket, with only the briefest glance at it.

"There are pictures on that drive," Father Perez said, gesturing toward it. "Pictures that Sati found of other tablets with markings similar to those on the gold books. Zaher found more artifacts in the Great Pyramid. But he hid them. I promised Sati that I would care for it. The Vatican and the Jesuit Order want what is on that USB. But I have not given it to them." Father Perez began to cry softly. "I've seen this star in the sky. The Vatican knows it's coming. I saw it at Mount Graham with my own eyes. But there is so much more you must know. All of you." He looked at each of them earnestly.

James could see through the small window in the conference room door that the light had gone out in the hallway. *We really must be alone in the building,* he thought. *Even the lights are on an automatic switch.*

"You cannot believe how big this conspiracy, or how long it has been planned," Father Perez said. "I can't be in the front, but I can guide you; I am ready to tell you what I know. We must alert the public. There is something deeply evil portended in the deciphered code Stan found in the DNA sequence, and in the golden books, represented by the number 666. In Hebrew the number 6 is the letter Wav. The three together as 666 means *hidden thing*. It appeared 70 times, and the number 70 in Hebrew means *desolation, a period of judgment.*

"The DNA finding and the golden books, if disclosed to the world, will force the global population to consider the real possibility that ancient Annunaki came to Earth and created man, leaving us evidence of their presence in code and in ancient technology. The evidence suggests that 'those who from heaven came, may be our true creators.' But that doesn't say *why* they came." He spoke slowly, as though himself hesitant about what he had to tell them.

Everyone sat in quiet contemplation. Nobody liked these implications.

Father Perez broke the silence, speaking softly and hesitantly. "Maybe they did not come here of their own volition," he said.

"What do you mean?" Stan challenged.

"Maybe they did not come from space, but were thrown from heaven."

Stan held the priest's gaze, shocked.

"This matches the story of the Fallen—those sons of God that rebelled, and were cast from heaven," Father Perez intoned. "Their number is 666, the number of the beast. Two hundred angels rebelled against God; they were cast from heaven and descended on Mount Herman, denied their first estate. Their leader was Azazel, or Lucifer, the Lightbringer. These fallen taught mankind technology, warfare . . . and corruption." Father Perez pulled out a small Bible. No one had ever seen him with a Bible before. He began to read from Genesis 6:

"And the sons of God (the Fallen) saw the daughters of men were fair; and they took them for wives all which they chose. . . and they bore children to them . . . and these children became the mighty men of old and renown . . . and God saw that the wickedness of man was great in the Earth.

"The Bible describes very literally the corruption of man by the Fallen—that was the corruption of our DNA. It was to purify this corruption that God sent the Great Flood. The Bible speaks about this corruption occurring again in end times: Matthew 24:37 says 'as the days of Noah were, so shall also the coming of the Son of Man be.' It also speaks of this binary star and the destruction it brings. Listen to Revelation 8:

"The first angel sounded, and there came hail and fire, mixed with blood, and they were thrown to the earth; and a third of the earth was burned up, and a third of the trees were burned up, and all the green grass was burned up.

"The second angel sounded, and something like a great mountain burning with fire was thrown into the sea; and a third of the sea became blood, and a third of the creatures which were in the sea and had life, died; and a third of the ships were destroyed.

"The third angel sounded, and a great star fell from heaven, burning like a torch, and it fell on a third of the rivers and on the springs of waters. The name of the star is called Wormwood; and a third of the waters became wormwood, and many men died from the waters, because they were made bitter.

"The fourth angel sounded, and a third of the sun and a third of the moon and a third of the stars were struck, so that a third of them would be darkened and the day would not shine for a third of it, and the night in the same way.

"Then I looked, and I heard an eagle flying in midheaven, saying with a loud voice, 'Woe, woe, woe to those who dwell on the earth, because of the remaining blasts of the trumpet of the three angels who are about to sound!'"

No one said a word. James's head was spinning; again he seemed to hear something in the hallway, but pushed away the thought. "What you're saying, Father, is that these Annunaki are the Fallen?" he asked in disbelief.

"What greater deception could there be," Father Perez whispered finally, with a small, forced smile. "These findings force us to accept these Annunaki as our creators, and to rewrite our history and our religions. After the passage of this sun they arrive as our saviors—as our creators—and who would not accept them as such with these findings? Mark 13 says, 'for there shall arise false Christs, and false prophets, and shall show great signs and wonders; insomuch that, if it were possible, they shall deceive the very elect.' The deception was also foretold.

"We must warn people. They must know. Sati had evidence that this is truly a deception. It's on that USB drive. There are photos there of ancient writings that reveal the truth."

Just then they heard a small squeak just outside the door, like the sound of a shoe against the marble flooring. They looked toward the door.

Suddenly the lights in the room went out, and the room was dark.

There was a deafening crash. The door to the conference room burst open with such ferocity that the air in the room compressed. The wood frame shattered. Debris flew through the air and landed on the table.

A figure dressed in black military uniform seemed to float into the room with a silenced M4 rifle held up against his shoulder, looking through the sights. His movements were fluid and trained.

Without a word, the man leveled his rifle at Stan. James watched in horror as he pulled the trigger. Stan's head burst into a haze of blood, splattering across the wall. Stan had been trying to stand when the shots hit him, and his body collapsed face-first onto the table and rolled onto the floor. James watched in utter confusion as the body slumped down; he felt as if he were in a dream.

Father Perez was somehow on his feet, trying to escape to the back of the room. James turned, trying to flee too, as he heard multiple clicks of the silenced rifle. Father Perez barely made a sound as his body went down, cut through by the shots.

James instinctively grabbed a wooden chair next to him and tried to lurch forward and strike the assassin. He froze in a state of shock as the man pivoted and began to turn the rifle toward him. Time seemed to slow to a nightmare crawl; James's mind was moving fast, but his body refused to respond.

God, no, he thought. James lunged at the man, using the chair as a weapon as he was moving forward with as much ferocity his coursing adrenalin could provide, he saw the man's eyes lock on him and he choked, panic exploding through his body.

It was him: it was the man he had seen so many times before outside his apartment, and watching from across the street and near the restaurant. His eyes reflected pure evil. Anger welled in him and the raw emotion erupted throughout him, enveloping his senses.

The shot came, just as the chair James was swinging reached the rifle. The leg of the chair exploded into splinters as the round slammed through it and continued on to James's forearm. He felt the heat of the bullet as it tore through muscle and bone. But it was too late: James's full momentum was behind the chair, and he slammed it into the chest of the man, knocking the gun down and the assassin to the floor. Coming down with the chair, James drove his knee down into the man's head with all of his might. A crunch emanated from the impact.

James could see at his periphery that Sofia was moving toward the door, the only avenue of escape. James jumped over the man and followed her through the door frame. This was their only chance at life. As they leaped through the door, James kicked the gun out of the assassin's reach, and into the corner of the room.

They entered the darkened hallway and turned to run down toward the exits. James desperately tried to trace in his mind the best avenue of escape through the maze of hallways to the exits beyond. But there, in the hallway, were two more men, outfitted identically to the man who had burst into the room. There was no pause. No hesitation.

In an instant, a shot rang out, hitting Sofia in the chest; another followed immediately into her head. Her body recoiled hard with the force of the impact, leaving a mist of blood behind it.

James couldn't move. His mouth opened slowly, but there was no sound. He tried to move toward Sofia, but he could not move fast enough. His mind raced but time seemed to stop. Slowly, Sofia's body fell toward the floor. James saw that the other man had his rifle aimed directly at him. James reached forward trying to get to the man—to get to the gun—to change what was about to happen.

A shot hit him directly in his chest. His body was spun sideways, and James fell forward into the wall, onto the floor. Every bit of air left his lungs and fire coursed through him. His thoughts raced as he fought against the darkness that overwhelmed him.

My babies—Sofia. This cannot be the end. I won't allow it. Dear God . . . No! Please!

The pain seared through his body, washing over him in waves. He struggled to suck in a breath that would not come, and everything went black.

* * *

Agent Stinson's car flew through the French countryside.

He looked over his shoulder at the blood-covered body lying unconscious in his backseat. Stinson knew he was working on borrowed time. He focused on keeping his breathing steady, knowing he must remain alert to save the life of this poor soul.

He had arrived at the ESA to find it an inferno. He knew that James, Father Perez, Sofia, and Stan had been there for a meeting. But the front door to the facility had been broken through, and glass was on the ground when he entered the building.

He'd slowly walked through the facility with this gun at the ready. The security guard at the main desk had been shot in the head; the electrical panel behind him was smoking where wires had been cut.

Stinson had found their bodies in the conference room. Checking their pulses, he found only one still alive. He'd fought against the flames to drag the limp body out of the building. How could he have let this happen to them?

Stinson slammed the pedal to the floor, the car's engine roared.

* * *

Le Figaro reported the following day that an electrical fire had occurred at the headquarters of the ESA on Sunday. Because of the lateness of the hour and the fact that it had happened on a weekend, most of the building was vacant, but for a small group of researchers. The article said it was with sorrow that the head of the ESA reported that the four researchers had perished in the fire after a beam fell, trapping them inside a conference room. Due to the large amount of accelerants and other flammable chemical materials stored in the labs, the fire burned very intensely, and the authorities were unable to recover any remains.

NOTES ABOUT THE ILLUSTRATED MATERIAL IN *OCCAM'S RAZOR*

The graphs in *Occam's Razor* have been adapted and redrawn for the book by Sason Kayyod. For information about the sources for the original images and more information about their subjects, please see the following:

Graph 1: Concentrations of Greenhouse Gases from 0 to 2015 (page 59) http://www.ipcc.ch/publications_and_data/ar4/wg1/en/faq-2-1.html

Graph 2: Chart by U.S. Geographical Survey of Destructive Earthquakes with Magnitude of 6–8 from 1900 to 2007(page 60) https://www.usgs.gov/products/data-and-tools/real-time-data/earthquakes http://www.i-nomad.net/2011/03/disturbing-chart-of-ever-increasing.html

Graph 3: Magnetic North Pole Shift Over the Last 420 Years (page 61) https://modernsurvivalblog.com/pole-shift-2/alarming-noaa-data-rapid-pole-shift/

Graph 4: Earth's Magnetic Field and Polar Shift (page 62) http://wdc.kugi.kyoto-u.ac.jp/poles/polesexp.html https://hubpages.com/education/Earths-Magnetic-Field-and-Polar-Shift

Graph 5: Fireball Events from 2005–2013 (page 102) https://space.stackexchange.com/questions/1486/what-existing-technologies-record-data-on-meteors

Picture 6: The Face of Mars (page 157) https://www.space.com/17191-face-on-mars.html

Graph 7: The Orbit of Planet X (pages 293, 342) https://science.nasa.gov/science-news/science-at-nasa/2001/ast24may_1 http://www.sitchin.com/

Graphs 8, 9, and 10: NASA Model of the Global Magnetosphere: BATRUS Magnetic Pause Reversal (pages 343, 344, 345) https://ccmc.gsfc.nasa.gov/models/modelinfo.php?model=BATS-R-US

Picture 11: Blocking Object in Virgo on Google Sky and NASA's SkyView Programs (page 361) http://www.ufos.news/2017-06-17-why-is-nasa-blocking-this-sector-of-space-what-are-they-hiding.html

ABOUT THE AUTHOR

As an attorney and technology entrepreneur, T. R. Ryden has built and sold companies to Motorola, Comcast, and other global institutions.

He received his undergraduate degree from Purdue University, received his law degree from Indiana University's Robert H. McKinney School of Law, and has a Certificate in European Legal Studies from Tulane University School of Law, Paris, France.

Occam's Razor demonstrates his keen interest in science and the unanswered questions that puzzle us all. As a dyslexic, he views fact patterns, information, and connectivity of evidence a little differently from most people, and he suspects that this contributed to his creation of this conspiracy thriller.

Ryden is passionate about philanthropies that focus on children facing adversity, and works with organizations that pursue educational reform in struggling urban communities and schools. He has served in a board capacity with Big Brothers Big Sisters of America, Christel House, and other children-focused nonprofits.

He is married to his high school sweetheart, and has three sons.